THE
R.AVENS

THE
RAVENS

TOMAS BANNERHED

Translated from the Swedish by Sarah Death

THE CLERKENWELL PRESS

The cost of this translation was defrayed by a subsidy from the Swedish Arts Council, gratefully acknowledged.

This book has been selected to receive financial assistance from English PEN's "PEN Translates!" programme, supported by Arts Council England. English PEN exists to promote literature and our understanding of it, to uphold writers' freedoms around the world, to campaign against the persecution and imprisonment of writers for stating their views, and to promote the friendly co-operation of writers and the free exchange of ideas. *www.englishpen.org*

Supported using public funding by

**ARTS COUNCIL
ENGLAND**

First published in Great Britain in 2014 by
THE CLERKENWELL PRESS
An imprint of Profile Books Ltd
3A Exmouth House
Pine Street
London EC1R 0JH
www.profilebooks.com

First published as *Korparna* by Svante Weyler bokförlag, 2011

Copyright © Tomas Bannerhed, 2014
Translation copyright © Sarah Death, 2014

10 9 8 7 6 5 4 3 2 1

Typeset in Goudy Old Style by MacGuru Ltd
info@macguru.org.uk
Printed and bound in Italy
L.E.G.O. S.p.A., Lavis (TN)

The moral right of the author has been asserted.

A CIP catalogue record for this book is available from the British Library.

ISBN 978 1 84668 899 7
eISBN 978 1 84765 857 9

There's Father, I thought. In his eternal cloud.

Bouncing along in Grandfather's old Ferguson with his body belt drawn tight and his hair growing greyer, and later he'll come home smelling of earth – because he has no choice. Because this spot is ours, this plot of soil, these acres of farmland. The lake, drained and turned into fields and banks. The marsh, Raven Fen, smoking like ashes and tinder as soon as the dry season sets in, the peat bog that can suddenly catch fire, smouldering and gasping in its depths, burning without a flame, glowing unseen, consuming everything from below until you dig trenches to cut it off.

This is our patch. We have no other.

This soil, observed by the sun and the ravens.

This plot beneath a sky criss-crossed by jet planes.

The tractor was scarcely visible, all you could see was the cloud of dust rising as he chugged past with the roller attached at the back. I got out the telescope and kept him in my sights for a good ten minutes, reluctant to let him out of view. Wondered what he was thinking about down there, what was going on inside his heavy head, why he kept licking his lips. Up and down with that infernal, peaty cloud all round him – length after length of the newly sown fields, back and forth between one ditch and the other, from east to west and back again.

The dust thickened into a dense, ash-brown mist as the telescope brought it closer. You could only make him out as a vague shadow inside the tractor's roll cage: the peak of his cap, the pipe in his beard, the hands on the steering wheel, the hunched back.

There he is, you think. Sitting in that cloud, breathing all that pulverised organic material into his lungs, coming home and coughing and looking like a Soviet miner – those subterranean half-humans they showed on TV, just restored to the light of day with helmeted heads and fluorescing whites to the eyes in their coal-black faces. Because he's got to. Has no choice. He'll never get away from here. He can't do anything else.

I panned slowly across the thousands of acres of reclaimed bog, from the football pitch to the south, past the clump of alders and the hay barns weathered to greyness on the other side of the Canal and over to the white arrow of the church spire where the sun always set at midsummer – – –

No, there was nobody else out there. Everyone had finished what they had to do. It was only Father left, in his cloud.

The fields, lying there waiting.

Sit on the stone wall and see how many different bird calls I can make out, waiting for the green woodpecker to show herself in her black hole, poke out her bayonet beak and at least say hello.

No sign of life. Dead as May Day in church. My greeny-yellow friend must have hacked out a home elsewhere, moved away and laid her gleaming white eggs in a dead pine tree instead. I had been sitting there for two hours, caught between hope and despair, swinging from one to the other, at my wit's end, and now it must be dinner time at home, too.

What shall I do, I thought uselessly. Show that I'm me or swallow my pride and lay down my weapon. I nipped a leaf off the Lightning Aspen and sat there holding it in my pathetic girl's hand. Compared the two sides of the leaf, studied the long, flattened stalk, the super-fine tracery of its veins, the irregular divisions of its blade, like aerial photos of paddy fields in faraway lands. The fresh leaf with its luminous green nerve fibres, as thin and fragile as the capillaries of an eyelid. The distorted yellow patch by the stalk, the rounded points and shallow serrations running along the edge.

I leant forward and sniffed it, put it on my tongue and took it into my mouth like a communion wafer.

The aspen and me, I thought. The least thing makes us shake. *Homo tremula*. That's me.

I gave a start.

The tractor heading this way, and no roller! So it's dinner time, the hour has struck. Soon they'll assemble in silence round the table and say a short grace.

Those heavy eyes on you.

Like something pulling at you.

You stay *here*, the voice ordered. You're not to be owned by anyone, not even the person who begot you. Today is today. You can do as you will.

Walk, see, feel, listen –

It's what you exist for.

I held the aspen leaf up to the sun, brought it gradually closer to my eye, little by little, and the veins turned into rivers spreading across a foreign land, waterways with natives paddling along in hollowed-out tree trunks among lethal caimans, rivers winding through steaming jungles where harpy eagles rose from the treetops with baby monkeys and sloths in their claws, sweeping off like their primeval counterparts on vast spreads of wing –

Again I was jolted back to reality. Father was sounding his horn – a long, insistent signal, as if he knew where I was and wanted to show me who was who.

Today's not just any old day. You are you and I am me and I'll come when it suits me. To the place you lot call home.

From a tree stump with a hundred rings:
If he drives the tractor into the Canal it's your fault. You'll have to live with it for the rest of your life.

I clambered down from the wall and shoved the aspen leaf in my back pocket. I went into the woods after all – to what's mine. To see if the songthrush babies have hatched, track down the wood pigeon with her incessant cooing, find out where the wood ants are swarming on a day like today.

That's how easy it is. Over the ditch and away.

I crept cautiously towards the young spruce where the thrushes lived, hid in a clump of thorn bushes a little way off and got out my field glasses. The male was babbling in the whitest birch and interspersed his fluting drills with oystercatcher and woodcock impersonations, whistled like a football ref and then did a retake, going for it all over again. And the female flew off! That means the eggs have hatched. A minute or two later she came back with a collection of worms in her beak, landed on the edge of the nest, distributed them among her brood and was off again.

I climbed onto a tree stump at about knee height and gently parted the branches. There were the babies in their smoothly plastered bowl of a nest, and all four had made it. Lying in a help-less, reptilian heap, their salmon pink throats gaping wide like fleshy collecting bags as if they thought I was going to feed them. The male had noticed me and didn't think I belonged there.

Tix-itix-itix! came his alarm call. *Tix-itix-itix!*

He advanced on me branch by branch, his call so shrill that it hurt my ears. He looked about him frantically as if hoping for reinforcements or planning his attack.

'Easy now, easy now,' I said. 'It's only me.'

Tix-itix-itix!

'Can't you see it's me?'

Tix-itix-itix!

'Calm down a minute and I'll go.'

Tix-itix-itix!

I went back to my thicket, broke off some spruce branches to act as a roof and made myself invisible. Instantly, peace was restored. The male carried on fluting and singing as before and the female came up to the nest to check all was in order, which it was. So she darted off for her next batch of worms and the male began talking to himself as usual.

In a fortnight's time, the baby birds will have flown the nest and be coping on their own. Fully qualified worm hunters and berry pickers with their sights set on France or Spain for the autumn.

And what about me?

I carried on towards the cooing wood pigeon, past Drowned Man's Pond where a teal with Indian warpaint on his face was wondering what kind of animal I was. Took a detour round the badger sett and was soon in the oldest part of the forest, in among the ancient spruces, keeping their thousand needle eyes peeled as I padded past, waiting for every step I took. The tall, rough trunks of spruce, like pillars in a great hall with a murmuring ceiling. The faint wind filtering through the treetops, the goldcrests whispering somewhere up there.

Ssshh –

Only a roe deer breaking a twig and bolting into the darkness, its white rump bouncing between the treetrunks.

The roe deer and the birds. Imagine living here. Turning into a spruce and growing bark.

I could hear the brook ahead of me now. The brook that rippled and flowed, however dry the woods and fields around – that *tugged* at you because it was without end. I looked down into the flowing water coiling round the rocks and stones in ever-changing patterns, impossible to keep up with. It's forever running here, I thought, every second and no doubt even in the middle of the night. Running and flowing, eddying on the bends as if it was nothing, frothing white as soon as anything gets in the way. The least little protruding root-end turns into a frothy tuft, like candyfloss tossed by the wind.

Entranced, I looked down into the stream as it ran and ran and ran, never seeming to rest. New water kept coming, yet still it stayed the same.

The brook here in the forest – *where did it begin?* – – –

Don't think like that!

Not about beginnings and endings, but just about what *is*.

Throw in a stone and make time stop.

I grabbed hold of a spindly alder that was growing right by the water but seemed to be dying anyway. I bent it over to use as a handrail and picked my way out to a rock in the middle of the stream. Like the Water Sprite, only without the fiddle and the dancing fairies.

Someone in the forest, not going home –

I put my hand down into the icy water and let it filter between my fingers, felt it sucking, tugging, numbing.

The aspen leaf, I thought.

I scratched a K with my little fingernail, put the leaf in the water and let it be carried away – out to the ditch that Grandfather and Father had dug, down to the Canal and off towards Marsh Pool through the narrow channel in the reeds, cutting straight across the long, thin bird lake, under the hundred-year-old echo of the humpback bridge, past the swidden land and the forest grazing, the water meadows and reclaimed farmland, through dark forest, outlying fields and boggy pools and all the way down to the coast, out into the mighty sea that you knew nothing about. Tens of miles over gliding black currents on the great waterway that never ends –

I can't see it any more.

The pigeon cooed and called to me – a hundred metres away or a thousand, it was impossible to tell.

Hoo hrooo hoo hu hu – – –

I left the brook and went in amongst the hairiest old spruces, where the Tengmalm's owl lived: the one with the eerie, dog-bark hoot that frightened the wits out of people at nights. Through undergrowth and thickets and over broken barbed wire fences, down into a brushwood hollow and up again, round a big mound of stones and in the end I scarcely knew where I was. Nothing but the cooing to steer by. Lots of scrub, and twiggy branches to scratch you in the face – but suddenly a ray of light cut through the forest darkness.

A narrow, unassuming roadway, forgotten after some bit of felling perhaps, but there was no trace of wheel tracks. If the sun had not been in exactly the right position I would undoubtedly have missed it. A moss-covered roadway where overgrown rocks and tree stumps made soft little hillocks. Small branches left lying under the thick carpet made bumps that stood out like the veins on the backs of Father's hands.

I took the roadway deeper into the forest with the sun on my back and my own shadow straight in front of me, as if showing me the way. The forest was as solid as a wall and the lighter roadway went on and on, jinked round an untidy bunch of boulders before emerging into a clearing I had never seen before.

An open space, almost like a circus ring, surrounded by huge spruces that seemed to be leaning in towards the hole at the top, watching over me and everything down below: the flat rock with the oak sapling beside it, the tree stump with springy haircap moss to sit on, the knot of birches on the other side, the little blueberry bushes now in leaf, the anemones with their flowers still white.

Stay here, something told me.

There is nothing here to be afraid of. No eyes boring at you, trying to get in. Just you and what is here, the forest murmuring its murmur, as it always has.

Now and forever.

Filled with a strange sense of peace, I sat down by the flat rock and brushed it clear, picked off some old spruce needles and partly rotted leaves and saw there was something written on it. Three letters that looked as if they had been cut using some kind of template or carved with a hammer and chisel, so clear and sharp were they, so perfect somehow.

I could make out a T and an A and a G.

Tag?

No, there were dots in between: T.A.G.

Father's initials.

Did he come here? Did he sit here, carving, when he was like me? Sometime during the war maybe, when Grandfather was in the asylum? Did he come here and chisel away? I ran my fingers over the letters, thought how old they looked, as if they had become one with the eternity of the rocks.

Something whispered: They are never going to disappear. In a thousand years from now, they will be the same. The oak sapling may become a tree and rot away, the stream may meander round more bends with every century that passes but the rocks will always be here, will never crumble away.

I felt suddenly light-headed.

I touched the letters again cautiously, as if they might burn me. I got out my bedroom door key and scraped away what I could of the ingrained lichens, and with a generous amount of spit and my sleeve I polished up his letters as best I could, trying to make them look good again.

T.A.G. down in the bottom corner, like the signature on a painting.

Father's rock in the clearing that belongs to me –

You must never say anything about this to anybody. Not Mum, nor anybody else, not a living soul. This is for only you to know.

I took off my shoes and climbed onto the rock. Took a few deep breaths and composed myself, as if to pray, squinted cautiously up at the heavens through the hole between the treetops. A few clouds paraded past. The wood pigeon cooed at a distance, the chaffinch and willow warbler trilled and sang, the robin made its urgent 'tic tic' and its high 'tsweee'. And the spruces! Now I could see they were blooming as if we were in Paradise. Every treetop boasted an array of reddish-pink female flowers like gorgeous tropical fruits – the nearer the sun the plumper and deeper in colour, as if flushing with excitement, extending their damp carpels towards the heat of the sun's rays.

Then there was a gust of wind, the spruces curtseyed and everything went silent and still as if at the snap of someone's fingers. I filled my lungs with air and turned my face up the bright hole.

'Yoo-hoo!' I shouted. 'Yoo-hoo!'

No.

'Yoo-hooo! – – –'

Nothing?

I cupped my hands into a funnel and shouted at the top of my voice, straight into the trees instead.

'*Yoou-hooou!!*'

Into the dense forest and everything that lurked in there – and an answer came.

And it was no ordinary echo, rolling off and dying away, it was the forest saying it *wanted* something of me – as if in a dream that had yet to be dreamed.

Spatters of fat hissed on the stove. The smell of cooking mixed with the smell of manure and permanently sweaty socks. It was warm and stuffy in the kitchen, in the closeness of evening, like when there was thunder in the air.

'So you didn't want any dinner, then?' said Mum, giving me a look.

But there was no reproach in it, just vague curiosity about what I had been up to all day, why I never said where I was going before I shoved off.

Important things, I thought feverishly. Something no one else is going to find out about. Something only I will know.

'Had some nests I needed to look at,' I answered, and it was no lie. 'The green woodpecker seems to have gone but the whitethroats have arrived. I heard one in raptures over by Broadleaf Brook.'

She gave me an indulgent, tender smile, came over and stroked my cheek with the back of her hand as if to comfort me. Her skin was glistening with sweat even though she only had on a short-sleeved tunic.

'You and your birds,' she said. 'Don't you ever get tired of them?'

Father wasn't listening. He sat there in his corner, entering the weather observations in his black oilcloth notebook, adding arrows and lines, drawing curves and cloud formations, shaking his head dejectedly. He seemed to be finding it hard to get enough air, or maybe there was something that didn't tally, the right connections were eluding him.

That heavy breathing.

We sat there on either side of the table, Father and I, as far apart from each other as we could get. It was a habit we had got into. He in order to keep the whole kitchen under surveillance, me for the view over the garden. Apple and plum trees in blossom, a patch of sky into which the swifts might come darting any day now.

'No rain is one thing,' he muttered, half to himself. 'But this infernal thundery heat in May. Something's not right.'

The tufts of hair in his ears were grey with dust from the roller. There was a rusty scythe hanging on the wall behind him, a memento of Grandfather.

'It's always something,' said Mum. 'If it's not too dry or too hot then it's too wet or too cold?'

'Though of course it's a leap year with thirteen moons,' he went on, engrossed in his own thoughts. 'I didn't think I'd see another one of those in my lifetime.'

Father had been keeping a record of the weather since he was fourteen. Three times a day he entered the readings for atmospheric pressure, temperature, wind conditions and precipitation, if any, and once he had finished in the cowshed he would sit down and summarise the day's weather. Whether it had been cloudy or clear, foggy or hazy, how the wind had changed and the cloud varied, the time any rain, hail or snow had started and stopped, how it all compared with previous years. Trends and signs, hundreds of different cloud formations and their consequences.

'The songthrush eggs had hatched when I got there,' I said. 'All four of them. They make the nest of cement inside and put the soft stuff on the outside.'

Father looked up, inspected me thoughtfully as if he had something to find fault with.

'That's not bad,' he said. 'They're sweet singers, and all.'

'What would you know about it?' said Mum in surprise. 'I thought you were only interested in pests? Spruce bark beetles and Colorado beetles and all that lot you're forever worrying about, day and night.'

'Oh there's room for a few birds in this head of mine as well.'

He gave a self-satisfied little smile and looked out of the window, the way he generally did when he was thinking about something special, something only he knew about, something that was a long time ago and might never come back. A smile in his beard, a little glint in his eyes. Then he slowly turned his head my way and fixed me with a look, and there was no way of telling if it was still a game or something more serious. He stared as if he wanted to get right into me, sat there for ages, glassy-eyed and unblinking.

Finally he parted those dry, shrunken lips.

'When I was a lad we had a songthrush behind the cowshed,' he said, raising his voice as if delivering a lesson. 'He was there for several years in that same spruce – they've chopped it down now, by the way – and whenever I came out with the barrow of manure of an evening he'd sing for a bit. Almost made you want to sit down and just listen, it was that sweet.'

He paused and looked up at the wall hanging, with the hymn verse embroidered on it.

'"Have you had a hiding today? Have you had a hiding today?" I thought he was singing. But maybe I just imagined that, too?'

He had that strange smile again, like a streak of sunshine across his face.

Mum checked she'd put everything on the table and poured milk into all four glasses as usual, before she sat down. Perspiration beaded her forehead and ran like tears from her neck down into her cleavage.

'Here we are then, help yourselves,' she said, with a nod to Father.

He took some smoked sausage and mashed turnip and got straight down to it, shovelling the food in with his fork, grubby fingers helping out as required. He never touched his knife, but there was always a clean one laid for him beside his plate, as she'd been taught at domestic science college.

Partway through the meal, Göran came dashing out of his room, jumped up onto his chair and started fiddling with what was in front of him: he speared a bit of bread on his fork and tapped his spoon against the serving dish and his glass until Father closed his eyes and took a deep breath. Mum went for a damp cloth and dabbed at Göran's brow, asked him to drink some of his soothing milk, put some food on his plate and pointed and whispered as if talking to someone retarded.

He gradually calmed down and we could carry on eating. Nothing but the sound of grinding molars, the scrape of cutlery on crockery and, once you became aware of it, the click and tick of Grandma's old wall clock. I made an effort to chew and swallow without a sound, to drink and not slurp. I would really have liked to put the food into my mouth without having to open it.

Above us, the sticky flypaper streamers twirled down from the ceiling, blacker with every passing day: hundreds of wretched captives in the spiral of death, most of them as dry and shrivelled as mummies. But some were still struggling, with a stifled buzz, their wings moving in slow motion, almost automatically, like Grandfather on his deathbed, playing a non-existent accordion. His fingers found only thin air, and moved much more slowly than usual.

After a while Father put down his fork and rapped the underside of the table. Göran flew up and looked out into the hall as if he thought we were about to have visitors, but there was nobody there. It was just Father, signalling that he was about to speak.

'So that's the spring sowing almost done for this time,' he said solemnly. 'Tomorrow I'll put in the last corn over on the leasehold. Then it's all in the hands of Our Lord. If we don't get any rain we'll lose the lot, if anyone happens to care.'

Mum forced a smile.

'Well at least that's the end of all that dust for now, eh?' she said. 'It'll do you in, swirling around like that all the time?'

He nodded in agreement and seemed content, then brushed down his shirtsleeves, releasing a big cloud of dust. Göran put on an act and started to cough, thumped his chest and sounded like a consumptive.

'Could we take a bit of time off when it's done,' asked Mum, 'before you start on the fences? Just a couple of days. Give ourselves something else to think about.'

She glanced encouragingly at Göran and me as a wistful look came into her eyes.

'What about a trip to Gotland!' she exclaimed. 'Wouldn't that be fun? A chance to see the sea.'

Father's expression darkened and he shot her an injured look.

'Take time off? There's more than enough to do here, if that's what you're all worrying about.'

He nodded out of the window several times and underlined what he had just said.

'In this place we're never finished, just so you're clear on that. There's the scrap pile waiting to be sorted if nothing else, you all know that as well as I do.'

Mum moistened her finger and dabbed up a few crumbs from the oilcloth.

'Never mind the scrap pile,' she said quietly. 'In a hundred years it'll all be forgotten.'

'Forgotten? I wouldn't be so sure about that.'

At that moment a fly fell off the spiral of death and landed squarely in the milk jug, where it lay helplessly on its back, floundering in the white well.

'Do you know why aspens tremble at the slightest thing?' I heard myself say.

'Aspens?' said Mum. 'What aspens?'

'The ones in front of the forest, I bet,' said Göran.

'It's because they're going to be made into matches and they're afraid of fire,' I answered for them. 'And because Jesus hung on an aspen cross. They're scared of death, too. Just like I am.'

Mum put down her knife and fork and sent an embarrassed smile in Father's direction, not sure whose side she should be on. Talking about the crucifixion at the dinner table. Father was not listening. He had not been allowed to finish what he had to say about sowing and Our Lord.

'As I said Klas, there aren't many acres left to do this time. When I was like you, I had to do the whole lot myself, with just a horse.'

He looked at me with a hint of triumph about his mouth, drumming his fingers on the tabletop. Had me where he wanted me now.

'Let's see, you're twelve now, aren't you?' he said. 'In that case it's high time. And you think you can get to the heavens with the help of those birds?'

'We live in different times now,' put in Mum, 'thank goodness. You can't go comparing now with during the war?'

'I wouldn't say that …'

He stopped chewing and stared out of the window. His eyes shrank as he screwed them up, as if a thought had suddenly struck him. He wiped the saliva from the corner of his mouth, smearing his dirty cheek, and sat there with a mouth full of food.

He's going to die soon, was the sensation that rushed through me. There's no one with grey tufts of hair in their ears who isn't going to die soon. And his eyes, there's something about his eyes that wasn't there before.

Die!

Why would he die? He's going to carry on farming this place that was left to him and provide for us if it's the last thing he does, he promised that himself.

'Everything's crowding in on me, as well,' he muttered. 'I've said it before and it doesn't get any better, not a bit. And the barometer's stuck where it is.'

Mum wiped a bead of sweat from the tip of her nose.

'Crowding in?' she said.

'Yes. There's not much air, either.'

He looked away.

'I don't know what it is –'

There was silence round the table. Mum cleared her throat and whispered something to Göran, reached over and switched on the radio.

'Forty years,' he went on. 'What have I got to show for it? Apart from sciatica?'

'You're talking in riddles.'

'I might have known it was asking too much for you lot to understand anything.'

Mum gave a routine nod and stuck out her lower lip.

'Have you seen the bunch of flowers?' she said, trying to change tack. 'Bearded iris, bleeding heart and some leopard's bane. Göran picked them in the fields. Pretty, aren't they?'

'Flowers? They'll be dead in a week. You'll only have to take them out again.'

At that moment my first pied flycatcher of the year alighted in the apple tree outside, perched on a blossom-laden branch, flicked his wings and raised his tail in greeting. Here I am!

Then he pulled himself upright and stared at me through the newly cleaned window, looking so long and so intently that for a while we could not tear our eyes away from each other. He fixed me with the white spot above his bill as if I were the female he was longing for. Here's where we'll live!

Can't you find the nesting box, I mimed surreptitiously. It's in the aspen by the raspberry canes, I built it for you, this spring. Send the great tits packing if they've got in first!

'I'll come with you to Africa in the autumn,' I whispered without thinking. 'I want to see the honeycreeper's radiant red breast, I want to see the hornbill that seals itself up in its nest, I want to see the fiery gaze of the crowned eagle as it tears the monkey's heart out of its body. See it all with my own eyes before it's too late.'

Father gave me a look, raising one eyebrow. The flycatcher flicked its wings in excitement, took off into the air and came back at once, brushed against some blossom and dislodged a lily-white petal, which floated down to the ground – like an answer.

'You could come with me tomorrow morning and take a look,' Father said after a bit. 'So you know how it's done. The sowing.'

He reached across the table and tapped my glass with the yellowing, clawlike nail of his index finger, as if to rouse me.

'But I don't suppose you'd even consider the idea, seeing as it's come from me.'

I couldn't think of an answer.

'It's been the sort of day that makes you feel lethargic?' said Mum, offering an excuse. 'Maybe the weather's going to change after all.'

Father looked at her as if that was the stupidest comment he had heard since the day he was confirmed.

'Change? It couldn't be more settled than it is now. We won't get a drop. The Devil couldn't have devised it any better.'

'It must be something else then? But I feel lethargic, at any rate.'

His eyes bored into me again. This time it looked as if he wasn't going to let me off until I had eaten humble pie.

'So what have we decided then? About the sowing and the rest of it?'

A lump of dough in my stomach, being kneaded back and forth.

I *want* to come with you Father, I wished I could have said. Learn how to harrow and sow and harvest and plough. Tend the fields and the animals.

But something inside me resisted.

His heavy, calloused, bloodstained hands on the table between us. I thought of that trembling mouth, the scabbed lips, those eyes swimming in something that could have turned into tears.

'I can't,' I said. 'I'm going over to Adder Hook to see Johnny tomorrow.'

The clock stopped. The walls closed in on us. My cheeks flushed as if I was feeling ill. Father pursed his mouth and squinted out over the marsh, sort of sinking into himself and nodding reflectively.

'Oh you are, eh?' he said calmly. 'Just mind you don't overdo it.'

Mum cleared her throat.

'Well I suppose I'd better –,' she said, and took Göran out into the hall as if there was something that needed doing out there.

Father just sat there, not moving.

'I thought you might enjoy coming out with me for once,' he said out of the window. 'One day it'll be too late.'

Then there was that hint of a smile again, and I felt it like a jolt running through me.

'Did you hear what I said, Klas?'

The long-eared owl nailed up over the front door: wings protectively outspread, its shabby plumage and hanging head, like the Redeemer on the cross. I knocked and waited for a bit, even though it was always left unlocked and nobody was going to come and open the door. Punch didn't even bother to bark.

There was a smell of home cheesemaking and mothballs in the hall. The rag rugs were all ruckled up as if the cats had been chasing mice or having a scrap. Round the chest of drawers hung her dried bunches of wormwood, to ward off evil.

This is where you should be, said the voice. He never comes here.

It was only five hundred metres from home, but even so he had never set his foot in here. He might go to their cowshed, but never into the house.

Johnny's gran was standing by the stove, splitting firewood, as small and slight as a fairy with her white hair hanging down to below her shoulders. On the windowsill mother-in-law's tongues, yellowing at the edges and wreathed in cobwebs, fought for space with sun-bleached hare paws and birch-bark boxes.

'It's only you then?' she said. 'I can't hear a thing these days. But maybe I've heard everything I need to?'

She blinked at me and made a little lunge with the knife.

'Oh we'd never think that, would we?' I said.

'Well be that as it may, I can't make head or tail of this wood.

It's as tough as juniper and as hard as stone, or maybe it's this knife that's no good any more.'

She glared accusingly at the pathetic pile of firewood in the stove corner.

'Well I can't fathom it and I doubt the parson could either,' she said. 'You know everything, so what do you make of it?'

'I don't know anything about this sort of stuff. Perhaps it's just a bit wet?'

'And I don't suppose you've heard the woodpecker shriek either? At least then we'd get a bit of rain.'

'The only one I knew has moved out. The others are always yelling and meowing.'

She shook her head, put down the worn, shiny knife and produced a bag of cough drops from her cardigan.

'Something's better than nothing,' she said, shaking out a few more for me to put in my pocket.

Then she snatched back the bag and shushed me. Opened her eyes as wide as if she'd seen a ghost in the apple tree outside.

'Thunder!' she hissed. 'Did you hear the crash? Here it comes!'

I frowned sceptically. She stood tensed, with her finger in the air and a quiver about her mouth. She looked at me and hardly dared to breathe.

'Listen! Thor's out with his chariot and billy goats.'

There wasn't a sound to be heard but I couldn't bring myself to contradict her. Eventually she took one step forward and put her hand on my shoulder, as if she was going to let me into a secret.

'Thunder before the seedcorn's in the ground,' she said, 'it can only mean misfortune. Sure as eggs is eggs.'

She nodded to drive home her words, taking up a stick of firewood and tapping the hearthstone with it three times to be on the safe side.

'I've had a feeling this was on the way,' she said. 'And now you know, as well! Last time it happened I was widowed that same autumn. Even though I drank wormwood every day.'

A shiver ran down my spine.

Johnny, I thought. Go in and see him now.

He was sitting on the bed in just his underpants, cleaning his shotgun, hair cropped as short as a lifer's, in a messy sea of cotton waste, bottles of oil, cleaning rods and little round pipe brushes. On the opposite wall he had hung his trophies in a row: the twelve-tined elk antlers with the chalky white fragments of skull, flanked by six little sets of roebuck antlers. Above his bed hung new posters, a scantily clad girl for every month.

There was a smell of gun grease and gunpowder.

'I knew it was you,' he said and carried on cleaning.

I stopped just inside the door and flicked through an old copy of *Field & Stream*: how to lure foxes with carrion; supplementary feeding for deer and partridge; ice-fishing strike-alert systems. Thrown on the chair beside me was a jersey with the black, sun cross logo of the Nordic Reich Party. Johnny was rubbing and scrubbing as if someone was about to come and demand to inspect the rifle. Outside and inside, lock, stock and barrels – every millimetre had to be cleaned and oiled and wiped dry.

'Have you heard the trollhound yet?' I asked in the end, to have something to say.

Johnny squeezed one eye shut and opened the other one quizzically wide. He didn't pause in what he was doing.

'I'm talking about Tengmalm's owl,' I explained. 'I heard her from three different directions at Easter. There must have been plenty of rodents.'

He didn't answer. He put aside the cleaning rod and cotton

waste and peered down the barrels, scrutinising them thoroughly with his moustache cocked sideways.

'Come and have a look,' he commanded.

I closed the magazine, took the gun and peered into it as he had done. Right eye, one barrel at a time, back and forth.

'Not bad.'

It was as shiny as church silver inside. The stock was silky smooth with a smell of linseed oil.

'No bastard can come along now and try telling me the parts aren't clean, so they can't,' he said.

'No, of course not.'

He reached out for two rounds and loaded, and hey presto he was a different person. His eyes set and narrowed to little slits. He put on a wily grin and his tongue explored his moustache.

'Don't suppose you've ever seen a cowgirl dance?' he said. 'Always got your head in a book, haven't you?'

I couldn't come up with a response. He raised his shotgun and aimed at my feet, nodded to me to move, get my legs going, do a little tap dance in my stockinged feet. I felt nailed to the floor and started to sweat. There was a lump rising in my throat.

Johnny looked up.

'So we gonna dance or not?'

He thrust his head forward and took aim again, shut the other eye and put his finger on the trigger.

Click –

He grinned so widely I could see the wad of snuff stuck under his top lip.

'I'm only having you on, you know that. You didn't really think I'd use live ammunition in here, did you?'

I gave a forced smile and tried to get my breathing back under control. Just stood there, empty and blank, staring at the pictures above his bed. Angelique down on all fours in a leopardskin tanga briefs, with whiskers painted on her face. She looked at me, fixed her eyes on mine, parted her lips, showing me the tip of her tongue between those pearly teeth. Her breasts were trailing on the floor like the udders of an American cow.

'You didn't really think I'd use live ammunition in here, did you?' Johnny said again. 'Get a bloody grip!'

I shook my head.

'They were only dummies, you know. I was just teasing.'

'Yes of course –'

He took the rounds out of the gun and held them out to prove it. I looked down into his outstretched hand and nodded mechanically: dummies.

I'll never forget it.

Johnny pulled on his camouflage jacket and stuffed the pockets full of ammunition. Pulled his cap well down over his cropped hair, popped in another wad of snuff and asked if I wanted to come along and shoot clay pigeons, test his new trap.

'Good practice, so it is. We're behind the cowshed.'

I could scarcely believe my ears. To be allowed to fire Johnny's Husqvarna, as if I was one of his proper mates.

'I've never shot anything in my entire life,' I said honestly.

'There's a first time for everything.'

'Just as long as you don't point it at me again?'

He glanced up, smiled uncertainly. Attached his knife to his belt and hung his ear protectors round his neck.

'Here, have some earplugs. So you don't go deaf like your father.'

I gave him a baffled look.

'Only joking,' he said, boxing me on the arm.

And off we went, Johnny first and me following along behind, neither of us saying anything.

The trap was in the old brewhouse along with a box of clay pigeons that looked like thick, bright orange saucers. Johnny whistled casually through his teeth as he set up the trap and showed me what to do.

'Then it's me giving the word and you following orders and releasing the target,' he instructed.

I nodded. He inserted two clay pigeons and walked over to take up his position.

'Hoy!'

I pulled the lever and off went the clay pigeon in a wobbly arc: he missed both times. A flock of terrified crows whirled up from the forest and dispersed in all directions, sounding their warning.

'Too low!' shouted Johnny and spat. 'You've got to get it higher.'

I put in another clay pigeon and cocked the throwing arm.

'Hoy!'

There was a bang and the clay pigeon turned into a little puff of orange smoke that hung there in the air until the wind gradually thinned it out to nothing.

'That's more like it!'

And he kept me busy launching targets and shot them in a steady stream. The forest was peppered with lead and the nests emptied of brooding birds, but Johnny grew happier and happier, every time he got a hit.

'That's the way to skin a cat! Right, it's time for you to show what you're made of, so it is.'

He handed me the gun.

'Don't bother about the bead,' he said. 'The presentation is what matters. The butt takes aim and the barrels do the killing.'

I nodded, without a clue what he meant. Slunk over to take up position and tried to tell myself nothing was going to happen, and it would all be over soon anyway. My legs would hardly carry me. As if my knees were full of carbon dioxide. I cocked the gun and put my finger on the trigger.

'Do I have to say anything in particular?' I called.

'You're the one who decides, so you are. But don't stand so bloody tense, you want to be like a sack of potatoes.'

Now or never.

'Yahoo!'

I screwed my eyes shut and pressed the trigger. I felt as if my collarbone had snapped and the whole Husqvarna was exploding. There was a ringing in my ears and the gunpowder smoke stung my nostrils.

'There, that wasn't too awful, was it?' said Johnny, patting me on the head. 'But you've got to aim better, so you have.'

He pointed up at the sky.

'Track the clay with the barrel, then overtake it and fire a metre ahead. And keep the butt pressed into your shoulder like nobody's business.'

He gave me a handful of shot and went over to the trap.

'Like a sack of potatoes, right! You hear me? You've got to be just like a sack of potatoes.'

I cocked the gun again and took some deep breaths. Just then I spotted Father out of the corner of my eye: the Ferguson and the seed drill in a cloud of dust, over on the leased land. He would be doing the last bit of sowing, alone with his cough, forward and back across the fields, lap by lap from ditch to ditch.

No, he's heading this way! He'll be here any minute, wanting to talk about my future, forcing me to take sides.

If you drive the tractor into the Canal it's your decision. I'm still not ever taking over.

The butt takes aim and the barrels do the killing – – –

Did I pass out? Had five seconds gone by, or ten minutes?

There was a rushing in my head. I was on the ground, my shoulder throbbing. Johnny was standing nearby, whistling absently and whittling away like mad at a bit of wood.

There was no sign of Father.

Maybe he wasn't even on his way? Hadn't I seen him coming?

'That fucker's got a real kick,' said Johnny. 'You're so puny you could do with some foam rubber down your jacket, so you could.'

I nodded, nonplussed. He spat out his snuff with a hiss and followed it with several squirts of yellow juice that landed right in front of me. He picked up an empty casing and sniffed at the splayed end.

'You can come along when I go for the wood pigeon in the autumn, so you can,' he said. 'We'll set out decoys and pot them on the ground. Even a beginner like you can't miss. I'll put up a new hide down by the Canal over the summer, so I will.'

'Great, sounds like fun,' I heard myself say.

I was sitting indoors, reading about the cuckoo's brood parasitism, when Father turned in past the cowshed to fill the seed drill for the last time. But he didn't back up to the barn door like he usually did; he parked the tractor outside the dairy and walked across to the barn. A little while later he emerged with a fifty-kilo sack on his back and carried it right across the yard, as if he didn't know what he was doing any longer, or his mind was not on the job.

I mounted my telescope on its tripod and tracked his progress as if through telescopic rifle sights, hugely magnified. Only the crosshairs were missing.

He's out there now. Limping to and fro in his own world, his face the green shade of the peak of his cap. His body belt on the outside, a piece of straw stuck behind his ear, the pincers in the tool pocket on the leg of his trousers. Back into the barn and out with another sack that looked even heavier than the rest. He lugged it across the yard, emptied it and put his hands on his hips, flexing the latter gingerly as if something was playing up again.

At the sudden sound of a circular saw in the distance he stiffened and his face assumed a worried expression; he looked paralysed, standing there with narrowed eyes and the empty sack in his hands. Frozen with terror, as it were.

The circular saw took a break but soon started up again, jointing the next tree trunk into little bits. Father screwed up his face and put his hands over his ears, as if he were the one being sawed to pieces.

He stood there by the well, scanning the fields. The saw had fallen silent and the seed drill was full. For arable land or pasture? I couldn't tell the difference. Maybe he was thinking that he'd had to do it all himself again this year, that I'd refused to come and help.

That nobody –

I thought he looked old. His hands hung mute and lumpen at his sides. The fingers were bent like the claws of a bird, shaped by all the handles he had spent his life holding. He got out his pipe, filled it and put it back in his breast pocket. He turned to look at the forest, squinting, moving his lower jaw back and forth as if in unendurable pain, or some sort of hatred.

What's eating you, Father, was the obvious question. Making you unsure whether to smoke your pipe or not. So you just grind to a halt? Sit at the kitchen table smiling to yourself and looking out of the window?

He turned his head towards me, stared intently in my direction and licked his lips, as if he had read my thoughts. I shrank back but realised at the same moment that there was no way he could see me through the window. Not in the middle of the day with the birches in between.

It's only me who sees everything.

Something's going to happen here soon –, a voice whispered in the air. *Something's not as it should be.*

He lay down in the grass by the woodpile with a block of spruce for a pillow. Put one leg over the other, stuffed his cap in his pocket and folded his hands on his chest. I could see every individual whisker of his beard, every little check on the horribly dusty fabric of his shirt, the wedding ring now so tight that he would never get it off again, however much he wanted. It had become one with him, like an iron hoop that's grown into the bark of an oak. Across his forehead ran a wide, black stripe of sweat and dust where the edge of his cap had been, a halo made of particles of Raven Fen.

The bumblebees were all around him, whirring among the glorious dandelions as if they were drunk. A viper went coiling past like a never-ending S on its way to its mound of stones, oblivious to the fact that Father was a live human being with an axe within reach.

I could not let him out of my sight. It nauseated me, watching him on the sly like that, getting excited at having him on my desk, forty times larger than life. Maybe he was yearning deep inside to go back to being grass and seed, hay and straw. Maybe his nerves and muscles were not ready for an encounter with so much that was unexpected.

After a while the flies were crawling over his face, drawn to the moist corners of his eyes as if he were any other animal. An earwig scurried up his chest, over his collar and through his beard, carried on along his cheek and stopped at the edge of his ear, where it looked down towards the semi-overgrown cavern. Maybe it lowered its abdomen and spread its pincers to attack before it thought better of it and ran back down to the ground. Left him in peace.

I wanted to rush out and lie down beside him, lie back with his arm round me and whisper something for his ears only, perhaps stroke his cheek with a cautious finger while he slept.

Father in the fresh grass, bareheaded, the spring breeze playing in his hair. Around him the thousand suns of the dandelions shone, the bees danced, everything was growing.

The words in my head:

I am as tough as juniper and as strong as a steer. You'll never be rid of me.

I could see the kite in my mind's eye, soaring majestically among the cumulus clouds and aerial plankton, gliding on outstretched wings, an object of admiration among the swifts. I had decided on a sea eagle, scale 1:1.5. Two thirds natural size so it would just fit in the empty cupboard in the changing room. Its wing-span would be a metre and a half and its body length seventy centimetres. That was a bit too long really, but it wouldn't fly properly if I made the body any shorter. Aerodynamically it should have been over a metre, but then you'd hardly be able to see that it was an eagle.

I stripped the bark off the chestnut branches and cut them to the right length, planed down the knotholes and sandpapered the ends so they were smooth and even. Measured to the middle of the long wing stick and put the backbone in place, fastened the two of them together with clove hitches and secured them with a reef knot, reinforced the basic cross with struts running from the wingtips to the backbone, like the hypotenuses of two right-angled triangles. I made the tail A-shaped and fixed it on where the two struts met.

And then the skeleton was ready. The frame that would have to carry my own weight.

I stapled the bridle to each end of the backbone and attached the bridle ring to it, for the kite line. Put a screwdriver through the ring and lifted the whole thing carefully, as if there was someone watching. The wings swept slowly up and down, swung like the pans of finely calibrated scales – and came to rest. The skeleton was evenly weighted, the kite balanced. I applied superglue to the knots: fixed forever.

But the hardest part was still to come: the sail. The surface that would catch the wind and turn the kite into a sea eagle. I unrolled the drawing paper on the floor, marked out the measurements and made a passable job of sketching the outline freehand, copying the flight picture in the book. The pointed head straight up, the enormous, rectangular expanse of wing with its seven splayed fingers, the tail like a half-open fan. I filled in the right wing, folded the left one over and made sure they were exactly the same, cut the whole thing out and coloured it. The wings dark brown apart from a lighter band across the middle and white patches under the wings, the tail brown-and-white striped with darker outer tips and the body a more tawny shade. Then I cut some more drawing paper into another shape exactly the same and reinforced the edges with wire. Glued the two pieces together and left it all to dry.

For the kite's tail I measured out five metres of twine, cut some scraps of sky-blue material and knotted them on at regular intervals. Checked the balance one last time now the covering and everything were in place before I carried my masterpiece out into the sun.

Ruler of the open skies, it said in the book. The heraldic emblem of empires. Messenger of the gods and fate. The raptors' raptor.

Nobody at school has ever seen such a glorious kite.

Mum closed her eyes and thanked God for the food she had prepared: a scarcely audible mumble into the lap of her frock. Helped herself to lung hash, rolled brawn and beetroot before passing the dishes over to Father.

'The mercury hasn't been below seventy-eight for nineteen days,' he said. 'Something isn't right.'

He took a deep breath and nodded into his black notebook several times. Mum turned up the radio in answer. Old favourites and some new ones, with all our regular travel updates if you're listening in the car. Bridges under construction and weekend traffic queues, bringing you the latest from Sweden and the world.

'Are you listening to what I'm telling you? Not a drop of rain for nearly three weeks! Even though the stars are bigger than usual. If the harvest fails it's the end for us.'

She cleared her throat, leafed distractedly through the knitting pattern she had sent away for and glanced over at Göran's door. The radio was playing 'Don't Cry for Me' by local band Thorleifs.

'Something's thrown the whole system out of kilter,' Father harped on. 'Whether it's atomic power or the neutron bomb or what –'

'You'll get your rain this spring, too,' Mum said in the end. 'Like every other year. There's no call for you to go around worrying about everything between Heaven and earth. I don't think it does any good.'

He shot her a look and stayed in his seat, squinting up at the skies through screwed-up eyes. The sinews of his neck were twitching.

'It's hard going for me at the moment,' he snuffled. 'If only somebody could tell me what was wrong.'

'Let's eat,' said Mum, 'before it gets cold. Man proposes, God disposes.'

The human anatomy wall charts covered all of one long wall. One of the skeleton, one of the muscles, one of the blood vessels and one of the nervous system. They all had the genitals missing. I had the picture of the nerves nearest my desk: a flayed man with his palms turned outwards and his ribs removed so you could see the intestines and everything. Thick cables from the brain and spine winding their way out to the arms and legs, branching into narrow threads that stretched down to the toes, out to the fingertips and forward, round the mouth. The stomach was a big muddle of tangled nerves.

Homo tremula, I thought.

This is the way you're going to be. A trembling, sexless human being.

The teacher coughed in a very obvious way and looked at the clock above the door; mouth open, he nodded in time to the second hand.

'Time's up!' he cried. 'Put your pens down and check you've put the right name on your papers. Nice, neat writing, please.'

He went round collecting up the test papers while we tidied the classroom and packed everything away for the holidays.

'Stand up!' he commanded. 'The school week is over and Sunday is almost with us. Time to pray, and God will give you what you ask for.'

He took his briefcase and left the room and a few minutes later it was only hard-boiled Bruiser Pelle and me left. He was doing something with his bag; he put a couple of sooty spark plugs on his desk and spent ages rifling through his homework sheets as if he wasn't sure about something.

'How did you do in the test?' I said, going over to the window.

He looked up and pulled a face. No answer. From the corridor came the echo of laughter and the clatter of clogs as everyone headed home. Between the two panes of the double-glazed window, a shiny, metallic bluebottle was careering up and down as if it thought it would be able to get out. The playground looked strangely deserted: the sun-bleached tarmac with plantains growing in the cracks and rickety basketball hoops with no nets, the empty hockey goalmouths, the heavy chains and worn tyres of the swings – it was as if I had never been out there, there had been no point in any of it, the thousands of playtimes had resulted in nothing but a hopeless sense of submission to those I either looked down on or was scared of.

'Don't you want to go home either?' I let slip.

Bruiser Pelle gave a start and then an enigmatic smile.

'Why wouldn't I want to? You think anyone would stay here unless they had to?'

'No –'

Outside the dining hall the caretaker was sprucing the place up, ready for the parents to come in for the end-of-term service, watering and edge-trimming, collecting up weeds and twigs on his carrier moped. The music master was inspecting his departing pupils from the headteacher's balcony, presumably with his fingers crossed behind his back and a sneer on his lips. Over in the churchyard, the witch dressed all in black was seeing to her graves as she generally did on Fridays. Polishing the headstones until they shone, watering the pansies, deadheading the petunias.

Summer, you thought. Inescapable, hateful, never-ending

summer – like a prison sentence, transportation to that place called home. A detention camp for lazy bookworms.

In a fortnight's time there wouldn't be a soul left here.

The playground looked incongruous, fringed by showy beds of tulips and blossoming chestnut trees. It was meant to be wet and muddy beneath drifts of autumn leaves, the rowans should be glowing red with bitter berries, acorn-gathering jays should be flying to and fro between the church oaks and their winter larders in the forest.

It should smell of apples and mushrooms, then you knew you had almost the whole school year ahead of you.

'Made a right mess of it,' Bruiser Pelle said at last. 'I didn't do any revision.'

'Nor me.'

'Yeah, right.'

He gave a laugh, put the homework sheets in his bag and brought out a carburettor he had been keeping wrapped in cotton waste. It stank of petrol. He raised it aloft and held the throttle and nozzle in his other hand, as proud as an astronaut on the moon.

'You mustn't ever drill through the throttle housing,' he said. 'You'll never get the right mixture coming through if you do.'

I knocked on the window. The bluebottle buzzed to and fro. The caretaker disappeared round the corner.

'Do you fancy coming flying?' I said on the off chance. 'I've brought my kite.'

He looked at me expressionlessly, as though he could never have imagined me suggesting anything in my entire life.

'If you're not doing anything else?' I added.

He looked surreptitiously towards the door to check no one else was witness to the embarrassing scene.

'Your bus doesn't go just yet?' he said guardedly.

'Odd weeks there's plenty of time.'

We went round the back, over the bridge across the river and out onto the grazing land where the dandelions grew so thickly that it made my mouth feel like a rabbit's. I checked the bridle was in place and hooked on the line.

'You have to launch it into the wind to get it up,' I explained, handing over my masterpiece. 'If the wind's behind it, it doesn't get anywhere.'

Bruiser Pelle fingered the skeleton and felt along the wire at the edge to try to work out how I'd made it, or to find some flaw in the construction.

'It's an eagle,' I said. 'A sea eagle. Just hold it up facing into the wind and let go when I say.'

I walked backwards, keeping the line taut. The wind rattled the wings of the kite.

This is it, the words darted through my mind. Now or never.

'Now!'

And the kite swayed and tugged, threw itself this way and that like an unruly lapwing in spring, rising and falling by turns, yielded to the wind and gained height – only to be thrown towards the ground again. But then a firm gust caught hold of it in earnest, filled it like a sail and took it higher and higher in a diagonal arc. I paid out more line and with a few twitches I had it climbing through the air as if up some invisible staircase to Heaven. It finally stopped resisting and hovered freely, without a struggle, sweeping round in slow, wide circles as it went on rising, wheeling ever higher on outstretched wings like a lammergeier riding the thermals.

'Come on then!' shouted Bruiser Pelle impatiently.

And we ran, with exaggeratedly high steps, as if tiptoeing through the fog of dandelions and grass, over to the curtain of foliage on the other side, me backwards with the wind in my hand and my eyes on the kite, he forwards so he could see where we were going.

'I've never flown this high before,' I called.

'Can I try?'

I felt a fizz of elation. My kite, and Bruiser Pelle wants to fly it.

'But make sure you keep back a bit of line. You've always got to have a bit of line in reserve.'

We found some rocks to sit on, wedged the reel firmly and let the kite fly itself. At a quick glance it looked as though the clouds were standing still and the kite was racing along on outspread, seven-fingered wings, so like a real eagle was it.

'You must have over a hundred metres of string?' Bruiser Pelle said.

'Nearly a hundred and fifty. It's fishing line really, for salmon. Good and tough.'

He nodded guardedly. Got out his tin of moist snuff by way of reply and started to pack a wad of it, a hard little pellet, shaping it so carefully with his yellowed fingers that it was as if he planned to keep it forever.

'It flies pretty well,' I said, trying to make it sound like a question. 'If we hadn't kept it on a line I bet it would have flown to Leningrad or something.'

'That wouldn't be a problem. Not at all.'

I couldn't work out what he meant.

'The wind's coming from the south west,' I clarified. 'West south west. Look at the clouds.'

He gave me a look. Wedged the pellet of snuff under his top lip and spat two thin yellow jets between his teeth as if it was second nature.

'People used to think it was the eagle that made the wind,' I said. 'Way up north where the sky ends.'

'Do you believe in all that stuff?'

'Well the wind's got to start somewhere, I suppose. When I was little I thought it was the trees that made it all happen. I couldn't work out how there could be wind on the plains on Öland or in Skåne.'

Bruiser Pelle made a face and raised his eyebrows to show he thought I was an idiot. Fished out and reshaped his pellet, added some extra snuff, tested it and repacked it again.

'I heard there's a Stockholm girl coming down here in the autumn,' he said as he did it. 'Think she's moving in somewhere out your way.'

'Oh?'

He put the snuff back under his lip and spat more thin jets to land at our feet.

'We'll bring her down to earth pretty damn quick,' he said. 'Won't we, eh?'

Something tugging at me –

Lie there among the dandelions and creepy crawlies. A jungle of flowers and life to be with. Lie among long-nosed weevils and sucking insects, flesh flies and springtails, to see the ants collecting the blue anemone seeds, to put a little finger into a foamy ball of cuckoo spit, lift a crane fly by its longest leg.

Why don't you come to me? Come and crawl on me! Come into me. Come robber flies, hawk moths and parasites! Be with me for a while –

He's sitting over there with his razor blade. Scratching and scoring the lid of his snuff tin, saying nothing. Ring in his ear and the Kawasaki logo embroidered right across his back.

Biker's scarf around his neck. Long suede tassels hanging from the yoke of his jacket, like a proper cowboy.

Why hadn't I got all that? A pierced ear, a souped-up moped and a Lee jacket with tassels.

I didn't know.

Why can't I join in, pinching pallets and siphoning off petrol to make some money for myself like everybody else! Have I got to spend my whole life going round on my bike selling packets of seeds and flower bulbs?

But fancy him wanting to come and fly the kite. Even though he's had girls and is starting to get a moustache.

'I want to lie here for a hundred years,' I said without thinking. 'And never have to go home.'

He turned round in surprise, as if he had forgotten my existence. Broke off a dandelion stalk and put the poisonous white juice in his mouth.

'Kids who like school have a helluva time later on,' he said. 'They're the ones with their heads stuck in a book, who never get nothing done. If you get top marks you end up in the loony bin or an office. Don't suppose you've any idea how a real cunt looks. It's not like in the books at school, if that's what you thought.'

I squinted at the veiled sun and thought about butterflies' brains, hoped for the peacock and the mourning cloak, held them in my mind, thought of how infinitely fine their nerve fibres and ganglia chains must be. To be drawn unconsciously to flowers and bees, live off nectar and honeydew, sleep when it's cloudy and fly in sunshine and warmth.

'Have you thought any more about what he told us in General Science?'

'Which bit?'

I propped myself up on one elbow.

'The bit about everything being made up of molecules that are moving the whole time. That nothing is constant, everything is in motion all day long. The teacher's desk and the chairs and books, the whole school, everything vibrating without you even thinking about it.'

He just sat there, busy with his tin of snuff, scratching and scoring.

'Or a rock in the forest that's been there since the Ice Age, the fact that it's quivering the whole time, like, inside, and never stops? Have you thought? That a school desk consists of billions of molecules on the go all the time, forever, even when it's stopped being a desk. I find it almost impossible to imagine.'

Bruiser Pelle gave me a couple of sceptical glances.

'Thought any more?' he said after a bit. 'There's not much anyone can do about it though, is there?'

I picked a dock leaf and slumped down onto my back again. Chewed on meadow oxygen and stared up at the sky, followed the continually shape-shifting clouds and felt a sense of boundless solitude. A kind of weightlessness, between waking life and nightmare. A transparent stone in a well by the sea. Nowhere to go.

The kite was straining against the wind, a hundred and forty metres above me: the silhouette of a sea eagle with a disproportionately long body. I shall show it to her when she moves here, the Stockholm girl, and we'll fly it every day, her and me.

Ruler of the skies. Messenger of the gods. King of the birds.

Bruiser Pelle gathered all his phlegm in his throat, hawked to produce a dirty yellow gob of it, tapped his snuff tin, tossed it across to me. He had carved two big, spiky letters on the lid, SS. Sara Sigfridsson or the Schutzstaffel?

'Red Lacquer, no rubbish,' he said. 'You can use my applicator if you want.'

I shook my head and passed back the tin.

'I already feel a bit dizzy. It must be the sun.'

He stuffed the tin into his front pocket and reached for the string of the kite.

'So shall we give it a go or what?' he said in a different voice. 'Then we'll see how far he can fly.'

I stared as if paralysed at the razor blade in his hand and the thin nylon string, thinking surely he wouldn't –

Then the blade swished and the dangling line went floating up before I had time to react. The kite got the wind in its sails and was borne away, twisting in the gusts but rising steadily away over the tops of the spruce trees to the east until it was no more than a dwindling black cross in the sky.

Bruiser Pelle didn't even turn round to watch it go. He contemplated me with a satisfied look, sat there with a pimply smile and his fringe hanging over his eyes, wondering what I would do next. Adjusted his wad of snuff with his tongue and goaded me with a kick to the shin.

'It happens sometimes,' he said. 'When you drop your guard.'

I looked away and said nothing.

'Pity you've no sense of humour, though. But I guess it runs in your family.'

I felt a lump in my chest.

'Fuck it Klassy! We'll go and get it back sometime, if you're that fucking bothered.'

Mum in the garden. How briskly and easily she moved when she could be outside and get on with her own interests, working among the flowers and vegetables, thinning and weeding and tidying. Putting in perennials, sowing beans and spinach, planting out dahlias and gladioli.

I thought I could hear her humming from way off, that purling flow so reminiscent of other times when she thought nobody was nearby.

No.

Father must have been there too. In among the gooseberry bushes, smoking a cigarette, with the tank of insecticide spray on his back. Mum called out something and vanished round the corner of the house but was back almost at once with the watering can in one hand and an axe in the other.

Is it so odd? For Father to want to help her in the garden now the spring tillage is all done?

I went to get the newspaper and sat out front where they couldn't see me. The nuclear power station at Barsebäck had to be stopped. Öster should have got a penalty. Red lead and arsenic found in the rubbish dump at Kosta. Full house at the parish hall for the sewing circle social evening. The letter I'd sent in about the next transit of Venus wasn't in there today, either, and I had almost given up hope of them ever printing the one I'd sent last winter about the difference between percentages and percentage points. But there was one signed 'Someone who knows', protesting against a statement from the National Board of Consumer Complaints that only the deceased have a right to complain about their funerals. The writer thought it entirely unreasonable to treat the dear departed as consumers and took the view that a relative should be entitled to speak out on the dead person's behalf if the funeral hadn't come up to scratch.

Something thudding on the ground? Father starting to go on about mildew and mites, infestations and parasites, all the minuscule life forms that are taking over. Shield bugs, rust fungus and whiteflies. Why we've got to resort to poison if we want to survive. Then he stopped abruptly, as if Mum had clapped her hand over his mouth. As if she knew I was here. Perhaps she'd seen me coming from the school bus but not felt up to waving?

Not worth thinking about. Look at the blackbirds instead, hopping along with their feet together and putting their heads on one side to hear where there's something crawling through the soil. How many worms does a blackbird pull up in its bird life? Three or four a minute, two hundred an hour. If it lives for seven years?

And the worms? They never run out. Two hundred per square metre, a billion in our marsh, I'd worked out when I was ill in bed one time. They'll be like the Chinese by the time I've grown up.

The worm: the subterranean farmer that never sleeps.

Another thud. Father's bass voice and suddenly there was Mum, her face hidden by her headscarf.

'We flew the kite today!' I called out to forestall her. 'Bruiser Pelle came with me and we went behind the school.'

She didn't answer. Her gumboots slapped against her bare legs as she walked.

'That's it, I've had enough,' she whimpered. 'I can't cope with any more.'

My throat felt as if it was closing up. Can't cope with any more? She came to a stop and showed me her face as I had never seen it before. Naked, red and puffy, almost entreating. One of her bra straps had slipped down her arm. She snuffled, half shutting one of her eyes.

Was she actually crying?

Are you crying, Mum?

Please tell me you're not.

'I tried everything I could,' she said in a low voice. 'Whatever you do, don't think I didn't try.'

I wanted to run over and hug her, rest my head on her bosom, do whatever it took to make her happy again. I sat there on the stone steps, fixed to the spot.

'For God's sake. Don't think I didn't try.'

She wiped her cheeks and gave me an imploring look, as if she wanted to be forgiven for something in advance. Then she vanished round the corner and closed the house door after her.

Can't cope with any more –, came an echo from the air.

You've got to. Do you hear me! You've got to cope.

The cat came up and rubbed herself against my legs, winding her tail into a question mark over her back. I picked her up and put her on my lap, stroked against the grain of her fur up the back of her neck and down towards her throat. A jumble of thoughts was pulsing round in my head. Imagine if I had to take over the farm and live alone with Father. Had to go out and do the milking, morning and evening, seven days a week. The cat's heart was beating. She squeezed her eyes shut and rumbled and purred, her whole body quivering, waiting for me to burrow my nose into her fur and mimic her purr as usual. If I had to sit at the kitchen table without Mum. I stroked her even harder, pressing right in to her ribcage with one hand and squeezing her throat with the other until she went quiet. Then she gave a yowl and pulled free, tore through the spiraea hedge and was gone.

Why did I do that?

It wasn't me.

She lay on the unmade bed in her gumboots, sobbing so much that her shoulders heaved. Her face was buried in the pillow. The bedspread of crocheted squares in a pile on the floor.

She's made up her mind, said a voice somewhere. It's too late to do anything now.

'Mum, are you crying?' I whispered through the crack of the door.

I said it as loud as I dared, but it sounded like the squeak of a mouse. I wanted yet didn't want her to hear.

'Can I come with you if you're leaving us?' I whispered. 'I can't manage without you.'

Fire on my cheeks.

I stood stock still with my ear to the crack for what seemed like half an hour, but the desperate weeping went on and on. It sounded as if it was going to last forever, as if something inside her had been worn to shreds.

'Was Mum cross?' Göran asked when I came into the kitchen.

He was at the kitchen table, practising my labyrinth game. His eyes were riveted to the ball and his tongue and whole upper body were playing the game. The stopwatch was on the table in front of him.

'Cross?' I said, with as much composure as I could muster.

I went over to the table and fixed him with a look. Scraped my nails hard along the oilcloth and kicked his chair.

No reaction.

'Go and comfort her for Christ's sake!' I shouted through clenched teeth. 'You being such great friends and all! Get in there and do something for once!'

He stared at me as if I was a stranger. The ball fell through a hole and rolled about inside the box.

'Do something then! We'll end up in a children's home if you don't do something! Like Johnny's brother! Get it? In a children's home!'

His eyes filled with moisture. He sat paralysed with his chin resting in his podgy hands and let the tears fall, crying soundlessly. Then he knocked over the vase and the contents ran all over the table as he ran to his room. Slammed the door shut and turned the key. I felt as if the air in the room was running out. Just the tap dripping, slowly, drop by drop, like in a torture chamber. Out in the garden Father was advancing with the insecticide spray, oblivious.

I wake in the middle of the night to find everything sopping wet. Get up and wash myself, put my underpants and sheets to soak in ammonia solution, wipe the plastic cover and make up the bed again, put on something dry and climb back in. The same procedure for the hundredth time.

The black water and the fluorescing, poison-yellow bubbles rising from my mouth, my futile efforts to get up to the surface with my hands tied behind my back. The feeling of being sucked ever deeper into the silent blackness. The emerald-green fish that dart by and vanish. Somebody standing up there in the sunlight, looking sort of wavy through the swift-flowing water. Father, but a hundred years old now and entirely bald.

What's wrong with me? The question fluttered through my head. Who is it, directing my dreams, sending down these images when what I need is a rest from it all?

I shut my eyes and clasped my hands on my chest, concentrated on my breathing, in and out, felt calm slowly return as my abdomen rose and sank and air reached my lungs. Tried to convince myself that everything was going to be all right one day, that it wasn't my fault things had turned out like this.

They're lying there just underneath me, right now, my floor is their ceiling, their walls are my walls, too. Beneath my head is the bedside table with the wedding photo and the bronze candlesticks on the crocheted cloth. The candlesticks with the candles that have not once been lit since she had them as a wedding present, as if they were never intended for use.

The brick channel of the chimney stack from the boiler to the chimney where the jackdaws started to build. It's all that will be left in the end. The chimney stack and the stone foundations, and the sick cries of the white-eyed birds.

Was that something down there? Mumbles muffled by a beard, springs squeaking. Had he dropped off and was shouting in his sleep? And was she hushing him, or tossing and turning because she didn't dare fall asleep? Heavy footsteps across some floor or other, a window thrown open.

'... *the moon as pale as a damned corpse ... the marsh will turn into a desert ... whiteflies ... get some help ...*'

Quiet.

Only the alarm clock pecking its way through the night, interminably, second by second, three thousand six hundred times an hour. Like a resting heartbeat.

I lie there and listen to it all.

Register every sign and sound, every vibration, like a human seismograph.

You can't fall asleep now. If you do, something dreadful is going to happen. Count the knotholes on the ceiling, take it panel by panel or imagine away the joins and try to spot constellations, see how many Ploughs and Dracos there are in the Devil's Room.

I jumped.

There was a black eye gaping at me – a bottomless hole, charred and dead. An eye of nothingness above my bed.

It's because something is going to come to an end, said the voice. That eye will swallow up whatever is left, stare and swallow until it has finished with you and the darkness has received its share. It will follow you wherever you go.

The wet weather did arrive in the end. The lethal drought was not going to last forever, the sun had finished baking the bog this time round. The spring sowing could spurt into growth at last and the clover could thicken, but Father had other things on his mind. He let the wet dung dry onto his clothes as he rummaged in the pile of old scrap, tugging at everything he came across as if he thought he had unearthed precious treasure. Rusty old metal sheets and piping, dented old car wings and oil drums sawed in half, battered shovels and dung rakes with no handles, discarded machine parts and dismantled engines – he wanted them all. He hacked away at things that had lain abandoned for so long they had started to revert to nature; then he levered them up, and if there was something he could not retrieve by hand, he hauled it out with his tractor and chains.

The scrap pile had served its purpose. Every little paint pot and remnant of barbed wire was to be gathered up, bottomless buckets and rusted milk churns, the steel bars that hadn't been needed when he extended the cowshed – nothing was to be left behind.

'Goodness knows what on earth it's all for?' said Mum. 'But I suppose he's got something into his head so it'll be impossible to talk him out of it. The other week he lay down and studied the vegetable garden through a magnifying glass. And now this.'

The clearing, I thought. Get in there once it brightens up. Check on the stones and see everything is as it should be, take the flycatcher's nesting box to the green chamber nobody knows about.

And it was all the same as ever, only dripping wet and full of birds, clicking and singing because the rain had stopped and the sun was coming through. The air was as fresh as the water in a deep-water spring, virtually steaming with the chlorophyll of everything that was turning green. I climbed up into the birch tree I had chosen and found a place where the entrance hole would be facing east: with sunrise on offer for those who woke early. Then I retreated to the mossy stump and waited for a black and white shape, one of the late arrivals, to come and inspect the new living quarters. Listened to the dripping of the trees, strained my eyes to see a chaffinch whose warning cry had got stuck on repeat a few spruces away, and suddenly the cuckoo started calling.

I had heard him a few times already that spring, but now there was something insistent about his calls that was unfamiliar – as if he *wanted* something. Maybe he thought he had waited long enough already.

It's you he's calling, said the voice.

I shaped my mouth into an 'o' and gave myself a couple of practice runs, working out how to mimic the cuckoo's cry. What seemed to work best was pulling my chin in towards my chest and forcing out the sound from as low in my throat as possible.

'Cuc-koo!'

Nothing.

Just the thin drizzle through the canopy of trees. A squirrel peeking out of the spruce opposite, a pair of restless robins busy round the uprooted tree on the other side, presumably occupied with the business of breeding.

I stood up and tried again. Leant back and pressed my chin down onto my chest, cupped my hands into a funnel and called as loud as I could, louder and louder, so he was bound to hear me wherever he was.

And he answered! Two balls of sound had been fired from the invisible giant catapult, loud and clear across fields and spinneys. Now he was coming, homing in on them with his beak in the air.

Cuc-koo –

And again.

I climbed up into the thickest spruce and hid. Hooted a couple of times and waited, tense with anticipation.

Here he comes! That long tail, those swift wings, and it's not a pigeon or a sparrow hawk – it's the cuckoo himself, skimming the treetops at speed. He gives a couple of coughs as if something's gone down the wrong way, falls silent and glides to the spruce on the other side of the clearing. He perches right at the top like a church weathercock, bobs his tail and looks nervously about him, turning his head as if expecting something.

Now it's you and me.

I've got him in my binocular sights, razor-sharp. The hawk-like, white-barred front, the shifty yellow eye, the raised feathers on the back of his head. Then he drops his wings, raises his tail in a fan and draws in his breast.

Cuc-koo – cuc-koo – – –

It came with such unexpected force that I felt like the fly that got shut inside Grandma's long-case clock. I thought I'd never heard anything so distinct in all my life, even though he was barely opening his beak, just sort of forcing compressed air from his throat. But there was something strange about the call, a discordant element when you listened closely. The singing call on its continuous loop was mixed with a screeching cry, and between the cuckooing there was a cross hissing of a kind I'd never heard from any bird before. It was as though he wanted to scare off every creature in the vicinity but lure in any who heard him from afar.

I can't help myself, I've got to try it now I've got him here. See if I come up to scratch as a cuckoo and a rival.

And he answers even more excitedly this time, ruffles up his neck feathers and calls until his whole body shakes. Extends his head and looks around, sticks his tail in the air and calls again – frantically, almost stammering in his eagerness: *Cuck-kuc-koo, cuck-kuc-koo!* The next moment the female comes swooping in with an unfathomable, bubbling call – and flies straight over to the uprooted tree where the robins were. Quick as a flash, she nudges out one of their eggs and squats on the nest, flutters her wings and gets up again, eats the egg she pushed out and disappears back the way she came. And the male cackles and crows and streaks after her into the trees, as if he can't wait to hear all about it.

I could hardly believe it was true. To get to see it like that. And everything happened so fast it was as if they'd planned and practised down to the last detail, or really wanted to demonstrate how it was done, initiate me into the noble art of parasitism.

It suddenly hit me: Why didn't you scare her off! Now the robins will sit out their full term on the nest and the baby cuckoo will kill their babies by way of thanks. And the parents will die of exhaustion.

I climbed down and went over to the fallen tree in two minds. The nest was small enough to fit into the palm of my hand. A bit of moss with a few root fibres bound round it, lined with hair, and three yellowish-white eggs with rust-coloured streaks and speckles. One of them was a touch larger and just nearby were the remains of what must have been the half-eaten nest egg.

Now's your chance! Destroy the nest before the robins get back, get rid of it and they'll lay a new brood somewhere else.

And the unborn cuckoo? Which could live a whole bird life if you don't interfere.

Who are you to play master of life and death?

I felt a sudden chill. If I leave things as they are, the robin will lay the rest of her eggs and sit on them for twelve days and nights, and the first thing the baby cuckoo will do is to make sure it has the nest to itself, that's for certain. The damage is already done. If I take out the cuckoo's egg the robins will notice there's something wrong and abandon the whole nest.

From up in the treetops: *The baby cuckoo or nobody* –

I simply didn't know what to do. Stopped, paralysed, staring at the wretched nest among the stones and gritty soil and mangled roots.

Thinking that down there –

Stamp on it, and it's all over.

I climbed down into the hole and planted myself there with my foot poised above the nest until my thigh muscles ached and the leg I was standing on started to tremble with tension.

Some barrier inside me.

Make yourself scarce and maybe the robins will jettison the unwanted egg for themselves. Pretend you are blissfully unaware. You didn't see what happened.

Better still: take the cuckoo's egg with you and run home. Put it in the stove and see a relative of yours come into the world.

As on edge as if I had committed some crime, I tumbled breathlessly out onto the old foresters' trackway. I sat down on a pile of logs and tried to regain my composure, bring some order to my thoughts, which were racing in all directions. Perhaps it was my fault that I always ended up in situations where I could only choose the lesser of two evils? Shouldn't nature itself have put a stop to the cuckoos' parasitism, made them take responsibility for their offspring like every other creature that wants its own species to carry on? Am I supposed to devote my life to hunting out cuckoo eggs and bringing the young up at home?

At the cut ends of the logs, the resin was pearling like beads of sweat between the growth rings: solidified sap that's going to be amber in twenty million years' time. There was a smell of tar and turpentine. On the ground below, the lily-of-the-valley were in bud, bowing to each other like the ones Grandmother sold on the market square when she was my age, walking the thirty kilometres to get there. Wrapped in wet newspaper, the wicker basket full of them, five öre a bunch. Among the fabulous marsh marigolds in the waterlogged patch of alders, the brimstones reeled around like new lovers, hunting for alder buckthorn to lay their eggs on.

'Someone's out and about in God's green world, I see.'

The dowser materialised in my path, long-necked as a crane, eyes peeled as usual. Before I had a chance to return his greeting he had pulled out his pipe and started to fill it, as if planning to keep me company.

'I saw a cuckoo lay an egg in a robins' nest,' I said, straight out, unable to keep it to myself.

He struck a match and cupped his hand round the flame. His axe handle was wedged under his arm.

'Not bad,' he replied without much interest. 'You've come from the woods, then?'

He puffed on his pipe and looked high up among the trees, as if he thought that was where the robins lived.

'I was on the lookout for a nice flying rowan,' he explained, changing the subject. 'Didn't happen to see one on your way, did you?'

I shook my head. I didn't even know what a flying rowan was, but there was no need to tell him that.

'You're meant to cut them on Ascension Day,' he said, 'but that depends on you finding one at all. If there's one thing this world's short of, it's flying rowans, let me tell you. In the old days, folk would at least keep track of where they grew.'

He took his pipe out of his mouth and waved it dejectedly in the direction of the woods.

'It was me that lured in the male cuckoo,' I said, 'and then the female came and laid her egg in the robins' nest. It was all my fault.'

He started to laugh, showing the unsightly teeth that he'd plugged with Plastic Padding so the dowsing rod wouldn't get any interference from the heavy metals in his fillings. You could hardly see his teeth any more because the whole row of them was hidden by the padding, like a crust of yellow plaster.

'Oh dear, that's not good, boy,' he said in a different tone, as if talking to a child.

'It took less than thirty seconds. Must have had plenty of practice, eh?'

He smiled indulgently and sucked on his pipe, puffing smoke out of the corner of his mouth. Wood pigeons called from two directions.

'Well be that as it may, I'm supposed to be finding a well up at Bliss Cottage,' he said. 'You need a good dowsing rod for that sort of thing. Seems to be some Stockholmers as have bought it.'

'Great,' I replied, as casually as he had, but he wasn't listening.

'The rowan was Frigg's tree, the mother of the gods, you know,' he lectured me, 'and a house that gets its water thanks to the flying rowan will be an abode of the gods. That's the way it is. The house is filled with holiness, the rowan gives protection and fertility to those who live there. Protection against thunder and corpses and a bit of everything.'

'What's more, the first woman on the Earth was made out of a rowan,' he added as an afterthought. 'Her name was Embla. That doesn't do any harm, either.'

I smeared a blob of resin under my top lip and jumped down.

'I've got an eye on my ceiling that's blacker than black and never blinks,' I said rashly. 'It's right above my bed. What do you think I can do about it? Plant a flying rowan and put it on my bedside table?'

The dowser looked grave and shook his head as if to impress his answer on me. The axe glinted like a freshly sharpened knife blade at his armpit.

'*That* wouldn't go unpunished,' he said. 'Putting a flying rowan in a pot is like burying a raven alive.'

He stepped forward and tapped me on the arm with the stem of his pipe, shutting one eye so he wouldn't see double.

'I'm going now,' he said. 'If you like, and as long as you can keep your mouth shut, I'll tell you one of the tricks.'

'I can keep quiet when I have to.'

'Lightning often strikes old oaks, even a whippersnapper like you knows that, but not everybody knows why, not these days. Well it's simple, see: the oak roots go deep, seek out the groundwater, meaning the oak conducts electricity better than any other tree. It attracts the lightning like a magnet. So if the rod doesn't come up with a decision, go to the oak and start there. That's where the water vein runs. Proof that fire and water belong together.'

He winked and gave a wily smile, so there was no way of telling if what he'd just told me was the truth or made up.

'Think about it,' he nodded. 'And as for that eye, don't you worry about it. One damned day it'll be gone. Tell your father I said so.'

Then he shouldered his axe and tramped off into the woods, in the direction from which I had just come.

I was ambling home along the track with my head full of bubbling cuckoos and flying rowans when I caught sight of somebody prowling round among our cows, grazing up ahead. I had no trouble making out Johnny's army cap and blue-and-white-checked flannel shirt between the trunks of the trees.

A spring, tightening. A feeling that trouble's brewing.

I set my sights on the old binder where I ought to be able to hide if he saw me, crept from tree to tree like an Indian until I reached the edge of the woods, carefully avoiding any dry twigs, and realised as I got nearer my hiding place that I would have to squat in a clump of nettles. It didn't matter.

The main thing is not to be seen.

Johnny was wandering nervously up and down, as if he'd arranged to meet a criminal. He looked round, clambered onto a rock but thought better of it and came back down. Thrust his hands into his pockets and paused uneasily, listening. Turned and walked the few steps to a heifer who was lying down, chewing the cud and swishing away the flies with her tail. Suddenly he had a cord in his hand, or a thin rope, as if he was going to lasso something. He kicked the heifer to make her get up and went after her as she slouched off, keeping a couple of metres behind her so as not to scare her. Then the cow stopped and started to graze again. Johnny moved in at once to snare her back legs and then looped the rope through a metal ring fixed in a block of blast rock, pulled it tight and knotted it. She pulled at it and almost fell over, but stayed upright with her front legs splayed, staring at the ground. Johnny cast a furtive look over his shoulder to make sure there was no one in sight.

Then he stepped up onto the rock behind her and let down his trousers. One hand was busy with himself while the other lifted up the heifer's tail. His right arm was going faster and faster. She bellowed and tugged at the rope and Johnny went down on his knees to position himself better, pressed himself against her and pushed for all he was worth. The heifer gave a gurgle and tossed her head, nearly losing her balance again, but then the fight went out of her and she just stood there, as if paralysed by the moment. Johnny wasn't satisfied though. He stepped down from the stone to pull her closer, and was bending down to take hold of the rope when the cowshed door at our place slammed shut. Johnny jumped and was instantly on the alert, looking my way.

I threw myself down into the clump of nettles and wormed my way under the binder. My heart was beating wildly, like a trapped bird's.

He's coming this way. Father's scared him off. If he sees the nettles have been flattened, I've had it.

I shan't tell anyone. Whatever happens. No one's going to find out about it, not ever, even if I live for a thousand years.

I lay stock still, straining my ears and holding my breath. I was itching terribly. There were throbbing nettle stings all over my body.

No more of Johnny's footsteps?

Swallowed up by the rustle and murmur of the woods?

I finally plucked up the courage to crawl out and rubbed my hands on the seams of my trousers until the skin was on fire. It didn't help. I found a binder strut where I could rub my forearms raw. Scrubbed my knuckles on some rusty sheet metal until they bled.

That's how easy it was.

I put on the ear protectors, span the random-number spinner six times to get two three-digit numbers, noted them on my pad, put down my pen and closed my eyes. Made sure I had the numbers on the inside of my eyelids.

Four hundred and seventy-seven times nine hundred and twelve ... four hundred and seventy-seven times nine hundred ... three hundred and sixty thousand plus sixty-nine thousand three hundred – – – four hundred and twenty-nine thousand three hundred plus twelve times four hundred and seventy-seven ... five thousand seven hundred and twenty-four plus four hundred and twenty-nine thousand three hundred – – – four hundred and thirty-five thousand and twenty-four.

435,024.

Note it down and check your calculations.

Of course.

You've got to get forty-nine right answers in a row, said the dangerous eye. Then you can dab on the soothing antiseptic and drink the cold milk. If you don't get them all right, something terrible will happen.

I had got hold of a book about reproduction in mammals and I couldn't put it down. I read about cross-breeding, stud farm boxes and insemination, artificial vaginas and particularly desirable sperm diluted into thousands of batches, learnt all there was to know about pregnancy testing, progeny testing and growth indexes, enviously studied pictures of the organs of bulls and stallions, half a metre long and swollen into monstrous barrels for sufficiently deep discharge into apparently indifferent females. I thought of Johnny and read about deformities and mutations, saw pictures of five-legged foals and double-headed calves looking two ways at the same time. And I read about castration by means of emasculators and Burdizzo castrators: 'If animals are to be reared for slaughter, bull calves are castrated by cutting or crushing the spermatic cords. The desired mood change resulting from an end to hormone production is then achieved. Grazing animals being reared for meat may also require castration, particularly if they share pasture with females and it is not practical to separate the sexes by walls the height of a man, heavy-duty fencing or similar.'

Father suddenly came into view beyond the trees. He was over at Oxmeadow planting potatoes, hunched over the dented old metal bucket as he set out the seed potatoes along the ridged furrows one by one and used the rake to cover them with soil until the scratch plough could complete the job. Sliced-off Bintje or sprouting King Edward? A few experimental rows of

President or Magnum Bonum? A boot's length between them, three or four to a metre. It only took a few minutes to empty the bucket and then he had to trek back to the trailer to refill it. Stretch his back, relight his pipe, pause and squint up into the sky as if he was listening for something that didn't exist.

He hadn't been asked when the neighbouring farms clubbed together for a new potato planter, so he didn't want to ask if he could borrow it when they had finished planting theirs. He would rather plant potatoes by hand, even if it took him ten or even twenty times as long.

'Going cap in hand isn't my way. I've always had to do it all under my own steam anyway.'

So should I have helped? Got a bucket and matched my steps to his. We could have planted the potatoes together, he and I, taken a row each and chatted about sciatica and low pressure, Colorado beetles and leaf fungus, pigweed and hemp-nettle, sulphuric acid and arsenic.

I could have seized my chance to ask you about everything.

If you know where the brook starts, up in the woods. What it is that makes the peat soil burn from inside. Whether you had any mates when you were a boy. Whether you've ever been in love. Why you carved your initials on the rock. If you and Mum really liked each other before I was born.

That sort of nonsense.

He sat there smiling for a long time, his clenched fist held up in front of me like a heart. In the end he asked me if I wanted to guess what it was.

'Don't you want to know?'

Then he slowly turned his hand, opened his fingers to reveal a tiny potato, no bigger than the robin's egg in the clearing. There was an enticing glint in his eyes.

'Have you ever seen such a tiddler?' he said.

I cleared my throat and looked at the puny little potato and the tracery of lines and creases on his trembling palm, making little angles and triangles, branching, running together and criss-crossing each other like the networks in a road atlas. His Life Line was as black as tar and ended abruptly in the Mount of Mars near his thumb.

'It's for you Klas,' he said. 'I thought you might like it as a souvenir.'

Mum gave him a sideways look.

'So that means everything that needs to grow is planted now?' she said. 'I think you could do with a bit of a rest before haymaking. That pile of scrap can just stay where it is for now.'

Father paid no attention. He looked at me and put the pointless potato on my plate.

'It's for you Klas,' he said. 'A present from me.'

Mum with her sewing patterns as evening came. A blue and white sailor dress for the little miss. This stemstitch cloth makes coffee time cosier. Shelf-edge trim uses Hardanger embroidery to create beautiful birds.

She read with her little finger as well as her eyes. She'd put a big cross in the margin by the sailor dress.

Father was peering down to the peat bog through eyes narrowed to slits, chewing and chewing as if he couldn't swallow anything. The sun was going down.

My name wasn't on the letters page today, either. But the vicar had joined the debate about swimwear and decency, exhorting all the girls not to presume on God's mercy and bare their breasts to his heavens. 'For women's breasts are the work of the Lord and shall not be used to arouse sinful lusts,' he wrote.

'Everything's crowding in on me,' said Father, wrapped in his own concerns. 'Something's not right. Could be the barometer –'

'Then I'll go and get Göran tomorrow,' said Mum by way of reply. 'Granny's going to see her sister-in-law in hospital. I don't think she's got long left, so it won't be much fun for Göran to tag along.'

Father glanced quickly at his watch, as if woken from a different world.

'Tomorrow?' he said. 'But you haven't got anything on tomorrow have you, Klas?'

I spluttered. He had caught me napping.

'We'll check over the rest of the wire fences, you and me,' he said. 'It all needs to be in order now the beasts are going to be out at night. And then we'll turn on the power. Might as well get it done.'

'Yes, that'll be fine,' I answered, managing to make it sound as if it had been my greatest wish in life.

Mum shot me a look of surprise.

'So the two of you'll fend for yourselves while I'm gone? It'll only be for the day.'

'It should've been done long since,' said Father, 'but it can't be helped. Everything needs electricity these days.'

The sun was already high in the sky when we came out. There was not a cloud to be seen, and it was going to stay that way, according to Father. There was a scent of lilacs and a delicate, almost imperceptible rustle from the aspens over by the potato cellar, like the swish of the reeds in the Marsh Pool as the morning mist dispersed.

It was going to be a lovely day.

I stayed a few steps behind as I usually did when it was just him and me, so we could both keep our thoughts to ourselves. So I could listen to the birds calling and chirruping. Identify the species and memorise them. Stamp my footprint in the yellow pollen porridge of the drying puddles.

This was *me* walking along.

But he had something to say. He stopped and turned towards me, took his pipe out of his mouth.

'Have you ever tried standing in a doorway and pressing your arms against the sides?' he said. 'They go up by themselves afterwards, it's funny really.'

He raised his hands until they were sticking straight out and he looked like a cross.

'You have to push as hard as you can and count to forty-nine. Then they'll go right up over your head when you let go. If you bring them down they'll go up again, it's like an invisible force. Wonder where that might come from, eh?'

He let out smoke with a smacking sound to underline what

he'd just said. Looked as if he was going to laugh, but then got out his handkerchief and blew his nose instead. I tried to imagine him alone in the cowshed with his arms going up and down by themselves, like some heavy-footed bird in slow motion.

'I've never tried it,' I said.

'It's never too late. It's just as funny every time.'

I loaded the newly sharpened poles onto the trailer and Father made sure we had the crowbar and the sledgehammer and all the other stuff. The roll of barbed wire, the toolbox and a heavy electrical unit.

'You all right driving?' he said. 'We'll start on the far side of the marsh.'

I felt all warm. Being allowed to drive on the road even though Father was with me. It was the first time.

You're growing up now, Klas, the voice whispered. Engage gear and off you go. The speed and steering are in your hands.

He didn't even turn round to check I was doing it right, just sat at the back on the bed of the trailer with his pipe at the corner of his mouth where all he could see was the road unfurling below him. Mum stood at the kitchen window waving, smiling broadly to see us like this.

Everything is as it should be. Father and I are going to mend fences together. Switch on the electricity and keep the animals in.

'You're fine in sixth,' he called. 'We've got all day.'

We started nearest the Canal where we had to be particularly careful it was all in good order so the heifers wouldn't go and drown. Father walked behind checking the barbed wire and the insulators and tested the poles one by one. Where they were cracked or rotting he spat on his hands, made a new hole alongside with the iron bar and put in a new pole, took up the sledgehammer and wielded it until the pole was as solid as a rock in the ground, as if he expected it to stand there forever.

The scarcely perceptible nod as he put the sledgehammer back in the trailer and relit his pipe and it was time to move on.

When we'd finished Calfpatch, which stuck out into the fields of tender crop shoots like a grass wedge, he said we would stop for elevenses even though it wasn't much after ten. We each sat on a rock and unpacked what Mum had given us. The Thermos flask of coffee for him and a bottle of milk for me, and the flowery cake tin filled with buns and pastries, plus a slice of Tosca cake each. He put a sugar lump between his teeth, poured the scalding coffee into his saucer and started blowing and slurping.

'When I was a lad I used to watch the trains going past,' he said after a while. 'I thought it was the best thing ever.'

He nodded a couple of times towards the overgrown railway embankment, as if to show me where the trains used to run.

'I bet you did,' I said.

'When I was like you I used to collect timetables, and tickets I found down by the station. Once I picked up a ticket all the way to Upplands-Väsby. I'll never forget it.'

We sat in silence, looking down at the grass and staring into mid-air. The fluting of the willow warbler from all directions, the falling umbrella of sound from the tree pipit, the ripple of the running water in the Canal, if you thought about it. The sun warmed the back of my neck. The cowslips were out.

Feeling that tension inside. At sitting here so quietly.

In a minute I'll ask about Johnny and whether there's anything really wrong with him. Ask why Father didn't tell me. But it's a question of finding the right words.

'It's Ascension Day today,' he got in first. 'But maybe you knew that, seeing as you're off school?'

I nodded that I did know, though in fact I had little idea what it meant. Ascending somewhere, presumably, like the swift ascending through the skies, eating and sleeping and even mating in flight. The carpenter from Nazareth as a space traveller with an aspen-wood cross on His back? The son of man on the verge of leaving us forever?

'It's the grandest time of the whole year, this,' said Father. 'Just as spring's giving way to summer and the ash trees are coming into leaf, I've always thought so. But it'll soon be on the turn. One day soon those leaves will have turned back to compost. It happens quicker than you think.'

I was paying close attention, trying to take in everything he said. To learn what he thought about one thing and another, but it was as if the words bounced back when they arrived so doggedly, as if they didn't *want* to stay. And he was so sure about everything that you lost the urge to say anything yourself. He never asked anything either, presumably because he knew it all already.

'Within a few weeks it'll be turning,' he said again. 'When the pollen's rising in clouds from the rye and the clover's in bud. Then the days start getting shorter.'

Then he sort of sank back into himself, sitting there with his coffee cup resting in his hand, staring out into nothing with wide, empty eyes. Far away in thought.

More willow warblers than people in this kingdom of Sweden – did you know that, Father? There could be fifteen million pairs. Do you want to hear what we learnt about the *Phylloscopus* family at school? Small, thin-beaked, creatures of the treetops, living in woodland, not gregarious, a night-time flier: it could have been a description of me. No one in the class knew what a willow warbler sounds like except me and the master. 'Dear, big, kind Father, can't the two of us have the day off today?'

Look at him.

Your father. He's sitting there. With his beard right up to his cheekbones and tufts of hair in his ears. His hands stained brown by resin, his shoulders hunched as if he's trying to hide his head or protect himself from something. His back bent and bowed.

A strange wave surged through me.

Father and me. A sense of belonging together?

Not a word.

We sit here in the pasture, he and I, and help each other put things in order for the animals. Replace poles and insulators and repair barbed wire. Mark off the bits of land that are ours.

What are you thinking about, Father, I felt like asking. Sitting there like that. Are you thinking about your arms rising up all by themselves in the cowshed? The weather, never anything but a worry? The scrap pile, calling to you day and night? Everything that needs doing back home and you're never finished? About the fact that it's a leap year with thirteen moons this year?

The never-ending toil.

Is that what you're thinking about now?

Work and illness. Everything that's against you.

'It was the dawn chorus picnic up at the community centre today,' he said. 'They always have it on Ascension Day, to celebrate the cuckoo's return. It would've been nice to go to that one year.'

What is there to celebrate about a creature that lives off others, it was on the tip of my tongue to say. Ask the robins and you'll see. He gave me a dark look, as if he'd heard what I was thinking and couldn't bear me contradicting him, even in my mind. Or as if I should have realised it was as much about me as about the cuckoo.

'They've had that dawn chorus picnic on Ascension Day for years and years,' he said. 'But I can never get away!'

'No, I know –'

'Not as long as the cowshed's full of beasts.'

He fixed me with his glassy eyes.

'I can't have had more than a week off in total since I took over the farm. You can't even begin to imagine what that means.'

No, I couldn't. But what I did notice was the air suddenly filling with dandelion seeds, drifting over on their miniature parachutes as a reminder that summer was inescapably on its way. The wind got up and whisked round in the grass and among the birches over near the spinney.

'I can't get away because of the beasts,' Father said again. 'Whatever I do. There've got to be two of us, it won't work otherwise!'

He shook his head slowly.

Was that what all this was leading to? Was that why he wanted me along with him today?

'I thought there *were* two of you,' I said hastily. 'Mum helps with everything, doesn't she?'

'It's not easy for her, either. Not for any of us now there's this as well,' he said cryptically. 'But it's too much to expect you to understand.'

I drank some of my milk. Father shared out the pretzel buns, split and buttered, passing me mine and breaking a chunk off his to dunk in the coffee.

'A lot of people have easy lives,' he said. 'But I never have.'

O-itt –

Like a droplet falling.

Again.

The curlew's call! The male hanging somewhere over the marsh and the female answering from the ground.

Had they even mated yet? Wasn't everything late this year?

'What she'd really like is to be spared the lot of it,' Father said, deep in his own thoughts. 'It might be just you left in the end.'

He turned and looked back towards the house, as if to check whether she was standing there listening, even though it was nearly a kilometre away.

'Our teacher said there wouldn't be any wars without boundaries and fences,' I said, trying to change tack. 'It's boundaries and laying claim to land that make people kill each other. Farmers and patriotism equal discord and war.'

O-itt –

Father did not reply. He put down his cup and compressed his lips, rubbing them together as if he had burned himself or was afraid of losing the sensation in them.

Did you hear the curlew too, Father, one wondered. It's on its way here now, coming to play for us on Ascension Day. He looked over to the straight stretch of road where Mum was just driving by. Pressed his teeth on his lower lip until the colour drained out. Stopped and then did it again.

Pou-itt! Litt, litt –

There it was again, more eager and sustained than before, passionate yet soft and quavering, repeated faster and faster until it exploded into trilling exultation that seemed to go on and on: *Lou-looui-lui-lui-lui-lui-lui-luuuui-luuuuui-luuuuuui-luuuuuui – – –*

The tremulous whistle made the whole marsh vibrate, and even the tiniest insects must surely have felt the notes that arched above us before they shot like an arrow through the quivering haze. Maybe he just wanted to announce that the eggs hatched today, trumpet his tribute to the female before she heads off and leaves him alone with the young?

Here he comes, on smooth gull's wings, and hovers around over the marshland using his unfeasibly long beak as a surveying pole. Warbles in that guarded way only curlews can.

'*There it is!*' I whispered, turning to Father.

He sat there with his head bent and his eyes screwed up as if he had a splitting headache. Put his hands over his eyes and pulled a face.

'What's the matter?' I said in alarm.

He looked up, caught off guard.

'Matter? I don't know. Is there?'

He looked at his watch. Looked away, with a slight quiver round his mouth.

'Did you hear the ravens?' was what he said. 'Felt like it was cutting right into my brain.'

I didn't understand what he was talking about. Rambling on about ravens when it was the curlew that mattered. The Eurasian curlew, who had got out his flute for us, and at this time of year.

'You should have heard the screeching,' he said. 'And last night there was one of them making a racket in the chimney. They've come to take my calves from me. Once they've pecked their eyes to bits they pull out their guts and leave them lying there to suffer a slow death. I read about it in a big book.'

I nodded my head and shook it at the same time, really not knowing what to do. Drink a bit more milk, quietly?

'You're the one who knows about birds?' he said. 'Aren't you?'

'Most of the crow family sleep at night,' I said in a friendly tone. 'It must have been something else in the chimney.'

He put his teeth to his lip again and bit down. Used his fingers to press even harder, as if he'd got to deaden something.

'What else?' he muttered. 'They're taking my calves I tell you! If it's not the ravens it's the County Agricultural Board. And they're not insured, either.'

He got up and limped over to the trailer, lit a cigarette and did several circuits of the tractor, trailer and me, looking in all directions as if he knew something was hunting him down. He had gone back to the unfiltered cigarettes, the strongest ones you could get, according to him. A few clouds moved across the sun. A little breeze sprang up again, carrying a swarm of dandelion seeds to sow themselves. The curlew's trills reverberated in the distance and the greenfinch wheezed and twittered in the top of his spruce. The chaffinch alerted everyone that a sparrow hawk was flying over: *pink – pink – pink –*

Father cleared his throat and spat.

'These poles are juniper!' he said loudly, as if he needed to drown out his thoughts or was addressing an old person. 'You hear that? Juniper. I sharpened the whole lot myself.'

He came over and sat back down on his rock. Took a deep breath, stamped out his cigarette and lit another one, sat there smoking and taking a good long look down at the Canal through screwed-up eyes. His veins writhed like bluey-green worms over his wrists.

'Juniper's the best thing you can get,' he said. 'It'll last fifty years or more. You'll never need to replace them.'

I gave an involuntary nod. He shifted closer and put his hand heavily on my shoulder as if to stop me running off. With his other hand he pointed like a statue to the poles, over in the trailer.

'It's juniper, you hear!' he said, as loudly as before. 'They'll last you a lifetime, I tell you. Be grateful it's juniper.'

I squinted up into his feverish face. The pressure on my shoulder increased, as if I were a spring he had to compress.

'It smells just like an old knife,' he said, and thrust his index finger right under my nose. 'Can you smell it? Like a knife.'

His body seemed to shake as he said it. He was breathing heavily.

'It smells just like Father's old butcher's knife,' he said. 'That was made of juniper, I recall.'

With Mum's *Housewife's Compendium* open on my lap I had it in black and white.

Enuresis nocturna. Involuntary night-time urinary incontinence after about the age of three when there is no obvious physical condition or nervous illness. Over-anxious mothering or an authoritarian father can lead to the habit in some cases being a symptom of so-called regression, meaning that the child copes with severe external stress by reverting to patterns of behaviour from an earlier stage of its development as a way of avoiding mental breakdown.

Night-time incontinence not infrequently occurs when the child has been in situations of conflict with friends or classmates, or becomes aware of insecurity, fear etc within the family. *Enuresis nocturna* often has deleterious mental effects, reduces the child's self-confidence and generates anxiety and apprehension. Invitations to spend the night away from home, planned school or camp trips etc in many cases strike terror into the child and affect sleep and appetite.

No drug exists that can provide an infallible cure for *enuresis*. If the problem has not been overcome by the age of 12–13, psychiatric treatment should be sought from the local paediatric clinic.

Scorching sun and no school to go to. The flies buzzed and the molehills readily sent up clouds of dust. Worse than the wasp summer of fifty-nine, said the old folk.

Mum spent her time at the sewing machine with a mouth full of pins and Johnny had no room in his head for anything except hunting and guns any more. By day he made hides and hammered away at a bigger one he'd use for foxes, and in the evenings he hunted woodcock. If he ever did want to talk, it was about the new double and triple-barrelled shotguns and elk rifles he had seen at the gunsmiths, or the hunting trails he could choose from for the weekend. Or military stuff. Voluntary Defence Training camps, civil defence exercises. Sub-machine-gun practice and first aid, bridge mining and bivouac building, eating out of mess tins and digging latrines.

'I'm joining up in the autumn,' he said. 'The thing is to have mastered it, the whole lot, so it is. If you mind yourself and do as you're told, you can get to Cyprus.'

But I had the library, at any rate, Father's old schoolroom that had been done up and turned into a branch library, open two hours a week. It was always an easy pedal on the way there. To all those things you didn't know about yet.

Gudrun was busy behind the counter with her card catalogues when I came in. With hair that had clearly been set in curlers and a glittering green tiara on her forehead, she looked rather like a queen.

'Lucky we've got two loyal customers, anyway,' she said, with a knowing smile in the direction of the magazine rack.

The retired schoolmaster was sitting there as usual, reading *Elementa* through a big magnifying glass. He was almost ninety and half-blind, but every week he came along to read the maths and science magazine line by line, column by column, as if he did not realise he would soon be dead.

'We've got to make the most of it,' I said ingratiatingly. 'The opening hours in the summer holidays, I mean.'

Gudrun's face brightened.

'If only more people thought that way. I don't know what they all get up to out here, but it certainly isn't reading books.'

She gave a shrug.

'Incidentally, do *you* know what people spend their time doing in a village like this?' she said.

'Nobody's opened a book at home for as long as I can remember. Except the Bible. Mum always read the Book of Job when she's ill. And the Prayer of Confession, even though she knows it by heart.'

Gudrun smiled and shook her head. Poor people who don't know any better, her clear eyes said. A woman who had scarcely done a stroke of work in her whole life – was I on her side now?

'And they don't get that much free time,' I added. 'They work a hundred hours a week. Take a Sunday off about once every five years.'

Her mouth twitched, as if at a bad joke, and she carried on with the library tickets.

I was left in peace with the latest issue of *The Birdwatcher*, which had a lot about the use of biocides in agriculture and the peregrine falcon being under threat of extinction. The ornithologists put part of the blame on cynical egg thieves, but the primary responsibility undoubtedly lay with the farmers and their irresponsible spreading of pesticides and other chemical preparations to maximise yields. It was the farmers who had poisoned the peregrine, and they had been getting away with it for decades.

In my mind's eye I saw Father setting off with the sprayer mounted behind the tractor and the gas mask over his face, lowering the long-armed spray mechanisms and turning on the tap. Chugging back and forth across the fields until every square inch was saturated with toxins. Leaving each stalk and blade glistening.

'If you don't kill off the weeds and pests they'll get *you* instead, in the end,' he said. 'They're like an illness, eating away at you from inside.'

And the peregrine falcon is dying out. 'One of the world's most fascinating birds, this inspiring aviator admired by man for centuries for its speed and grace, this perfect flying arrow of the billowing skies, with a mastery of his element unmatched among our winged friends,' one column waxed lyrical. 'Kubla Khan of China and Marco Polo may be long dead, the tourneys of the age of chivalry have faded away and the Provençal troubadours fallen silent, but for as long as we have the peregrine falcon, his very existence is a reminder to us mortals of all the wondrous things that once were.'

'It's Dower Agne's boy, isn't it? So you've found your way to this house of learning, eh?' the schoolmaster interrupted, trying to fix me with his watery old eyes.

'Looks like it.'

He put down his magnifying glass and cupped his scrawny hand behind his ear.

'You take after your father,' he said, loudly enough for the sound to echo from wall to wall. 'He liked reading better than anything, I recall.'

I said nothing.

'And maths, of course. There was no one as quick as him at mental arithmetic. We had our first slide rule by then, but he never needed it. He had it all up here.'

The schoolmaster tapped his skull with his fingernail and a nostalgic smile crept over his face, as if he were summoning images from his mind.

'He could have gone a long way, Agne. I don't think I ever had such a studious pupil as he was.'

'No,' I blurted.

'He should have been a clergyman.'

'Yes.'

'Or a meteorologist. But perhaps things weren't very easy for him at home. With all that was going on?'

'Oh?'

The schoolmaster shook his head, looking anxious, and went back to his magazine. The magnifying glass trembled over the fine print of the cryptarithms and the wonderfully mysterious mathematical symbols.

'Oh by the way, there are a few volumes here I ordered with

you in mind,' said Gudrun, coming over with an armful of books.

I started leafing through them greedily.

Russian spacecraft and Halley's comet, the husky dog Laika, on her way to death in Sputnik 2, a yellowish-green galaxy cloud spiralling in towards a dazzling light as though metamorphosing into a shell. The picture of how the Plough would look in a hundred thousand years: a knife with a broken haft.

Gudrun, clearly pleased, stood looking over my shoulder.

'Astronomy,' she said. 'I thought that might be something for you to get your teeth into. The origins of the universe and whatnot.'

She gave me a pat on the head and went back to the counter. The schoolmaster watched out of the corner of his eye as she sat down and pushed back the tiara in her hair.

'Dainty as an escritoire', he said, and dug me in the side.

And his face split into a wide, toothless smile that brought tears trickling down his cheeks.

I read about Galileo Galilei, the first human being to turn a telescope to the skies, creator of the new philosophy that could prove the Earth was not the centre of the universe, and thanked for it by lifelong house arrest. About his discovery of the four moons of Jupiter, the construction of his Jovilabium to work out their positions and his conclusion that the Earth was one planet among many. There he was in a whole-page picture, pale and emaciated with a big, white beard and dark, sceptical eyes. In his hand he had a long telescope, not much thicker than a fishing rod.

What are you waiting for, whispered the voice. Do it now, if you want to get away! You've got to lift yourself up by your own bootstraps, no one else is going to do it for you.

I was reading about the birth of our planet and the real origin of everything when the outside door opened and in came a girl I had never seen before. She had black platform mules and tatty dungarees with flowers and stars sewn onto the legs. Her hair was dark, thick and wavy, hanging right down her back. She walked tall as she wandered among the bookshelves with what looked like a slight smile, but it wasn't that she was trying to impress anybody, you could see that a mile off. It was just her way.

Walking straight-backed with her arms hanging at her sides, absorbed in her own thoughts.

'Hello,' she said.

I smiled awkwardly and looked away. She sat down in one of the armchairs and looked through the cassette tapes, put on the headphones and nodded in time to the music. She didn't even need anything to read at the same time, just sat there with her hands in her lap, fiddling with her bracelet and smiling to herself, her lips moving every now and then.

That's how relaxed some people were.

Here I am, sitting here listening, humming along. This is how I am. You others look by all means, I don't mind.

I skimmed aimlessly to and fro through the space books and tried to find something to fix my mind on, but my eyes kept straying back to the checked armchair. There was something about her face, the smooth cheeks and the well-defined eyebrows, the lips permanently on the verge of laughter though she seemed neither happy nor sad. The long, slim arms sticking out of her jumper sleeves.

Bet she was raised on a diet of beech sap and doves, I thought. You don't turn out like that otherwise.

She wasn't looking in my direction at all. Just swaying along to the music as if I didn't exist, or as if she were sitting at home in her bedroom with the door shut.

I fastened the library books onto my carrier and positioned myself at the bottom of the steps, waiting. Instantly the nerves started. I tried to think of something to say that would sound fairly natural but I felt like a criminal waiting for his victim. However, I had made up my mind. No matter how reluctant I felt. You only get a chance like this once.

The door opened and there she was.

'Are you the Stockholmers at Bliss Cottage?' I said, straight out.

She turned round but didn't laugh in my face and run off as I feared she might.

'How did you know?' she said, cool as a cucumber.

'There aren't that many people round here,' I said to the ground. 'Two hundred maybe, in the whole parish. Word got round that some Stockholmers were going to buy it.'

She gave a quizzical frown, as if there was something she didn't understand.

'I don't know anybody here,' she said. 'Scarcely know where I am, in fact. We came down on the train at the weekend, Mum and I. Dad's been here for a while.'

'Have you had a new well dug yet?'

'Well? I don't think so.'

She gave an embarrassed laugh. Lowered her eyes and twisted the leather cord she was wearing round her wrist.

No ordinary girl this one, you could tell right away. Saying all that stuff about her parents, just like that. And she *talked* differently, too. Everything she said was so clear and distinct, and sort of refined. The words seemed to come out of her mouth by themselves, as if she never had to work out in advance what she was going to say.

'It'll be rather nice to be out in the country for a while, actually,' she declared in a grown-up way. 'But we don't come from

Stockholm, by the way; I've lived in Upplands-Väsby all my life. I've never set a foot here before.'

I nodded, listening intently to every word she said as if she would be testing me on it afterwards. As if I'd be expected to prove myself. But almost before I could register it, she had her hands on her handlebars and was about to go. No books, nothing. About to desert me and cycle off home.

You've got to stop her, said the voice inside me. Show her the books you've borrowed, tell her about the Horsehead Nebula and the Andromeda Galaxy, Galileo and the speed of light, anything you can think of. Teach her the difference between the song of the willow warbler and the chaffinch. Or of the garden warbler and the blackcap. The two of you can sit by the gatepost and count the thousands of flowers on the biggest cow parsley.

She'll be off any second now.

'I'm going the same way for a bit,' I lied. 'If you're off home, that is?'

I felt a sudden shiver, as if my whole life was hanging on the thin thread I had just cast in her direction.

'I wouldn't mind a bit of company,' she said casually. 'I only came out on my bike to help pass the time.'

Like a beam of light. And she was the one who said it.

Company – – –

'But don't go out of your way for my sake,' she said.

'No, don't worry!'

I leapt onto my bike and she came along behind. Out onto the oil gravel road, past the Landmark Pine by milk-churn stand and into the village, and this time I wished every single person would be hiding behind their curtains and looking out of the window so they'd see us go by with their own eyes. The Stockholmer from Bliss Cottage and him, the work-shy boy who's hardly the gilt on the gingerbread. Maybe they were already at their stations, spying out of their nice clean windows, but I couldn't be bothered to look. Let them lurk there and ring each other and talk as much as they like. It's her and me now, keeping each other company with the holidays stretching ahead of us. Over the brow of the hill by the church, then it's downhill nearly all the way to the river, where fate smiled on me and I saw my first ever golden oriole.

'Hey, you're in a hurry,' she puffed, coming up alongside. 'Are you trying to get rid of me or something?'

She had a large, old fashioned ladies' bicycle and could scarcely reach the pedals, but she zipped along fast enough to make her tyres sing. And her hair stream out.

'Just wanted to see how fast I could go today,' I said, nodding towards my speedometer. 'This is the longest downhill stretch in the whole of Stoneacre. They built the church at the top so they'd all be reminded of the existence of God and not risk committing any sins.'

She smiled.

'Now it's my turn to decide how fast we go. We'll have to give up on keeping each other company otherwise.'

We continued side by side, each following a rutted wheel track in the road like some old couple out for a little bicycle ride. The headwind pressed her jumper tightly to those breasts of hers. Then she suddenly started ding-dinging a tune on the old bike bell, twisting it to and fro and tapping it with her nails and knuckles.

'Can you hear?' she said, humming and wagging her head in time.

'Of course I can.'

'Pretty good, huh?'

'Oh yes –'

And we rode on in silence.

We stopped at The Crossing where the road went over the river and our ways would have to part if the lie about my route home was not to be exposed. A buzzard mewed from the watermeadows and a few hammer blows echoed in the distance. I thought of a thousand things but couldn't find a single one to talk about. She looked at her watch and twirled one of her pedals back and forth with the toe of her mule.

'There are stars in the sky that could have died before the birth of Jesus,' I said finally. 'It's just that the light hasn't got here yet, even though it's travelling at three hundred thousand kilometres a second. The Pole Star could have imploded in the Middle Ages.'

She tossed her head.

'I don't go round thinking about that kind of thing. Do you?'

'Oh no, but I do sometimes think about the way nothing lasts forever, not even a star. About whether everything has to disappear or turn into something else?'

She looked towards home as if to reassure herself she was on the right road. Stretching away in a straight line, through the elk forest and past the disused sawmill.

Why can't I keep my eyes in check? To and fro, hither and thither, like a passerine spying out food.

'Is that where you live, over there?' she said, pointing over to the Manor where they kept eighty cows and had fancy woodwork round the cowshed windows.

'Not exactly. I live over by Raven Fen. Quite a way from here. Beside a drained bog. Our place isn't that big.'

Just go ahead and say it. That wasn't so bad.

She nodded as if she didn't care, spinning her bike pedal.

'Well I've got to get back and unpack my things,' she said, and seemed bored by my lack of enterprise. 'My room's full of suitcases and removal men's boxes.'

'Shall we do something together when you've unpacked?' I heard myself say.

Curious. It just popped out, as if it had been brewing away inside me since she made herself comfortable in that armchair. So now I'd said it, for better or worse.

'Why not? I don't know anyone here, after all.'

'You can come with me and listen to the birds that sing at night, if you like. We've got the best bird lake in the district, near here.'

She looked doubtful and scratched the back of her ear as if she thought I was having her on.

'Might be fun, I suppose,' came her unexpected answer. 'But I don't know the first thing about birds. Hardly even recognise a magpie. Just so you don't get the wrong idea.'

She gave a laugh.

'At the weekend maybe, if the weather's fine?' I said. 'Or next week?'

'I'll have to ask Mum first.'

'Nothing much can happen out there, tell her. The lake's shallow and the birds keep an eye out.'

She looked up and smiled an enigmatic smile. As if she had a secret to keep – or as if she were making fun of me.

'You promise you'll come, then?' I said, holding out my thumb.

'So this would be at night, yeah?'

'We can ride out there at dusk and stay a couple of hours.'

I lowered my thumb. She just stood there, still with that smile, looking at me until our eyes were locked together. She looked right into me and didn't drop her gaze, and I did the same to her, neither of us blinking; we stood there, eyes suckered fast to each other as if in some mutual dream. Eyes wide-open, looking and looking.

'All right,' she said, breaking the spell, and this time she was the one holding out a thumb.

A warm feeling inside me.

'I'll come along,' she said.

How had I managed it? Her promise to come with me and hear the night-time chorus –

She lined up her pedals and was ready to go.

'You know you'll get home fine if you go thataways?' I fussed.

'Thataways? Oh, er, all right.'

I felt a rippling inside me. Looking into those eyes and then pressing our thumbs together to seal the promise.

Imagine that happening.

And then she was in the saddle, pedalling off towards Bliss Cottage. The gritty road surface crunched under her tyres. The thrushes sang.

'I'm Veronika, by the way!' she called over her shoulder.

I could hardly see her for all the bushes and trees on the bend, but her voice came plain and clear.

'Klas!' I called back, as loud as I could.

She turned again and gave a quick wave.

'Bye Klas!'

'Bye!'

Father could think of nothing else. Day after day he charged to and fro across the cowshed yard with armloads of scrap metal. Scrabbled through the contents of sheds and lean-tos and dragged out every conceivable bit of junk, as long as it was rusty enough. It made no odds to him if it was pouring with rain or the sun was blazing down, he just couldn't leave the scrap metal alone.

I thought back to the last day of term, when I got back to find him bashing away furiously at the old threshing machine, going at it with a cloud of powdery rust rising around him like smoke. His sore, red shoulders, the dirty bandages and the leather thumbstall covering where he had cut himself. The other parents sitting in the end-of-term church service in their best clothes and coming into class to see the reports handed out. Even the duffers had somebody there who couldn't wait to look at the sheet of paper with the nine grades and the head-master's illegible signature.

For Father the scrap metal was all that mattered.

All the rust has got to go *here*. Let the weeds grow as they will. Let her deal with the animals. The firewood will have to wait. It's this and nothing else. Old tine harrows and mowers, corroded molasses troughs and garden chairs with no seats, dis-carded axes and scythes, pitchforks, spades and shovels eaten away by rust – it's all got to be brought out into the light.

He had made short work of the scrap pile behind the henhouse;

now it was the cart shed and the roof space in the barn that were to be turned out and emptied of all those abandoned objects, serving no useful purpose. But the aim of all his frantic activity in this heat wasn't to get rid of it. By the end wall of the barn, a new scrap pile towered aloft. Everything had got to be assembled in a new place. Not even Grandfather's old binder was left in peace. It had to be dismantled and dismembered. The seat there, the wheel there, the axles and beams somewhere else, the control levers in this pile and the struts in that one, the bodywork over here and the mudguards over there. Out came the angle grinder to cut through bolts and bars, making the sparks fly. The extension cable coiled across the beaten dirt like a black snake.

Never a moment's rest.

Off on the tractor to fetch more. Car windscreens and bonnets, wheelbarrows and rusty cement mixers.

'Surely there's no end to it?' said Mum with a quizzical puckering of her lips. 'He's driving round all the abandoned farms now, dragging out old car wrecks. Horse rakes and hay tedders and goodness knows what else. It can only be a matter of time before the police turn up?'

As if she had received some sign from above, a few hours later a car crawled up, curious faces visible through the windows. It was the Salesman out for a nice little drive, the biggest blabbermouth that ever wore wellies. The car drew to a stop a little way from the scrap heap and the heads nodded to each other in confirmation, like when you see for yourself something you've only heard speak of and scarcely believed possible. An index finger came jabbing out and the Salesman's wife turned to explain something to the children. They instantly pressed their noses to the window, eager to see the spectacle.

Look at that clown, bashing and sawing. It's him, the one who isn't right in the head.

After a while, the Salesman climbed out of his car and went cautiously towards Father, the way you might approach an unpredictable or wounded animal. He was wearing a short-sleeved shirt and plus fours and smiling that crooked smile of his. Father neither saw nor heard him; he had the ear protectors on his head and the whining angle grinder in his hands. The sparks were whirling round him like a swarm of fireflies in a tornado. The Salesman put his hands behind his back and slowed his steps. Then he suddenly seemed in a hurry to get back home, climbed in and said something to his wife as he started the engine.

Almost at once the car came back the other way, sending up a cloud of dust, and was gone. Father turned round, the dust making him wrinkle his nose.

Where did that come from?

It doesn't matter, anyway. Time to get on, so much to do. There's no end to it.

Who wants to lie under an eye that never blinks? That keeps watch and demands answers interminably?

To have that hanging over you whatever you do – – –

The words in my head again:

I am as tough as juniper and as strong as a steer. You'll never be rid of me.

I could scarcely believe my eyes. Where not long ago the grass grew half a metre tall and the lupins were flowering, there wasn't a green patch to be seen. Nothing but trampled earth and a huge jumble of rusted bits of scrap metal in different shades of brown. Piled in the middle were the things he hadn't yet found time to attack, but all around them it was possible to detect the beginnings of some kind of permanent order amid all the nonsensical chaos. Every item was to have its place, and only the signboards were missing.

Machine parts.

Appliances.

Tools.

Girders.

Flat bars.

Corrugated iron.

Engines.

Gearwheels.

Generators.

Radiators.

Cables.

Iron piping.

Rods.

Struts.

Chains.

Reinforcement bars.

Barbed wire.

Chicken wire.

Guttering and drainpipes.

Milk churns.

Oil drums.

Wheels and wheel rims were propped against each other in long rows. There was an assortment of big cans into which he had sorted screws, bolts, nuts, springs, hinges, fittings and other small items I didn't know the names of. All as rusty as each other. I was trying to fathom what possible purpose all this could serve when the sound of a souped-up moped suddenly cut through the air.

Funny. First the Salesman and now Bruiser Pelle. As if there was a rumour going round.

He skidded to a stop, grinned broadly from inside his helmet, revved the engine and bent down to adjust the carburettor jet.

'Seven horsepower now!' he shouted, putting it into gear at the same time. 'Only the rods and head gasket left to change!'

I nodded, though I had no idea what he meant. He rode the moped a bit closer and held out his oily hands to prove it. He'd been working on it every hour of the day since the end of term. Chromed the swing arm and polished up the silencer, put on the new Cuppini handlebars, notched the pistons and changed the liner, cylinder, contact breaker and drive sprockets.

'Goes like a rocket, I bet?' I said.

He gave me a smug smile and engaged gear noisily, leaned way over to one side on the Zündapp like a speedway rider, and went skidding round in circles on the road. Stones and grit sprayed in all directions.

'Reaches sixty-five kilometres an hour!' he yelled.

He looked as if he owned the world and could do anything he wanted. Burgundy saddle cover and cowboy boots with heel-irons that sent sparks flying round his feet. I imagined Veronika jumping on behind and putting her arms around him. Her hair streaming out, breasts pressed against his back as he sped off.

Then he planted his feet in front of the footrests, revved up and let the back wheel spin until it had gouged a deep hole in the road. There was a smell of burnt rubber and petrol. The exhaust fumes got up my nose. Show over, he swung the bike gently up out of the hole, turned off the ignition and hung his helmet on the rearview mirror.

'You've got a bit of everything here,' he said, nodding in the direction of the vast scrap pile.

'You're right there.'

He inserted a wad of moist snuff with his thumb and pushed his fringe out of his eyes.

'Fancy doing something?' I said swiftly. 'I found the kite. It was hanging in an aspen.'

'The kite? You still on about that?'

He went up to the scrap metal, yanked at a couple of pipes and rummaged around in the tin cans.

'Your dad goes hunting, doesn't he?' he said. 'Can't we borrow his shotgun and pot a few pigeons? Make a fire and cook them? Or some chickens maybe?'

His eyes glinted.

'But I s'pose you're scared you'll get a hiding? Tell me where the gun is and I'll go and fetch it. You can have a test drive for every bird you shoot.'

At that moment, Father came round the corner, as if he'd been standing there eavesdropping. He grabbed up a crowbar and made a beeline for Bruiser Pelle. His face looked like thunder. His jaws were working.

This is it, the thought ran through me. He'd be capable of

anything, looking the way he does. Bruiser Pelle dropped the bit of scrap metal he was holding and a look of terror came into his eyes, for all his toughness. The cocky grin had gone. But Father stopped a few metres short of him and just glared.

'Can't you leave my scrap alone, either?' he said finally. 'Four years ago you broke one of my cowshed windows. Who had the job of putting a new one in, do you reckon? And now this. The scrap's about the only thing I've got left.'

Bruiser Pelle opened his eyes wide and threw me an uncomprehending, disconcerted look. He backed a couple of steps nearer his moped in the hope of making an exit. Father walked over and prodded around in the hole with the crowbar.

'Is that all you can do, make trouble?' he said. 'I've been slaving away at this road since Father died. Then you come along and wreck it.'

He gestured with one arm as if trying to drive away a cow.

'I thought we had public roads in this country,' said Bruiser Pelle, plucking up some courage. 'Isn't that where the taxes go? But maybe the road to Dower's not included?'

Father glanced in my direction to see whose side I was on.

'Shove off home and rip up the roads there as much as you like,' he said, raising his voice. 'But this one's mine and you'll keep away from it! I'll ring the police next time.'

Bruiser Pelle turned on the ignition with a self-confident smile.

'I'll go where the hell I like, you can be fucking sure of that! You need help, you do.'

That was too much for Father. He strode up to Bruiser Pelle, raised the crowbar to strike and opened his mouth to tell him a few home truths. The crowbar shook in mid-air. Then suddenly he lowered his arm and cowered back, looking from Bruiser Pelle to me and back again through terrified eyes, like someone who had just woken from a nightmare. He rubbed his nose with the sleeve of his shirt and slunk quietly back the way he had come. His hand opened and the crowbar dropped to the ground with a dull clang.

Bruiser Pelle snorted several times and shook his head. Tapped his knuckles on his forehead.

'Is he cuckoo, or what?'

'I don't know what it is,' I said honestly.

'They should bloody well lock him away.'

'Maybe –'

He picked up a stone the size of a clenched fist and threw it at the diesel tank, as hard as he could.

'He'd better watch his fucking step!' he yelled. 'I don't take any old shit, he needs to bloody well know that.'

Bruiser Pelle was bright red in the face as he got on the moped and folded out the kick start.

'Someone's going to pay for this!' he yelled, and roared off at speed in a spurt of gravel.

I stared hard at the dent in the tank. Something that will never go away. Something that will always be there. Like an everlasting scar.

The racket of the souped-up Zündapp gradually receded, getting fainter and fainter as it disappeared into the distance. In the sparse foliage of the white birch across the road sat an irritating magpie, laughing its head off at me.

The ravens fly over the farmer's house, shrieking, predicting death. That's what is written, I've got it here on the desk in front of me. *Fly over the farmer's house, predicting death.* Just like that. The Romans knew it and so did the Vikings.

Do you know it, Mum? Do you think about it when you're kneeling in the garden, sowing radishes? When you're standing in the old washhouse, making blackcurrant jam? When you're sitting alone and sleepless on autumn nights, darning socks and knitting thick winter sweaters for the three of us?

Corvus corax corax.

The hawk of wounds.

The jinx of the wilds.

The Småland vulture.

Old Poker's coaly courier.

The Grim Reaper's envoy.

The funeral watchman.

The jet-black bird from Hell.

Hrafn!

Shuns human civilisation, lives off carrion and refuse, drinks the blood of the fallen, flocks to scenes of slaughter and mass graves, pecks eyes to pieces and tears out the rectums of newborn mammals, nests in winter to harden up its young.

I live in the farmer's house and I shall not die.

Why should I die? I'm going to Marsh Pool to listen to the night singers.

I loaded the wheelbarrow full of footballs pumped up hard, took it round the corner and put it in the penalty area like Ove had told me – and thought I was seeing things. Over on the substitutes' bench, sitting cross-legged like a tailor and wearing a hat, was Veronika. She was looking at something cupped in her hands, maybe a twelve-spotted ladybird she wanted to show me, because they're supposed to bring you luck?

It must be her. There's her bike. And the dungarees with flowers and stars on them.

My stomach knotted. I wanted her to be there and yet I didn't.

'Come here,' she called. 'Come here and I'll show you something.'

She held out a milky, transparent stone with little specks and streaks inside it.

'Moonstone,' she said. 'It's my lucky amulet, my grandma gave it to me. Isn't it lovely?'

It seemed to me to be reflecting the whole sky, an ethereal, blue colour that came and went as you looked at it. She put it in my hand, as if she wanted me to share in what was hers, to feel how clean and smooth it was.

'It's the stone of undreamt dreams,' she said, making it sound like some kind of incantation. 'You can make a wish if you want.'

'Can I?'

'I have.'

Not like other girls, this one, came the thought. Riding round on an old bike with twenty-eight inch wheels, amulets in her pockets and a straw hat on her head. I felt like sitting down beside her and asking her about the night singers, which evening she had in mind. Whether she'd asked permission yet.

That was the moment Ove blew his whistle to make us all gather round, and waved to me to get a move on.

'I've got to go now,' I said, feeling torn. 'The session's starting.'

'Hope you shoot a lot of goals or whatever they're called.'

She laughed.

'Are you staying long?' I said.

'I'll have to see how bored I get.'

'Look lively, we haven't got all day' shouted Ove.

I'd no sooner got there than Bruiser Pelle stuck an elbow in my side.

'Anybody you know?' he hissed.

'I think we're third cousins. She's here every summer.'

I was out of breath and the taste of sick was burning my throat. My heart was pitter-pattering like a baby bird's. Veronika didn't even seem to have noticed that I'd won the interval running even though I was the smallest of the lot. Must have been really engrossed in what she was writing in her notebook?

'Good work, you lot!' shouted Ove, bringing out the crate of pop. 'We'll have a quick game to finish off.'

Right, this is where it really matters. You can be as fit as anything, kick as hard as anything and run as fast as anything, but everything depends on the actual game. Ove gave me a yellow vest and Bruiser Pelle a red one. Him and me, one side each. And Veronika's still sitting there.

This is it.

'No fixed goalies today lads, since numbers are a bit low,' called Ove. 'Short shots and let the ball do the work!'

And I win the ball from the off and dribble it briskly through the midfield, see Fishface who's found a gap and is signalling from the far right of the field, wants me to place it forward of where he is now, and I'm just getting lined up to curve it in when the tractor suddenly comes into view on the other side of the fen – – –

Is he coming here?

I lose the ball. Fishface, thwarted, lets out the croaky yell of someone whose voice is breaking. Throws up his hands. That's it, finished. There's no way back. The Ferguson, still coming this way. This is where he's heading. Like a burning fuse. I hear my name from far, far off, as if through a welter of noise. Titch is looking for someone to pass to. Less than half the straight stretch of road left. He comes past the Landmark Pine and emerges from the shade. In a few minutes he'll be standing here. Everything's spoiled. Veronika and the night singers, everything. It's a throw-in to red because I was off in a dream. I hear myself call out that I'll fetch it. My childish squeak. Stride into the tangle of grass. Pretend to search, even though I know where the ball is. Wander round, panicking. Six years old again. Can't think straight. Anything, doesn't matter what. I'm lying down now. I'm not here any more. Inside the nooks and pathways of the grass, one with the caterpillars and beetles and parasites. *Klas!* I don't exist any more. I'm a tiny insect in the endless greenery. A ruminant that never gets any further. *Stop messing about! It's not funny any more!* Ove's grip on my shoulder. I squint through my eyelashes. See his face from the side, his serious look. See the green-coated doctor waiting for the anaesthetic to take effect. 'My foot's gone,' I hiss, 'or the ligament'. 'Gone?' *Come on! We can manage fine without him. Play on!* Ove's smooth, accountant's hand round my ankles. Prodding and testing. The tractor over there. It turns off. Three hundred metres to go. 'Does it hurt?' 'Yes, awfully.' He *is* coming here. The road doesn't lead anywhere else. It's not a dream. It's here and now. Ove's expression as he scratches his forehead, not sure what to do. One eye almost closed. 'You'd better go in and rest, and keep your foot propped up. Put it under cold running water first, and it'll ease off.' The smell of clover and timothy deep inside my brain. I put on a limp all the way, lock the doors and huddle down in front of the window, pressing myself against the wall like a young hare. My temples are throbbing. Footsteps in the fine gravel, going past.

He can't have seen me. I carefully part the slats of the blind, make a slit for one pupil. He's standing over there, shrunken, shoulders drooping, with his pipe in one hand. The protectors still over his ears. Old manure caking his boots, almost to the tops, and his boiler suit with the pig breeders' association logo on the back. My father. Looks around as if he's searching for something. Walks over to the corner flag and back, nodding like a moorhen with every step. Stops on the margins of the oat field and scrutinises the glittering stalks. Bends down, on the alert for insects and other crop pests. Puffs out a cloud of smoke which hangs in the air around him, blue with cadmium. Drums his hand against his thigh and looks down to the Canal, over to the other side. Veronika's gone! Ove goes across to him, gives a forced smile, lifts one of his ear protectors, says something and points this way. Gives him a slap on the shoulder, as you would to an old schoolmate. Father turns round, gives Ove a quizzical nod. Where's Veronika? The radiator so cool against my sweaty thighs. The flies buzzing round the half empty pop bottles. He scrapes his boots and comes up the steps, pushes down the door handle. *Klas?* It was his feeble voice, begging and somehow empty. *Are you there Klas?* How intense silence can be. Like physical pain. Just the pipe smoke seeping in. You can plead and beg as much as you like, but you can't get to me. I've locked up all round. He knocks again. Wheezes and coughs. *Can you open the door Klas?* I shrink as small as I can, into a foetal position. Gabble the seven times table inside me, as fast as I can. Turn at forty-nine and recite it backwards, to and fro, back and forth. The mantra in my brain. *Can't you do it? Are you there? You're injured aren't you, Klas?* He's knocking harder now, really bashing. Scrabbling at the window frames as if he thought I'd forgotten to shut them properly. I scarcely dare breathe. Surely he must have been out there for three minutes *now? What must Ove and the others think? Why are you doing this to me? I'm not that strong any more. I only wanted to say sorry.*

Strange and warm. A relief that wasn't supposed to exist. He's gone now. I can't hear the Ferguson any longer.

For the first time I went naked into the shower room, with my towel over my shoulder like a boxer. Hung the towel on the hook and paused in front of the mirror on the wall.

Stand and look.

It's just you now. No eyes boring at you, trying to get in, no leering, nosy, acne-ridden faces. You don't need to cover yourself or come up with explanations. There's nothing to be afraid of.

I turned on the hot water and stepped in, let my shoulders sink and relaxed my stomach. Took long, calming breaths, felt the jet of water tickle the back of my neck, the hot cascade down my back, the splash as it hit the floor.

A knot untying itself. A marvellous sense of peace inside me.

Feel the gush and the spurt of it, the water hitting my forehead and eyelids, hear my ears chirping, see the steam spreading and the mirrors misting up. Dare to soap my body all over, turn my face to the steady torrent and let myself be filled with an incomprehensible calm. Feel my muscles soften and my pores open. See the veins swelling on my hands and in the crook of my elbows, along the insides of my thighs, in my groin, feel my breathing deepen and expand, my testicles descend into the scrotum, my blood pumping and coursing just as it should.

I want to stay here all my life.

It's a great feeling, that flowing and pulsing in your body. I'm expanding inside. I'm growing by the second, everything's so serene – – –

I unlocked all the doors and crept out the back way, through the club room, stopping to fill my lungs with the evening air, clear as spring water. The breeze was rustling the sycamores, which had strewn their helicopters on the gritty ground. A songthrush was perched somewhere, singing and talking at the same time, trying out melodies over and over again, while the swallows wheeled on their hunt for mosquitoes. Out in the pasture, the cows were ambling towards the clump of spruces where they liked to lie down at night. Each made its own separate way yet they still always seemed to belong together, bound to each other in some naturally ordained fellowship.

As if through a haze, I heard Ove blow his whistle and say that was all for today.

I gave a start.

Someone had left a note on my bike carrier. A piece of white paper, folded as many times as it would go.

That was why he came, said the voice. It was time for a serious talk.

I was shaking as I pulled out the note and unfolded it. 'See you at the Library at 8 tomorrow evening,' it said, and it wasn't Father's handwriting.

Who has the willpower to lie awake waiting for disaster, night after night?

I switched off the light and shut my eyes, following the vibrating circles of light as they moved slowly to and fro across my non-existent field of vision. I lay there as taut as a steel spring, listening for sounds in the house, still strange and warm after all I'd been through. The bedclothes stuck to my body. The protective mattress cover gave a plastic rustle if I so much as thought about it.

A fly swatter down in the kitchen?

Restless creaks across a floor?

The cap of a pill bottle being unscrewed?

Nothing – – –

I had kept the window closed all evening, but the mosquito was in the room. It had scented my overheated head and its life revolved around one thing.

From the dangerous eye above: make sure you don't get bitten tonight. If you fall asleep it could be the last thing you ever do. That mosquito's carrying a fatal disease, that's why it's come. One bite and you're done for. You can hear yourself that it's not whining the normal way, must have chosen its victim carefully, knows who it's going to share the disease with, whose blood it wants.

Ssshh!

'... *the cowshed ... like a sow ... the hell I will ... pigsty ...*'

Several thumps on the wall. Something falling on the floor?

'... *inventing it ... this is serious now ... the whole lot ...*'

The slam of a door, making the whole house shake.

When I came down, Göran was walking up and down outside his room with his eyes shut and his ears covered, but he wasn't sobbing or crying as he usually did. He looked as though he was reciting something silently to himself. He was wearing my tatty old rabbit pyjamas. His top lip was glistening with snot and saliva. I felt the urge to hug him, touch him without giving him a Chinese burn or punching his arm black and blue. He had his eyes as tightly shut as they would go and his hands were pressed hard against his ears.

Mum was standing in the kitchen, leaning against the bedroom door in just her nightie. She turned her face away and put her hand over her mouth when she saw me. Father was breathing heavily and drumming his left hand on the draining board. His grandfather shirt was hanging out. He kept clenching his right hand and then half straightening his fingers, as if he was on the point of smashing something to bits. His jaw muscles were pumping; his carotid artery was stretched taut and looked as if it might explode.

Eventually, Mum cleared her throat and gave me a long look. I couldn't make out whether it was one of resignation or of warning. She wasn't wearing a bra and you could see her breasts through the fabric, hanging down over her belly like two enormous dugs. All at once, Father turned his head towards me and stopped drumming, stood stock-still like an actor and parted his scabbed lips.

'I'm going to sleep with the pigs from now on,' he said, and smiled. 'There's a spare pen I can use. It makes no difference to me. There's plenty of straw and hay.'

His fixed, introspective smile made shivers run down my spine. His eyes were clouded and red-rimmed from lack of sleep or whatever pills he's been taking.

'My place is with the animals, who haven't got any feelings,' he explained. 'That's where I belong.'

There was a sudden intake of breath from Mum, who was watching him from the side. He ignored her, put a cigarette in his mouth and limped over to the cellar door.

'Then we'll see who's sorry,' he said before he disappeared down the steps.

Mum didn't bat an eyelid, simply stared at the wall in front of her with a distant expression. Her eyes seemed to be getting bigger with every passing second, as if a thousand thoughts or none at all were surging through her. I didn't have time to open my mouth before Göran rushed over and threw his arms round her. He was crying uncontrollably, snuffling and sobbing until his whole body shook.

'Take no notice of Dad,' she said. 'I don't know what it is. He's not really himself.'

She wiped something from the corner of her eye. We sat down at the kitchen table, Mum and I on chairs and Göran on her lap. She patted his back, looked out of the window and shook her head ruefully, as if she was crying inside. Göran pressed himself close against her bosom and whimpered like a puppy.

'Try to get a bit of sleep, boys,' she said. 'Tomorrow's another day. You need any sleep you can get with all this going on.'

I left the door of my room unlocked, raised the blind and opened the window. Sat there, looking out over the dark yard in front of the cowshed. The shapes of the woodpile, the well pole, the Dung Birch. From the pigsty you could just about hear the nocturnal rumblings of the sows, but there was no light showing anywhere.

The windows were black squares. Blind holes.

There were thin trails of mist hanging at the forest margins, dancing with the spruces along the outer edge, a strict line of them to witness what could not be allowed to happen. I listened in suspense, incapable of intervening, ready for anything. A rifle going off. A car engine starting. Flames, growing and taking hold. One match in the hay and the cowshed is alight within a minute. Soon the flames will be licking out of the windows, sparks and glowing fragments will whirl up to the sky, visible across the whole fen, and everybody around will see what's going on. The chickens will fly for their lives, feathers on fire, flapping between the outbuildings like burning rags until they fall to the ground, cackling frantically, and fall silent. The calves bellow from their pens. The tethered cattle tug at their chains and gurgle with terror. The pigs shriek as they do when the slaughterman opens the door, trying to climb up out of their sties or force open the gates in their panic. The roof trusses collapse and the sheets of corrugated asbestos cladding come crashing down. Tomorrow there's nothing left but the brick walls, the bed of ash on the floor, a few load-bearing uprights and crossbeams like a charred skeleton round the roasted bodies with their shiny leather crackling –

The moon was reflected in the uneven glass of my double-glazed window, a twin image so diffused it was almost unreal. The night air was cool out there. The curtains hung motionless. There wasn't even a hint of a breeze.

That's how quiet it can be beside a drained marsh in the middle of the night. Not a sign of life.

But wait, here it comes.

The robin has woken up and sent out his first arabesque.

He has sung at so many sunrises that his whole breast turned orange in the end. Here came the first, fragile rockets of sound, glitteringly clear, as if he were scattering silver over the dumb-struck forest.

Then you knew that dawn was coming.

That time they found the car beside Marsh Pool and the soldiers assembled with their maps and compasses.

The dogged search parties vanishing into the coniferous gloom. Laminated and on a scale of one to fifty thousand, the dotted paths, bogs and ravines. Police questions about knowledge of the local terrain and any favourite spots. Crackling two-way radios, yelping Alsatians –

The flashing blue lights at dawn and the sound of the hovering helicopter.

The letter they found in his pocket later. The one only Mum was allowed to read.

I polished my shoes with a pair of Mum's old nylons until they shone and put the steel comb in my back pocket. Rummaged in the back of the wardrobe for my Terylene jacket and set off. I've scored a hit here, I thought as I pedalled. She's not interested in Bruiser Pelle or anybody else, it's only me she wants to be with. That's why she came to the training session, to set the date for our outing as soon as possible.

How keen can you get?

The old village school stood on its own at the edge of the forest, as if abandoned to summer. In the evenings, it looked like a haunted house. The big, schoolroom windows gaped vacantly. Weeds and grass had reclaimed the yard where Father used to play marbles and tag. Not a human soul in sight. Only the jackdaws, perched there tchack-tjacking as they geared up for that night's aeronautic display. The ground beneath the copper beech was strewn with hundreds of black feathers, as if there had been a massacre.

There were twenty minutes to go to the appointed time. I tried to stop myself chewing my cuticles to shreds. Peeled some scaly, lichen-coloured spots off the flagpole to help pass the time, grabbed the halyard and waved it to and fro, imagining it was the mast of a boat that was moored there, waiting for its sails to be hoisted.

Her and me, on our way to an unknown island –

Then the flock of jackdaws took flight. Hundreds of daws

reeling drunkenly into the air with a deafening cackle, spreading across the sky like flakes of soot as if they had heard a shot.

Like a sign, the voice breathed.

But of what?

I had no idea.

The shadow climbed infinitely slowly towards the gilded finial of the flagpole, forced upward by the rotation of the earth. When the summer solstice arrives, we shall sit there, leaning back against the pole and watch its shadow move round the schoolyard like the hand on a twenty-four-hour clock face. See it emerge from the greyness of dawn, grow sharper and shorter hour by hour until midday and then extend again and slowly fade away, melting back into the great shadow that swallows everything. Her and me.

'Evening,' came a voice from the road.

I jumped.

It was the verger, standing beside his black bicycle. He had been to ring in the Sabbath and get everything ready for the service tomorrow, he told me, though I hadn't asked. There was a red velvet collection bag fastened to his bike carrier.

'Someone's taken the trouble to look his best, then?' he said, clearly keen for a chat.

'I wouldn't say that. But you never know.'

I kept an earnest look on my face and looked ostentatiously at my watch.

'So how old are you, these days?' he asked. 'You'll be coming along for your confirmation classes soon, I daresay?'

'Maybe next year.'

He nodded thoughtfully, while I started whistling an unchristian tune so he would realise that I wanted to be left alone. That there might be sensitive things afoot.

'Whatever you do, never turn round in your pew,' he said. 'You might have to live with it for the rest of your life if ...'

'It'll be fine,' I interrupted him.

'Don't be so sure of that. Well, I've warned you now. And I suppose you already know the commandments, with a head for learning like yours?'

I didn't answer.

'It's Trinity Sunday tomorrow, you know,' he droned on obliviously. 'Trinitatis, as they used to call it. They'd gather round Holy Spring and throw cross-shaped sticks into the water to find out how long they had left. Whitebeam and alder floated and rowan sank, but not many people knew that. Take your grandpa, he came along with rowan sticks year after year, and look how things turned out for him. But I expect you know it all, eh, just like your dad did? He spouted it all like running water when it was his turn to come forward.'

The verger nodded, as if he thought he ought to answer for me, since I wasn't saying anything. Then he raised his cap and said goodbye.

'I'm taking the collection bag home with me for a few running repairs,' he added, 'if that's what you're wondering about. Everything comes at a cost, even charity.'

It was almost quarter past eight. I wandered up and down in front of the branch library like an abandoned elk calf. My cuticles were sore and bleeding. I had promised myself I wouldn't wait more than half an hour; after that it would be her hard luck. Even I must have some pride, however suppressed it was, I persuaded myself.

There she was!

Standing up in the saddle, pedalling her old, big-wheeled bike, pinging her bell a couple of times when she saw me.

'I've just got here!' I said as she freewheeled the last bit.

'Wow, you're all poshed up,' she said, her face brightening. 'Are we going to a party?'

I cleared my throat. She was in tatty old cord jeans and gym shoes, with a scarf round her neck.

'We were invited somewhere, earlier,' I invented. 'I wouldn't have got here in time if I'd gone home to change.'

Veronika gave a sympathetic smile and leant her bike against the corner of the building.

'Do you realise how far it is for me to come?' she exclaimed. 'Must be at least twenty kilometres!'

'About three, I'd say,' I said in a friendly way.

It's all the same to me, she answered by means of a quick glance. Then she said nothing. And just like the last time, I couldn't come out with a single sensible word. Thought it was up to *her* to suggest something, since she was the one who'd proposed the meeting.

Everything I'd had in my head on the way here –

'Have you always had such long legs?' I asked stupidly.

'Are they all that long?'

'No –'

Eventually she sat down and drew a five-pointed star in the dirt, the sort you can do all in one go. She went over the lines several times with her finger, as if it had some special meaning known only to her. Then she drew a circle round it, linking all the points into a single figure.

'Pentagram,' she said. 'Earth, water, air, fire, spirit. Protects you against anything. My dad wears one round his neck.'

I forced out a smile.

Incredible. What is it that makes you different from other people? How do you get away with not having to pretend? Dressing how you like, saying whatever you like without having to think it out in advance?

'Me, I've got a staring eye on my ceiling,' I said after a pause. 'Black as a raven and right above my bed. Feels as though it's swallowing me. Or suffocating me.'

Veronika looked at me as though it was the most natural thing in the world, or as if it was all the same to her.

'Can't we listen to those birds you were telling me about?' she said, getting up.

That sent a jolt through me. Cycle to Marsh Pool now – in my best clothes with no boots or binoculars. We'd have to call in at home on the way there.

'It wouldn't work,' I said, groping for the right words. 'We said next week, didn't we?'

'Do the birds only sing some weeks, then?'

I swallowed.

'Let's look in at the church first,' I said, chancing it. 'The verger's just gone home.'

'The church?'

'It's always open. We can practise getting married.'

She gave a laugh and set straight off.

'All right!'

We left our bikes by the stone wall and were making our way to the gate when I noticed there was something written on the wall of the hut that served as a chapel of rest before burials. In big, untidy letters, like straggly rock carvings, covering half the wall.

It can't be possible.

For a moment I thought I was seeing things or had been transported to the middle of a dream.

AGNE HEADING FOR THE LOONY BIN

Just that.

As plain as anything. Spray-painted in bright red on the whitewashed wall, clearly visible from the road. Veronika had seen it, too, and gave me an enquiring look, as if she expected an explanation. I just stood there, my lips glued together.

'That's not nice,' she said. 'Is it?'

I averted my eyes.

'Why does it say that?' she persisted.

'I don't know what it is,' I said in the end. 'I've never seen it before. Somebody must have painted it on there today.'

'Is it about a person called Agne?'

'Seems to be.'

'What an odd name.'

'Yes.'

We walked over to the chapel of rest, side by side, unable to resist going closer for a better look. The coloured lettering had run, as dark as clotted blood on the rough wall. Veronika read the message under her breath, the way you might mumble a prayer.

'That's a really low thing to do,' she said. 'Is he the local village idiot or what?'

I sort of choked and put my hand on the wall for support.

'I don't exactly know what you'd call him –'

She gave me a look, losing interest.

'Shall we go?'

Out on the road, a car slowed to get a better look. They must have driven over just to read that poisonous message. It's going to spread as surely as if it were on the front page of the paper. The minute I thought of it, I could hear the cackle of all those old crones, see them sitting in their rocking chairs, gassing on the phone for hours.

'Can they really leave someone like that on the loose?'

'Well that's what it said, and there's no smoke without fire, is there?'

'Maybe they won't even let them keep the animals?'

'You saw what happened to his father, back then.'

And tomorrow they'll all be here for the service.

Bruiser Pelle, I thought. He must have done it. I'll get my own back tonight, go over there on my bike and set fire to their pigsties.

'Do come on,' said Veronika.

We heaved open the solid church door and paused in the porch, looking at each other. As silent as stone and as cool as a potato cellar. Long shelves of hymn books and catechisms, cardboard collecting boxes for charity, and a yellowing Jesus Christ, framed and under glass. In the window niche there was a traditional brown vase of dried everlasting flowers.

I had no appetite for doing anything any more.

We walked up the aisle, cautiously as if somebody might hear us, first me and then Veronika, half a pace behind. I hoped she'd forgotten we'd planned to play weddings.

I'd got to get rid of that writing. Come over on my bike when there was nobody around to see.

I stopped beside the font, where the vicar nearly drowned me when he had to read out my names. It was made of granite, solid and heavy enough to support a statue to the prestige of the whole district, rather than hold a few measly drops of water. Around the edge wound a pattern of winged lions and large-billed birds of prey, each with a snake in their jaws.

'Klas!'

Veronika was calling from the vestry.

'Hurry up!'

She was fiddling with some things in a cupboard. Her eyes were shining as if she'd found a secret passageway to some priceless treasure. I was still on my way over when she took out a bottle of wine and held it up for me to see.

'Nineteen percent proof. Do you think it's real?'

She pulled out the cork and smelt the wine. The bottle was almost full.

'There's money here, too,' she said, handing me a rattling biscuit tin full of old coat buttons and coins long out of circulation.

'The collection,' I said. 'Definitely not worth taking.'

'Do you think it's the real thing?' she asked again, holding out the bottle.

The smell was a cross between cough mixture and fruit squash, but it was so strong that it even reached your ears. I sniffed again, wondered if she –

Live for the moment, said the voice. It won't kill you, at any rate.

Veronika nodded eagerly.

I took a mouthful and had hardly swallowed it before there was a stinging sensation in my belly. A burning shaft through my chest, warmth spreading right down my arms and legs.

'Good stuff,' I said nonchalantly.

Veronika could hardly contain herself. Grabbed the bottle and drank, made a face and ran her fingers over her mouth. But you could see it wasn't the first time; she knew exactly how to put the bottle to her lips and how much you could drink in one go.

Another gulp, smaller this time.

'Agne's actually the name of a king,' I said, to get it off my chest. 'It was the name of one of the kings in the Yngling dynasty, the kings of the gods. He was hanged using his own torque. He symbolises fire and can mediate contact between the human race and the cosmos.'

'Sounds more like a lamb or something,' she said casually.

'You think so?'

My turn again. My veins had opened up and my blood was sluicing round at double speed. The evening sun was coming in through the window glass, casting long ribbons of colour across the sacred space and onto the opposite wall. The communion chalice was shimmering red and yellow and the candles in the candlesticks were dappled with blue and green. I thought it was the loveliest thing I had seen in my whole life.

'Look, can you see?' I said.

I could feel my cheeks burning. Everything was swaying inside me, but Veronika didn't seem to feel it. She sat there unperturbed, wanting more.

A membrane rupturing – – –

As if someone had loosened every restraint, all inhibition had gone, every ganglion losing control. I can say whatever I want! Who cares about a few words on a wall? Maybe there wasn't really anything there, after all?

I'm here, and Veronika's here.

There's the bottle.

I'll read the lesson, 'Love is patient, love is kind', if you play the organ. Choose a hymn and I'll sing it so loud that I raise the church roof. We can run up into the tower, ring the bells and look out over the whole village and beyond. If our farm's in flames I don't care, things will just have to take care of themselves. Let him set light to whatever he wants and burn it down, I'll cope on my own from now on.

It's you and me now. We'll jump from the tower and see how far we can fly. I'll point out where they found a skeleton with a seven-inch nail in the back of its head, show you where a great fissure opened up when a coffin disintegrated, the one containing the remains of the choirmaster who was hard of hearing.

She took the wine and raised the bottle in a toast to herself.

Soon I shall brush your arm, feel how smooth it is in real life. And you've got to promise not to get up and walk out.

My insides are sparkling, turning somersaults. Nothing's difficult any longer, or resistant; there are no hard edges anywhere. Everything's so soft and nice here, nothing but rounded, yielding corners.

But my thoughts had started to get muddled up. They merged into each other or dissolved into thin air the instant I thought them, like when you're trying to work out a dream.

Now I'm going to think about *this*, then I must say *that*.

Gone –

I turned to Veronika and tried to focus on one of her eyes.

'Does it show?' I found myself blurting.

She looked up, puzzled. She had the bottle on her lap and her cheeks were not even flushed.

'That I'm getting tipsy?' I said.

She laughed and pulled a funny face, shaking her head floppily. I took the wine off her and drank what was left. Felt as if I had wings on my back and an eye that could see into the future.

Was that a crunch on the gravel? The big door creaking?

From the oval window in the gable end: They've come to get you, the police and the vicar and your parents. It'll be in the newspaper on Monday.

'Anybody there?' I heard myself calling. 'Somebody's coming!'

Veronika gave a vacant smile and shrugged her shoulders. She kept on blinking, as if she was having trouble staying awake.

Doesn't really matter.

A second later she was on her feet, making unsteadily for a tall cupboard. She rummaged around among what she found there and tossed a few hymnbooks and a plastic bag full of discarded tombola tickets and crocheted butterflies to the floor. Then she came towards me with two of the vicar's vestments, handed me the green one and put the purple one over her own head.

'Come on,' she said, holding out her hand. 'Weren't we going to get married?'

I awoke with a shudder. We were sitting against the church-yard wall, slumped there in our shimmering vestments, and her damp, lifeless hand was in mine. Thirst was gasping in me. I felt as if my brain was about to be turned inside out.

Veronika was still asleep, breathing through half-open mouth, like a child.

It was almost dark out there now, but the message still shone as if written in letters of fire on the white wall of the chapel of rest. From the fields at the bottom of the slope I caught a sweet waft of hay.

'A cloudburst this week wouldn't hurt,' said Father, glancing up at the clear blue sky. 'But I suppose that's too much to ask?'

'The weather'll change soon, you'll see,' said Mum in her conciliatory way.

He leant over to the barometer again, glared accusingly at its hapless pointer and tapped the glass.

'Change?' he said. 'It's going to be like the summer of '17, this one, I swear it. There was nothing left but the thistles by the end. Thistles and dust clouds and pure hell.'

Father in a vest and a flannel shirt in the heat. Scabbed lips, flecks of powdered rust mottling his face, the much-thumbed oilcloth-covered notebook on the table in front of him. A hairpin for cleaning out his pipe. Had he heard about the graffiti on the little chapel of rest? Did he know that the verger had shown his solidarity and painted it over before the service?

Mum suddenly came over to the table and scrutinised him suspiciously, lifted up his hand and pulled a face. Dark patches up the arm of his shirt and a black leather thumbstall. His hand was covered in blood.

'I caught it on some sheet metal,' he said by way of an explanation. 'It's nothing.'

She stuck out her lower lip doubtfully.

'We're going to go and get that properly washed before we eat,' she said.

The hint of a smile flitted across his face. He left the notebook where it was and followed her out to the toilet without the slightest protest. When they came back he had a clean hand and a white gauze bandage under the thumbstall.

'It's not every day you get that sort of fuss made of you,' he said, beaming contentedly at me. 'And I agree it was looking a bit nasty, that gash. I think it went right to the bone.'

'That's all we'd need, you with blood poisoning on top of everything else,' mumbled Mum.

'I'm going for a run on my bike down to the Marsh Pool tomorrow,' I said to change the subject, and because it was the only thing in my head.

Veronika. Cycling there, her and me.

'There's a surprise,' said Father.

'The last species that migrate to the tropics will have arrived now. Rosefinches and marsh warblers. Maybe even honey buzzards.'

'You and your birds,' said Mum. 'Don't you ever get tired of them?'

Father's expression turned grave. He looked alternately down at his bandage and out of the window: over to the right, the mountain of metal and rust; over to the left, the dry fen with its clouds of pollen. Then there was that fleeting smile again, like a flash of fire in the night. As if he were in another world.

'Birds,' he said. 'They fly any way they like, don't they?'

I lay there with my hands clasped between my thighs, not knowing what to do. I listened to the alarm clock pecking its way through the night, stared at the meaningless flower pattern on the wallpaper and found myself thinking about Veronika and her eyebrows, the way they slanted and tapered at the sides, like swifts' wings. About it being a sign of perfection.

Soon I'll be able to tell you that. I'll show you the aerobatic tricks of the swifts and common snipe at Marsh Pool. The marsh warbler's inimitable mimicry. The hobby hunting dragonflies at twilight. Everything that's *mine*.

Was that really the sound of the cellar door, at this time of night? Heavy steps up the stairs, a semi-stifled burst of wheezy coughing, a match being struck. So there's someone else in this house not sure how to pass the time. Someone on his way out to talk to the pigs, forcing me to stay awake until I hear the door open and shut once more.

It wasn't long before I heard crashing and banging from the scrap pile. The usual racket, but in the middle of the night it sounded as though the gates had been thrown open wide to the lake burning with fire and brimstone. Then there was a hissing, snakelike sound I'd never heard before. I crawled out of bed and cautiously pulled aside the blind.

There he is. In the middle of the mountain of scrap with a headtorch on his head and an ice-blue flame in his hands. Half his face was hidden behind a black mask and sparks were shooting out on all sides. The steel was melting and running like red-hot lava around his feet, lumps of metal hitting the ground as if it was some kind of production line. The fizzing jet of fire was evidently so unimaginably hot that it could eat through absolutely anything. Bridge girders and sections of railway track were lined up on the sawhorses, ready to be divided into pieces and then cut into little bits.

The time's come to deal with all the stuff I've been putting off. Now we'll see what *this lot* can take. I'm going to wrench it all apart and not a thing's going to be left unchanged. What does it matter that it's the middle of the night, since I never get a moment's peace anyway?

This isn't Father.

It's a fire-spewing savage who takes over when people are asleep. The maverick with the cutting torch who's going to destroy everything.

Between us, Mum and I dragged the kitchen settle down to the boiler room in the cellar. The settle was a heavy and incredibly unwieldy bit of furniture, made of pine with threadbare ticking and high arms at either end. All the colour had come off the slatted wooden back and the whole thing was worn and scratched after almost a century in the same kitchen.

'Don't blame me,' said Mum. 'He was the one who wanted to move down here. He doesn't belong with us any longer, he says.'

We shifted aside the paraffin cans and cylinders of bottled gas, the chopping block with the axe embedded in it, Father's battered old xylophone and the pram that Mum refused to put in the car and take to the tip – and finally succeeded in wedging the settle in between the oil tank and the neatly layered woodpile, creating a sleeping alcove among all the junk.

Imagine living here, I thought. Bare concrete walls and spiders' webs with mummified flies in the corners, the floor covered in splinters of kindling and chips of bark from when we'd brought the wood in, the window so overgrown outside you could scarcely see through it. Not a single bit of furniture. Just the Russian lightbulb with its sizzling white glare, as sharp as burning magnesium. Together we opened the hinged seat of the settle, pulled off the sweat-stained sheets and put new ones on, changed the wool blankets that the mice had been nibbling and put the pillow into a freshly laundered pillowcase with Grandfather's monogram. I laid a rag rug on the floor, straightened out the fringed ends and put an ashtray to hand, to be on the safe side, and Mum hung up the embroidered sampler that she'd made herself.

My dear, my native soil,
For whom my dearest wish to Heaven is sent!

Ornate lettering, a red wooden house with white paintwork and a flag flying from the flagpole in front of it, the sun shining down on some apple trees and an old man ploughing, his back bent.

'He'll have to sort the rest out for himself,' she said. 'Then it'll be the way he wants it. I suppose he thinks the boiler's got to be kept going all night now, as well?'

She threw the old bedclothes down on the floor outside and stood back to inspect his new abode. She put her hands on her hips, surveyed the boiler room and gave it and me a look of misgiving. To me, the bed we had made up looked like a coffin.

'Right, so that's that then?' she said.

I shut the lid of the settle and went over to her side. It was on the tip of my tongue to ask: How long's he going to live here? And surely he's got to eat? The fourth *and* the fifth chair at the kitchen table will be empty from now on, if he doesn't join us?

'As long as he doesn't set fire to anything,' I blurted out.

Mum snorted and gave me a severe look.

'You think he'd set fire to his own house? That's the stupidest thing I've ever heard. It's his whole life, this place.'

'I was only thinking.'

So I'd been invited round to *hers*. I had no idea what the etiquette was. And what's more, it meant Bliss Cottage, where there'd been no one but the melancholy warrant officer's widow and her emaciated dachshund for as long as anyone could remember. She'd put sacking over the windows and never showed herself among people except when it was First Communion. So miserly that the magpies flew upside down whenever they passed overhead, so it was said. I hadn't even bothered stopping there when I was out selling my flower bulbs and bags of seeds and had almost forgotten the place still existed.

But it did. Because now *she's* there, waiting for me.

I parked my bike and went up the path, as docile as if on my way to have my fortune told by a palm reader. The sign on the door said FORSSMAN, with a double S.

Veronika Forssman, I tried out to myself. *Klas and Veronika Forssman –*

Okay, here we go.

Her mother opened the door. Tall and dark haired, with a yellow dress and her hair in a ponytail.

'Do come in!'

She held out her hand and gave an easy smile.

'I'm Helena.'

'Klas,' I said, looking at the floor.

I went red. It wasn't an everyday thing for me, shaking someone's hand like that and introducing myself. But in this house you were somebody as soon as you stepped through the door, it seemed.

'I hope you've got time to stay a few minutes and see round?' she said. 'Since you've cycled all this way?'

I nodded uncomfortably.

'Yes, that'd be interesting.'

There was nothing in the kitchen remotely reminiscent of either an old warrant officer or his widow. There was a fresh, clean smell like newly washed clothes, the wooden floor was bare of rag rugs and on top of the old, wood-burning stove was a milk jug someone had filled with buttercups and bright blue viper's bugloss.

'I expect you'd like something to drink?'

'There's no need,' I said automatically.

She went to the fridge, poured two glasses of carrot juice and gave me one. And Veronika? Why wasn't she sitting at the window waiting for me, making corkscrew curls in her hair with her finger? Hadn't she been looking forward to this all week, longing for it to the point where she, like me, nearly popped?

'We're so happy with this house, you know,' said Helena. 'I fell in love with it just like that. Veronika's not quite so enthusiastic, but then she's got her friends up in Väsby. I'm sure I would have felt the same myself.'

She smiled and blinked her brown eyes.

'But we've kept our flat in town for now, just in case,' she added. 'I mean, you never know.'

'No, of course not –'

Here she is, coming downstairs! That thick hair, and those dungarees with the flowers and stars.

'Hi,' she said and poured herself a glass of juice, too, looking down and not even smiling.

All at once I felt as feverish as if I was running a temperature.

I leant against the wall and gripped my glass hard with both hands, as if it was full of nitroglycerine.

'It must be fantastic to be able to grow up here,' Helena went on. 'With nature all around you and no exhaust fumes. Be able to grow your own food and sit outside in the evenings.'

She looked me in the eyes.

'Er, yes.'

'And the silence. Get away from all those wretched planes coming in to land. To me it seems simply wonderful. Absolute paradise. Don't you think, Veronika?'

Her face took on a sulky look.

'For fir trees, maybe.'

Helena stroked her cheek tenderly, went over to the door on the far side of the kitchen and gestured to us to follow her. In the front room, Veronika's dad was sitting listening to piano music with a book on his lap.

'This is Klas,' she said. 'That nice boy Veronika met.'

No reaction.

'Leo?'

He raised one index finger in the air and plainly didn't want to be disturbed while he was listening to the music. He closed his eyes and swayed slowly from side to side in his armchair as if in some sort of trance, his arms on the armrests and his fingers playing an invisible keyboard. Helena shook her head lovingly.

'Le-o –'

'Mendelssohn!' he exclaimed. 'Isn't it wonderful? *Lieder ohne Worte!*'

He looked up, gaping at me, presumably in some kind of ecstasy. Veronika gave an audible sigh and whispered that we could go up to her room if I wanted. I didn't know if my answer was yes or no.

Give it a bit longer. A few more minutes, at any rate.

'Have you ever heard music more beautiful than that?' he said. 'Songs without words.'

I gave a cough and tried to think rapidly.

'Probably not. At home they mostly listen to singers like Jan Sparring, or Mia Marianne and Per Filip. And Lill-Babs sometimes, on Saturdays. My brother and I are named after that song of hers, "Do you still love me, Klas-Göran?" I'm sure this is more beautiful than those.'

He gave a loud laugh and reached for the wine.

'Veronika,' said Helena, over on the sofa. 'Perhaps you two should get going soon?'

'I just want to show Klas my room first.'

'So you're Klas!' said Leo, taking the floor. 'I recall Veronika mentioned you at some point. And now you're both off to play ornithologists?'

'I wouldn't call it playing,' I said. 'We're bound to hear marsh warblers, reed warblers and nightingales tonight. Probably some common snipe and spotted crakes as well.'

'Oh, will you? Well well, fancy that.'

'On the way there we pass a place where we'll hear corncrakes and quail, if we're lucky.'

'Quail!' he exclaimed. 'Darling, what do you say to hard-boiled quails' eggs for breakfast tomorrow?'

He gave her a wink. Looking as though she wanted to avoid a fuss, she took out a newspaper. Veronika stared out of the window, fingering some piece of jewellery she was wearing round her neck.

'It's a bit too early for that, I'm afraid,' I said. 'The quail breed virtually last of all the bird species in Sweden.'

'Is that so?'

He put down his wine glass and held his book up in the air, like a signboard.

'You ought to read this,' he said, changing the subject. 'Ever heard of *Steppenwolf*?'

'I don't think so. What happens in it?'

'Happens?' he said, nonplussed. 'There's a lot of crap talked about what happens in books. If you see a great painting, do you ask yourself what's happening in it? Or a piece of music?'

'No?'

'Of course you don't. What's interesting is how the work of art has been executed, its intrinsic power, colour and form, rhythm and tone, linguistic nuances. Things like that. But I suppose one might say Hesse problematises the relationship between instinct and spirit, the battle between human and divine, how we relate to time and infinity.'

He licked his finger and leafed through the book.

'Here, listen: "The desperate clinging to the self and the desperate clinging to life are the surest way to eternal death, while" – he raised his finger in the air again – "the power to die, to strip one's self naked, and the eternal surrender of the self bring immortality with them".'

It was as if somebody on television had read it, or a vicar in the pulpit. He wasn't just rattling off the words like anybody else would. He knew exactly what everything stood for and where to put the stress in the various words.

'And here, another passage: "I, too, once put too high a value on time. For that reason I wished to be a hundred years old. In eternity, however, there is no time, you see. Eternity is a mere moment, just long enough for a joke".'

He snapped the book shut.

'What do you all say to that? Live, I say, eternity is the here and now! But we're so terribly afraid of dying that we fill our days with anything at all, just to pass the time and distract ourselves from thinking; we scurry round in our hamster wheel, desperate for recognition and full of sexual inhibitions. And so life passes us by and amounts to nothing more than a fleeting dream in the desert.'

'Oh steady on, darling,' said Helena.

'But then we're the first generation in the history of mankind that hasn't anything to believe in. No God, nothing. No fairies or wights or wood spirits, we haven't even got the brownies and trolls left to us nowadays. That's the price of knowledge: we know everything, but we've nothing to believe in – and the more we know, the unhappier we get. Of course we put our lives in God's hands in an age when nobody knew any better. We created a chimera to escape our own responsibility and help ourselves bear our meaningless existence.'

Helena cleared her throat and tucked her legs up under her on the sofa.

'People seem to believe in whatever they want to these days,' she said. 'Though I don't know if that's an improvement. Sect leaders making their followers commit mass suicide, for example. "The People's Temple", wasn't that what they called themselves?'

He wasn't listening.

'Have any of you ever heard of a chimpanzee suffering from angst?' he rattled on. 'No, of course not. They eat, dance and breed, in that order, blissfully unaware that it'll all be over in a few years. Can you think of a worse fate than that of a human being? To have been born with an oversized brain and unlimited opportunities for self-contemplation.'

He filled his wine glass to the brim and regarded us one at a time, but nobody answered. Veronika and Helena gave the impression of having heard it all before.

'And you won't find anyone who can give a sensible answer to the question of what purpose our lives actually serve – for the simple reason that there *isn't* one,' he added. 'Homo sapiens is a brief parenthesis in the mighty book of evolution, a will-o'-the-wisp in the infinity of the universe, a mutation that accidentally proved too robust. And what's more, we shall have to endure that insight all alone, because we'll never be able to share our thoughts with another creature like us. Is it any wonder people end up in the madhouse?'

I swallowed and gave an awkward nod by way of answer. The piano music had finished. The pickup crackled with each rotation of the turntable.

'You've got your birds, at least,' he said, and my insides gave a lurch. 'What do you think I've got?'

Helena put her head on one side and gave him a smile of sympathy, or habit. For my part, I felt I'd just experienced something that was going to change my life.

'Isn't that the question?' he said, turning to Helena.

'We mustn't assume Klas is all that interested in books or in your expositions of lord knows what,' she said. 'Not everybody is, Leo.'

A look of tenderness came over her.

'I like reading books,' I said, involuntarily siding with him. 'I'm sure it's good for my general knowledge.'

'Just so!' he said. 'Eh, Veronika?'

She tugged at my arm, already on her way out of the room.

So this is where she lives.

Fabrics with African dancers on them, on the walls, clothes lying all over the floor, collapsing stacks of cassette tapes. There was an advent star hanging in the window, alight although it was the middle of summer. She closed the door behind me.

'Take no notice of Dad,' she said. 'That's just the way he is.'

'He seemed rather good fun. He knows all sorts of stuff, too, doesn't he?'

She picked up a Buddha figurine from the bookcase and sat down on the bed with it, as if she needed a protector. Put a cushion on her lap and stroked the Buddha with her thumb.

'He won't be such good fun in an hour or two.'

For a moment the area round her mouth looked strained and distorted, like when you taste something bitter on your tongue.

I forced a smile. I felt as stiff as a statue, standing there in the middle of the room, palms sweating. I looked down at the floor and all round the walls and up at the ceiling, like an idiot with his head held at a strange angle.

'Imagine sitting meditating all day long,' she said. 'Some people do. In northern Thailand, I think, near the Golden Triangle.'

'It wouldn't surprise me.'

She shuffled closer to the wall, took a corner of the bed-spread and started polishing the Buddha.

Look at her.

Those smooth cheeks. Those brown arms with their downy covering that shone like gold.

I live here. I've nothing to be ashamed of.

As relaxed as you like.

Yet I could sense she had something on her mind. The thing she wanted to show me.

'Do your parents ever touch each other?' I said after an eternity.

Veronika looked up, as if to check I was being serious.

'Why ask a stupid thing like that?'

'Just something that occurred to me.'

I wiped my hands and looked to check that the edges of the wallpaper were neatly aligned all round, and the pattern had been properly matched, and it had. Everything was as it should be.

I could feel something pulling and tugging at me.

Out and away!

'Nice Buddha you've got there,' I said.

'It was a present from Dad. He says it symbolises calm and concentration. If that's true, then he's Buddha's opposite here on earth.'

I gave a laugh.

Are you going to just stand there? she asked, tossing me a glance. You *are* allowed to come and sit down if you want. We came up here for something, after all.

I summoned my courage and sat down at the foot of the bed. Hands trapped under my thighs.

'Are you staying in Stoneacre all summer?' I asked, managing to keep my voice from shaking.

'I expect we'll be going to Gotland before long,' she said carelessly. 'And then the Riviera; we know some people with a house there. We usually spend a couple of weeks in each. What about your lot?'

A candle flame, snuffed out.

The whole summer holiday –

'Oh, I have to help out at home. We've got some hay to get in, we usually spend a couple of weeks on that, too.'

'Sounds fun. I've got relations up in Roslagen who keep horses and rabbits and things.'

I nodded, looking down at my lap.

'That's if I haven't run away before it's dry enough to cut,' I said.

A look of confusion came into her face. She put the Buddha down on the bedside table and found a loose thread in the seam of her dungarees to fiddle with. Seemed to have something preying on her mind that she was keeping shut up inside.

'Do you want to see my catalogue of class photos?'

Before I could answer she was over at the chest of drawers, opening one. Then she came back to the bed and sat so close that our knees were almost touching each other.

'This is me!'

She was sitting cross-legged in the middle of the front row with her hair pushed back behind her ears. To me she seemed to be glowing, and looked as if she was laughing even though her mouth was closed.

'I was a little bit in love with him,' she said, pointing to a long-haired boy in a black-and-white Yasser Arafat scarf. 'But I'm not sure if I am any longer.'

A stabbing blow.

That's how easy it is for someone with nothing to be ashamed of, someone who can bring their friends and boys home, just like that, someone who's ready for anything.

'Though he is quite cute,' she said, half to herself.

Pssh.

The sort that plays the diva in the school corridors, you can see it a mile off. Do you think he knows how sharp an eagle is? Or an osprey with his eye of fire trained on the glittering back of a roach? I bet he wouldn't even know the difference between a tern and a gull.

She carried on leafing through the catalogue. Class after class standing against the same wall, boys with stony faces and arms crossed, girls smiling or holding onto each other. At the back she'd stuck in a picture of her parents trying to kiss and look into the camera at the same time, taken at a party somewhere. Then she put the catalogue to one side and shifted back into the corner of the bed, sort of inaccessible again.

So that was all?

I cleared my throat and made a big show of looking at my

watch. Looked at the poster she'd sticky-taped to the wardrobe door: a man in a suit being led out into a sunlit forest clearing, his eyes blindfolded. Perched in the trees all around him were birds of paradise with every conceivable kind of plumage and adornment, each more gorgeous than the next. Head plumes a metre long, elongated tail feathers and matchless colour combinations: Darwin's idea of sexual selection. As for the man, he was as pale as a corpse.

'You've got your own room, have you?' she said, not looking up.

I nodded.

'So what about your brother?'

'At the other end of the house. So we don't kill each other.'

She smiled to herself, as if at something else, or as if at somebody who didn't get a joke. She heaved herself off the bed and went back over to the chest of drawers. Applied some lip gloss, leant forward to study herself in the mirror and knotted that scarf nonchalantly round her neck.

'If you'd had no brother or sister we could have pretended I was,' she said.

I didn't know what she meant, or whether to be disappointed or glad.

'Then you and your family'll have to adopt me instead.'

'Is that what you'd like?'

'The other night I dreamt we were joined together like Siamese twins. I could never get a clear look at you, because we were so close.'

She didn't answer. Just pouted at herself in the mirror.

'Let's go,' she said.

When we got back downstairs, Leo was standing by the

bookcase, pouring brandy into his wine glass. He looked even taller than when he was stretched out in the revolving armchair earlier.

'You're sure this isn't going to be too late for you Veronika?' said Helena, lowering the newspaper onto her lap.

'Oh no, it'll be fine,' I answered for her.

Leo put his glass on the table and sat down with a thud.

'You read everything you can get your hands on,' he said, trying to locate me in the narrow gap between his spectacles and floppy fringe. 'Veronika's started reading Agnes von Krusenstjerna. The Tony Hastfehr novels, do you know them?'

I shook my head. Helena made an apologetic face at me.

'And it's not that remarkable,' he went on. 'Jan Myrdal read Strindberg's *Inferno* when he was only ten and felt a great affinity with a lot of it. Krusenstjerna isn't all that difficult either, is she Veronika? Somewhat erotically outspoken for her time perhaps, but I don't suppose that's ever done any harm.'

He laughed at his own joke.

'Do you think you need to impress him, too?' Veronika snapped. 'Can't you just be normal for once?'

'The two of you don't need a lift, then?' said Helena, going over and putting her arms round Veronika.

She rested her head against her daughter's and swayed them both gently to and fro, stroking her hand through Veronika's hair.

A shiver went through me.

Imagine standing like that, so close together – like in a film.

'Isn't it getting a bit late?' she whispered into Veronika's ear.

'It's not very far,' I said hastily. 'I always go on my bike. And we've got to get home afterwards.'

'Of course you should go by bicycle!' came a voice from the armchair. 'On such a wonderful summer's evening.'

He swivelled round and tried to look at me and Veronika at the same time.

'Well let's hope you see lots of birds at that lake, given all the trouble you're going to.'

'It's mostly a question of hearing them, like I said,' I corrected him. 'Some species basically only sing at night.'

'Yes yes, of course. Did you say corncrake, by the way? Strindberg in fact doubted it existed at all, but perhaps you knew that? Since no human being has ever seen it fly, it can't possibly get itself to southern Africa every winter, he reasoned. It simply wouldn't be able to cross the Sahara on foot.'

'Well I've certainly heard him, lots of times,' I said, as confidently as I dared. 'Sometimes for hours at a stretch. It sounds like *crex crex*, over and over again. He's saying his name in Latin, so that's easy to remember.'

This seemed to subdue Leo.

'Is that so? Well, well. You know more about it than Strindberg did, I can hear that.'

He clasped his hands over his thin stomach and sank back into himself, into the piano music that was playing again. Helena came out to the kitchen with us, put Veronika's packed supper into the bag and stroked her cheek.

'Ooh, I think I've got butterflies,' said Veronika.

'You needn't worry,' I assure her.

'No, of course not,' said Helena. 'You're going to take good care of my daughter, I can see that.'

The door closed behind us and we were finally free to set off. The rest of the evening and the whole night, her and me.

'I'll just go and get my bike,' she said, and hurried off across the grass.

I waved to Helena at the window, mouthed 'bye' and pulled the bag strap over my head.

So serene, so nice and easy here –

Nothing but the gentle patter of the water sprinkler and the yellow bunting counting to seven: *chizz-iz-iz-iz-iz-iz-zee* –

We rode side by side, each following our own tyre track, like a proper couple, but we didn't say anything to each other for a long time. Maybe we didn't need to, either, with it being so quiet all around us. The trees were as immobile as a guard of honour standing along the sides of the road, the milking machines and pressure tanks had stopped humming and the tractors had all stopped for the day. Here and there the hay had been arranged into rows to dry and wait to be baled and brought in.

It was that time now.

'Can you smell it?' I said. 'It's honeysuckle, it only has that scent in the evening.'

So it was quite easy after all. Just say something.

'Does it?'

'So the moths can find their way to it. The hawk moths are out and about now. They're the only ones that can reach the nectar, with their long proboscis.'

'Yes, now I'm getting it!'

'You can make dens inside honeysuckle bushes and live there.'

'Oh yes?'

Yes, and we're going to do it, you and me, I was on the point of saying, but stopped myself. It's best to take things slowly to start with. There was so much stuff inside me, wanting to get out, and I had to save some of it for tonight.

'Have you heard about the marsh warbler, by the way?' I ventured. 'It can imitate the birds it lived with in Africa.'

Veronika laughed; she couldn't help herself.

'What did you say it was called? I don't know a single thing about birds, I told you. I scarcely know what a magpie looks like.'

'No, of course –'

Not too fast on the downhill stretches. Nice and easy, that was the idea.

'I lived in Africa, too, actually,' she said, as if it was no big deal. 'But I don't remember much. It was before I started school.'

'You've certainly been to lots of places and done lots of things,' I said ingratiatingly.

'Don't know about that.'

But did I detect a blush? A hint of extra colour because I was the one saying it?

'So you'll be starting at our school in the autumn then?' I pitched in.

'Maybe,' she said, unconcerned. 'Have to see. I'd far rather stay in my old school.'

'Obviously.'

'I mean, I haven't got any friends here.'

'No –'

But we can change that, and sooner than you think! Soon we'll be sitting down by the Marsh Pool, you and me and nobody else, and I'll show you everything that's mine.

We passed King Orre's Oak and the track that led off to the dowser's isolated cottage, and turned down the old railway line where they'd removed the sleepers and along which I'd ridden hundreds of times with my binoculars round my neck and the bird book and thermos flask in my shoulder bag.

Now is now! Something bubbling up inside me. We'll be there any minute. Veronika and I are on our way. Come on, out of your nests and hiding places. Up from your tussocks and roosts and show what you're made of!

Osprey dive! – – –
     Red-footed falcon hover! – – –
       Horse gowk whinny! – – –
         Woodcock chee-wick! – – –
       Nightjar purr! – – –
    Curlew trumpet! – – –
  Crake whistle! – – –
Tawny owl cry! – – –
   Quail sound your call! – – –
     Nightingale rattle! – – –
       Water rail grunt! – – –
         Marsh warbler sing! – – –

We followed the fence down, the way I usually did, balanced our way across the narrow plank bridge over the boggy part and set our sights on the mound with the clump of birches, where you got a good view and could sit without getting wet. The setting sun was making the cowshed windows on the far side of the lake sparkle like copper.

The shooting hide on stilts was empty and the flat-bottomed wildfowling boat was drawn up on the shore. Not a soul.

I spread my raincoat beside a rock and sat down. The slope just in front of us was smothered in frothy white cow parsley, the tussocky meadow running on down to the lake spangled with yellow flag irises. A few mayflies were still in flight, moving up and down through the air as if each was on a piece of string someone was playing with. Rising and instantly falling, dancing as fast as they could in their effort to attract a female before they floated to the ground and became food for others. The absolute opposite of the cuckoo: created to reproduce and be eaten, never eating anything themselves.

At that very moment, a roebuck barked from the depths of the trees. A powerful roar, a rutting cry that echoed out over the murmuring lake.

'Almost like a lion,' I hissed enticingly.

'D'you think so?'

She cast a listless look over the reed beds in the sheltered inlet to the other side, as if she was wondering if this was it, if there was really a prospect of anything happening here. I tried to stop myself sneaking furtive looks at her standing there, but it wasn't easy. The whites of her eyes were shining like fine china in the soft evening light. Her wavy hair reached way down her back. She was wearing a striped anorak with a hood and her mum's old blue-and-white wellies. She'd stuck an oxeye daisy with an uneven number of petals into her hair at one side.

'D'you think we'll see anything exciting, then?'

She yawned and sat down, less than a metre from me. Pulled up her knees and held them tight together at the top so she looked like a splay-legged calf.

'There'll be no better chance than this, that's for sure. The weather's perfect, the night-time singers have come back from their winter grounds and the air and water are full of food.'

And as if someone had clicked their fingers, the starlings came flying in for that evening's performance of aerial acrobatics, appearing from all directions so the group grew larger by the second. Soon a great, flickering host of them was billowing back and forth over the lake, tightly packed together so nobody felt left out. It was constantly shifting form – stretching out into a narrow ribbon, compacting into a ball, changing back into a big oval balloon again – as if every starling knew how to move so they could collectively create a particular shape, or as if they were under the control of an invisible force. Then the right moment arrived and the whole flock swept down over last season's yellowing reeds, keeping low and close –

Something wrong, maybe a marsh harrier in sight?

Slicing towards the forest again and back out over the lake, coming further this way now, like a huge streamer without a flagpole.

'Look now!' I whispered. 'Look!'

They vanished into the reeds without a trace. Only a faint rustling sound as they found the right perch – then all was still. Not so much as a waving frond. A thousand sleeping starlings.

'Almost as if they'd rehearsed it,' said Veronika.

I nodded proudly.

'And we can assume these are only the males,' I filled in. 'You'll see what I mean in September.'

Further over by Osprey Holm, where the sun was still spreading its coppery gleam across the lake, the swifts were busy netting mosquitoes in their wide open beaks, diving and turning at such a tearing speed that it made you dizzy trying to keep up. I passed the binoculars to Veronika and pointed.

'They can do everything in the air,' I said, though she hadn't asked. 'Even mate, and sleep. They spread their wings wide and glide in a sort of trance. In Australia, no one's ever seen a swift on the ground.'

She closed one eye and tried to adjust the focus.

'I can't see a thing,' she said.

'Yes you can!'

Once the screech of the gulls had died down, the proper night-bird orchestra could finally come into its own. Deep in the sedge bog, the spotted crake started up, providing the beat; behind us perched the nightingale, its fluting and rattling like a whip to the ears; the sedge warbler grated and scolded and whistled as if in complete ecstasy behind the osiers. The common snipe, out courting, hurled themselves headlong from the sky, bleating for all they were worth; the great crested grebes rasped and the lapwings beeped and whined; the water rail was standing somewhere, hammering out *his* beat, his insistent *kypp, kypp, kypp, kypp* –

And so it went on. And there was the incidental stuff besides. The curlews having to shuffle up and make room for some trumpeting cranes who came flying in at the last minute, the voles in the little pool, paddling away with their wakes frothing behind them, scared to death that the marsh harrier might be awake, and as a background to them all, the soft, monotone purr of the nightjar. Every now and then the marsh warbler chimed in, so even the nightingale had to admit defeat as a soloist.

'That's the one that imitates its African cousins,' I whispered, digging her in the leg. 'Incredible mimic and improviser, both at the same time.'

Veronika was scarcely listening. She was sat there, looking through my bird book, leafing randomly backwards and forwards as if it were a Bible with nothing in it to catch her eye.

'What time is it?' she asked irrelevantly.

I pretended not to hear. At that very moment the coots started shrieking and splashing, deep in the reeds, the black-headed gulls awoke from their slumbers and started cackling in each other's faces, the water rails grunted and the spotted crake set up a warning cry of life-threatening danger.

'That'll be the long-eared owl,' I gambled, trying to make it sound enticing. 'It hunts at dusk, that's why there's all this racket.'

'What does it look like?' said Veronika, perking up.

'Like a great horned owl, but in miniature. Burning eyes and big ear tufts. Long wings, controlled flight.'

'You think that helps me?'

'You can hear the young begging all night, too.'

I wanted to show her and scanned the lake with the binoculars, but a minute later everything was as it had been and the birds had already forgotten they'd been alarmed. The ducks and grebes were floating there as if nothing had happened, and a few gulls and lapwings were swooping around lazily in the pale darkness; on a tiny island of mud, the young cranes stood sleeping, their heads under their wings. There was no long-eared owl to be seen.

'It must have gone off the other way,' I mumbled.

Instead, Veronika started telling me about the African village where her mum used to work. About the girls mostly having babies when they were fourteen and the boys being expected to kill a lion with a spear or steal a cow from another tribe to earn the right to be called warriors; about how they lived on blood and milk from the cattle, and all slept in huts made of mud and dung, shared with the animals, and the fact that the nights were so dark you couldn't see your hand in front of your face, but only the fires that were forever burning and all the white teeth.

She paused, and lowered her voice as if in prayer or reflection. Asked with her eyes if I wanted her to tell me something.

'One evening a leopard came and took a boy when he was going to the well. We heard him scream and then it all went dead quiet; leopards always go for the neck first. Then we all sat there together in a ring round the fire, talking and singing until it got late. At dawn, the men all set off with poisoned arrows and spears. Because they had to take revenge on the leopard and eat it. They walked miles and miles and hunted for days and didn't find it, but in the end they came across some bloodstains under a tree that must have been a thousand years old – baobab, they called it, it's a sacred tree – and when the boy's dad stuck his spear in the trunk, a big white bird flew up and vanished. When they got back to the village they said it was the boy who'd flown away. He'd turned into a bird.'

I felt I could visualise it all. The lean men in loincloths with their spears and the bird flapping off without a word, like a mocking angel. The bright blue sky, the sun at its zenith, the brick-red soil, and Veronika sitting by the fire under the stars, forced to listen.

'That was sad, wasn't it?' she said. 'But kind of wonderful, too.'

I didn't know how to respond. The whole thing seemed too big.

Like being let into a confidence.

The stars were starting to emerge from the dulled light. To the north west there was still bright, fiery light on the horizon, but the scattered clouds above it were as dark as lead, as if the remnants of a distant thunderstorm had been left hanging there as the earth turned on its way.

Only the night all around us here. The reed warblers down in the reeds, and everything else that was humming and rasping, squealing and croaking from all directions.

I want to sit here all my life. Sit and sit and sit.

Soon I shall say something to you about it. Maybe move a little closer and get to sit shoulder to shoulder for a while.

Little by little, that was the idea. Nice and easy.

'How long do you think we'll be staying?' said Veronika, puncturing the whole thing.

She stifled a shivery yawn and rubbed her eyes like a tired child.

'We've only just got here!'

'We might as well have something to eat.'

We made room for the packed suppers between us. We each

had a rustling little packet and a thermos flask, hers was tea and I had hot chocolate. Mum had given me homemade bread with brawn and mustard, and a hard-boiled egg, pre-sliced and salted so it was all ready to eat. Veronika had a couple of rolls and a box of salad that had bits of a thick white cheese in it, without holes.

'Don't you ever get scared of the dark?' she asked as we ate.

I shook my head.

'I don't believe you.'

'Well if I ever did, it would be at home. Having to lie there staring at that eye on the roof, with nowhere to go.'

After that we sat in silence for a bit, listening to all the sounds of the night. Our cups steamed. Veronika put up her big hood and leant over her tea, as if she wanted to catch all the vapours, not let any escape.

Then all of a sudden, mist had descended over the lake, billowing white and sort of luminous against the black spruces on the far side. As if out of nowhere.

There was no wind, not even the slightest little sigh in the aspens, but the mist was sweeping to and fro in a mysterious dance, as if it was *alive*.

Can you see, Veronika, was on the tip of my tongue. That this mist isn't right. It's billowing and rolling though there isn't any wind.

Pssh –

And there's something up with the moon, too. Way off over the marshes like a big yellow cheese, swollen and blotchy like I'd never seen it before.

From the darkest depths of the woods: It's all the people who've drowned, dancing; the restless souls that have woken at midnight. That's why the mist can't lie still – because *their* hour has come.

Boh –

Veronika peered at me from the side.

I didn't know the answer. Put the binoculars to my eyes for want of any better solution.

Boh!

We heard it again, strange and dark, like something from another world. Veronoika sat up straighter.

'What – was – that?'

I shrugged my shoulders, feigning calm. Thinking that I must have sat here in the middle of the night hundreds of times and never heard anything like it or seen the mist dancing when there was no wind.

This is a night like no other, said the voice. Because at home at this moment there is someone spraying icy fire and hacking away like grim death. Someone with the deep gashes in his fingers, a way in for all that rust.

And that was the church bells ringing.

Nonsense. Surely you couldn't hear them from right out here?

Don't be too sure. It depends on all sorts of things, what you can hear or not hear on a night like this. And bells don't ring for nothing.

'You can die of blood poisoning, can't you?' I asked without thinking.

She gave me a sharp look.

'Why bring that up now? Haven't you noticed there are loads of weird noises everywhere?'

At that moment an unfathomable groaning and snorting issued out over the lake, as if a bull had fallen into a well and was bellowing for his life. Veronika's mouth dropped open.

'Did you hear? There it goes again!'

Even louder this time, dull and majestic, seeming to set everything quivering. And this time it wasn't individual snorts but a whole stanza of them pumping out.

Uh uh uh uh uuh-boh, uh-booh, uh-booh, uh-booh – – –

'It must be the bittern,' I concluded. 'The strangest bird in all Sweden. The male can apparently boom all night to attract an available female; the sound carries for several kilometres. It looks a bit like a heron, but it's brown and ungainly, with a thick neck. It flies almost like an owl.'

'It doesn't really sound like a bird at all,' said Veronika, relieved. 'More like some prehistoric creature that's come back to life. Listen!'

'Apparently they were pretty common in the eighteenth century. I don't know anyone who's ever seen one in real life. It lives deep in the reed jungle, like a hermit.'

Veronika cupped her hand behind her ear and held her breath.

'You could almost imagine it was somebody at death's door,' she said naively. 'Or a water spirit.'

And the bittern went on with his peculiar boom, over and over again – as deep and dark as a slide trombone. But it was impossible to hear where it was coming from; it was everywhere and nowhere, as if the mist was groaning.

Oh-boh! O-boh! O-boh!

'Wonder where it is,' I thought out loud.

Veronika started spying all round her.

'Let's see if we can find it,' she said, as if we were talking about a woodpecker up in a tree in broad daylight.

But she wasn't joking.

'Like I said, it lives deep in the reeds. It'd be totally impossible to find it now.'

'If I just sit here I shall fall asleep. We've got our boots, after all.'

I climbed up into a birch and tried to get a hint of where he might be. It seemed to come from somewhere in the reed bed around where the Canal ran out into the lake, but whether it was this side or the other I couldn't tell. It could be a long way off.

'Right, I think I've got a general idea,' I said, slithering down the tree trunk. 'You're not having second thoughts?'

Veronika gave me a crafty-looking smile.

'You're really not like other boys,' she said.

I scanned her face for clues, but there was only that smile, and eyes concentrated on doing up the bag. Then she got to her feet and was on her way down the slope to the water, half-swallowed by the mist and the foaming cow parsley.

'Aren't I?' I called.

'Don't think so!'

I just stood there and stared blissfully after her, thinking for a second that I was in the middle of a lovely dream. That the Marsh Pool and her and me –

Not like other boys.

Did you hear what she said?

'You coming or not?'

I ran to catch up with her and took the lead across the waterlogged grass by the shore, trying to find the tussocky bits that could take our weight. Eagerly broke off some thin alder branches in passing, to make us a stick each.

'Is this where we've got to go in?' she said when we reached the reeds.

I nodded, torn. An impenetrable wall of night. The bottom of the pond invisible, and a dense mass of last season's rigid reed growth high above our heads.

Out there where the ghosts and creatures live –

That's enough of that. This is your lake and you're going to show her tonight. The two of you are going to track down the bellowing hermit together.

This is your chance.

I put down the binoculars and checked the position of the Pole Star: the heavenly marker that has guided hominids and the human race for millions of years.

'We'll have to be really quiet out there so we don't scare it,' I said.

Veronika nodded and poked an impatient finger into my back.

Right then, here goes.

I parted the wall of reeds with a swimming motion, bent my head and groped my way forward, step by step, feeling with my feet for firmer spots, or trampling down stalks to step on.

'You can cut yourself on the leaves,' I whispered, trying to clear the way for her.

'As long as my boots don't start leaking I'll be fine.'

The vegetation closed in around us. This year's reeds were tough and tangled and hard to get through, and the stalks seemed to get higher, the further out we went. In the end the plumy tops were so far above us, silhouetted against the sky, that I felt like a field mouse in a flooded field of oats. Here and there the reeds were flattened into great floes that held your weight when you stepped on them, but if you went through you found yourself up to the waist in broken stalks and could hardly scramble out again.

And the bittern played. Sometimes a whole sequence, or several in a row, sometimes as if he lost it before he'd even started, or was just tuning his instrument ready for the real performance.

'Is it far off?' whispered Veronika.

'Who knows.'

'We won't get sucked down and stuck in the pond, will we?'

'Sucked down? I don't think so.'

We squelched on, one step at a time, like two Indians with our shoulder bags like quivers and our sticks like spears. The mosquitoes were singing above our heads. The bats were darting about, swift as arrows in the darkness.

He gave another snort, even mightier than before, so deeply and loudly that it made you jump even though you were waiting and ready. It sort of resonated within itself and came at us from all round. Over in the inlet where the fish traps were, up in the forest on the other side and back through the mist.

Uh-hooh! Uh-hooh! Uh-hooh!

That's where we're trying to get to.

'Sounds totally crazy!' hissed Veronika, on the ball this time.

A few steps later she held out a finger and wanted me to hold it while we went along, gave my hand a gentle scratch with her fingernail in greeting.

Go ahead. Prod and tickle as much as you like.

'Ssshh!'

Was that a rustle up ahead?

'Careful now.'

A coot talking in its sleep? A couple of great crested grebes, snoring open-beaked?

And there's an explosion at our feet! Water splashes and Veronika gives a cry, the huge, primeval bird flaps wildly up over the reeds – and flies away as softly and silently as an owl, its wings in a shallow 'V' and its long legs trailing down.

Away into the dark and mist.

Not a sound.

I stood as if turned to stone. It brushed me with its wing! I got to feel its wing quills against my shoulder!

We just stared at each other.

The bittern's wing – – –

She grabbed at my jacket, splashed over to me and wanted to link arms.

'There must have been another one,' I hissed. 'A female we startled, I bet.'

'Well it certainly put the wind up *me*! Think if it'd attacked us.'

'I expect her nest is here. They stand stock still until you virtually trample on them. Bitterns are known for it.'

'Weren't you scared, too?'

'Not really. It was a bit of a shock, that's all.'

I got out the torch and shone a beam of light – and there it was. The bittern's nest, with five big eggs and what looked like the remains of a pike. Made of lengths of stalk and reed, lined with feathers and down. We pulled back the reeds and squatted down. The eggs looked like ordinary hens' eggs, just a slightly more greeny-grey colour.

'Is it all right to touch them?' Veronika whispered reverently.

She cautiously tapped one of the eggs with her little fingernail. I nodded, though I wasn't sure. Wood pigeons always notice and abandon the nest.

'You'll have to put it back exactly as it was,' I said, to cover myself.

She stroked it gently against her cheek.

'Feel! It's all warm. Feel!'

I weighed the egg in my hand. Felt I could sense the pit-a-pat of a bird heart through the shell – or was it pecking away with its beak, trying to get out?

Incredible to think that there was a bittern in there – – –

'As long as they're not rotten,' I blurted. 'If they've been lying in water, it can happen. Should have hatched by now, if they were okay.'

You two mustn't stay here too long, I heard in my head. She'll come back and peck your heads if she sees what you're doing. The harpooned pike is proof enough of the sort of thing she can do with that beak of hers.

'Maybe just as well for us to go now?' I said. 'So she can risk coming back.'

Veronika placed the egg back as it had been and stroked all five of them delicately with her fingertips, as if she was trying to baptise them. We stood silently for a brief moment, looking down at the abandoned nest, as if fixing the image of it in our minds.

'The mother will find it again won't she?' she whispered.

'Yes, of course.'

We crept a few metres into the jungle of reeds. Switched off the torch and held our breath. The male that was so eager to mate had started bellowing again, further out, but you still couldn't tell how far away he was. Perhaps on the other side of the lake, even? An eternity to squelch through. The Pole Star had vanished into the mist. The moon had set.

'Shall we go back?' said Veronika.

She took hold of my arm and pressed herself close. A thrill ran through me.

Nothing but the bittern booming rhythmically and our panting breath. The sedge warbler whistling, somewhere up on the bank, as if to show us the way.

'We can't get closer than this, anyway,' she whispered.

Don't say you're scared of the dark, Klas? You're too big for that now.
You're not to be scared of anything.
You hear me?

I could see from a long way off that the lights were on in the windows. That means there's a body sitting up knitting socks in the middle of the night because she daren't sleep. Or a body wandering up and down the house because he doesn't know what to do with himself. Biting his lip and licking the spittle from the corners of his mouth.

It's because you've been out without leave, said the voice. There'll be no peace in this house as long as you're running around at nights. It's all your fault.

In the hall, the rag rugs were all ruckled up as if someone had been in a hurry to get out and had tripped, then left us and disappeared. The cleaning cupboard where the medicine bottles were kept was standing open.

No.

The toilet door opened and Father came out, fully dressed in his work clothes, with a gauze bandage wound round his arm. He stopped and peered at me through pinprick eyes, as if he thought he was seeing things, or as if blinded by a bright light.

'You don't get rid of me that easily,' he said in a slow drawl.

'I've been at the Marsh Pool. I saw a bittern.'

He nodded gravely and showed me his bloodied hands. Opened his mouth wide and shut it again, like a moray guarding its cave.

'It's uncanny sometimes.'

He took a few steps towards me and laid his big, damp hand

on my brow. Did he think I was delirious, sick perhaps? He smelt of smoke and Vademecum mouthwash.

'I've got things to do at the moment,' he said. 'You know that as well as I do.'

'In the middle of the night? Can't it wait until tomorrow?'

He gave a disdainful snort.

'Tomorrow,' he said. 'Who cares about tomorrow, when it's now that matters? I told you, I've got this hanging over me all the time! I'm sure they came and let the animals out this evening, for instance. Can that wait for tomorrow?'

I felt my throat constrict.

'There's no such thing as tomorrow,' he said. 'Do you hear me? They're all after me now.'

He blew his nose on the sleeve of his shirt and limped towards the cellar door.

I was sitting in the kitchen reading the death announcements when Father came up from the boiler room, his face swollen and grey although it was the middle of the day. He was breathing heavily through his nose, as if he was finding it hard to get air, or as if he was losing his senses. The smell of pig manure and socks dried to stiffness, the dusty peaked cap with the weedkiller logo on both sides. The same old shirt blotched with rust and blood.

'I'm having a rough time of it today,' he said. 'The ravens were screeching from the minute I woke, not that I'd been able to sleep anyway.'

Mum pretended not to hear. She turned off the stove and brought the smoked sausage and potatoes in cream sauce to the table, sat down and said the briefest of graces.

'And the scrap metal pile grows taller with every passing night. It doesn't help that I'm killing myself with all this hard labour. Is there anyone else apart from Sisyphus who can tell me how to do it?'

'Let's take things one at a time,' said Mum. 'The hay's got to come first. "When the timothy's ears grow steady, the scythe must be sharpened and ready", wasn't that what you used to say? And I think we can forget about the scrap metal once and for all; none of us get any pleasure out of you carving old spring harrows and threshers into little bits.'

He just sat there, staring down at the labyrinthine patterns on the oilcloth, his right hand pumping almost indiscernibly as if to remind himself of the rhythm of his heart. Then he allowed his eyes to move over the table, and bored them into me instead.

'Seventeen acres,' he said, making it sound like the start of an order. 'What'll that make? Ten thousand bales to get in this year. In this heat.'

'Let's eat,' said Mum. 'The potatoes are getting cold.'

'That means no time for you to go running around listening to birds half the night. Eh? Do you hear that?'

He smiled a crooked, grudging smile. I took a gulp of milk and wiped the lip-shaped mark from the rim of the glass.

'Were you very late back last time?' Mum asked in her conciliatory way. 'Don't you ever get tired of those birds?'

'No danger of that. Last time I saw a bittern's nest. No one else round here has done that.'

'Wouldn't it be more fun if you took someone with you next time? So you didn't have to sit there on your own all night?'

Before I could answer, Father cleared his throat and tapped hard on the table. But then he seemed to lose his thread and suddenly start thinking about something else. His mouth dangled half open, waiting for what was to come.

'The hay's one thing,' he said, 'but the Colorado beetles are on the advance too, I can feel it. If they find their way here, the potato field'll be stripped bare in a week.'

'Let's eat while it's still got some heat in it,' said Mum.

'The females lay a thousand eggs, and the caterpillars do nothing but eat. So you can work out for yourself how it ends. An unprecedented invasion, like the locusts in Egypt.'

He squinted out of the window with a pained expression. His jaw muscles were working inside his beard.

'I can't cope with yet another setback,' he said. 'Hear that, Gärd? If the beetles come, I've had it.'

She can go off to Gotland and the Riviera and do whatever she likes. This is something *we* share.

Amazing. From one day to the next. And yet it had only just started, you could sense that a mile off.

Exultation inside, trying to get out.

And I thought it was lovely at the lake –

Did you hear that was what she said before we parted?

Like a promise.

The mechanical red jaw of the baler chomped the crackling hay with a rhythmic thump that made the whole equipage rock its way round Black Bog. Lap after lap of hay laid out in windrows, waiting to be baled and got in under cover as fast as possible. The tractor roaring at full throttle. The weather could turn at any moment and ruin the lot.

'If we have to put the ruddy stuff on the drying racks we'll never be done,' Father had said. 'It can take all summer, maybe even longer.'

He was up on the loaded trailer, toiling like a savage in the heat. Catching the bales and throwing them into place at the same time as he stamped round compressing the hay to make way for more. He was coughing in the dust that was so bad for him, grimacing at the sun that irritated his eyes, swearing when the machine didn't send the bales through at the proper rate. Mum was with him, helping wherever she could. Keeping an eye on the twine spools, straightening the bales that were out of line, and jumping down to retrieve any that had ended up on the ground because I'd taken the corners too fast or Father hadn't kept up. But when the twine broke, it was him that had to crawl in under the machine. It took someone with strong hands who could tie a knot that would last through anything.

'If you go near that switch now you'll have my arm off,' he shouted as he crawled his way under. 'You'll keep your fingers to yourself, won't you Klas? If you don't want to make an invalid of me?'

It was close and dusty and quivering with heat in the boggy field. Black as tar in your nose when you blew it. I leant forward over the wheel as I drove, watching out for broken eggshells between the rows of hay, tying to imagine how many brooding females and unhatched chicks had paid with their lives this year. In my mind's eye I could see the birds cowering in the protective clover and not having time to get away when Father came along with the harvester, see the hawks and foxes fighting over the scraps and the crows drinking from the exposed eggs. Now there was nothing left but broken fragments, the corncrakes' pale yellow, the pheasants' grey-green – because they weren't to know that we mow the hay several weeks earlier now than a hundred years ago.

'Right, we'll take five minutes!' called Father, with an imploring look at the sky. 'We'll sit under the Shady Oak, like we did when I was a lad and Father decided everything.'

Mum was already on her way to fetch the basket of coffee things. Father shook a cigarette out of the packet and went to get the small beer from the ditch. In the pasture, the cows were lying down, shaking their heavy heads indolently, apparently indifferent to what we were doing. But the heat did nothing to hamper the horse flies; the hotter it got, the more furious they grew. And they were attracted to you as if you were a pile of dung.

'See the stone wall over there?' said Father. 'It's Agne who broke the stones for that. Father's father. It was all he ever did and he still didn't get it finished.'

He slurped down his coffee, peering at me reproachfully through the gap between his cup and the dusty peak of his cap.

Splat!

That was Mum, flattening her first horse fly right in the middle of her thigh, bloody and filled with a diarrhoea-like gunge.

'They always go for people with thin skins,' said Father.

'You'll be all right then,' retorted Mum, vainly trying to lighten the mood.

'He kept at it year after year. To shift the biggest ones he had to lay down planks and lever them out, or get the stoneboat and harness up the oxen to pull it. And then he had to fill in the holes, wheeling tons of earth out there by barrow and tipping them in. Not everybody realises that today.'

He shook his head as if there weren't enough words to describe such misery. Broke a bit off his plaited bun and dunked it in his coffee.

'Infernal slavery, that was what it was. A ruined back for the rest of your life by way of thanks. People drive round now thinking stone walls are for decoration.'

He looked at us, craving sympathy. Mum couldn't even be bothered to listen; she was batting away the horse flies and trying to rub her arms with a bunch of yarrow.

'It was like a war in those days. The farmers on one side and the stones on the other. A war, I tell you, and that's no exaggeration. It was a matter of survival.'

'Or maybe he was like Pharaoh,' I said to the ground. 'Some people want to make big piles of stones and build monuments.'

Father winced.

'Is that supposed to be funny? If it weren't for his drudgery, we wouldn't be sitting here today. Especially not you.'

'Surely he could have sold the place and moved somewhere else if it was all so awful? If everybody just stayed put, where they happened to be born, we'd still be inbred half-apes walking round the savannah.'

'Just as long as the weather holds and we don't get any thunderstorms,' said Mum, looking for a way out. 'It hasn't felt this sultry all summer?'

'Do you hear what I say, you two?' Father hammered on regardless. 'Like a war, it was. The Devil couldn't have arranged it better himself. But Agne, he beat those stones.'

'And what do you want us to do about it? Go up to Heaven and thank him? Or down to Hell, maybe? It seems the more obvious choice, actually. Time goes by and the stone wall's just a stone wall.'

Father could scarcely believe his ears, but Mum acted as if nothing had happened. Poured more coffee and gave me the last bun.

'I don't suppose you really remember him?' she added. 'Surely you'd only just started school when he drowned himself? Anyone would think it was yourself you were feeling sorry for.'

Father put down his cup and took several deep breaths. Then he started rubbing his lips, first slowly and then more and more frantically, digging in his nails and pressing his teeth against his top lip as if he wanted to perforate it.

'My gob's on fire,' he muttered. 'If it's of any interest to you lot.'

Mum leant forward and tried to take his hand away.

'You were going to stop doing that. Wasn't that what we agreed?'

'Agreed? You have no idea how I'm feeling. You never did.'

She didn't answer. Tossed the drooping yarrow aside and sat there with glazed eyes, staring blankly at nothing. The sweat poured off us and the horse flies swarmed around us. The cows swished their tails, oblivious to it all. The air shimmered like petrol fumes over the fen.

Did I think it would turn out like this?

Was this what I signed up to when I came with him?

Is he the one I'm to love until death us do part?

Is that what you're thinking, Mum? When your eyes go moist and you don't say a word. When the beads of sweat run down your neck between your breasts?

I looked out over the fields of oats and the mound of stones still sticking up in the middle, like an island of rocks to save yourself on if the water level started rising again, the Canal broke its banks and the fen turned back into the bottomless bog it had once been.

Splat!

I got that one right in the middle of my calf.

'But I suppose you think I've imagined that, as well?' said Father, glaring at her. 'Like everything else.'

'Let's not talk about it any more.'

'When I say my jaw's burning –'

'There's thunder in the air and things are never the same as normal then.'

He fished out his pocket barometer and tapped the glass with the claw-like nail of his index finger. Lit a cigarette and blew the smoke out through the hair in his nostrils.

'A shower might actually be quite nice,' said Mum, trying to move on.

'So the hay's ruined, yes. But I suppose that's what you're secretly wishing?'

Something snapped inside her. She opened her hand and her cup toppled sideways and the coffee spilled out. She looked at him with sharpened eyes I had never seen before, as if she'd reached a decision.

'That's enough. I don't want to hear any more.'

'Oh you don't, eh?' came the provocative retort.

Then she got to her feet and walked away. Hid her face behind her headscarf and went up towards the forest and the overgrown wolf pit. She had her red shorts on. The varicose veins at the back of her knee looked more lumpy than usual, maybe because of the heat. You could see her bra through the damp back of her blouse. Father didn't watch her go.

'She'll come back when she's finished blubbing,' he said after a while. 'They can be a bit sensitive sometimes, women.'

He drew up one knee as a prop for his elbow, took the last slice of sponge cake from the tin and looked out across the fields. His eyes screwed up small, as if he was trying to suck in all the light.

'But she *can* milk,' he said. 'I've always said so.'

I put my nail to my horse-fly bite and pressed as hard as I could, dug it in until there was a deep, wine-red line across the swelling, a score mark full of trapped blood. The itching finally stopped, and it hurt instead.

Father was sort of whistling, through his teeth, probably thought it was too quiet and could sense strings being stretched taut. I looked away. A caterpillar was crawling along between two blades of grass, doubtless on its way to bury itself and pupate somewhere. It was going so slowly that you wondered if it would ever get there. And it was acting as if it was divided in two: its head was trying to go first one way and then the other, but its body trailed along behind like some passive, disproportionate appendage.

'You ought to learn to scythe, Klas,' said Father.

I poured some strawberry cordial, thinking about when Mum had been to the pick-your-own and the whole house smelled of the jam and cordial she was making. Allowed myself to wonder if it would never happen again.

'There was nobody could handle a scythe like Father. The grass fell without a sound. The best idea is to start at night, the blade bites better when the grass is wet. And you need to put a cap under your left arm when you're scything. As long as it stays in place you've got the grip right. It's mostly a question of technique, the whole thing.'

Spin a cocoon and await complete transformation.

So simple.

He reached for the small beer, took out the china stopper and swigged it down, straight from the five-litre flagon, as if he hadn't drunk a drop for days.

'And you need a good honing stick,' he droned on, 'so you can sharpen your scythe when you're out. Preferably black oak, I know that's what Father generally used. Then you dip it in glue and carborundum powder every so often.'

He put down the flagon and leant back against the rough trunk. His jaws were working slowly, as if he was sinking into old memories. Then he turned away, towards the forest where Mum had disappeared from view, where the wolf pit lay with its column of stone, sharp as an awl.

'I never forget a thing,' he said, smiling to himself. 'Have you ever thought about that? Not a thing –'

I dreamt I was peeping through a chink in a door that opened into a great, light hall. Sun was flooding in through the arched window and outside the door where I was standing, the red light flashed its warning, as if secret experiments were being conducted inside.

The hall was empty apart from a pristinely made bed in the middle. In it lay Father, his hands clasped on his chest. His eyes were closed and the expression on his face was serene, as if he had been set free from something. Both the bed and his clothing were white. Mum was sitting by him with a black hat on her head and a heavy veil over her face, a crocodile-skin handbag on her lap. On the bedside table a lighted candle stood beside a tin vase of dried everlasting flowers.

'We'll soon be home again,' she whispered consolingly, 'and everything will be like it was before. The doctor will be here any minute.'

Then she rose from the visitor's chair, just as you do when you've been putting someone to bed, and vanished silently through the window arch. She was replaced by a team of doctors, who formed a circle round the bed. They were all wearing black butcher's aprons and scrutinised him for a long time with concerned faces. They took off the bedcover and carefully examined his naked body, furrowed their lofty brows and stroked their chins as if faced with an insoluble puzzle. After some intensive discussion in Latin the eldest doctor, whose hair was completely white, took a syringe out of his coat pocket. The others helped by holding Father down while the old doctor injected him in the temple.

'Now you won't have to be afraid of me any more, Klas,' said Father, looking up at the ceiling. 'Do you hear that. Not any more –'

Then his face smoothed out and the doctors closed his eyes and mouth. A faint smile lingered as they nailed his arms and legs to the four corners of the bed and the youngest of them, a slender-limbed medical student, pulled out a pair of long red rubber gloves. His colleagues nodded in unison as he took out the scalpel.

I gave an involuntary cry and ran off down the echoing corridor, ran as fast as I could so that nobody would know who I was.

The clouds were massing themselves into a leaden wall behind the tops of the spruces. The swallows were flitting round like mad things over the yard by the cowshed and around the roofs, chasing flies and mosquitoes in dizzying swoops and dashes, and in the henhouse the cock was crowing non-stop. Because the storm was on its way.

Father planted himself in front of the barn doors and examined the sky with the air of an expert.

'All hell's going to break loose,' he said. 'But then that hardly comes as a surprise.'

Mum dusted herself down and gave him a guarded look, as if she was trying to work out what the implications were for her. He produced the stick of chalk and put another mark on the inside of the door: another load under cover.

'That's the fun over for this time,' he said.

The tethered black-and-white calf gave us and the overturned water pail a shamefaced look, as if wondering how it had happened.

'Well I'd better go in and get some dinner ready while we've still got the power?' Mum said anxiously.

Father nodded his approval and went to get an adjustable spanner. Shifted his cigarette to the corner of his mouth and climbed up on the conveyor to close the roof opening before the rain came. When he reached the top he sat himself down and turned his head in all directions like an owl, reading the sky and wind and interpreting cloud formations.

A finger that wanted to press the start button. Just a little jab, half a second and the machine's running.

No it didn't, not at all! Wherever did I get that from?

You must never start the conveyor when he's up there – on no condition. You could kill your own father.

'It hardly bears thinking about, how this is going to end!' he shouted.

Thunderstorm twilight and a foreboding patter of raindrops. The sound of Mum's needles. The ball of wool in the lap of her dress and the pattern in the folder on the kitchen table, the needles flying like drumsticks in her stubby hands. Stitch by stitch, pick up and cast off: a thick jumper for Father to wear in the forest in winter, navy blue with eight-petal daisies in white on the chest.

How many thousand stitches are there in a jumper? How many plains and purls?

Inside two minutes, the whole sky was black, the rain came sizzling down and the wind tugged and tore at the trees. The rowans turned their white sides out and the aspens flickered like shoals of herring. I went to get the stopwatch and sat looking out over Raven Fen where the lightning flashes came.

'I thought the fermented milk was particularly watery today,' said Mum, half to herself. 'It always gets it right, doesn't it?'

Father wasn't listening. He was tapping the barometer and shaking his head.

'It's falling every time,' he said. 'How much lower can it go? But I don't suppose there's anybody can give me a sensible answer to that.'

'If it's the hay out there you're worrying about, most of it's still uncut, isn't it?' Mum said soothingly.

'There are other things as well. I'm not that happy to see the bottom falling out of the barometer like this.'

He lit a cigarette and checked the damper was shut.

'If we're really unlucky, the whole atmosphere's got out of kilter,' he mumbled on, into his beard. 'Atomic power and the neutron bomb and everything that goes with it. It's not good.'

The thunder rumbled again, sounding angrier each time, running like a train from west to east across the sky with a dull echo behind it. Father went over to the window and took a couple of deep pulls at his cigarette, and drummed his fingers impatiently on the draining board, beating out a march for the rain as it teemed down.

'It could all go to blazes, let me tell you,' he said, sucking out the smoke. 'But it's no more than I expected, the way the pressure's been plummeting.'

'We have had thunder before,' said Mum. 'Man proposes, God disposes.'

Then the first naked flash of lightning flared, and the rumble followed four seconds later: a kilometre and a half. The bluebottles swarmed round the stove as if they'd gone crazy.

'What shall we do about dinner, do you think?' asked Mum.

Father just looked at her.

'How can you think about food with all this going on? These aren't just any old discharges, you know. We could be talking about a hundred thousand amperes a time.'

He nodded out of the window to emphasise his point.

'It's the Storm Bird coming,' I said, to have something to contribute, and because there was a picture I would never forget. 'It's been to the other side of the sky and looked into the sun, and that's why its eyes flash lightning whenever it blinks.'

Mum, busy counting stitches, glanced up quickly as if she was momentarily scared that I was serious. The rain hurled itself down in ramrod shafts. The lightning flashed and the crash came in less than two seconds: right above the fen where there wasn't anything to strike. On its way here to set fire to us.

'The Storm Bird carries a whole lake on his back,' I explained, 'so all it has to do is turn for the rain to pour down. The roar is when it beats its wings together.'

Father nodded, though he hadn't listened. He threw his cigarette butt in the dishwater, took his oilcloth notebook and a bottle of pills with him and made for the cellar door.

'This isn't easy for me,' he said. 'The tensions we had were more than enough. You both know that!'

He pulled the door to behind him and went down to the boiler room. The next instant the lights went off and Göran came running out of his room with my gumboots on, as if he thought an electric current was going to surge through the whole house.

'Is it right above us now, Mum?' he whimpered.

He curled himself onto her lap and put his thumb in his mouth, resting his head against her.

'There's nothing strange about a power cut in a thunder storm,' she said soothingly. 'The lightning might have struck an overhead cable, or the transformer substation.'

He nodded, but was clearly thinking otherwise as he sat there kicking the air with my boots.

'Why do we have to have the thunder just here?' he asked.

'Oh it thunders on the herb garden and on Gehenna, you know.'

Just then there was a terrific crash, as if the sky was being torn in two. Mum closed her eyes and rattled off some words to God, hoping we wouldn't notice.

'Maybe we *should* go out to the car, anyway,' I found myself saying.

We'd just sit there, Mum and us in the dusky light, like when we were little. Her and us and all the doors locked from the inside.

'Do you want to, boys?' she said unexpectedly, lifting Göran down onto the floor.

He nodded eagerly. All three of us got ready, and waited to see the next lightning flash before we dared risk it.

'Time to get cracking, as the squirrel said to the nut,' said Mum, putting up her hood.

Straight out into the cloudburst, first her, leading Göran by the hand, and then me, hunching over as we crossed the track and scrambled into the car, Mum and Göran in the back seat and me in her place at the front. We left Father's seat empty.

'Now it can thunder and lightning all it likes,' she said, breaking into a smile.

There was a flicker, and something hissing down into the tops of the spruces behind us before I'd even counted to one. The rain drummed on the metal roof and streamed down the windows, came and went in billowing gusts; it would slacken off a bit and then suddenly come gushing down again as if the bottom had fallen out of the biggest bucket in the world. The lightning and the crashes were coming so close together it was impossible to tell which belonged to which. It didn't matter. So nice to be sitting here now, Mum and us. Inside the house it was as dark as the grave, not even the light of the paraffin lamp down in the boiler room.

'Tell us a story, Mum,' said Göran. 'Will you?'

'A story? I don't know?'

She reached for the blanket and tucked it round Göran and herself, trying to think of one we hadn't heard before.

'It isn't really a proper story,' she said apologetically, 'but I can tell you about a tree with supernatural powers that protected people from thunder and all sorts of things.'

Göran nodded, wide-eyed.

'Well this tree was at my grandparents' up at Little Hult, where my mum grew up. 'It was a big, knotty lime tree, must have been a hundred years old and five metres round, with big black bumps on the trunk and deep holes. It was called the Storm Linden, and that was because it got in the way of a ball of lightning once and saved the place from burning down.'

She was almost whispering the words, as if they were secrets that might sprout wings.

'But the lime tree didn't only keep you safe from lightning. It protected you from fires of any kind and all the evil forces you could imagine: witches and ghosts and nightmares, ailments and illnesses. You could make a tea with the flowers that was good for nerves and rheumatism.'

Göran looked at her as if he wondered whether she was having him on, or perhaps he too had noticed she was somehow different.

'And do you know what the explanation turned out to be? It wasn't really the tree that had those powers, but a snake who lived down in the roots. It was called the Lindworm, and I promise you it was no ordinary little grass snake. It was seven metres long and as thick as my thigh. It pulled the lightning flashes down to earth and swallowed them if they struck nearby. It had big fish scales all over its body and a black mane down the back of its neck, like a horse. Its skull looked like the head of a pike with protruding red eyes that stared in all directions at the same time, and if it got frightened it reared up and came towards its enemy with its venom all ready, or it bit its own tail and rolled off like a big wheel.'

Göran sat there dumbfounded.

'But it only showed itself at the full moon,' she added. 'So it wasn't anything you had to worry about from day to day.'

I wiped the condensation off the window. The thunder was still growling and roaring, but the lightning had subsided and the rain was pattering down like any ordinary rain. The discharge was over, and it had only taken a few minutes for the storm to move on, leaving space for something else. I wound down the window and breathed in the fresh air, filled my lungs with it and smelled the mock orange from across the driveway.

'Do you think it's over now?' said Mum.

'Go on,' said Göran. 'Tell us some more.'

She popped a couple of cough candies in her mouth; as she sucked them they chinked against her teeth, and a knowing look came into her eyes.

'Do you know what my dad, your grandad, said a boy had to do if he wanted to make up to a girl?' she said.

We didn't.

'He had to pick some linden seeds and sprinkle them outside the girl's door. If it worked, she'd get up in the middle of the night and come to him in her sleep. That meant they'd be happily married.'

'So did Dad have seeds like that with him when he came to you?' said Göran.

Mum could hardly stop herself laughing.

'Oh, he isn't the superstitious kind,' she said.

She wiped the condensation off the window with the blanket, and all of a sudden her eyes glazed and tears were welling up. She sat there, just letting them fall, looking out of the window and saying nothing.

'You're not crying, are you Mum?' exclaimed Göran, tugging at her arm. '*You're* not allowed to be sad.'

She looked down into her lap and slowly shook her head.

Strange, I thought. From one second to the next.

'It's nothing serious,' she managed to say. 'It'll soon pass.'

'It's got to,' said Göran. 'Promise?'

'I don't know what gets into me sometimes.'

Then a smile flitted across her face and mingled with everything else there. She mopped her cheeks with the sleeve of her cardigan, laughing and crying at the same time and seeming to have no control over any of it.

'Actually, I remember another time,' she snuffled, 'when my sister and I were at Granny and Grandad's and there was a thunderstorm.'

She tried to look at me and Göran, both at the same time.

'But it may not have anything to do with the lime tree?'

'That doesn't matter,' I said quickly.

'Doesn't it? You're so kind to me, boys.'

She reached forward and stroked my cheek.

'It must have been one of my first school summer holidays,' she said, 'so I suppose I was a little bit older than you, Göran. Grandad was off digging up peat the way he used to, so it was just the two of us and Granny.'

She fished out a bit of kitchen towel and blew her nose.

'We all went out to the earth cellar together, I remember. Granny had the carbide lamp with her and we sat there waiting, pretty much like we are now. Granny recited the Prayer of Confession and we tried to join in, as best we could, and hey presto, when we came out again it had cleared up, and evening had come and the stars were winking. Then she said, "Do you know how the stars came to be, girls?" but of course we didn't know. "It's Our Lord, getting old and walking with a stick," said Granny, "and every time he rests on his stick he makes a little hole in Heaven. What we can see is the light from the other side." I thought that was lovely.'

Mum was crying again, as if she'd been reminded of something she'd lost, something she could never get back.

'How can God see everything we're doing if he's only got those tiny holes?' said Göran anxiously.

'That's what they used to think,' Mum explained, and she had to smile behind her crumpled bit of kitchen paper. 'But Our Lord's never needed a telescope, if that's what you're wondering. It's only people looking in the opposite direction, out into space, who need one of those.'

Galileo, I thought. Him and me.

'And us birdwatchers,' I said.

The darkness had intensified and the rain started again. I tried to spot the lights from the farms on the other side of the marsh, but all I could see was my own reflection, a dark outline in the yellowy glare of the car's interior light. The exaggeratedly large eyes, the long nose, the crooked mouth. A fake, sheeplike smile.

Veronika and *her* smile.
  I didn't know.

Soon I shall tell you you've got the smoothest cheeks I've ever
seen. Ask what you were thinking when our eyes blended that
time, suckered onto each other for several seconds, just looking
and looking, our pupils wide open.
  But you've got to promise not to just get up and walk off.

I woke to booming and shuddering, as if the ground was about to crack open. The walls were thumping and shaking. The windows rattled and the colour photo of Göran and me fell onto the floor.

It can't be possible. For the earth to start quaking beneath an old, drained bog.

Tell me it's not true. Who knows what might be concealed down there? Sliding plates and fissures gaping all over the place, the same here as everywhere else.

What holds up a fen, ran a sudden thought in my head. No load-bearing base, no primary rock to absorb impact. A reclaimed quagmire that could give way and collapse in on itself any time, be swallowed up by yawning chasms widening to infinity, never to close up again.

That's why nobody ever lives out in the middle of a marsh – because everything could be sucked down into the underworld. Down into a dark and bottomless hole.

I got up and looked out into the night. The aspen by the outside light was rooted to the spot, the leaves asleep on their long stalks.

It was the water pipes and radiators wheezing and banging, and the expansion tank just the other side of the wall. It wasn't continental plates colliding, a volcano erupting through the earth's crust, or sudden deep subsidence about to swallow the fen and everything else.

It was Father, stoking the fire to the point where the house was coming to the boil, as if he wanted it to blow up.

Mum was sitting alone at the kitchen table with the pink flowery coffee cup in front of her. Her rough hands rested heavily and as if forgotten on an open magazine. Father's bowl of porridge stood untouched, though it was past eight o'clock.

Something's happened, her eyes said.

No. In that case she would have woken me straight away. She hasn't got anybody else.

I sat down, not daring to ask. Unruly fears and misgivings fluttered about my mind, each worse than the one before. All the things I'd lain there at nights thinking about. Mum said nothing, just leafed vaguely through the magazine like a patient in a waiting room, running her eyes up and down the pages and making that little clicking sound with her tongue, the way she did when something was the matter.

Out with it then! It's something between the two of them. He's kicked up a mighty row and gone off with his shotgun, leaving her to keep it all pent up inside her.

On the radio there were seven LPs in the prize kitty and a retired major from the Kronoberg brigade who had to give a foreign phrase meaning purification of the soul achieved through tragedy. Mum wasn't listening, the radio was just playing to itself the way it always did now. Left on for days on end, so it wouldn't be too quiet.

She stopped clicking and gave me a hasty glance.

'The lightning's killed Maja and Beauty,' she said.

I took a spoonful of my cereal and yogurt and looked down at the pattern on the oilcloth. Rectangles and angles, the start of a never-ending labyrinth.

The thing that was not on any account to happen.

'Both of them?' I asked like an idiot.

'They were lying under the Spreading Oak when I went to fetch them in.'

Bruiser Pelle must have done it; he said he'd really get his own back this time. He's so different now, he'd be capable of anything. Bet he was here last night and jabbed a hypodermic in the cows.

'I don't think we'll get a thing for them. Maja was our best milker and Beauty was in calf.'

'Are you and Father sure it was the lightning?' I asked tentatively. 'If it got them both in one go?'

She raised her eyebrows.

'What else would it be? They were lying there, I told you, struck dead and without a scratch.'

'God's mercy,' guessed the old bloke on the radio after several minutes' thinking time.

I spooned my way through my rapidly warming yogurt.

'Catharsis,' said the presenter. 'Catharsis is the answer we were looking for, but it wasn't an easy one, not even for a former commanding officer.'

As his consolation prize, the major was allowed to choose the next record, pop group Jigs Orchestra playing 'Hello You Old Indian.'

After dinner the slaughtermen's emergency lorry pulled up. Father stood at the kitchen window chain smoking and didn't want to go out.

'You think I enjoy it any more than you?' said Mum at the door.

'I'm not coming.'

She hurried over to the man in the cab and pointed over to the Spreading Oak, where the cows lay. He gave the nod of one who's seen it all before and closed the cab door.

I looked at the dead animals through my telescope. They lay there with heads outstretched and legs sticking straight out, as if someone had knocked their hooves from under them. Their blackened gaze, gentle and empty, stared out on nothing. The flies were crawling over their muzzles and clustering round their eyes as if they were meres to drink from.

The slaughterman went over and inspected them, lifting one head up by a horn and then letting it fall back, as if to make sure she was really dead. He said something to Mum that made her give a brief laugh. She had the camera with her and wanted a photo of them before they were taken away. Then he got the lorry and hoist ready, fixed a chain round the cow's back legs and hooked on the winch. Mum took a couple of steps back and the cow went jolting away over thistles, stones and cowpats, over the back flap and onto the flat bed of the lorry, as limp-limbed as a shot elk.

Almost the same thing again. Mum didn't move a muscle, just stood there with her hands clasped, like a mourner in church, waiting for it to be over. He put up the back flap and secured it, wiped his hands on his trousers and put a wad of snuff under his lip.

'It's the Devil's work, this,' roared Father, making me jump. 'And I hadn't insured them, either.'

He turned round with a look of despair on his face.

'There's no end to the setbacks I have to suffer. Do you know that?'

I had no idea what to reply. I sat down at the table and leafed aimlessly through Mum's magazine. Pictures of the Queen's precious diamond diadem, a summer saver pull-out with barbecue hints for the holidays.

'You hear that, Klas? Everything's against me now.'

'Yes –'

His mouth was trembling. His eyes looked all dry and set, as if there were no tears.

'One more bit of bad luck and I've had it,' he said.

A lump came into my throat.

He hid his face in his big hand, massaging and pressing his temples.

Something about to snap, that was how it felt.

'You mustn't say that,' I tried. 'As long as the harvest brings in a decent amount you can buy more cows. You said that yourself.'

It didn't help. He was sunk deep into himself.

'I can't take much more Klas,' he said, his voice scarcely holding. 'That's just the way it is.'

Then he disappeared from view down the steps to the cellar. Outside, the lorry rumbled off with the dead animals piled on the back. In my mind I could see them being cut up and turned into scraps and meat and bone meal, as if they had never lived.

'I want to go swimming!' beamed Göran, leaping up from his seat and throwing his arms round Mum. 'When can we go?'

She ruffled his hair and gave Father a furtive, uncertain glance.

'I wouldn't mind coming along too,' I said.

There was no response from Father. He sat there with the oilcloth notebook in his hand, looking tired and washed out, stirring his coffee as if the sugar simply refused to melt.

'I'll stay here,' he said. 'I've got a few things to do.'

'Everybody's got to come!' declared Göran innocently. 'It's no fun otherwise.'

Mum studied Father's face, put her head on one side and tried to catch his eye. I thought I saw a look of tenderness steal over her.

'Are you really sure you don't want to come along?' she said. 'We needn't stay long.'

He put down his teaspoon and looked out of the window. Bit down on his bottom lip with his front teeth, as if to restrain himself.

'It's not that I don't want to. Blowed if I know what it is. If I could only see an end to it –'

He gave her a gloomy look and turned away again, squinting out at the glaring sunlight.

'The boys and I will go on our own then,' she said, laying it on. 'And you'll have to spend the evening here on your own?'

'Everybody's got to go for a swim!' repeated Göran.

Father stretched out a trembling hand for an envelope and opened out some sheets of paper as if he wanted me to look at them: 'Instructions for the installation of a lightning conductor.'

'I've managed to get hold of some good copper strips you can use for the roofs,' he said, 'and then you've got to get the earthing system buried in the yard. You'll have to dig by hand round each building.'

I nodded, nonplussed.

'You've got to protect us against everything,' he said.

Mum went over and sat down beside him, moved the papers aside and stroked his thin, hairy arm several times. He didn't push her away.

'You always thought it was so nice to go for a swim when we'd got all the hay in,' she entreated. 'It was the best moment of the year, you said?'

He found a half-smoked cigarette in his breast pocket and lit it.

'Don't you remember, Agne? How lovely you thought it was, throwing yourself into the lake once the hay was in?'

He regarded her for a long time through the spiralling smoke. His mouth hung half open. It looked as if he didn't know what to do next.

'Remember?' he said. 'I never forget anything, do I?'

The bathing place was deserted, except for a few thrushes pulling up worms for their second broods. On the beach stood a pair of black boots, neatly laid out as if someone was about to come up out of the water and step into them. Scarcely a ripple on the surface, just a few little insect rings spreading and fading, as silent as stars. High above Ness Point, the gulls wobbled on outstretched wings, and in the woods a tardy songthrush sat babbling to itself, doubtless on the top branch of one of the highest spruces.

I thought of Father, when he and I came skating here. The solid, thick black ice and the grooves we carved into it, like chalk lines on a pristine school blackboard. First Father, leaning forward with his hands clasped behind his back, taking long, confident strides. Newly sharpened skates strapped on under his ski boots, trouser legs tucked into his thick ski socks, his frosted breath like smoke and me in his slipstream. Scarves fluttering.

'You keeping up all right, Klas?' he shouted, holding his hand out behind him, wanting me to skate alongside, not after him.

Is it really almost four years ago? When we clambered ashore at Fishtrap Holm and made a fire, sharpened some sticks and cooked the smoked sausage we had in the rucksack. Saw a sea eagle heading for the boar bait.

'We've got the whole lake to ourselves!'

Mum was calling from down by the jetty. She was holding her hand up as a shield against the sun, had taken off her shoes and was squatting down to test the water. A hay drier switched off in someone's barn on the far side of the lake and you noticed the silence.

'This is when the water's warmest,' said Mum. 'Just before the sun sets. It's as warm as anything!'

She took Göran's hand and hurried up to the changing huts, not wanting to waste a minute of being here. A reward for spending half the summer in the hay.

The sun's dazzling trail of glitter right across the lake, from beach to beach, like a bridge of light. I couldn't take my eyes off it, felt as if it was me it had in its sights, me it was attracted to, that it was following me wherever I went.

That's where you've got to go, said the voice. Swim in the trail of sunlight as far out as you can. Out to where you can't touch bottom, and then see if you can get away with it.

I'm sitting naked, dangling my feet in the water, when the damselfly lands just beside me on the jetty, shimmering blue like Mum's brooch against her grey wool cardigan. Its incredible gossamer wings, the veins thinner than the ribs in a newly unfurling leaf, the body as slim as a rod, with the turquoise patch at the back. It spreads its wings out to dry and scrutinises me with its enormous eyeballs, bringing its front legs repeatedly to its mouth as if it had something invisible to eat.

There's Mum on her back, apparently weightless and looking up at the sky, her hair streaming out around her face and her big breasts bobbing on the surface, as if they were buoying her up. The swimsuit with yellow flowers that I'd chosen for her from the Ellos catalogue. Göran with his styrofoam floats on his back, his new fishing net poised, lying in wait like a heron that has spotted its prey. He'll no doubt be bringing some tiddlers home to see if he can feed them up without them killing each other, like brothers and sisters.

I cross my legs to cover myself. The dowser's come slipping into view round the clump of reeds, his oars dipping soundlessly as if he were rowing in oil. He looks around and glides the last few metres to the shore, pulls up the boat and ties the rope round the whitest birch. A row of perch on a forked stick and his fishing rod over his shoulder. His floppy hat protecting him from the sun.

He turns towards me: long-necked, legs planted wide apart, mouth primed.

'You just watch yourself, eh, boy. Your family don't get on very well with water, you know.'

Then off he goes. Disappears behind the changing huts in his socks.

'Your boots,' I call after him, unable to stop myself. 'You forgot your boots!'

As if in some strange dream. Of having seen it all before, knowing exactly what was going to happen. That the boots would be left standing there.

Cautiously I bring my hand closer to the damselfly, a centimetre at a time so she won't get scared, encourage her up onto my little finger and raise it as slowly as I can to the quivering sun on the other side of the lake. See the rainbow suddenly flicker in those transparent wings.

Gone – – –

'Get up, right now! We need to get Dad to the hospital!'

Mum was bending over my bed, shaking me with something wild in her look. The light cut into my eyes like a searchlight.

'You've got to come down and ring 90 000!'

Her nightdress fluttered out behind her as she rushed off down the stairs.

A patch of black.

It's happened. The thing no one was allowed to speak of, the thought you scarcely dared to think.

I dialled the number and explained as best I could where we lived and how to get there, said it was my father, and that he was likely to die unless they were quick.

'Tell them it's the pills,' shouted Mum.

I dashed to the kitchen but came to a stop in the doorway: Mum on the floor with Father lifeless in her arms. She was kneeling, trying to lift him under the arms and get him to sit up. He collapsed like someone blind drunk, his head hanging loosely, his mouth open and drooling.

She slapped his face.

'Agne! Can you hear me Agne!'

His head hung as before. She stuck her fingers down his throat, but he showed no sign of being sick.

She tried again and again.

As long as they don't put the flashing blue light on, I thought.

Standing waiting on the front step, not knowing.

Stars between the scattered clouds, the air completely still, warm although it was the middle of the night – as if the whole world was holding its breath. The dragon's back of the spruce forest on the other side of the marsh. Mum's anguished cries from the kitchen.

She was calling his name over and over and over again, as if refusing to acknowledge it made no difference.

Try anything at all –

'God help us!' I heard. 'Oh Lord my God!'

She's on the edge of the abyss now. When there's nothing to cling on to. Screaming into the void.

Then a vehicle came along the straight stretch of road in the distance. Its headlights bounced over the marshland, pointed into the night-time gloom with their rigid beams of light, found a telegraph pole and turned off the road towards us. No blue lights or sirens.

I rushed upstairs and sat down by the climbing plant that twined on its never-ending way, rested my cheek against the coarseweave wallpaper and waited for the car to pull up. Two doors slammed, and then another: they were taking the stretcher straight in. Mum opened the door and explained what had happened and what he'd taken. How many pills did she think he'd swallowed? How long ago? What had she done? They went out into the kitchen and opened a bag, and got to work with various instruments, scraping their chairs. Is this the first time? Yes, at least like this. Could he have been drinking, too?

'There've never been any spirits in this house,' came the offended reply.

Now they're looking for a pulse in his neck. Now they're listening to his heartbeats – if there are any. Now one of them is putting his mouth to the patient's and blowing, just as Father used to with the newborn calves.

'At least like this' – what did that mean?

Now they're carrying him out on the stretcher; you can tell they're in a hurry. Mum comes out into the hall and pulls out some drawers, gets something from the cloakroom.

'I'll ring as soon as I can! You two will have to fend for yourselves in the morning.'

My stomach clenched. Göran and me.

'Please don't argue. And make sure the cows get milked.'

The door closed and she locked it from the outside, tested the handle to be sure. The ambulance turned round and drove off quite decorously. Perhaps things weren't too critical after all? Unless it was already too late!

I went over to the window and saw the tail lights disappearing round the bend into the forest. No blue lights now, either, but they seemed to have the light on inside, where he was lying. Like an illuminated hearse on its way through the silence of the night.

How empty it is.

I tapped my fingernails gingerly on the glass, tapping out Father's rhythm without thinking. Over and over and over again, like a signature. *Pa-pa-dam-pam-pam, pa-pa-dam-pam-pam, pa-pa-dam-pam-pam –*

I deflated. Suddenly it was as if all the strength drained out of me, an internal switch was flicked, my backbone and muscles slackened. My whole body was cold and shivering. A terrible powerlessness overcame me, as if a thousand volts had run through my body or an inhuman tension had suddenly eased.

I opened both windows. So dark and quiet it hurt your ears. The faint stars of the Milky Way spattered across the sky, the devouring black hole somewhere there in the middle. A few invisible greenshanks flying south, eagerly attracting and calling to each other in the vastness: *tew-tew-tew, tew-tew-tew* –

A glimpse of eternity.

Then gone.

Father lying lifeless in an ambulance, it was somehow impossible to imagine. The fact that he didn't know what they were doing with him, couldn't make the decision himself, was completely in their power.

And Göran just slept on? Or didn't dare show himself. Lay there with his hands over his ears, going la-la-la so he wouldn't hear.

Whatever will we do? The question seared through my exhausted brain. Who have I to turn to when my legs won't carry me? Who can I lie beside or cling to when my whole body is chattering?

If you're there, make yourself known!

Call to me! Whisper something!

I padded down the stairs without a sound, like a burglar. I had an urge to go into the kitchen and warm some milk, but there was an invisible wall across the kitchen door. I couldn't even bring myself to peep through the crack. Father lying half naked under the kitchen table, his head hanging like a crucified man. The wild look in Mum's staring eyes.

Something that needed forgetting for all future time, wiping from my retina and my whole being.

I fetched the phone and plugged it in up in my room. It was almost half past two. I sat there staring at the point of the second hand, followed it tick by tick as it counted down to something unprecedented. Moment after moment, slowly amounting to time.

They must be there now. Corridors with bells and red lights, nurses almost breaking into a run and beds on wheels, white coats and syringes and bits of equipment. Father lying there unconscious, hoping he doesn't exist.

I stare at a black telephone.

Pull open a drawer and push it shut again.

Think of the root of two, to as many decimal points as I can.

Reel off the seven times table, forward and back as fast as I can, turning at forty-nine and taking it in reverse, forward and back, to and fro.

If she doesn't ring within the hour it's because she can't leave him. She wants to be at his side to the last.

I went over to the upstairs living room, sat on the arm of the sofa and felt the night air streaming in. Mum's pelargoniums on the window ledge, the star-sprinkled sky, the bend in the road on the edge of the forest where the ambulance passed out of sight.

Shine a little for me –

Now Mum's taking the lift down to a green public phone. He's out of danger. She'll ring soon and say everything went all right.

Not yet. She's got to hold his hand for a while, make sure his chest is rising and falling as it should, look at the twitching of his eyelids, the veins coiling up his neck, the tufts of hair sprouting from his ears.

You do like each other don't you, in spite of everything?

Say you do. Say you're genuinely fond of each other and will soon both be home again so we can go off and watch the football together, like *before*. Or drive to Granny and Grandad's to fish for tench in Ghostchild Brook.

I'm too big for that now. Everything's got to get back to normal, that's all, so Veronika can come and visit.

It's just me now. Not a sound in the house. I can leave the door to my room open, try to drop off without locking it, read myself to sleep without having to listen. There's nothing to be afraid of here.

I turned onto my stomach and closed my eyes, thrust my hands between my thighs, rubbed them slowly to and fro on the smooth pyjama fabric and breathed deeply. I grew warmer and heavier inside, as if an inexplicable calm had come over me.

Warm, gentle currents inside me.

Thin streams of magma along my arms and legs.

The torrent welling forth and catching fire – – –

Mum at the corner of the stairs, those times.

'He's gone now, Klas. Can't you come down and have something to eat! I've kept you some meat and potatoes.'

Mum with that patient, peacemaking tone. Coaxing and trying, as you do with a toddler that doesn't want to put any clothes on.

'You need something inside you with all you've got to do. You can come straight down, he's gone now –'

I'm not imagining it am I, it is all much greener and fresher this time? Luxuriant tussocks of moss and wet, waist-high ferns to wade through, pearly dawn dewdrops in the spiders' webs and the ground strewn with late-blooming, seven-petalled chickweed wintergreen.

You can stop here, said the voice. There's no threatening eye to see you here. Stop for a while and do what you have to.

Be here now, while everything's at stake.

There's Father's rock with the oak sapling beside it – and it's already time: the sun's shining on the topmost spire of the tallest spruce. So there's no going back.

I took off my shoes, climbed onto the rock and breathed in deeply. Raised my eyes and looked into the spruce trees, the millions of this season's delicate green shoots.

Now or never.

'Father mustn't die!' I called. 'Everything's got to stay exactly as it is, I'm too little to take over at home!'

I clasped my hands tightly together and waited for an answer, sneaking a look at my whitening knuckles. I called the same thing again, and felt it sounded like a helpless squeak among the mighty trees – as if it wasn't me, as if somebody else was calling out of my mouth.

'Granny and Grandad mustn't die either!' I went on. 'Nothing's allowed to change! All the trees have got to stay standing where they are! No one's to set fire to our house! Not even the cats are allowed to die, or the rats! Everything's got to live forever!'

I paused for a while, as breathless as if I'd been marching at the double. I made a funnel with my hands and turned my face straight up to the glaring light of the oculus that was the sky above.

Intoxicated, I shouted, 'Agne's got to live! Do you hear that? He hasn't done anything wrong!'

'So save him! Everything's got to be like it was before!'

I felt a sudden pang.

Agne? Had I ever said his name out loud before, articulated it like any other name? Not as far as I could recall.

Sitting on a mossy stump with an inexplicable ringing in my ears. As silent as when an echo has died away.

Only the spruces were keeping watch.

The distracted whistles of the blackbirds. The high-pitched little sounds of a goldcrest.

You are one with heaven and earth, sighed something in the air. You are the damp grass and the sun shining over sea and land, the wind that never ends. You are all this, and I have listened to your words.

'I am Klas,' I answered giddily. 'I have nothing to be ashamed of. Nothing can be taken from me or held against me. I have done what I could.'

And I hunted out the best chickweed wintergreen there was left and stuck it carefully in a crack in Father's rock. The rosette of dark green leaves formed a wreath beneath the threadlike purple stem of that solitary Arctic starflower. The flower with its seven petals provided a lily-white chalice for the anthers to rise from.

Do you remember when we were sitting there fishing for tench and you explained the times tables and what fractions and percentages are? When we were by the circular saw and you showed me how many inches there are in an ell, and how you can tell from the annual growth rings in a tree stump which way is south – do you remember that?

You could stand up there outside the church and point out over the village like a statue, and tell us where this person or that person grew up, who got the first combine harvester in the parish, where the best footballer in the county drew his first breath.

Do you remember when you gave me a lift on your handlebars and the way we laughed at our faces, stretched wide and unrecognisable in the newly polished surface of the bell? When you belonged to the chess club and the local history group and people still rang to talk to you, to ask you for advice?

Gone now.

Electric shocks to the brain, Mum said.

Not anything one would want to talk about.

Göran could scarcely wait. He was on tenterhooks as the taxi pulled up, calling to her before she'd even got out. She reached the front steps almost at a run, and swept him up as if she'd been away for weeks.

'Now let's see about a bit of tea,' she said, chivvying us ahead of her into the kitchen like a couple of chicks. 'I expect you're both starving?'

Göran nodded so hard he almost dislocated his head. She got going on the potatoes and conjured up a dish of leftover pork ribs and chipolatas. Göran wanted to show her how you lay out the cards for Idiot's Delight, the patience game that never goes out, which Grandad had shown him in a futile attempt to make him sit still.

Was she going to say anything about Father, I wondered. What had happened, and when he would be allowed back home. What was wrong.

An empty cloud vibrated over his place at the table, and for some reason the fifth chair also felt emptier than usual, even though no one ever sat there. It was as if it was begging and pleading to be sat on at last.

In the middle of the meal, Göran put down his fork and looked at Mum with wide eyes, as if he had worked something out himself for the first time in his life.

'Who's going to write down the weather, while he's not here?' he said.

Mum forced out a smile.

'Klas will have to do it,' she said. 'You know how good he is at that sort of thing. And Dad'll be back soon, just you wait and see.'

'When's soon? Can't we go and visit him before that?'

'I don't think you'd enjoy seeing him just now. It's not exactly a nice place where he is at the moment, you see. And he's terribly tired, as well.'

Göran frowned and puffed out his cheeks, not really understanding what she meant. Kicked his feet under the table while he was thinking.

'He needs to sleep properly, then,' he said. 'So he mustn't wander round doing things in the night.'

'You're right there,' said Mum, and a sympathetic sort of look came into her face. 'Now who's going to help me finish this up?'

Once it was dark and Göran was asleep there was a knock at my bedroom door, shy and tentative as if a little girl was disturbing her father in his office.

'Can you come a minute, Klas?' Mum asked through the door. Like a jolt.

That means it's worse than she dared say.

I got up from my chair without a sound and straightened out the fringes of the rug, made sure they were all lying parallel and none were tucked under. Combed out the strands and separated them according to which knot they belonged to.

'Klas?'

'Just coming.'

She was sitting in the rocking chair with her knitting on her lap and cleared her throat ominously as I came in. Didn't meet my eyes, as if she had something terrible to tell me.

He can't cope any more. I'm going to have to step in and take responsibility for supporting the family.

She's leaving us, taking Göran and vanishing out of our lives forever. Forcing me to stay with Father so he can get by. Is that what you're going to tell me, that you can't take any more?

Psssh. Where did you get all that from? She just wants a bit of company before bedtime; perhaps it's her first night here without Father?

She turned her face in my direction but then changed her mind and knitted a few more stitches, as if she wanted to test the crucial words inside her before she let them out.

'I don't know what's to be done,' she said vaguely. 'I can't manage it all on my own.'

I sat down in the armchair and wrote my signature in the deaths column in the paper that was lying open, over and over again, as identically as possible. The long-case clock slowly chimed ten in the room below us. Mum carried on knitting as she waited for my answer, unwound a bit more wool and put the ball on the table.

'All what?' I stammered in the end.

'Dad's not all that good. Nobody knows when he'll be able to come home.'

My stomach gave a lurch.

'And it'll be harvest time soon, you know that.'

She reached for one of our translucent summer apples and cut it in two with the knife we kept in the fruitbowl. Cored it and passed me half.

'Of course I do, but I mean, I'll have school and …'

'So we're going to have to hire someone to keep things ticking over for now,' she said soothingly. 'And then we'll have to see. Adder Hook Johnny's pretty good with animals and machinery, isn't he?'

Johnny! I only just stopped myself spitting it out. Were we going to let *him* get near our heifers and sit in Father's place and have dinner with us?

'He'd be no good,' I said, as firmly as I could. 'His head's full of guns and hunting and he's off on military service any day now. I'll ask somebody to have a word with the dowser instead. He could do with a bit of a change, I bet.'

'Alvar, over at The Point? Well all right, if you'd rather. It'll be the crops first and foremost, then the straw and the autumn ploughing. And a bit of help with the animals wouldn't come amiss.'

I stood up and went over to the window with a sense of relief, popping the last bit of apple in my mouth. The insects were flitting to and fro on the other side of the glass, attracted to the outside light and clearly convinced it was the moon. Mum picked up her knitting again. The sound of her rapid movements, the faint rustle of her dress material against her wrists as they worked.

'What am I to say is wrong with him?' I said, my eyes averted.

I felt my cheeks burning, detected her puzzled look out of the corner of my eye.

'Who needs to know? Isn't it enough to say he's in hospital?'

'Yes, of course –'

A hornet zigzagged across my blurred reflection, crawling from my neck, over my nose and up to my forehead. I tapped my fingernails on the pane to say hello. No reaction from the hornet, which just crawled on obliviously with its amber wings folded down along its back, its oversized eyes and spiny legs.

'Do you think they said on the police radio that the ambulance was coming here?' I asked, facing the window.

My ears were throbbing. The knitting needles stopped. I looked out over the marsh and into my own eye sockets. Way over to the north west, the evening sky was as streaked as a hawk's breast.

Was Mum sobbing silently to herself? I didn't dare look and see.

'Is that what's on your mind, when we've all this to worry about?' she whispered, her voice hardly holding. 'When we don't even know what's going to happen?'

I am as tough as juniper and as strong as a steer. As unsquashable as a cockroach and as big as a mountain.

You'll never be rid of me, just so you all know.

Boiling hot and not a breath of wind. The crows were lurking in the darkness of the spruces and the wagtails were gasping open-beaked as they sat up on the gutter waiting for the next drop of water. Not a leaf quivered, not even the aspen's. But the potatoes were flowering and the dill had formed its heads.

I lay by the south wall and tried to conjure up an image of the Riviera, wondering what it looked like there, whether it could really be all that much hotter, whether I might not eventually get a postcard, after all. I could taste the sweat round my mouth, reckoned it must be saltier than the Mediterranean, saw Veronika in front of me in her white bikini, alone at the water's edge with her long, wet hair hanging down her back.

I went back to the chapter about the species complex of the Western yellow wagtail – 'long seen as one of the hardest nuts to crack in bird taxonomy'. At least eight different races were so alike that it seemed impossible to distinguish between them in the wild: all with pale yellow underparts, greenish backs and a white stripe under the eye. But the trickiest thing of all was that you couldn't even rely on the adult males' summer plumage. There were certainly some marked differences – *Motacilla flava flavissima*, for example, had a yellow-green head and *Motacilla flava thunbergi* a grey-blue one – but identification was complicated by local colour variations within the various races, and by the fact that individual specimens had been observed to spread blithely into other races' breeding grounds and created perplexing crossbreeds that looked halfway between the two originals.

'Is that you, Klas?'

I propped myself up on my elbow. Johnny's gran was out on the road, waving her stick.

'Plenty of time to laze about, I see?' she grumbled. 'Well maybe you can tell me what time it is, then? My watch seems to have stopped – and that doesn't bode well, I can tell you.'

She held up her left arm, as if to certify that the hands really had stopped moving.

'The hay's in and the birds have stopped singing. What would I be doing if I weren't reading? Breaking stone and building pyramids?'

'I don't think I've ever seen the like,' she said. 'As hot as Gehenna and not a drop of rain, though this is meant to be the most humid week of the year. But it's Seven Sleepers' Day on Sunday. If it rains then, we can reckon on it pouring for seven weeks. Maybe that would be no bad thing?'

She loosened her headscarf and wiped her perspiring forehead. Took a few steps onto the grass and stopped in the dappled shade of the cherry tree, puffing.

'Agne's left his axe in the block down by the woodpile,' she said inconsequentially. 'But maybe you knew that?'

I nodded and smiled.

'It brings bad luck and that's a fact. Just so you know. And you and I agreed back in the spring that lightning was no laughing matter.'

She gave me a wily look and hit the trunk of the cherry tree three times with her stick – in warning, I wondered, or because the cherries had started to ripen? Then she cleared her throat as if to make an announcement.

'I was sorry to hear about Agne,' she said. 'I suppose the

chances are he won't be able to keep the lease after what's happened.'

I looked down.

'Daresay the main burden will fall on you, now,' she ploughed on. 'But if you and your mum can't manage, I can always ask Johnny. He could do with a bit extra coming in.'

'We'll cope,' I said with determination. 'Like I said, between the clover and the barley there's not that much needs doing.'

She mopped her brow again, screwing up her face as the sweat ran into her eyes.

'No call for you to lie here bare-chested under God's Heaven, even so,' she said. 'There's enough misery in the world already. And Our Lord sees everything, you can be sure of that. He sees and He punishes.'

I didn't answer, just flicked to and fro between the pipits and the wagtails in my book to make her go, compared the aerial display habits of the tree, meadow and tawny pipit, studied the peculiarly fragmented distribution pattern of the grey wagtail. A good three minutes must have passed but she was still there, rubbing her chin.

'So we'll have to see if it rains on Sunday then?' she persisted. 'But we can't bank on it, that's for sure. And I'm thinking you won't have heard the fox shriek in the night, either?'

I shook my head. Finally she pulled her headscarf back over her hair and stumped off with her stick, bent over like a witch.

'Fare you well, then. I'm off.'

'Don't forget to wind your watch,' I shouted after her. 'Whatever you do, you can't stop time passing.'

I could imagine Mum and Göran running out of the shallows, splashing about and throwing water at each other. Floating on their backs for a while in the sun-warmed surface water, swimming and diving and hunting for tiddlers together.

And me? Why didn't I want to go with them?

Whatever it was that kept tugging at me, always demanding a no, never a yes. To lie in the garden studying taxonomy while the others go swimming.

Ask me to. Say I'm not like all the rest.

Try to persuade me. Put your head on one side.

Comfort me.

A cloud of microscopic insects was suspended above me, thousands of tiny, winged creatures dancing round each other in a big, bewildering swarm – up and down, forward and back, hither and thither with incredible speed – but the cloud itself did not move, it remained still, vibrating internally, extending one way a little and then retracting as if pulled by some invisible force.

As if they *wanted* something from me. Like the annoying molecules inside me.

I want to see the Andromeda galaxy tonight. Show me the light that was sent out two million years before mankind came into being. And our closest neighbour, Centaurus. Human and horse combined, like before the tractor came on the scene. Explain to me how far forty thousand billion kilometres are.

A few kilometres up: a jet plane heading north, with its chalk line behind it, as white as unfallen snow, dead straight as if Our Lord used a ruler to draw it. Streaks of condensation that can make crosses in the sky.

I thought about that last training session, Bruiser Pelle's swollen penis swinging from side to side as he towelled his back, twisting and turning to show off the bush he'd acquired.

'I heard they took your dad in on Sunday? High time, too.'

The superior sneer. The flick of his towel against my bare

legs, the penis that was now engorged, pointing straight out, ready for anything. The red-veined foreskin stretched over the taut glans.

'Why else would the ambulance have come in the middle of the night?' he said. 'Can you tell me that, seeing you're such an expert on everything?'

Twelve pairs of eyes on me. Greedy, staring, gimlet eyes all around me. The smile on Bruiser Pelle's pimply face as he scented victory. Twisting his towel again and again, flicking it at my thighs until they were mottled red; triumphantly scratching his crotch, raking around in the black pubic hair, tugging at his cock like an overgrown kid.

'They locked him up on Sunday then, eh? You think the news hasn't got out?'

The smell of sweaty shin guards and liniment, the raspberry soda on the bench just by me. The rapacious eyes on my back when I walked away for the last time.

Standing by the electric fence and thinking of Father, of the poles and insulators we'd installed together, the barbed wire he'd fixed to keep the cattle in. I saw him lying sedated on a narrow bed in a separate room with bars at the windows, thought about the electricity pumping through human substance, travelling on into muscles and blood. Direct current pulsing between his temples, epileptic activity in his brain tissue. Unconsciousness, convulsive fits, sleep without dreams – – –

The electric fence Bruiser Pelle boasted he could hold onto as long as he liked and still feel nothing. I found a rusty end of wire and squeezed, felt a jolt and forced myself to hold on. Felt it pumping through me, twitching at my arm and running to my chest and down my legs in the form of dull, numbing thuds. Stood there thinking that I'd finally got electricity in my blood.

Then I lay down among the stones in the dried-up ditch. Above me and around me the meadowsweet grew so thickly that hardly a scrap of sky was visible. Rose chafers everywhere on the sprays of flowers, an impossibly glittering green as they took off with their wing sheaths unfolded.

The frothing, steaming, waving meadowsweet. The overpowering scent of almonds. Lying here listening to the swifts' despairing shrieks – – –

Without the leasehold we'll never get by, it just won't work.

We've got to keep on good terms with the Salesman. You hear that, Klas? We won't survive without the leasehold.

I was out in the blackcurrant bushes when the dowser came. He left his tractor by the pigsty and advanced on me slowly, hands clasped behind his back, as if to show he wasn't one to intrude without due cause. He had a leather cap on his head and a worn and shiny jacket that made him look like a scarecrow.

Did *he* know about Father, I wondered. The real reason? It didn't matter, anyway. He was generally seen as a bit of an odd customer himself, and always stood right over by the corner flag when he came to watch the football. Turned up when the game had already started and slipped away before the ref's final whistle went, so he didn't have to talk to anybody.

'Last time I was here you were kicking your little feet on a rug,' was his opening gambit. 'Red as a crayfish you were, if I remember rightly. But that must be eight or ten years ago now?'

'Well eleven or twelve, really, if I couldn't even walk.'

He nodded.

'But things are the same as ever here. Nice and quiet, I daresay. And you've a good well, eh?'

His head twisted and turned as he looked about with a nostalgic smile, as if something particular had occurred to him from back then.

'Twelve years,' he said dreamily. 'That's a fair old time.'

'It feels like a lifetime. For me, at any rate.'

'And you didn't find any flying rowans?'

'No, but I did find the bitterns' nest, way out in the reeds at the Marsh Pool. I've written in to the paper about it.'

He nodded again, swayed back and forth on his long feet and smiled even more broadly. There was something comical about him with those darting, yellowy eyes of his and his ears sticking out like wing nuts. But he wasn't stupid, you could see that. And he was well in with supernatural forces and beings, so they said. Knew everything there was to know about cleft trees, grave earth and smoking out evil spirits.

'The Marsh Pool's one thing', he said, unflappable as ever, 'but if I haven't said it before I'll say it now: you watch out for Raven Fen. It's chock full of holes and they've swallowed up more than enough over the years.'

A cow came ambling over to the bathtub on the other side of the fence, lowered her head and drank in great gulps, litre after litre, whisking her tail in a vain attempt to get rid of the flies. Then she came up to the barbed wire and stopped to stare at Alvar with her empty, shiny eyes, as if she was wondering what manner of thing he was: the first stranger at Dower Farm. As for her, she had a white patch on her forehead the shape of South America. She even had the little kink that was Tierra del Fuego, down by her muzzle.

What about Mum? She was taking her time coming out, wasn't she?

'Look at this,' Alvar suddenly said, bending down to pick up a large black slug. 'Do you know what to do with one of these?'

'Maybe feed it to the ravens? You'd scarcely find a blacker food than that.'

He gave an ambiguous smile. Pushed his cap to the back of his head and tried to look at me and the slug at the same time.

'He that lures forth the raven does not go unpunished,' he

said. 'Blackcoat portends death among the innocent. You can do better than that.'

'Mash it up and use it to lubricate wheel bearings?'

'Not such a daft idea. They did that, in the war. But there's something better.'

I shook my head. Alvar looked sly.

'You take it by one feeler like this,' he showed me. Then you raise it over your head and drop it down the back of your neck, inside your shirt. And when you've counted to seven, you can wish for anything you want.'

There was an alluring glint in his eye, like you might see in a magician's, as he held out the slug.

'It's the same as with shooting stars,' he said. 'Slugs and shooting stars all come to the same thing where wishes and success in this life are concerned.'

It crawled slowly up his wrist, its tentacles waving in their separate directions. Just looking at it gave me goose pimples on my arms and sent shivers down my spine. It came to me that the slug was the image of a human being turned inside out: as black as gall and as slimy as a sea creature.

'Now's your chance,' said Alvar with a wink. 'If nothing else there'll be some lassie you've got your eye on?'

I took a step back.

'That stuff's no good to me. If wishing this and wishing that had helped, I wouldn't be standing here today.'

'Oh is that so? Hard words they are, from such a tender mouth. But it's no skin off my nose if you don't want to.'

Alvar chucked the slug in among the rhubarb and was about to put his arm round me when Mum finally came running out, and he thought the better of it. She tied her headscarf as she came dashing over, and there was a nervous smile on her lips before she even reached us.

'So you want to hire someone for the drudgery?' said Alvar, laughing his strange, hissing laugh.

Mum forced a bit more of a smile.

'It was kind of you to come,' she said, fingering the hem of her cardigan. 'We can more or less manage what the animals need by ourselves, but then it's harvest ...'

Her eyes didn't know where to look. Alvar gave a nod and smiled his Plastic Padding smile.

'That'll be fine,' he said. 'If there's one thing I know how to do, it's harvesting.'

'Klas has promised to harrow as much of the stubble as he's got time for,' Mum went on, 'and then I suppose we'll have to see about ploughing when the time comes?'

Alvar raised his cap.

'At your service,' he said ingratiatingly, 'and we've got all autumn.'

'All autumn?' I blurted out. 'How do you know that? Has somebody said when Father's coming home?'

Mum gave me a peppery look and smiled apologetically at Alvar.

'So that just leaves us with the hourly rate to agree on,' she said.

'Don't you worry about that. As long as there's a meal to be had and the occasional bed for the night, that's more than ample. Hired labourers aren't exactly big game these days. You have to make do with what you can get.'

Mum nodded thoughtfully. Came over and put her mouth close to my ear to ask if I'd mind coming with her to show Alvar round.

'Then I'll help you with the currants later,' she whispered.

We headed to the barn, where Father kept most of the machinery. Mum lingered in the doorway while Alvar went round and inspected everything as if it was an auction viewing. He felt the mower blades and ran his hand over the worn, shiny mouldboard and shares of the plough, inspected the counter in the baler and opened up the seed drill so he could peer down into the hoppers, all the while with that strange smile plastered onto his face like a mask. He hadn't said anything about the mountain of scrap and rust piled up outside, just cast a quick glance at it and nodded understandingly.

'Yes, this is all going to be all right,' he said, coming over and putting his arm round me. 'Looks like everything's been kept nice and tidy.'

'So we're done in here, then?' Mum asked uncertainly.

'And I've sorted out a harvester I can borrow when it's time.'

Mum shut the door and fastened the hook, listening carefully to everything he said, as if our future lay in his hands.

'It's only an old one with a bagging platform, but as long as there are two of you it works pretty well.'

He winked at me and laughed again.

'I suppose we might as well have a look in the cowshed while we're about it?' said Mum. 'So you can see how he keeps the place.'

It was so quiet and shut in, abandoned somehow. The flies buzzed but the stalls were gaping empty. A brown rat darted away along the wall, petrified we might be bringing the cats in with us. Caked dung and spiders' webs wherever you looked. Father's record folder with all the feeding tables set out in neat columns lay on the table outside the dairy. He had put black crosses in the margin next to Maja and Beauty. Over in the far corner stood the solitary stud bull, tossing his head and rolling his eyes, as if he knew his days had long been numbered.

He gave another crazed bellow and jabbed his horns into the wooden partition, sending wood chips flying.

'My word,' said Mum, her whole face frowning, and Alvar looked the same.

When we came out to the grain bins we found Göran all ready to jump from up in the hayloft. It looked as if he'd been standing there for hours, waiting to show off what he could do.

'Look everybody!' he cried.

Too stupid to be afraid, I thought. Or too small.

He plunged into the void and landed in a pile of loose hay on the concrete floor. Turned to us, beaming.

'Not bad, not bad!' cheered Alvar.

Göran looked so exhilarated it made you almost want to join in. He ran towards Mum but then had second thoughts and scrambled back up the ladder before we had a chance to go out. Right up under the ridge of the roof this time.

'Nimble as a monkey,' said Alvar, looking at Mum.

She gave a proud smile.

'Look now everybody!' called Göran from up in the roof timbers.

He threw himself headlong and disappeared down into the pile, the giggles bubbling out of him. Alvar clapped his hands and shot me a crafty smile, as if he was cooking up something.

'Let's all jump,' he said.

Göran couldn't believe his ears, but Alvar meant what he said. Mum brightened up and nudged me in the side. Göran was already back on the ladder.

'Come on then! What a load of dawdlers!'

'Just you wait,' said Alvar, putting on a burst of speed. 'I'll give you dawdlers.'

He took the whole ladder in three strides and Mum went straight up after him. I rummaged round for a few extra bales to improve the landing pile and hurried up after them. Göran was so eager he was jumping up and down on the spot.

'It's certainly been a while,' said Alvar with a laugh. 'But it's too late to back out now.'

I looked at the lethal beam sticking out of the wall down there. Göran took a run up and carried on running into thin air, like a cartoon character. He landed with a hoot. Alvar looked over the edge and waved to him, then held his nose with one hand and his cap with the other, as if he was jumping into a lake. Mum and I made do with girly jumps, knees drawn-up so we landed on our backsides, and then we were all lying there in the prickly hay, laughing together.

'That takes me back,' said Alvar.

'Again,' cried Göran, over the moon. 'Everybody's got to do it again!'

Mum smiled at me and was already on her feet.

'Bagsy first up!' hollered Alvar.

We wiped our sweaty foreheads and went to get a drink each from the cool of the potato cellar, all except Göran who wanted to get on with the hut he was building, so he could live in it and guard the cowshed for Father until he came home again.

'And when do you think it'll be time to start harvesting?' Mum said after a while.

Alvar nipped off an ear of barley from the other side of the ditch, rubbed out a few grains and bit into them with his front teeth.

'A couple more weeks and we can go ahead,' came the practised reply. 'They're still doughy inside.'

He gave me a few grains so I could try, too. Mum cleared her throat and looked alternately at him and down at the ground a few times, as if there was something she'd got to say before he went.

'Out with it then,' said Alvar. 'It'll have to be really something to make these big ears of mine fall off.'

She gave a strained smile.

'I think it's best for this not to get out,' she said. 'You know how it is. One careless match and you've got a forest fire.'

Alvar nodded but took his time answering.

'I'm not one for loose talk,' he said, 'but to be honest I've got to tell you there's already been plenty said about Agne, and now this ...'

He looked away and stroked his chin in embarrassment.

The graffiti on the chapel of rest, and the police radio, I thought. They all know the whole lot. Their blah blah blah spreads like wildfire.

'Just so you know not to blame me,' said Alvar.

Mum plucked a few bits of straw off the sleeve of her cardigan and did up a couple of buttons across her chest.

'I might have known it,' she said quietly. 'All we need is for them to mess everything up for us so we lose the leasehold or the animals. Then we'll be back to nothing.'

Today's the day.

If there's nothing in today's post either, then I'm riding over to Bliss Cottage, just to see. I had promised myself not to wait any longer than forty-nine days. Seven weeks since we were at Marsh Pool and not a squeak out of her. No postcard, nothing. As if it had never happened.

If only I hadn't sucked up to her and showed off like an idiot, I thought for the hundredth time. Let her sit there with her Buddha figurine and her thick hair and be as relaxed as she likes. Let her dad read as many books as he wants and listen to as much piano music as he cares to, and let her mum hug her like that every evening, she still won't get as good marks as me. She'll never grow up to be a great anything.

In spite of myself, I stopped just past The Crossing and picked her a bunch of flowers, spent ages wandering round selecting those I knew the names of, in case anyone asked. Scabious, autumn hawkbit, oxeye daisies and agrimony, knapweed and bladder campion, and a couple of stems of yellow bedstraw because they had such a nice smell. Down in the ditch I even found a few veronicas, speedwell, with small, partially withered flowers – but at least they were veronicas, there was no mistaking that. Faithful unto death, as Granny always said.

I could visualise Veronika as I gave her the bunch of flowers at the front door. Suddenly shamefaced and embarrassed.

'Are they for me? Come in!'

I left my bike a little way off and cut across through the clump of trees out of sight, so it would be a real surprise when I suddenly presented myself, but I noticed straight away that something wasn't right. The lawn needed a scythe taken to it, the flowerbeds were semi-overgrown and the Venetian blinds were down. The croquet hoops were still set out, with the double one in the middle, and a stepladder was balanced all askew against the gutter at the corner of the verandah. It looked as if they had had to leave in a hurry, abandoning everything to its fate.

And no well had been dug, nor had Alvar been here with his dowsing rods. The house hadn't been filled with holiness and fertility, but there was a lovely scent of ripening apples.

I hid the flowers behind my back and decided I might as well ring at the door now I'd cycled all this way. After a bit there was a shuffling sound inside the house, as if an ill person or semi-invalid was struggling to the door. Leo stuck his head out, his face grey with a crumpled ball of bloody paper sticking out of one nostril. He was in khaki-coloured pyjamas with some emblem on the breast pocket and he squinted suspiciously at me as if I were a travelling Polish picture seller, or as if he hadn't seen daylight in weeks. But then he recognised me and his face broke into a smile.

'Hesse!' he said. 'Now I remember.'

He held out one hand but hung on to the door handle with the other, as if to stop me slipping inside.

'Did it rain last night?' he said, sniffing the air like a tracker dog, still with the ball of paper in his nostril.

'There were a few showers this morning,' I answered with exaggerated politeness.

He took a few steps from the doorway, reached out for the Angel Trumpet shrub and stroked a leaf between his fingers. Went down the porch steps and over to take the post out of the box.

'Hesse, yes,' he said, parking the pile of letters on the porch rail. 'You can start with *Steppenwolf*. A melancholy hermit beyond all fellowship, human being and wolf in one skin and therefore a presumptive suicide. Never able to fit in, all his life wanting to be someone else. The dualism of instinct and intellect. Hesse himself was intended for the priesthood as a young man you know, but he trained to be a watchmaker instead – though perhaps it all comes to the same thing in the long run.'

He smiled at himself.

'The mortal dread remains constant, as we all know,' he added.

I could already feel my patience running short, so I gave a couple of little coughs and tried to catch his eye.

'I wonder if Veronika might possibly ...'

He stiffened, like a warrior suddenly pierced in the back by a spear and having to come to terms with the consequences, or as if he had just been woken from a dream.

'Veronika? Ah, yes of course ...'

He laughed nervously and scratched his neck.

'The idea was that she ... would move here ... this summer. But it seems as if she ... I don't know ... after all ...'

A big door clunked shut.

She won't be going to school here. I'll never see her again, it's all been for nothing. And it's this lunatic's fault, still in his pyjamas in the middle of the day, rambling on about old German hermits.

'Incredible as it may sound ... she apparently prefers to live with her mother in Väsby for the time being,' he explained. 'But she's bound to think the better of it ... when she gets more of a perspective on ... things. If nothing else, she'll have to come down here to visit me?'

He lowered his eyes and started twisting his wedding ring, sliding it up and down his long piano finger. He pulled it off and put it back on again.

I stood there paralysed, the flowers behind my back.

Kick him in the crotch and leave him to his fate. Cycle over here tonight and throw a flaming brand through a windowpane. Ring the police and report him for idling.

'Was it anything particular you wanted, by the way?' he said. 'I can let Veronika know you were looking for her, if you like.'

'It was these.'

He looked from the flowers to me and back again, to and fro for a good half minute before he took the bouquet. Tears welled in his eyes as if he were a little girl in distress. The clear drops merged into thin rivulets that found their way down into his

bushy beard. He looked as if he had been reminded of something that was forever lost.

'It's the yellow bedstraw that smells so strong,' I said. 'It's
sometimes called Our Lady's bedstraw as well. You can tell
Veronika the flowers are from me. You'll have to dry them for
her, if the worst comes to the worst.'

He shook his head slowly, trying in vain to force out a natural
smile.

'It's not right that it turned out like this,' he moaned. 'I don't
see what I've done wrong. Why should any kind and decent
person have to endure this?'

I could find nothing to answer. Simply turned round, avoided
looking him in the eye, took the steps any old how and ran over
to my bike. Leapt on and pedalled off without waving, standing
on the pedals and going full pelt in a spray of gravel, as if I had
some lethally dangerous animal at my heels.

If only a terrible storm would blow up, I thought over and
over again. If only I could be struck by lightning.

Cycle to the deepest bit of bog behind the sawmill, said the
voice. That's where you've got to go, to the Marsh Wife who's
been waiting a thousand years for the right one to come and
keep her company. Be with her and count the disgusting bubbles
of gas rising up from the water.

I laid my bike down at the edge of the road and went round
to the back of the sawmill, strode out into the alder bog and
was soaked above my ankles before I was halfway to the hole.
There was a stench of decay and stagnant mud, as if the very
earth had split open and its seething intestinal mass had started
to ooze out.

I don't care. It's the deep bog and the Marsh Wife who matter now. Whatever it is, sucking and dragging me down because it has no end.

A lifeless eye in the forest –

Completely dead and still. As black as gall, with little islands of fir cones and needles. At the near edge, a mush of half-rotted aspen leaves had collected. A broken rowan with drooping leaves leant out over the water.

Stare down into a mirror.

No sign of life. Just my own blurred face and the tiniest ripples if you looked really carefully, like vibrations in the air from the silently whirring wings of the circling gnats. A pond skater came shooting across the water on its sewing-thread legs. Here and there, gas bubbles percolated gently to the surface and popped with a wet sigh.

Is that all?

No toothless Marsh Wife leering down there, no long arms and yellow nails like claws to draw you down into the black hole?

Go and get a lath of wood from beside the sawmill and poke it down to find out what she wants! In fact, that long oak twig there will do just as well.

Actually, don't bother with laths or sticks, just take a couple of steps out and see what happens. If she's there, she's there.

I felt a sudden light-headedness as I sat there. A current surged through me, making me go hot and cold. An icy hot current of longing and terror.

Sitting by a bottomless hole in the forest, counting the bubbles rising up from everything that's been rotting down there since the dawn of time. Listening for the Marsh Wife's breathing from the deepest depths –

I listened hard.

A raven somewhere? That raw croak which only a raven can produce.

Odin's soot-black thinker.

Death's unannounced messenger.

Corvus corax corax.

And it came. Swishing right over me with its beak pointing to the fen back home. *Kronk, kronk* it went, continuing on its way with wingbeats that ate up the distance.

Like a hello.

The smooth, soft, loose-jointed body dressed only in white lacy knickers. Eyes without whites, the irises as bright a blue as those of an innocent child, the mouth a dark flesh colour with a round hole between its lips, as if for holding something tight rather than sucking. The eyebrows like two thin lines, high on the forehead.

That infuriating smile.

I put her on her back and pulled down her knickers, turned her arms up behind her head and twisted her legs one at a time so her heels were pointing to the ceiling like a gymnast's. In the slit between her legs she had another hole, just like the one in her mouth. I thrust the four-inch nail into the hole and hammered it in with my wooden clog until only the head was left sticking out.

As if to seal her.

She lay there the same as ever, subjecting me to relentless scrutiny from those wide eyes of hers. Lay there on her back and should have been asleep, but only one eye was shut, the other fixed me with a demanding stare, as if there was something wrong with her.

Whatever it was, effervescing and simmering inside me.

'Shut your eyes then!' The words escaped my lips like a cry. 'Shut your eyes and do what I want!'

I didn't recognise my own voice.

I tried in vain to press in her eyes. I yanked the head off the body and put it down at my feet. A few bits of skin-coloured plastic and a length of wire came out of the hole in the neck, and a disc with an embossed cross in the middle. I pulled off her arms and legs and laid them out at right angles round the head, like a frame round a portrait. The head merely stared into thin air, like a decapitated hare's head before the hunting dog gets its teeth into it.

That only left the sealed torso, and the rusty four-inch nail sticking up into her belly.

Mum stepped back and studied the last pane with a satisfied nod: sparkling clean, right into the corners, not a trace of fly-dirt however hard she looked, no newsprint disfiguring the white window frames. She had cleaned every single window in the house, upstairs and down in the cellar yesterday and the ground floor today, as if trying to convince herself spring would soon be on the way and we could make a new start.

Clean glass. Like when the doctor syringed the wax out of your blocked ears and you could suddenly hear everything, making the world crisp and crystal clear. That sense of nothing being in the way any longer. The cowshed and outbuildings all looked newly painted, the marigolds in the garden shone a more orangey orange and the sky was almost unfeasibly blue between the clouds. The black lines and patterns on the bark of the silver birches stood out as sharply as if someone had marked them in with felt pen.

'I expect you both want to come along and surprise Dad now he's on his way home?' Mum said, clearly in high spirits. 'I'm sure he'd like that?'

Well I wouldn't exactly say want. When I ought to be down at Marsh Pool. Counting geese. Sitting in the flat-bottomed rowing boat I'd finally made watertight so I'd have a front-row seat for watching the autumn migration flights. The cranes and geese and teal, all the passage migrants, the plovers and sandpipers, which could only be viewed for a few weekends. A chance to see the young lapwings flocking in from all directions so they could fly together.

'It must be a couple of months since you've seen him now?' she went on, partly to herself.

'Don't blame me,' said Göran. 'I must have told you twelve times that I wanted to go and visit him when you had time.'

Mum smiled indulgently and put the basket of coffee things by the hall door, like when we were little and off on a Sunday outing.

'We'll have to get going,' she said, 'I promised we'd be there at two. He's quite particular about timekeeping, as you know.'

Göran ran into his room and came out clutching his toy white rabbit in one hand and his new plimsolls in the other, as expectant as if it was his birthday.

Father's coming home again. Everything's going to be like it was *before*. Though we can hardly remember what that was.

One rain shower succeeded another as the kilometres mounted up, but just as the spruce forest began to thin out, the sun sliced through the gloom and came out properly. A mysterious smoky haze steamed from the sedge mire along the roadside, and above a hayfield of sway-backed, dirty grey racks of drying hay the rainbow stretched in such searingly sharp and vivid colours it made me want to ask Mum to stop so I could get out and touch it. One end of it was planted among the racks of hay and the other was deep in the forest, but there was no way of telling if it was three hundred metres away, or thirty kilometres. Alongside the main arc ran a feebler, back-to-front copy, like a little brother or sister.

'I wonder if it would be just as well for you two to stay in the car?' said Mum as she turned into the car park. 'It won't be much fun for you in there.'

She put on the handbrake and turned round to us.

'Now you both promise to behave and not squabble, please. He could be a bit sensitive to noise to start with, the doctor said.'

She patted each of us on the cheek and hurried over to the pale yellow building with a black clocktower on the roof. She ran lightly up the steps like an actress and vanished through the heavy front door. The thought ran through my mind that maybe she'd rather have stayed in the car, too. If she'd only had the choice.

'Hope it doesn't take too long,' said Göran, starting to kick the seat in front of him.

'She could be quite a while. It's only half past.'

And there seemed nothing more to say to each other. Göran turned round and thumped the back of the seat behind him for something to do, boxing it with his fists until the dust particles skittered in the sunlight. Thumped and thumped as if something inside him was fighting to get out.

The gardens looked like the parkland of some grand manor house, pedantically neatly kept, with closely mown lawns and bushes pruned into square boxes, planted in some geometric pattern designed for viewing from above. On the gravel walks between the barrack-like buildings, people were strolling about arm in arm or with their hands behind their backs, apparently in normal conversation like anybody else. Others were sitting on the benches round the non-functioning fountain, enjoying the afternoon sun, most of them with faces as pale as sheets even though the whole summer was behind them.

At the far end of the row sat a solitary woman, looking down at the gravel in front of her with empty eyes and a distant smile. There was something entirely transparent about her, as if her facial features had dripped off her and her eyes had been mixed with water. Over on the gravel terrace, an elderly gentleman in a blazer and cap was marching up and down, trying to execute smart military about-turns without overbalancing, as if he thought another war was coming. Every time he approached the flagpole, he stood to attention and saluted the non-existent flag.

I tried to see Father out there among them, see him sitting chatting to someone or walking round by himself, chain smoking, but I couldn't. It was impossible to imagine him sitting on the same bench as her, or walking the same gravel paths as him.

They took it slowly as they came towards us, each carrying a suitcase. Mum was holding his arm, making them somehow reminiscent of the other couples in the park – but Father was scarcely recognisable. His face was all puffy and he had a big bushy moustache and dark sunglasses. His hair was slicked back like a film star's.

Can you see it's Father over there, I was on the verge of asking Göran. Father, who's coming home with us. Here he is with Mum, arm in arm, like a blind man and his guide. Soon he'll be opening the door and wanting to shake hands.

Mum stowed the cases in the boot while Father flicked out a cigarette and looked in through the open slit at the top of Göran's window.

'You don't get rid of me that easily,' he said, and smiled. 'If that was what you were thinking?'

I forced a smile in return, but Göran went all shy and ducked down to hide behind a cushion. Father remained unruffled and opened the passenger door, stuffing a bag down into the seat well in front of him before he got in and sat back. Mum was going to drive, even though he was with us.

'Right then?' she said, turning the key in the ignition.

Father nodded approvingly and lit his cigarette, and off we went. Past the lake where the brittle willows were leaning way out over the water as if to admire themselves or look for fish, through newly built estates of identical, boxy detached houses in a variety of different colours, and then out onto the plain where tractors were busy pulling loads of straw and disk harrows. Two hours in the same car, then we'd be home.

'You two count the cows if you're getting bored,' said Mum. 'You take the brown ones Klas, and Göran can do the black ones.'

Göran squirmed.

'But I always lose count. It's no fun having to keep starting all over again.'

'Too right,' mumbled Father.

He got the road atlas out of the glove compartment and looked something up in the index, as if he wanted to see where we had got to, or where we were going next. The cigarette smoke curled its icy blue way up to the roof upholstery that was already a brownish yellow and blended with the pungent smell of Brylcreem and aftershave.

'Your hair's certainly grown, the pair of you,' he said to the atlas. 'So you've not been to the barber's all summer, then?'

Göran gave me a quizzical look. I didn't answer.

'Well isn't it nice that they're finally letting you come home?' said Mum, changing the subject. 'So we won't need to have that Alvar around any more. Makes me uncomfortable, the way he's always grinning.'

Father nodded without interest from behind his sunglasses.

'I think it's kind of Alvar to help us,' said Göran, gullible as ever. 'He's been at our place nearly every day driving the harvester.'

'He certainly has,' said Mum, trying nervously to catch

Göran's eye in the rearview mirror. 'But now he's finished for good, eh? He's got lots to do at home, too, you know.'

'Do you know what, Dad?' Göran persisted. 'One day when Alvar came we all jumped into the hay, everybody together. Can we do it too, when we get back home?'

Mum shot a glance at Father, sort of passing the question on, but there was no answer. He shut the atlas with a bang and closed his hand round the handbrake between the seats instead. He gripped it and kept pressing and releasing the button, as if it was the end of a giant ballpoint pen to be clicked, or as if his mind wasn't on what he was doing.

'So term's started for you both now?' he said.

Mum looked at him.

'It started over a month ago now, you know that?'

'I've almost reached the end of my maths book,' I put in quickly. 'It was nice to get going again.'

'I didn't think it was,' said Göran.

'Don't suppose you did,' said Father, continuing his dangerous game with the handbrake.

A voice from an oncoming car: He could take it into his head to yank it without warning! Then you'll go into a skid and crash head on before Mum has time to react.

'We're going to visit Granny and Grandad soon,' said Göran. 'And you're coming too. Mum said so.'

'Well, it was mentioned ...'

'Are you going to stay with us for good now?'

Mum frowned by way of warning and gave Göran a look over her shoulder. Father said nothing.

He's just waiting for the right moment. For us to meet a fully loaded timber truck or get to that bridge across the lake, where there are no barriers. Maybe that's what he was looking for in the road atlas.

A hand that felt the urge to poke him.

He cleared his throat and slowly turned his head towards me.

'You've always been scared of everything, Klas,' he said, giving me a look from inside those awful sunglasses. 'It doesn't achieve anything, let me tell you that.'

'No –'

I looked out at the trees and the telegraph poles swishing past as blurred shadows and lines, the nearer the road, the vaguer the shape. On the far side of the fields of stubble, the aspens were dancing like yellow-flamed torches against the drab green of the spruces. The aspens: always at the front, adoring the light, torn through by every wind, trembling at the least little thing.

Father held up his hand as if to count on his fingers.

'Scared of the bull and scared of the cows, you were. Scared of the harvester and scared of the chimney sweep and scared of the slaughterman.'

Mum tried to nudge him with her elbow without letting go of the steering wheel.

'If we had a thunder storm you were scared of fire and if we were going down to the Canal you were scared of water,' he went doggedly on. 'It wouldn't have surprised me if you were scared of us, too. Your own parents.'

'Whatever are you up to?' hissed Mum. 'I hardly recognise you, Agne?'

'Do you remember when the air-raid warning sounded and he was lying outside in his pram? He must've been under a year old, but he shrieked until it cut right into your brain. Reckon I can still hear it today.'

Mum looked at him as she might at a stranger.

'You remember that, Gärd? That siren howling as if all hell was breaking loose? But that's asking too much, I suppose?'

'I don't know what's got into you?' she mumbled, half to herself. 'Is it those pills, don't they suit you?'

He didn't answer, but turned round and stared at me through the black glass lenses.

'You shouldn't be so fearful all the time, Klas,' he said. 'That was all I wanted to say. I don't think I've ever been scared of anything that exists.'

Then we were coming into the more built-up area round the station, the place with the slavering dogs and the boarded-up general stores that were rumoured to be a weekend pinball venue for the mob that ride round in beat-up old cars. The cylindrical silo of the central grain store towering halfway to the sky, like a temple to the newly harvested crop. The girls playing hopscotch at its base looked like living dolls by comparison. Where the road crossed the disused railway track, a white-haired man looked up from chopping wood. He instinctively raised his axe in greeting, even though it was embedded in a heavy chunk of spruce. Father said hello and gave a slightly reticent smile, as if to an old acquaintance.

'It's just ahead,' he said all of a sudden. 'Take the next right.'

'Is there really a lake down here?' asked Mum. 'It's hard to believe.'

'Ancient Monument. Burial Site,' read a barely legible sign at the roadside.

'Believing's for in church. A map never lies.'

A bumpy dirt road between new summer cottages. Wheelbarrows with handles poking skywards, empty sets of swings with concrete blocks for feet, an abandoned, cushionless swing seat. A man digging, a woman hanging up washing. Down by the water, the road circled round the flat, grassy area, so Mum was able to loop round and stop the car, facing back up the way we'd come.

'This'll be fine, won't it?' she said, and was already out of the car.

Göran ran down to the wooden jetty and lay flat on his stomach to look for tiddlers. I got out my binoculars and stood on the biggest rock. A family of swans basked in the pleasant warmth, the male with wings raised like sails, the female dipping for underwater snacks, the youngsters dirty grey and far from pretty. Beyond the reeds the great crested grebes were busy with this years' flying lessons, running along the water and flapping wildly but still not managing to get air under their wings. In the end they gave up and swam dejectedly back to their parents, as if to ask if they would be expected to paddle all the way to Portugal.

'It's ready, boys!'

Mum had spread out the rug under a white birch and laid out everything she'd brought with her. Father was sitting on a stone in the shade, chain smoking and squinting towards the lake, lost in thought again.

Not a soul. The changing hut gaped empty and forlorn, and down by the lifebuoy floated a rowing boat, moored by a rusty chain.

'What good boys for not being at each other's throats,' said Mum, reaching over to Father with the big coffee flask, handing out glasses of cordial and passing round the basket of freshly baked buns and her array of homemade biscuits.

In the forest a juvenile thrush, one of that year's clutch, was busy with its sub-song, as if doing a bit of private practice before things like females and territories got serious in the spring. Off at a distance, the cranes trumpeted farewell to all those who had to stay behind.

'Well this is nice, isn't it?' said Mum.

Father nodded absently.

It's that time now, I thought. Migrating cranes and sub-song. Before winter comes and everything is over and done. From the birches down by the lake, the autumn leaves fluttered to the ground one by one, as if we were supposed to count them.

All at once, Father came to life and stood up. He walked round us a few times with a pastry in his hand, compulsively licking his lips.

'Right, we're not staying much longer,' he said. 'I can feel my legs itching to go.'

'Me too,' said Göran, getting to his feet. 'We can get in the car and go home instead, can't we Mum?'

No reaction. She was sitting there with her head tilted back, enjoying the autumn sun.

'I've got to climb a tree first.' The words flew out of my mouth. As if by some compulsion.

Father nodded behind his dark glasses.

'Just mind you don't fall and kill yourself, you hear?' he said, and did another circuit.

'Is it birds again?' Mum asked.

I shook my head.

'You've got the harrowing to think about, if nothing else,' said Father.

I ran across to the alders on the far side of the jetty and opted for the one closest to the shore, pulled myself up to the lower branches and aimed for a fork near the top, where I'd be able to sit. And sure enough: the glitter grew brighter and brighter and the light more and more intense, the higher you got. The radiant channel widened into a glinting shower of light, the whole lake filled with a million little silver lamps winking on and off at their own rates with dazzling clarity, so the water looked almost carbonated, sparkling with bubbles. The light squeezed my eyes harder and harder, forcing my eyelids shut.

And the eagles? Who can look straight into the sun without being blinded, keep looking without a blink. Who will kill their own young if they don't make the grade.

The eagle is an eagle and you are you, the voice said soothingly. All is as it should be.

There's Mum, sunbathing on the chequered rug, lying stretched out on her back with her head on one side, as if she'd dozed off. There's Göran at the water's edge, skimming stones but not getting the right flick of the wrist.

Sitting here in the black alder, looking out over it all.

The robin's ticking contact calls from the bushes beside the boat. Spain is waiting, Portugal, maybe Morocco. In a month or less we'll be there!

Doñana, Extremadura, Monte Aloia, Algarve, Cap Rhir, Tamri, Ouarzazate, Oued Souss, Oued Massa – – –

The rusty-red songster, who brought fire from the heavens to the human race and can safeguard us against lightning, the protector who has a drop of God's blood running in his veins and who covers the faces of the dead with moss and leaves.

The cuckoo's egg in the clearing, came the rustling voice. Why didn't you do anything!

'So did he say where he was going?' I asked, pretending I wasn't worried.

Mum had her eyes closed and didn't hear, or didn't want to hear. She was lying there in the sun in a sort of torpor, her cheeks reddening. On the stone where he'd been sitting, Father had left a crumpled cigarette packet and a half-eaten almond biscuit. Göran came bounding up.

'Where did Dad go?' he demanded, kicking Mum's foot.

She screwed up her face at the bright light.

'How should I know? Isn't he here?'

She yawned and rubbed her eyes. Looked towards the forest with an air of resignation.

'Didn't he say we were going soon?' I ventured.

She got her shoes on and folded up the rug.

'It's always the same. Suddenly he's off, without a word.'

'Da-ad!' called Göran. 'We're going now!'

'That won't help,' Mum said in a shushing sort of voice, taking his arm.

We went up to the edge of the forest, stood in a little opening between the trees and held our breath. A raven kronked his vigilance from a distance. There was a smell of fungi and mould. The heather was in flower.

'Where did he go, do you think?' asked Göran in a whisper, as if we were in church. 'He can't just disappear, can he?'

'Try telling him that and see.'

We advanced a little further in, clambered over a tree blown down by the wind and fought our way through tangles of spider's webs and clumps of rusty ferns, Mum in the middle with Göran and me on either side, like a miniature search party. The ground fell away sharply without warning, down to a mere in front of us. Mum looked at the water and then at me, with something like rising panic in her eyes.

'He's probably already back at the car,' I said. 'He could've come out further up the road if he took a wrong turn.'

'He might not be able to see very well with those glasses on,' said Göran.

She forced out a smile of agreement but insisted we go on a bit further now we'd come this far. We followed the path round the edge of the drop and saw a ridge ahead of us. We scrambled up the steep slope and stood on top, looking all round.

'Ag-ne?' she called half-heartedly.

'Daddy!' called Göran, keen to get involved. '*Dad-ee!*'

I couldn't quite bring myself to say anything, just stood there behind them like a pole of wood, straining my ears.

The murmuring of the trees and the calling voices were sort of suspended in the air for a moment before they dissolved.

'*Ag-ne! –*'

'*Dad-dy! – – –*'

I could feel my throat constricting.

'We'll go and wait in the car,' Mum decided after a bit. 'We can't stay here making fools of ourselves.'

'What if he's fallen and broken his leg?' said the ever-innocent Göran.

She took his hand and turned to go back.

'Yoo-hoo!' we heard from the opposite direction. '*Yoo-hooo!*'

Mum gave us a look that was simultaneously relieved and exasperated, and led Göran down from the ridge.

'Not out looking for me, are you?'

Father was sitting on a tree stump in the clear strip of forest where the power lines ran, with a collection of rowanberries in one hand and a magnifying glass in the other. He had tucked his trouser legs into his socks and buttoned his shirt right up to the neck for protection against something.

'Oh you're here, are you?' asked Mum, pointlessly.

He smiled broadly under his moustache and held out the rowanberries. She gave a firm shake of the head. Göran went up to her and hugged her leg, peering shyly at Father.

'Has it ever occurred to you that a person who's rowing away never has to turn round?' he said. 'He can see everything he's leaving behind him. It's a funny thing.'

He regarded us one after another.

'Rowing?' said Mum. 'Nobody's going to be doing any rowing here, are they? How long were you planning to sit on that tree stump?'

He looked at her as if he'd just realised she'd never understood a word. He twisted the magnifying glass to and fro between his fingers and licked his lips.

'It was good for me to get away from the lake, anyway,' he said after a while. 'I don't like it when things are too pretty to look at –'

'Well you'll be fine here then, with the electricity poles and all this scrubby wood. And you've certainly chosen the right person to marry.'

He turned to Göran with the rowanberries and nodded to him to come and take them.

'They're good for scurvy and gout,' he said encouragingly.

Göran looked down and shrank back.

'Come on then,' said Mum, holding a hand out to Father. 'We can't stay here all afternoon, can we now?'

'You lot just go, if you're in such a hurry. After all, nobody's ever cared how I'm doing.'

Mum laughed out loud.

'What about you then, Klas?' he persevered. 'Aren't you going to try them? But maybe it's only to be expected, seeing as it was me that picked them?'

I shook my head, in spite of myself.

'I haven't got the plague, if that's what you're thinking. Though some people reckon I'm putting it on, pretending to be ill.'

'Right, let's go home and get some supper inside us,' said Mum in a different tone of voice. 'We're just messing about here.'

Father wasn't listening. He got up and came staggering over to me with the rowanberries, holding his giant paw in front of my eyes as if to force me to take some. I felt paralysed, just stood there with my hands thrust into my pockets, looking at the bitter berries, the heads and stalks and leaves, the tiny, pale brown snails crawling along with their houses on their backs. After a few seconds he slowly closed his hand, squeezed it tighter and tighter until the juice ran over his wrists and dripped to the ground. Waxy yellow pulp oozed between his fingers.

'See what can happen,' he said with a strange smile. 'It's a bit like crushing a brain.'

'Right, time to go,' said Mum, 'we all want to get home now. This isn't fun any more.'

What's wrong with your eyes Father, I wanted to ask. Where did you get them? With that empty, glassy look that was never there before, as if they're looking inwards instead of outwards. That opaque film over them, getting in the way.

And that cloud you've got round you, making me shaky whenever I get near you – where's that come from? How long are you going to have it hanging round you, be *inside* it?

Until something finally comes to an end, said the voice. Because that is all it can do.

At five to twelve Göran and I were in our seats, almost bursting with expectation. Mum had kept the kitchen door shut all morning, as if she was hatching something in the warmth of the stove. She'd set the table with the silver cutlery and the wedding-present dinner service, with one of the posh, cut wine-glasses for each of us; put out some freshly baked cumin bread and made thin butter curls, which she'd arranged in the little crystal bowl. In the middle of the table was Father's heirloom Orrefors vase, filled with red and yellow dahlias. It all looked so lovely that I wondered if the vicar was coming round to welcome Father home, but the table was only laid for four and the spare place was as vacant as ever.

Father came in and sat down on the stroke of twelve, dressed for work and still in those awful sunglasses. He read off the temperature and the barometric pressure and entered the readings in the oilcloth notebook. He didn't notice the specially laid table.

'Everything's crowding in on me. I've said it before and it's no better now.'

Mum threw him a look from over by the stove.

'If you mean the boiler room, I didn't force you. You were the one who wanted to sleep there.'

From his breast pocket he fished out a cigarette that was mended with sticky tape, and lit it. He blew two dense streams of smoke out through his nostrils.

'There's more to it than that, but I don't expect anybody in this house to have realised. What's more, I was out going through the scrap metal last night and it couldn't have been worse. And the potatoes have got to come up soon – unless the Colorado beetles have ruined the lot.'

'I thought peace and quiet was what you needed, these first days back home?' Mum said guardedly.

He gave a disdainful snort, as if that was the stupidest thing he'd ever heard in his life.

'Peace and quiet! When it's gnawing away at me day and night?'

Mum took off her apron and brought over the serving plate of fish, garnished with lemon slices and sprigs of dill, then a dish of radishes and the green salad with rocket and tomatoes. She'd sprinkled chopped parsley and little sticks of cooked carrot over the potatoes, and there were four bottles of Pommac on the table instead of the milk jug.

'Well then, dinner's ready. I thought something a bit special might be nice, now the family's back together again. It's the first time I've made this, but I hope you'll all like it.'

She sat down and whispered thank you dear God for the food we eat, with a smile of satisfaction on her lips. Father leaned further over the serving plate and moved a couple of the fish pieces aside with his dirty fingers as if to see what was underneath.

'You expect me to eat this?' he frowned.

Mum looked at him with a blank expression, as if she'd just had a bucket of water tipped over her or was trying to persuade herself she must have heard wrong.

'This is Valborg's Party Salmon with Butter Sauce and Radishes,' she said, still keeping that expressionless face. 'I got the recipe from a posh cookbook.'

He pushed the plate away and sat back in his seat again, smoking and looking out of the window as if he was waiting to be coaxed, or simply wanted to be somewhere else. He drummed his fingers on the table.

'I'm not eating that,' he said. 'But then I expect that's why you made it.'

She swallowed and put one appetising portion on Göran's plate and another on her own, calmly and methodically as if it might help her retain her self-control. She passed me the serving dishes one by one, showed Göran what to do and poured the soft drink into our glasses.

'If you don't fancy it then I suppose you'll have to go without,' she said after a long while. 'There's fresh bread on the table and cold meat and cheese in the larder if that's what you're in the mood for. All the more Party Salmon for us.'

'In the mood? You think this has got to do with being in the mood? There could be DDT and PCB and all sorts of things in that, in case you didn't all know. Neurotoxins, probably.'

'Well I think it's pretty tasty,' she said, looking enquiringly at Göran and me.

'Me too,' I said. 'It's one of the nicest things I've eaten all year.'

Father smoked and squinted out across the fields that Alvar and Mum had harvested. His jaw muscles worked and tensed.

'I think it's really nice, too,' said Göran, and his face brightened as if he'd suddenly been asked a question.

Father slowly turned his head and regarded him through the sooty black lenses.

'You could learn to sit still in class for a start,' he said, 'then we wouldn't have to put up with those never-ending complaints from your teacher. There's enough misery round here as it is.'

Göran stopped chewing and restlessly swung his dangling

feet. A minute passed. Then his chair crashed to the floor and the door of his room slammed so hard it made the windowpanes rattle.

All was silent at the table. Mum put down her knife and fork and looked out into the garden. Her eyes started to look moist. Father kept turning his matchbox round and round in one hand, and drummed his *pa-pa-dam-pam-pam* with the other. The clock on the wall ticked louder and louder.

'Was that really necessary?' Mum finally said.

He looked at her.

'Is it asking too much to expect him to sit still in class? Or to be served something edible now I'm home?'

Mum didn't answer. She fixed him with a look and fought to keep back the tears that must not flow.

'I was only trying to make things a bit special,' she snuffled. 'And I paid for it all out of my savings. The bits I make from my sewing.'

Father jabbed his cigarette end into the flowerpot and stood up.

'He could start by going to school on his own two feet like some of us had to,' he said. 'Then he'd have no problem sitting still in lessons.'

It was all going round and round in my head. A heavy, threatening mass surged through the night, rolling through me as if our house were a captainless ship on the black ocean of eternity. I didn't want to think about it.

I don't want to be part of this, he seemed to have been thinking. The evil will has taken over. I have no control over what is happening.

Something that sent shivers through you whenever you met his eye. The thought that he's come home to end everything.

He came tramping into the kitchen in his boots with the canister of insecticide spray on his back. Wiped his nose on his synthetic fur-fibre sleeve and panted as though he'd had to run away from someone out to get him.

'Pests and insects everywhere,' he said, throwing up his hands. 'What shall we do? They'll be the ones taking over come the spring.'

His forehead was glistening with sweat. He looked from Mum to me and back again, as if we were throwing a ball to each other. Mum didn't answer. She just lifted the canister off his back and took it out into the hall.

'What enjoyment is there in life when you can't get a wink of sleep at nights?' he muttered.

'Come and sit down for a sandwich,' said Mum. 'There's jam, and I've made some of my cheese, you like that.'

He gave her a disappointed look, but let himself be prevailed upon and sat down.

'If only someone could explain where they all come from,' he said, almost to himself. 'But I suppose that's asking too much.'

'Why not make a few of your weather notes instead,' she said, as if talking to a child. 'I wonder if we're going to get a frost tonight? We'll need to cover the dahlias, if so?'

He didn't reply, but took a couple of bits of paper out of his pocket and started to read them out.

'Spinning mites – silverfish – cockroaches – springtails

– furniture beetles – deathwatch beetles – longhorn beetles –
mildew – bedbugs – crab lice – mould – larder beetles – biscuit
beetles – clothes moths – whitefly – thrips – blight – amoebas
– itch mites – nits …'

He shook his head the way he did if there was an area of low
pressure coming in at haymaking time.

'There's no end to it, is there?' he said. 'And it's going on
round the clock. The itch mites are laying their eggs under our
skin. Did you know that?'

I nodded automatically. He wiped the sweat off his brow.

'We'll have to fumigate the old place with hydrogen cyanide,
the way things are going,' he said. 'Rip out all the fitted carpets
and burn them. Don't forget it was the fleas that brought in the
Black Death.'

Mum gestured meaningfully in my direction. Father's eyes
were shifting wildly as if there were insects everywhere.

'Have you ever looked at the carpet in here with a magnifying glass?' he said. 'I didn't think so. In that case you can only
imagine.'

'I think you ought to go and lie down for a little rest,' said
Mum, forcing herself to sound calm. 'You haven't had much
sleep at all these past few nights, have you? Then we'll have our
sandwiches a bit later.'

He lit a cigarette and observed her through the smoke.

'I've done enough lying down for one lifetime,' he mumbled.
'We did nothing else in that place.'

She stroked his arm gently, folded his pieces of paper and
tucked them at the bottom of the newspaper pile. Father stared
down at the floor in front of him and left his cigarette smoking
in the ashtray.

'I don't know what it is,' he said after a long pause. 'They've
just got to be exterminated, the lot of them.'

He went over to the window and looked out over the marsh. Ground his jaws from side to side like a ruminant.

'It isn't easy for me now,' he said to the windowpane.

He leant towards it and breathed on the recently cleaned glass, breathed so heavily that the patch of condensation grew each time he exhaled. As if he couldn't bear the sight of his own face.

'If only someone could tell me what was wrong –,' he screamed silently.

I'd been lying there for hours with the ear protectors on, studying the list of birds that only rarely pay Europe a visit. Lingered over a few names, placed them in the taxonomy, tried to conjure them up in my mind's eye, imagining how they looked and sounded. Drew their outlines with my finger, in the air or against the wallpaper, invented songs and warning cries and mating calls for them.

The Chinese pond heron. The Tennessee warbler. The Eskimo curlew ('formerly declared extinct'). The bufflehead. The hoopoe lark. The lesser crested tern. The white-capped noddy. The yellow-bellied sapsucker. The yellow-headed blackbird. Moussier's redstart. The magnolia warbler. The painted bunting ('unconfirmed sighting, possibly escaped from captivity').

The yellow-bellied sapsucker. *Sphyrapicus varius.*

That's me. Tomorrow I'm going to find out what it looks like.

There was a rumble like thunder in the walls, and the pipes spluttered and banged as if something was about to blow up. The expansion tank bubbled menacingly.

That must mean there's somebody in the boiler room who won't be satisfied until the whole house comes to the boil. Somebody who's stoking the fire to see how much the system can take.

His exhilaration in the car that time.

'Look, we're driving straight into the light! Aren't we, Gärd? You can't see a thing, can you! You're driving into the light!'

The glitter behind the black sunglasses.

We were all going out to do the potatoes. Make the most of having Father at home, which meant we could use the potato digger; promise to behave ourselves and work as a team to get them all in before the frost.

Nothing for it but to grit my teeth and tell myself we'll get through it this time, too.

'We've only got thirty-six rows this year,' said Father. 'Three days' picking should do it if we put our backs into it. Four at most.'

He reached for the pencil and made a quick calculation in the oilcloth notebook. Scrutinised the barometer and nodded his approval.

Four days, I thought. At least thirty hours' picking. One thousand eight hundred minutes.

Stuck there in a quivering, threatening storm cloud. Crawling along, side by side with nowhere to escape to.

'Especially as we've got some extra-special help,' said Mum, putting her arm round Grandad. 'It's going to be as easy as pie, just wait and see.'

'It'll be nice to make myself useful,' he said. 'And get some time off from home into the bargain, it'll be like a holiday by comparison.'

He turned to me and blinked. Showed me what he'd got in his inside pocket and beamed like a child.

'Just as long as Our Lord doesn't get it into his head to damn

well mess me about again,' said Father, 'but nothing would surprise me. If it rains, the whole lot's going to rot. *Then* what are
we going to live on?'

'Surely we mustn't think like that?' said Grandad. 'And if He
did want to, it's bound to be for a reason, just like with everything else in this world.'

Father didn't answer. He tried to catch Mum's eye and tapped
the glass of his watch with his fingernail. Put his fists on the
table and pushed himself up.

'You take one tractor then, Klas,' he said. 'The trailer's
already attached so you can just go.'

He fastened the catskin to his back, thumped the doorframe
three times and hobbled out.

'The old goats have the stiffest horns,' said Grandad, and
poked Mum in the side, making her giggle like a little girl.

Father was already in full swing with the digger when we got
over to Oxmeadow, his head twisted right round to check the
machinery was operating as it should. I scarcely had time to
stop the tractor before Grandad chucked down the baskets and
was off to get started, stooping in his eagerness as he always did
when there was work waiting. Mum took a couple of baskets
in one hand and Göran in the other and she wasted no time
getting into position either, as if she wanted to show she wasn't
the sort to stand around with her arms folded waiting for
someone to tell her what to do. I stayed in my seat, staring out
over the sticky black field, and couldn't bring myself to climb
out. I bent over the ribbed steering wheel and felt the lump of
distaste growing and surging in me.

Something I had no control over. Whatever it was that kept
tugging at me, resisting. Like a heavy weight in everything.

To me they looked like three overgrown insects, kneeling there grubbing in the earth: Mum in her quilted jacket and bright red headscarf, Grandad in the oilskin that had once been yellow, Göran in his new beaver nylon boiler suit. It was so quiet all around, as if the marsh itself was trying to say it was done for this year, had already prepared itself for snow and ground frost. My eyes tracked the windscreen wiper as it tick-tocked across the dry surface, listening to the pointless rasp of rubber on glass.

The heavy soil and the shrivelled, colourless stalks out there. The rows of potatoes were so long you couldn't see the far end; they disappeared over a hump, halfway down to The Canal. Like an insult.

I thought about when I was harrowing the stubble, and Father was up on the concrete drain cover, pointing out over the marsh. The way he yelled into the tractor cab as I came abreast of him.

'It's the couch grass you need to kill off! It's as bad as what tape-worms do to humans! You hear me!'

He wanted the fields completely taken apart, every root fibre severed, so I had to go up and down and across several times before he let me finish.

'Nothing spreads like couch grass! Once it takes hold you can never get rid of it!'

He went down on his knees and dug with his hands to show me all the roots and runners, and how deep the harrow had to go to kill them and do any good.

'They're like vermin the lot of them! You can get twenty thousand buds to a square metre!'

'Klas?'

I gave a start. It was Mum, waving. Peering over at me with an enquiring look.

'Are you off in a dream again? We've got four rows waiting here!'

On with my cap and down into the muck, then. Scrape the mud off the potatoes and toss them into the right baskets, throw aside the stalks and the goosefoot for a bonfire at the end. Try not to think about the raw cold trying to penetrate my marrow.

And Father lined up the digger for the fifth row. The potatoes bounced up the belt, tumbled out along with stones and lumps of mud and lay there with their demands, glowering at me.

'Big ones in here and little ones in there,' Mum pointed. 'The ones for the pigs go in there. The green ones are poisonous, but you know that.'

Through the morning haze I caught glimpses of cackling wild geese overhead, their skeins all pointing south like back-to-front compass needles. The last of the swallows were perched on the telephone wires, waiting to set off.

He stopped the tractor after the seventh row. The spark arrester flickered and everything went quieter still around us. Only Grandad's wheezy breathing and the sound of the potatoes hitting the baskets, the rustle of waterproofs, our hands attacking the wet soil, the shuffle of boots and knees. Father, bent over almost at a right angle by his bad back, tore away stalks and gathered the potatoes like a machine, picking them up and rubbing them clean with one hand while chucking them with the other, sorting and throwing right on target without even raising his eyes. If he happened to get big and little potatoes in the same hand, he was still somehow able to toss them into their respective baskets. It was as if he'd done nothing else all his life.

'There won't be any horses left before long,' he said, trying to meet Grandad's eye while still picking up potatoes. 'Tractors have completely taken over.'

Mum gave him a sideways look.

'There's something in what you're saying,' Grandad responded vaguely.

'Who's going to drive them when war comes and all the youngsters are called up? There aren't many old folk that can drive tractors today.'

'Well you'd be the one to drive in that case, eh Klas?' said Grandad.

'And what about when the diesel runs out? Are we going to run the tractors on milk, is that what they think?'

He shook his head and looked at us one by one, as if to satisfy himself that we realised the seriousness of what he'd been saying.

'Is there going to be a war, then?' said Mum, chastened.

'Well you won't have to worry about famine, like in my time,' said Grandad.

'Don't say that,' muttered Father.

'Johnny at Adder Hook can't talk about anything but armoured fighting vehicles and heavy weapons and anti-aircraft guns these days,' I put in. 'What the Warsaw Pact's got in the way of attack fighters and tanks. Apparently they could land their Spetznas units by helicopter right in the middle of the fen under cover of darkness, if they wanted to.'

'We surely can't be expected to believe *that*?' said Mum.

Grandad nodded and clicked his tongue as if he'd been reminded of the horse back home.

'It's taken five thousand years for us to get this far,' said Father. 'Five thousand years of work and sickness and so-called hardship, and now it's not worth a fig. It's only machines and tractors that count today – and oil, for as long as that lasts. Machines and oil. And neutron bombs.'

Mum cleared her throat and gave Grandad an apologetic smile. She stood up and went to get another basket.

'Blimey, it's not what you'd call hot today,' said Grandad, fishing out his pocket flask.

At twenty past ten it was finally time for elevenses. We hadn't got anywhere. The knees of my trousers looked like mud-caked swallows' nests and were soaking wet; my feet were as heavy as flat irons. The tips of my fingers were sore from all that soil trying to force its way under my nails. We spread the tarpaulin by the telegraph pole, brought empty baskets to sit on and used the drinks crate as a table. Mum put the cups on their saucers and handed round little plates as if we were on a Sunday outing.

'Listen to my guts, grumbling for their coffee,' said Grandad, winking at me.

Father stood there smoking, looking out over the fen with indifferent, glassy eyes, as if he was still five thousand years back in time.

'Nothing beats schnapps in your coffee,' confided Grandad in an undertone. 'You have to put a little five-öre piece in your coffee and pour in the schnapps until you can see the coin, then you know it's decently laced.'

'We're going to get roughly two hundred and fifty kilos a row this year,' said Father. 'It could have been a lot worse.'

'That would make nine tonnes all told,' I said without thinking.

'You're impossible,' said Grandad.

'The blight wasn't as bad as we might have expected, either,' said Father. 'And there was no brown rot to speak of.'

'And no beetles came all the way across the Atlantic to gobble up your plants, either,' Mum observed wryly.

'King Edwards are good spuds,' said Grandad. 'And just the right size, too. Only stupid farmers end up with oversized spuds.'

Father gave a genial smile and pushed his peaked cap to the back of his head.

'You know, don't you Dad, that Klas is doing really well at school?' said Mum. 'In mental arithmetic on Fridays he wins every time, isn't that right?'

Three heads turning this way. Eyes gleaming, as if they expected me to come up with the answer to an insoluble mathematical problem.

'He's a born scholar,' said Grandad. 'I've always said so.'

'It's multiplication you're best at, eh?' said Father, finally coming over to sit down. 'Or have I got it wrong again?'

I wriggled uncomfortably.

'He can do it all,' Grandad said for me.

'His form teacher says he's never seen anything like it,' boasted Mum, 'and he's been a teacher and a music master for over twenty years.'

Father nodded proudly, as if the praise was for him.

'How do you do it, with so little effort?' said Grandad. 'It must be inherited, as the carpenter said about his wooden leg.'

'Give me two numbers then.' The words just tumbled out of me.

Grandad looked around, nonplussed, and then put down his cup and thought for a bit.

'Twelve times seven?'

'Too easy. Three-digit numbers.'

Mum turned to Father, passing the baton to him.

'A hundred and nineteen and seven hundred and three!' he said, raising his voice like an auctioneer. 'One hundred and nineteen times seven hundred and three!'

There's something for you to get your teeth into, said

Grandad with a wink. I closed my eyes and set the numbers up on the insides of my eyelids, did a hundred and nineteen times seven, put two noughts on the end and added three hundred and fifty-seven.

'Eighty-three thousand, six hundred and fifty-seven.'

'You're absolutely impossible,' said Mum, shaking her head.

'He'll be a professor,' said Grandad. 'I've always said so.'

'Seven seconds,' said Father, and carried on nodding in time to the second hand of his watch. 'Eight at most. I timed it.'

'I'll drink to that,' said Grandad. 'If all spuds tasted like this I wouldn't mind picking them seven or even eight days a week.'

The well-laced coffee was making him loud and rosy-cheeked, and a broad grin was plastered across his face. It was as if some stone inside him had come free, or a block of ice had started to melt.

'Wonder how many basketloads I've picked in my time?' he said, still beaming. 'When I was young you we had to go labouring for other farmers once we'd finished at home. Sometimes we were still at it well into November. You'd start at dusk and pick like mad for as long as you could see your paw in front of your face.'

'Eugh, dreadful,' said Mum.

'How about that then, Klas! You needed a pickaxe, and it ruined your back. And then it was the turnips, before the snow came. Different times, they were. We even got days off school to help out with the picking. Not that we earned much. If you got a krona a day you were lucky.'

He gave my leg a little kick with his boot and laughed until his false teeth rattled and the juice ran from his snuff.

'You had the same in your day, didn't you Agne? Potato break in October?'

Father didn't answer. He sat empty-eyed, staring at the earth in front of him with a jammy biscuit in his dirty hand. Deep inside himself again.

'Thank the Lord for that,' said Mum. 'For the way times change. Where would we be otherwise?'

'A person whose eyebrows grow together in the middle will die by drowning,' said Father irrelevantly. 'Someone said that, in that place where I was.'

It all went quiet. Grandad nodded and put his little finger to the bridge of his nose, as if Father might be talking about him. Mum cleared her throat and took a slice of Swiss roll but had scarcely taken a bite before a potato came flying through the air and hit Father in the back of the head. A terror-struck Göran stared down at us from the back of the trailer, his face as rigid as a board.

'I didn't mean to! I was aiming at Klas!'

Father closed his eyes and took a deep breath. His head fell forward in slow motion, as if he was in indescribable pain. Göran had already ducked down to hide behind the trailer flaps.

'It was only a joke,' he implored. 'I'll never do it again, I promise.'

Father's face darkened. He rubbed his lips together and fumbled with his coffee cup, spilling the liquid on the plate of cakes and biscuits.

'This'll be more of the Devil's work!' he shouted, turning to Mum. 'Won't it, eh!'

The saliva was spraying from his mouth. He reached for a stone to throw at Göran, but dropped it just as quickly. Mum moved closer to Father and helped him with the big plate, putting a soothing hand on his shoulder.

'He didn't mean it, you know that. He was just larking about. It's not much fun for him out here in the cold all day.'

Father looked at her with those awful eyes.

'Fun? Who the hell said it had to be fun? It's our survival at stake here!'

Just then, Göran seized his chance and ran off, arms and legs pumping as he charged across the stubble field, on his way home to lock himself in his room and never come out again.

'Here, have a nip and it'll soon pass,' said Grandad, holding his pocket flask out to Father. 'It's good for any kind of ailment, I can vouch for that.'

Father glared at the outstretched flask. Took off his cap and felt his head to see if there was a bump. He sat there for a long time, watching Göran go, rubbing his lips together more and more frantically, licking them and biting the bottom one as if to keep something in check.

'He'll be back out with us this afternoon, you wait and see,' said Mum. 'We'll just have to manage without him for a bit.'

'This afternoon? Now is what matters! Who cares about this afternoon?'

'Well I'll have one for you, then,' Grandad said eventually.

On the other side of the barbed wire fence the cows stood looking at us with vacant eyes, apparently blissfully unaware of everything. They swished their tongues over the balding yellow grass a few times, keen no doubt to get into the warmth of the cowshed and feed on hay instead. The swallows had departed, leaving the telephone wires hanging slack and empty like a winter clothesline with no pegs.

When I turned round, Father was hunched over his knees, and had squeezed his eyes shut with a grimace as if his head was about to explode, or as if something had already burst. Mum put down her cup and looked uneasily at Grandad, and Grandad looked at me. I reached for a crispy oat biscuit and tried to eat it without crunching too loud.

'Listen,' was Father's next word. 'Listen to those devils –'
It was his feeble, hollow voice. Mum frowned.

'What is it, Agne? What are we meant to be hearing?'

He was breathing heavily through his nose, squeezing his
eyes tightly shut and rocking back and forth with his big hands
pressed to his ears.

'The ravens,' he said with an effort. '*The ravens, for God's sake!*'
He gave Mum a look of despair. His chin was trembling.
Grandad dropped a sugar lump into his coffee and stirred as
slowly as he could so he had something to do with his eyes.

'If they could only leave me in peace,' Father whimpered. 'I
can't bear hearing them any more.'

'What are you talking about, Agne?' Mum tried again.
'There aren't any ravens here, are there? You would have
heard them Klas, wouldn't you? What with you so interested
in birds?'

'Well *I* can't hear anything,' said Grandad, taking her side.
'But maybe I'm too old for it? I haven't heard a cricket in
twenty-five years.'

He laughed. Mum gave him a look of complicity and shook
her head in resignation.

'Can't you hear what I'm saying!' said Father, working himself
up. 'The ravens are screeching I tell you! The bluest ones are
the worst fiends of the lot!'

'Of course we can hear what you're saying,' said Mum, as
calmly as she could. 'But I don't understand what ravens it is
you're talking about. I don't think I've heard you talk about any
ravens before?'

'Depends what you mean by talk. But I'm talking now, at
any rate. There's one hell of a racket and it's coming from all
directions!'

Mum put her arm round his shoulders, leant forward and

whispered something in his ear, went to fetch the small beer and got some of his tablets ready.

'Did you hear anything, Klas?' asked Grandad, rather missing the point. 'You've got good ears.'

I pulled a discouraging face. Mum stroked Father's cheek and asked if he wanted to go and rest for a while, take five minutes and unwind a bit.

'We'll carry on, Dad and Klas and I,' she said, 'and you can come and join us when you feel up to it. Wouldn't that be a good idea?'

Father shook her off and glowered indignantly.

'Up to it? First there was something wrong with my ears and now it's my stamina. It's as if I wasn't to be relied on any more –'

'What the ravens want, they get,' said Grandad. 'That's the long and the short of it.'

'This won't do,' said Mum. 'We can't let ourselves starve to death in the potato field?'

'An army marches on its stomach,' said Grandad, his face cracking into a wide grin.

Father gave an absent nod.

'I'll just do something easy,' Mum decided, and was off.

'The easier the better,' said Grandad.

He winked at me and fished the flask out of his pocket, listening hopefully for a liquid sound, and he was in luck: a little drop to produce a glint in his eyes.

'Your job to remind me we need to fill her up once we've eaten,' he whispered.

'Klas, you take the tractor,' said Father. 'We might as well unload while we're back at the yard. Nobody knows how long it'll be till next time. I'll stay here and take up a couple of rows while she's cooking. You two go on the tractor.'

'I'll walk, said Grandad. 'I've done it before.'

I turned the tractor round, used the hand accelerator and let the tractor drive itself, taking my hands off the wheel and steering with my thighs like a proper driver. A full load on the trailer and dinner waiting. Into the warmth and change my long johns and see if the post's come, if Veronika's answered the letter that took me several weeks to write, fiddling around with how to phrase it and looking up difficult synonyms, taking out clauses where I wasn't sure I'd used commas properly and resorting to dictionaries to make sure I'd hyphenated in the right place, using the biro from the word go and rewriting so it'd look as if I'd got it perfect first time. Beside my signature I'd done a sketch of the bittern flying up, traced from a bird book so it would look as if I'd drawn it from memory. The rounded wings and the plumage, mottled like an owl's, the truncated tail, the dangling legs with the implausibly long-toed feet.

I could see her in my mind, in her room in Svärmaregatan in Upplands-Väsby. The fabrics and posters casually pinned up on the wall, the washed-out dungarees with the flowers and stars on the legs. She's sitting in bed like a buddha, painting with watercolours on her big, unlined pad of paper. She's alone, and regretting that she didn't stay at Bliss Cottage after all.

Her smooth cheeks with that little dimple when she smiles and looks down, her hair falling over her breasts that she's –

You're dreaming again!

One wheel of the trailer missed the bridge and the potatoes came tumbling out by the thousand, the whole thing was close to tipping over. Thirty baskets mixed up in a big heap, everything we'd picked and sorted.

I engaged first gear and stepped on the gas, declutching and breaking by turns, but the tractor kept sliding and heaving and the more I tried, the further the trailer slipped into the ditch. Suddenly Grandad was at the cab door.

'This is a pretty sight,' he said, laughing.

'Something must have gone wrong?'

I broke out in a cold sweat. My heart was racing.

'I've seen worse mishaps in my time,' Grandad said consolingly. 'If we take a pitchfork each we can have the whole lot up in a jiffy.'

'But the trailer ... if Father comes ...'

'With spruce twigs under the back wheel we'll soon get some

purchase. If the worst comes to the worst, we can use the snow chains. It'll be all right, never you worry.'

Father killed the engine of the Ferguson and went over to the ditch with heavy tread. He took off his cap and slowly shook his head, sent me a look of boundless sorrow.

'I can sort them again later, tonight,' I said, looking at the ground. 'It was my fault, I must have been in a dream as usual. Cut the corner.'

'It's nothing,' said Grandad. 'It'll be done in a trice if we all pitch in.'

Father chewed his lip. Shook out a cigarette and lit it, dragged until his cheeks were deep hollows and blew out the smoke in a long sigh.

'There's no justice in this world,' he hissed. 'What have I done to deserve all this?'

Grandad gave him a sharp look.

'Done? If anyone's at all to blame for this it isn't you, Agne. And there's no serious damage done anyway.'

Father gave a hopeless flap of his arms and looked down into the ditch and over to the trailer, which was hanging there with the back axle wedged against the side of the bridge.

'What's my next punishment going to be?' he said. 'Stones instead of grain, plagues of insects, potatoes in the deepest ditch –'

At that moment, the Salesman came gliding by in his new company car, right on cue as if someone had telephoned to tip him off. The car shone like newly polished brass as he pulled up at the side of the road.

'Someone's been demobilised right in the middle of potato picking, I see,' he said, sticking out his neatly combed head.

Father didn't answer, just shot him a black look and took the pitchfork down into the ditch. The Salesman opened the car door and got out, as if he wanted to inspect the devastation at close quarters now he'd bothered to stop.

'It doesn't look hopeful,' he observed to Grandad, clasping his hands behind his back. 'I assume some of the potatoes are already ruined?'

'Oh, together we'll soon get things shipshape again,' Grandad said blandly. 'We'll just have to get stuck in.'

'It was my fault,' I said again. 'I don't know what happened. It's my punishment for daydreaming.'

'And how were you thinking of getting the trailer out?' said the Salesman. 'I should think you'd need a crane.'

He smiled his stuck-on smile and wiggled his foot, sort of marking time for Father who was throwing up potatoes at a furious pace.

'So you may not have heard the news about the fen?' said the Salesman, changing tack. 'The Manor's planning to do away with the leaseholds down here, and they seem to have the County Agricultural Board on their side.'

Father pretended not to hear. He gritted his teeth and puffed, and kept on throwing.

'It's all about large-scale production these days. There'll soon be combines with twenty-foot headers and they need decent acreage to operate in,' lectured the Salesman. 'I daresay you'll have heard yourself about rationalisation and mergers. More efficient farming units. Increased yields. They can always find some paragraph about neglect or negligence if they need to terminate a lease early.'

'You think so?' said Grandad, stroking his chin.

The Salesman just stood there with his hands behind his back.

'The land round here's in demand these days, you know. Open country and not too stony. The County Agricultural Board are sitting there with a map and a ruler doing their calculations and concocting plans, buying and selling land and making sure those who've already got some acquire more. Better a big, prosperous estate than a hundred small farmers hardly making ends meet. And reputation comes into it, too. The Manor's got a good name and wants to lease to respectable, trustworthy folk, the sort they can rely on.'

Father gave several snorts down in the ditch. He didn't deign to so much as look at the Salesman.

'Landowners are always the winners in the long run. And if the estate owner gets fed up with sitting on his combine a couple of weeks a year he can always plant Christmas trees or put in a golf course or crayfish ponds. Pretty much anything would be more profitable, really, than a couple of thousand a year for a leasehold. Trees wouldn't be that exciting when I come to think of it – but a golf course! I'm sure they'd let you be an honorary member, Agne.'

'Let's take one thing at a time,' said Grandad, straightening his back as best he could. 'We've got to think of these spuds first and foremost. Agne's very likely going to get a krona a kilo for them come the end of the winter.'

The Salesman wasn't listening. He just smiled even more broadly and went a couple of steps closer to the ditch.

'You'll have to look for something else, that's all there is to it,' he said, as if it didn't matter. 'But find someone who can tow out the trailer before you do anything else.'

'We'll deal with this ourselves now!' snapped Grandad. 'If there's one thing we don't need it's bystanders and clever dicks.'

The Salesman carried on smiling as he wiped his shoes on the grass.

'Mind you don't overdo it now, Agne,' he said, and went back to his car. 'You've got your scrap pile to think about, too.'

He wound up the window and nodded to Grandad and me before he backed and turned. Father leant on his pitchfork and watched the car for a long time as it reached the bend and disappeared out of sight. His eyes narrowed and his jaw tensed, as if with bottomless hatred.

'I'm sure he's the one behind the whole ruddy thing,' he said. 'This earth we've been toiling over for a hundred and fifty years –'

Grandad turned to me.

'Wasn't that Sonny from Sunnyside?' he said, as if the name burnt his tongue.

'It certainly was,' said Father, raising his voice. 'And he's a nasty piece of work, I can tell you! He'll stop at nothing if there's cash to be made. Takes advantage of other people and stoops to anything, yet somehow he still gets folk on his side. He should be sent to Bog Island to fillet mosquitoes.'

Grandad nodded uncertainly and stroked his chin again.

'Last time I met him at the bottle shop he said he didn't know you. He scarcely knew where Dower Farm was. That's my son-in-law, I said, Dower Agne, but it didn't help. He just shook his head.'

Father chucked away his half-smoked cigarette and stared at us with a wild look in his eyes.

'But it suits him when he wants to borrow my machines,' he gasped. 'Then he comes here all smarmy and chummy. And the bastard drives them into the ground before he brings them back. Who do you think has to stay up welding all night when that happens?'

He flapped his arms.

'The farmer's lot is the foulest,' muttered Grandad to the ground.

'A nasty piece of work, that's what he is! Borrowed half a load of gravel off me on the twelfth of April this year. You think I've had so much as a sniff of it back?'

Grandad didn't know what he was supposed to answer, so he shook his head and nodded at the same time.

'I thought maybe I was getting senile and made a mistake,' he said. 'So it was Sunnyside Sonny, after all? He denied he knew who you all were.'

'Yes, you said,' I replied, trying to deflect him.

'Seems a bit odd –'

All of a sudden the pitchfork fell out of Father's hands. He tottered and sat down heavily in the middle of the heap of potatoes, bent his head and pressed his hands to his ears as if to make the sound stop. He sat there with his hands over his ears, rocking to and fro.

I felt my stomach knotting. Grandad gave me an anxious look and stalked down into the ditch.

'Have you hurt yourself, Agne?' he said. 'Agne? Have you hurt yourself?'

There was no answer. Just a whimpering sort of crying that could not exist, like nothing I had ever heard before. Like something coming from a different person.

Big, dirty hands over his ears. Shoulders shaking.

Mum had made the creamed liver Father liked so much, with lingonberry preserve, but he didn't even come and sit down. He went straight to the boiler room and locked the door, without a word.

'He's got to eat to keep his strength up for all the work,' said Göran with his mouth full. 'If you don't eat you can't do anything.'

'We'll let him rest for a bit and then see. Maybe it was too much for him, the ravens and then the potatoes in the ditch?'

'That's well said,' said Grandad, ruffling Göran's hair. 'You're not as daft as you look.'

He found the schnapps bottle and filled his glass to the quivering brim. Then it was empty again.

'Spuds are actually best in liquid form, I've always thought,' he said, and started humming along with the Jan Sparring song that was on the radio.

Mum gave an embarrassed smile, served up a portion for Father and took it down to the basement. A few minutes later she came back up the stairs.

'We can't go on like this?' she said, putting down the tray. 'I'd better drive him back there, straight away.'

Göran stuffed his fingers in his ears and started singing la-la-la out loud to himself, swinging his feet and making his chair squeak to and fro.

'It's my fault,' I said.

Grandad looked enquiringly at me and Mum, trying to get one of us in focus with his watery eyes.

'But what about the spuds?' he said. 'The spuds have got to come up.'

'If you two can do some picking while I'm gone that would be great,' said Mum. 'We'll all have to pitch in as best we can.'

'Of course we will. You'll have to drive the digger, Klas. Unless we're going to get out the mattocks, like in the old days.'

'I'll be as quick as I can. I'll just go straight there and back.'

Göran stopped going la-la-la and looked at Mum as if something important was just occurring to him. He looked and thought until his eyes were as round as saucers.

'Will Alvar be coming again?' he said after a while.

Grandad flinched.

'Alvar? Are we going to hire in labour when we've got Klas here! He'll be the one in harness, putting his back into it.'

'We'll have to see what we're going to do,' Mum said soothingly. 'We'll take it a day at a time to start with.'

'It's no problem for Klas, all this,' declared Grandad. 'He can do anything, and what he can't do he'll learn quick enough.'

The pungent smell of urine and the soaking wet underpants in the middle of the night. The big, round wet patch in the middle of the sheet, the bedwetters' very own flag. The wave of self-disgust rising within me.

Up and rinse them through and wash them off and hide them out of the way, get out dry ones and remake the bed. Hang Wunderbaum trees above the bed and convince myself it was the last time, something's got to change soon.

Enuresis nocturna. 'If the problem has not been overcome by the age of 12–13, psychiatric treatment should be sought from the local paediatric clinic.'

But at least I hadn't drowned this time, either, only sunk and struggled for a while in the bottomless black sea of my dream. I had been restored to favour and allowed to live. Allowed to carry on yearning to do it all.

To take Veronika to Africa on the back of my new Kawasaki, climb Kilimanjaro and see the elephants turn into toy animals down on the savannah. Hear the mating roars of the lions at night, find a baobab tree that's been standing for a thousand years. Carve our names into the bark.

I never forget a thing.
 Have you ever thought about that? Not a thing –

As if somebody had called to me in my sleep.

Today is the time to go – before Alvar gets here and starts on the autumn ploughing, blacking out the fields ridge by ridge, preparing for a new year that can never be the same. Before he comes clomping in with his boots on and sits down at the kitchen table with that silly grin of his.

An act of defiance? Because I couldn't stand seeing him in Father's place?

I didn't know.

Out and off with you, was all the voice said. Away from all this –

Of course I will, I mean that's sort of been the idea all along. And what better day than All Saint's, when the candles and little lanterns are flickering on every gravestone because people persuade themselves the dead can come back to life again?

I put some clothes and some tinned food in my rucksack along with the little spirit stove, the wool blanket, my survival knife and some rope, and strapped the tent to it. Left a note on the kitchen table and tied my walking boots with double knots.

The note with the truth and the lie: *I'm with the birds. Back soon. K.*

Out on the road it was so immensely silent and still that I came to a halt and just waited for something to happen, for a hunting dog to bark, a power saw to let rip or a gun to go off.

Something that could puncture the roaring silence, cleave the mist apart like an axe of now.

Nothing –

As weighty and still as an omen. Not a pine needle moving, not even the last leaves on the aspen. Just the smell of manure from the unploughed fields.

I was all shaky inside when I got up into the forest, as if I had been fleeing for my life, trying to escape a dangerous animal. But I hadn't had anything after me, anyone to run from; I hadn't seen or heard a living thing. I had only my trembling self, and the rucksack that was already digging into my shoulders. On the tree trunks around me hung the abandoned nesting boxes, their holes gaping blankly like an extinct choir.

But what about you, poor little harebell? Fancy having to bloom all by yourself, at this time of year! Isn't it too late on this earth for you, too?

I gave a start.

Birches with black armbands! A whole clump of them up ahead by Broadleaf Brook, there must be thirty or forty – and each with a broad black bandage at eye height, just where you couldn't miss it.

It's a message for you, whispered the voice. A choir of extinct birds and the smooth white trunks with black bands.

A message from someone who knows –

I summoned as much courage as I could and started arranging what was to be mine. Put up the tent between two bushy spruces, broke off plenty of soft spruce twigs to make a mattress, collected stones for a fireplace, just in case.

This is where I'm going to be, I persuaded myself. In the green chamber nobody knows about.

Alvar's there and I'm here.

All of a sudden it seemed to be getting dark, even though it was the middle of the morning, as if a dark shadow had been drawn to me, made me the forest's heart of darkness. Heavy, dripping branches, dank and wet everywhere, slippery roots and piles of squelchy leaves, tangles of fern umbrellas lying there, longing to rot away. The seeping shrouds of the spiders' webs, close to the ground, the mist hanging in the air, the smell of pepper and earth, mould and decay, eternity. Dead aspen leaves everywhere, mere skeletons as delicate and transparent as ladies' stockings.

It's that time now, I tried. All is as it should be.

The songthrushes have landed in France, the robins are halfway to Spain and the cuckoo's made it to Africa.

And Father? Lying on a plastic-covered bed in a bare room with bars over the windows, listening to the ravens screech. Shutting his eyes and holding his ears because he doesn't know what on earth to do. Rubbing his lips together and biting them with his teeth until they bleed.

You mustn't tie him down with those leather straps Mum talked about! Mustn't send the direct current through his brain or bore holes in his skull! Mustn't destroy him for all time. He hasn't done anything.

Just shine a little light. Say everything's going to be all right.

I went over to his rock, cleared off the debris and brushed the letters clean. Squatted down and felt his T and his A and his G. The keen edges, still sharp after all these years. The full stops he'd made like upside-down triangles, balancing on their own points.

'Tom Agne Georgsson –' I heard myself whisper.

A shiver ran through me.

Had I ever said it before? Taken his full name in my mouth, pronounced it so it could really be heard, syllable by syllable? Not that I could remember. Dower Agne I'd said, if somebody forced me, but never his proper name. I whispered it over and over, slowly and experimentally to see if I could conjure him out of the rock. As if that was what I wanted.

When he was like me, and sat here carving. Was it the same wind filtering down between the treetops? The same water purling over there in the stream? The same irresistible urge to get out and away? Grandfather admitted for treatment and he himself alone in the forest.

I sat there on the mossy stump and stared down at the rock as if I was bewitched: quartz, feldspar, mica, hornblende. The hundreds of shiny little splinters that looked as though they had been strewn there before they stuck, the irregular patches of red, the grey shades with greenish streaks, the pale lichens spreading into saffron and verdigris – it all appeared to me in a new light, every detail somehow rising up out of the rock and transforming into patterns and forms, as if they *wanted* something of me, were significant. I felt I had never seen anything so clearly in my entire life. Every little fragment and fracture, the clumps of moss growing there, the patches of lichen and the variations on darker hues in the granite itself – everything shaped itself into images and signs that no one else would be able to see, that were only for me. Uninhabited islands in the ocean. Paths that crossed, on a deserted fen. Starry skies and galaxies fixed like tiny dots on a negative from another time. It was as if something was moving in the rock, as if I could see every teeming molecule in it – the ones that will always be there and can never die, even when the rock has stopped being a rock.

It can't have lasted longer than a minute, but I had been

admitted to something I'd never experienced before, opened the door to a secret room a tiny crack, and glimpsed something no one else is to know. The oddly soothing feeling that the struggle was over, that nothing mattered any more.

Hunger was gouging away at me. I thought of the enormous young cuckoo I'd had to help out of the spotted flycatchers' nesting box, too fat after all its begging. It must be there by now, looking for grubs among the lianas and umbrella trees of Zaïre or Zambia instead – but how did it know where it had to go, and that it ought to stop among the ibises and openbills and flamingoes rather than fly on and on and never land anywhere?

Did the cuckoo's call sound the same down there? The thought flashed through my mind. Has anyone heard a cuckoo call in Africa? Seen it perching in an umbrella thorn acacia by Lake Edward with its tail spread like a fan, hurling its echoing ball of sound across the Albertine Rift?

Can you imagine a cuckoo that never calls? What does that make him, if so? A long-tailed grubhawk? A yellow-eyed parasite pigeon. Droop-winged prankjay. Loathsome slyhatch!

I thought of all the young cuckoos who had grown up round Marsh Pool and on Raven Fen, each on its own without siblings or proper parents, fed by whitethroats, wagtails and robins; I tried to understand how they could know what a cuckoo looks like and where a cuckoo needs to point its beak when summer's over and all the grubs are gone. Is there any member of the human race who can explain how a cuckoo knows it's a cuckoo and not a whitethroat or wagtail! – – –

Rustling and footsteps from the other direction. Twigs snapping.

Up the spruce and hide! It could be a highly-strung elk that hasn't had a moment's respite since the hunting season started, or a badger who needs to feed himself up before he retires to his sett.

Nonsense, it's just the foresters out marking trees ready for felling this winter.

'Hello,' I called, without meaning to. 'Who's there?'

I held my breath.

'Hoy,' came the answer. '*Hoy there!*'

Johnny.

I didn't know what to think. When you want to talk to people, there's never anyone to go to, but when you run away they come and seek you out in the clearing nobody knows about.

Here he comes, traipsing along with a big sack over his shoulder. He's presumably going to lay out apples for the roe deer, which are what he likes shooting best.

'So the slacker's on a field trip?' he said, with a nod towards the tent. 'Any special reason?'

He hawked up a gob of phlegm, leaving it perched on his outstretched tongue before he spat it out.

'It's just as well to start practising for military service in good time,' I said, pleased that I'd come up with a good line.

'Good,' said Johnny, not realising I was pulling his leg. 'Join up as soon as you can, if you get the chance. I've never had it so good, so I haven't.'

He sat down on the sack of apples and put a wad of snuff in his mouth, then spat a couple of yellow jets at my feet.

'They talk a lot of crap about the officers, but I think they do a good job. The company commander can be a bit of a bastard at times, but I'd rather that than too soft. The warrant officer was in the Congo hunting natives and lions and all that; it's a right hoot hearing all his stories. The food's good, as well. Two hot meals a day, which is more than I ever get round here.'

He was wearing his usual military cap – but with the earflaps down and that blond moustache he looked a right idiot.

'I'm going to be squad leader in the first infantry when we're on manoeuvres this winter,' he rabbited on. 'Second platoon. Those conscripts won't know what's hit them, so they won't.'

'I bet,' I said, not caring.

'If you play your cards right when you choose your trade, you could find yourself going to Cyprus and earning real money, there's wages and board and the whole caboodle. But for that you need good marks, ten seven seven for starters, probably ten eight eight when it comes to it.'

I nodded and hadn't a clue what it all meant.

'Think about it,' he said. 'You won't get another chance like it in your life, so you won't.'

He brought out his hunting knife and ran his thumb experimentally along the edge of the blade, checked its sharpness against his nail, took a little steel out of his leg pocket and worked away at whetting it as if he might need to use it any minute.

Squad leader, I thought. Ten eight eight. Cyprus.

'You staying here long?' he asked, keeping his eyes down.

'Well stamina's the main thing, isn't it?'

He gave a grave nod.

'Roots and moss are good to eat,' he said. 'Frogs and birds and snakes if you can find them. They all taste pretty much the same, so they do. There was plenty of that on the survival course.'

'Oh yes, I'll be fine,' I said cockily.

'And then you brew up some pine-needle tea and drink as much as you can, but maybe you knew that? If you've got to stay awake, chew some resin.'

He got up and went over to inspect the tent, picked at a mended patch that was peeling up at the edges, pulled the zip up and down and tested to see that the canvas was pulled as tight as it should be and the guy ropes were taut.

'But beware of this one,' he said, kicking a fly agaric so it exploded into little bits. 'They used to give them to the horses and drink their piss when the schnapps ran out. Eat one of these and it could be the end of you.'

I didn't answer. He sat back down on the sack and started whistling through his teeth as if he was waiting for something. Took out his knife again, and used a corner of his military tunic to polish the blade.

'It should be so sharp that you don't notice when you cut yourself,' he explained. 'If the blood just flows, you know it's sharp.'

Then he reached over and cut clean through Father's oak sapling at ground level. With a little *chpp* sound, quick as a pinprick. It only took a couple of seconds for him to trim it and start paring off the bark with long, confident knife strokes.

'I heard Alvar at The Point was starting at yours again,' he said.

So that was it. That was why he'd hung around – to pick up a titbit to take home, so as not to leave empty-handed, to force me into a tight corner.

'So they locked him away again, eh, Agne?'

He looked up.

'You lot'll have to watch out you don't lose your animals. There are regulations now. They don't let just anyone keep live-stock in our communities these days.'

Was that a sneer plucking at the corner of his mouth as he smiled?

If you don't shut up I'll be the one making a report to the

police, I almost said. If it gets out what you were up to behind the cowshed last spring, you can forget Cyprus, that's for sure, and plenty of other things in life besides.

'It was something to do with his sciatica,' I improvised hastily. 'Some more tests, I think. You can get paralysis if you go back to work too soon.'

Johnny didn't react. Just went on calmly paring his oak switch, sharpening it into an arrow at one end. A black wood-pecker flew up with its warlike cry. Black as death itself between the tree trunks.

'Makes you feel a bit sorry for him, really,' Johnny said unex-pectedly. 'And getting all that shit thrown in his face.'

I didn't know what he meant.

Kree –, echoed the martial cry, receding into the distance. *Kree* – *Kree* –

'But he's always been a bit odd,' he went on. 'Scarcely answered when anyone spoke to him and went round snigger-ing to himself. That was probably why someone wrote what they did on the corpse shed, so it was. No smoke without flames, or whatever the saying is.'

So he'd seen it too. Everybody in the district must have heard about that graffiti, thought to themselves that it was the plain truth but just pretended they hadn't seen. Gave me a cheery greeting as I cycled past, then hid behind their curtains and whispered and pointed as I came back.

'What would you know about it?' I said, trying to keep my cool. 'About whether he's odd or not? Just because he's not the type to go nattering on about nothing in particular and what-ever's right in front of his nose, like other people. Anyway, it's generally those that spout the most who have the least to say. The old schoolmaster says he's never taught anyone with such a head for learning.'

Johnny looked surprised.

'Well in that case, why does he stand in your dairy singing opera, or whatever it's meant to be? Why does he prowl about with a headtorch and a shotgun in the middle of the night? Is that so clever, eh?'

I cleared my throat.

'I didn't see those words myself, by the way,' he added as an afterthought. 'It was the Salesman who told everyone.'

'There's a surprise.'

Johnny slid his knife into its leather sheath and threw the switch away. Adjusted his wad of snuff with his tongue and gave me a look.

'Our warrant officer says it's the longhaired, intelligent types who end up locked away. You'd better watch yourself.'

I waited for him to grin and take it back, but he clearly meant what he had said.

'By army regulations, you'd more or less need a hairnet,' he said. 'It isn't supposed to come down over your collar at the back of your neck, so it isn't.'

'Plenty of time to get my hair cut before then.'

'Here, feel this.'

He took off his cap and ran his fingers through his stripes of fringe, bending his head forward for inspection. His scalp was pink and scaly and covered in scars, as if somebody had marked him with a branding iron like we used for the pigs.

'Want to feel?' he said. 'I cut it myself, with the vacuum clippers at home.'

'I've never had mine that short, and I never will. I don't care about Cyprus.'

He pulled on his cap, flattened down the peak and glanced at his watch.

'Well, this isn't fixing any screws,' he said, letting his laugh lighten his mood. 'But the deer need a bite to eat, so they do.'

And he heaved the sack of apples onto his back and set off the same way he'd come, stamping on a puffball as he went and whistling a waltz tune that might have been 'Life in the Finnish Woods'. Just as the old spruces were about to swallow him up, he stopped and turned round.

'If you haven't got anything else on this winter you can come along and watch for foxes. I've made a hide down in the cowshed and there's room for two.'

I nodded, feeling torn.

'It'll be mostly at night,' he said, 'ideally when the snow's settled and the moon's out. If you can keep your gob shut, that is. Fox hears everything, so he does.'

'I'll have to see. I've got sixty or seventy nesting boxes to make before spring comes. And an eye in the ceiling to get rid of.'

I said that last bit more to myself.

'See you,' said Johnny. 'I wasn't planning to shoot you this year, if that's what you were thinking.'

And off he went, whistling.

Sleep would not come. I lay there trying to make out the mesh vent up by the top ridge of the tent, wondering whether the storm that was whipping around out there had decided to stay or just wanted to scare me and then move on. I listened to the rain hissing down, the branches scratching at the canvas whenever there was a heavy gust of wind, the trees creaking like the doors of a haunted house.

How can it be so black? It makes no difference whether my eyes are closed or not, there's scarcely a streak of light for the brain to register. Only the phosphorescent pigment that is my watch hands, like two pale green dashes.

It must be worse now. Listen to it whining and whipping, never-endingly. Squall after squall, almost merging into each other.

Those branches breaking –

This is the real storm coming now, the sort that tears down all in its path, determined to take everything with it, to uproot and destroy and lay waste.

Heaven's brush over the birthplace of bondage on this earth, as Father put it when the wind from the fen got up and the impossible happened: the hay on the drying racks blew over, with all their struts and supports. That's what's coming now, I thought feverishly. Sweeping its broom over everything that's still left here.

I thought I could see the clouds rushing over the treetops like driven phantoms, the spruces swinging wildly back and forth in the dark, tossed to and fro by the wind that tugged and tore at them.

A lethal-sounding crash somewhere!

How can walls be so thin?

You must lie awake and be ready tonight, said the voice. If a fully-grown spruce should break, that will be the end of you. You can hear for yourself the roaring and creaking all around you now. Bellowing and blustering, the whole forest through.

Of course I can lie here awake, if that's all it takes. Chew resin and put my hands together for Veronika.

I stared at the scarcely discernible shadows flapping this way and that across the tent canvas. They seemed to be mocking me, darting at me from all directions and then vanishing just as swiftly. Then they came at me again, slapped the tent and were gone.

This isn't just any night, it's the night of dead souls tonight. Night of the blackcoats. Grandfather has risen from the unconsecrated ground to bid you farewell, the man they kept locked up all those years so you wouldn't have to see him. It's him swooping around out there with his raven-wing cloak; he's come to the rock to find out about Dower Farm and you, whether you've decided, once and for all.

Of course it is. This is your punishment for going off without permission again, always just running away.

I jumped. *Something moving beneath me –*

As if the ground itself was billowing or bulging, on the point of cracking open. The fen was collapsing in on itself, dragging the forest and farms down with it! Black chasms that have been waiting hundreds of thousands of years to open up and finally swallow everything, send every last thing sweeping downward. Now it's my turn to be despatched into the marshlogged peat that can only bury and preserve, never let anything rot to generate new life. I shall have to go down to my forefathers who lie there waiting with distorted, leatherlike faces, conserved like mummies in layer upon layer of bog since the beginning of time, covered in ash from Hekla and Laki. Unless the Lindworm's woken up! He knew there was going to be a storm tonight and wanted to be here when the lightning strikes for the last time. It's him rooting about and trying to get up through the soil, with that red-eyed pike's head of his, staring in all directions.

I could see him in my mind, rearing up on his tail, eyes staring wide, fired up by the storm like a rutting stallion, seven metres long and as thick as Mum's thigh, his body covered in sharp fish scales. The spikes running down his back and that forked tongue flicking in and out of his jaws.

From up by the invisible vent: The earth is not going to split open; it's just the roots of the spruces bracing themselves to hold the trees steady in the high wind. That's why the whole clearing is tossing and heaving like the sea, so the mighty trees won't blow down and kill you.

You and the ground are one.

You and the spruces, you and their roots –

Lie here tonight. Feel the rhythm of the spruces and let myself be rocked by it, become one with it, trust those elastic roots.

Was that more footsteps I could hear? That rustling and cracking, which wasn't the gale?

It's Johnny, come back to stick his knife through the side of the tent. Has he found out I saw him last spring, so he needs to get me out of the way while there are no human witnesses around? He's standing out there now, with that sneering grin, his earflaps down and his mouth full of snuff, brandishing his newly sharpened hunting knife.

I curled up in the very middle of the tent and pulled the blanket over my head – for protection I thought, vainly. I slid my hands between my thighs and listened to everything. The roar of the wind, the murmuring and drumming of the trees and the rain.

I felt like a caterpillar in a coal sack on a rocking ship. Thought to myself: if I survive this, I'll never just shove off again.

Like an obsession in the hour before dawn.

Beware of this one, Johnny had said. But I won't.

It's your turn to try it, commanded the voice. If you don't, something terrible will happen – and you'll be the one that has to live with the guilt, you'll have to bear it like a cross on your shoulders for as long as you live and you'll never be rid of it.

I switched on the torch, struggled out and went over to the dangerous fungus to pick as many as I could find. I wrapped myself in the blanket and sat in the tent opening like a buddha, cut the fungi into slices and dice and stirred them into the ice-cold pine-needle tea I had left. I drank it in small, even mouthfuls and helped with my fingers to make sure I got it all down. It tasted of forest and turpentine.

Was that all?

Sit there like a buddha with danger weighing in my stomach. Let the poison do its work and take its time.

Lie on the bed of spruce twigs and listen to the demented storm, wait for the thing no one knows anything about –

I am as big as a mountain and as sharp as a raven.
  You'll always be proud of me.

I awoke with wild animals in my guts. Starving beasts squeezing and wringing me to get the final drops, sharp-toothed jaws pulling and tearing and wanting their share of my poisoned intestines. I crawled to the tent opening and stuck my fingers down my throat, let it all come heaving out of me over and over again, meat hash and digestive juices, stinging right up into my nose; I hunched there on all fours and vomited like a fox, puked and spewed until there was nothing left.

The tent and the ground were swaying like the devil. The whole forest. The hydrochloric acid burned in my chest. My brain bubbled and writhed in agony. I lay down on my side and brought up the last of it, greeny-black. The convulsions ran through me in waves, seized hold and let go, squeezed and slackened, came and went incessantly, like bouts of inconsolable weeping. Thirst flickered like a ground fire, perpetually smouldering, impossible to extinguish, burning and destroying everything from the inside, invisibly.

Now I don't know what to do. Now my stomach is being wrenched inside out. Now my brain is exploding into tiny pieces. My intestines are shrivelling like worms in the desert.

It's because the poison is coming into its own. What you've already been through was a mere foretaste, but now the toxins have had time to get into my bloodstream and nervous system, into every cell and synapse. This is how it's going to feel before your guts wither and shrink, your muscles are paralysed, your throat swells and closes up, your airways are choked off. That's the way it goes for someone like you.

You're to vomit bile until you die.

Shimmering yellow and blue, the second I opened my eyes. Rainbows and soap bubbles reeling and roving at will across my field of vision. Hundreds of diaphanous snakelets trying to penetrate my skin. White-eyed Alsation dogs howling, the foam frothing from their shapeless jaws –

I can't stand any more of this! How can I make it stop? Help me make it all stop!

Give me a hand.

Anything.

Psshh –

Make it stop? Oh, but it's now we can really see what you're made of. The one who always keeps away and tries to get out of things, never lifts a finger or pulls his weight, just lives like a cuckoo on what other people have toiled to bring in – you surely don't think that anybody cares about you now? That there is a single human being or higher power which might feel sorry for you or sympathise with you? When you've refused to help your own parents and have let Alvar come and take Father's place?

You can lie there writhing and whimpering as much as you want, like the pointless insect you are. This is a fine time to beg and plead for forgiveness – when it's all too late anyway, the damage is done, it's all over. You'll have to take the consequences now.

Moan and groan and live off other people, that's all a slacker like you is good for!

Klas – – –

Are you there, Klas?

Today you're the one doing the writing. It's finally your turn to inscribe your name in Father's stone. You are to carve your letters as he once did. You haven't forgotten that it was why you came here, have you, that it was the intention behind all this?

There are seven-inch nails in the tent bag and big pebbles to strike with. It will be time when the sun is shining on the topmost spire of the tallest spruce.

But he's already standing there! Behind the black woodpecker's desiccated spruce. Standing there grinning with his canines extending way down his chin and gleaming, dangerous, empty eyes.

Of course he is, anybody can see it's him. He's come to make sure you do what you're meant to, as the day dawns. You can't find any excuses this time and make yourself scarce the way you usually do. Today is today.

By the way, it's you he's grinning at; he knows what it means to have your name in a rock like that and be glad it's nearly all over.

Can you see the way the hair has grown over his face? Matted grey hair up round his eyes and right down his neck, and his whole brow is covered. His nails sharpened into claws and his back rounded and bowed. That's how you're going to be. You'll be exactly like him, that's been the intention all along.

– – – *keeang-ank, keeang-ank-ank, keeang-ank* – – – *keeang-ank,*
keeang-ank-ank, keeang-ank – – –

The trumpeting of the wild geese from the fen. Males, females
and juveniles at once, all together in the unmistakeable goose
chorus.

I heard them through a distant haze, cackles and honks
coming and going, growing stronger and gently fading away,
depending on the wind. I thought I could see the skeins coming
through the mist one by one, like when we were grubbing in the
potato field and I would have given anything to turn into a goose.

It was broad daylight outside and the storm seemed infinitely
far off. For a moment I doubted whether it had existed at all.
Was it perhaps just another product of the dreams conjured up
by the evil substance?

I lay there looking up at the roof of the tent and let my
thoughts roam free, lost myself among all the needles and little
twigs that had blown down and stuck to the damp canvas,
looked for signs and patterns, was put in mind of constellations
and the clutter of bird footprints in the mud by the Marsh Pool
in spring. I clasped my hands behind my head, watched my
toes moving at the bottom of my sleeping bag, the furrow that
formed between my legs, my stomach rising and falling without
me thinking about it.

I had never been so thirsty in all my life. I had heartburn right up to my ears, and my guts were screaming from dehydration.

It didn't matter. I'm lying here now and it's all I want to do. Smell the fragrance of spruce twigs, hear the sighing of the wind, never need to die.

I boiled up some water from the stream and drank it spoonful by spoonful, lay there hour after hour with my head out of the tent and followed the clouds as they passed in procession, drank the water and saw the spruces swaying confidently to and fro as if nothing had happened.

Like a state of grace.

The goldcrests' cautious little whispers among the treetops, the wren rattling from the other side of the clearing as if he thought spring was already here.

To be allowed to lie here. To feel the wind on my cheek, fill my lungs with the fresh air, hear the murmur that runs through it all, all, all –

Suddenly, as if somebody had pointed and said there, and there, a whole phalanx of tits came sweeping out of the forest. A hundred birds alighted in the birch, thick necks jerking nervously, moved a few inches and set a branch swinging, put their heads childishly on one side and wondered who would dare to make the first move.

A bluetit with an extra-wide blindfold. He was there like a flash to grab a few seeds before zipping round the corner out of sight. Then a few great tits and a nuthatch darted down, and the ice was broken. Almost at once my well-laid table was alive with humming and whirring, birds flitted to and fro between the branches and the food or perched for a few seconds to feed before they had to move on. To and fro, up into the tree and hide in a crack. Down to fetch more. Peck open a few seeds. Crack a nut. Never a moment's rest.

I had been sitting there all weekend admiring the birdtable I had constructed and the wire hook device I had set up so it could hang outside the window rather than be fixed to a pole in the ground. Octagonal, like a summerhouse, with unobtrusive uprights and a column up the middle. The perfect gradient of the roof triangles, covered with roofing-felt overlapping the joins, and the shallow tray at the bottom with perches all round the edge.

Come and eat! Food's up! I've got ten kilos in the wardrobe and a long-handled soup-ladle to refill with. Hemp seeds and oats, peanuts and raisins in a special mix of my own. I've put out buckling for the woodpecker, like last year, thawed some cherries for the hawfinch and tied little sheaves of oats for the yellow buntings.

And I was as elated by all the blue tits, great tits and willow tits as if they were exotic rarities lured out of steaming tropical jungles; for me, the greenfinches and bullfinches were more vivid in their colouring than all the world's parrots and birds of paradise; I admired the pinky-red breast of the male redpoll, now resplendent in his adult plumage, as if it was my own creation.

By the gable end of the barn, Father's scrap mountain lay covered in fresh snow, as white and clean as baby powder. Of the iron and the rust there was nothing to be seen.

I was busy making a sketch of a three-dimensional model of the Plough and the other stars in the Great Bear that were of at least the fourth magnitude, converting light years into millimetres and trying to find a scale that would be suitable for a glass-bead mobile, when the phone in the hall rang and pricked the bubble.

Like a needle lancing a boil. The Christmas grind is over and people can risk ringing each other again.

But whoever would want to ring here, it suddenly struck me. Probably some distant relation I'll never meet, who sends a Christmas card every year out of duty and habit, and wants to check the Post Office has earned the price of the stamp.

'It's someone called Veronika?' Mum called up from the bend in the stairs.

I felt paralysed.

It can't be possible. Has she changed her mind and decided to come here after all? To live with Leo and go to school here? She's ringing from Upplands-Väsby to tell me she's coming.

'I'll take it in the front room,' I called, in a voice loud enough to reach the telephone receiver.

'Is it someone you know?' whispered Mum, blinking as I passed her.

I pulled the door to after me and hurried over to the phone, which stood there trembling with the power to decide everything. My heart was thumping as if it was about to jump out through my ribs.

'I haven't got a thing to do,' was how she started. 'It's totally dead round here. Can't we come up with something?'

So she's already here! Maybe she moved in when school finished for Christmas, and just hadn't let me know?

Are you starting with us this term, I almost couldn't stop myself asking.

Nice and easy. Little by little was the way to do it.

'Fine by me,' I faltered.

She was breathing rather loudly, snuffling as if she had a cold, or perhaps she'd been crying.

'I don't get how anybody could live here,' she said. 'Nothing happens, not a pissing thing.'

But that's soon going to change! The thoughts rushed through my head. You can come with me and put up nesting boxes if you want, or clean out the old ones and see if we find the sparrowhawk's larderful of field mice. We can lay out bait on the ice to attract the ravens, and watch through the telescope while they tear the meat into scraps, like the vultures in Africa.

'Shall we meet up tomorrow then?' she said again. 'Think of something to do, anything?'

'Sure.'

'You can come round here if you like.'

My hands were sticky with perspiration as I put the receiver back. I scarcely dared believe it was true.

There, that's it! She's already sitting there waiting, that's why she's come back to Bliss Cottage, to see you again.

That's how easy it is. Go around in an agony of not knowing all autumn. Then talk on the phone for three minutes.

I felt like a newly opened bottle of Pommac. I wanted to throw the window wide open and shout the news to everyone who had ears to hear with. Run out to Mum in the kitchen and tell it like it was: this spring wouldn't be like other springs.

It was white everywhere, white and sparklingly cold, so your nose glued up as soon as you breathed. The cold nipped at your cheeks. Tree trunks and fenceposts were shaggy with frost. Even the rusty barbed wire was glittering white, as well as the grass stalks and seed heads that were sticking up out of the snow. The spruces had their winter furs on and stood as unmoving as sentries along the sides of the road.

I felt as if I was part of a historic moment, as if by cycling here at just this time I was allowed to be in on something that would last forever, that my wheel tracks were being inscribed in a vast book and my breaths contained messages to another world.

The sky was ice-blue and immensely still, the columns of smoke were rising from the chimneys as straight as pipe cleaners and the seven-branched candlesticks were twinkling in the windows. Hare tracks wound across the fields, like secret nocturnal paths to aspen copses and autumn-sown rye.

I tried to summon to mind all the things I had rehearsed about Hesse and his work, in case Leo was in the mood. Apart from the factual information I had also chosen a passage from *Steppenwolf* and learnt it off by heart, to make an impression. I replayed it now, saying it over and over again with different expressions as I pedalled. 'He felt himself to be single and alone, whether as an odd fellow and a morbid hermit, or as a person removed from the common run of men by the prerogative of talents that had something of genius in them. Deliberately, he looked down upon the ordinary man and was pleased that he was not one.'

Like running water.

And again.

I can do it now, no matter how nervous I get.

And I've got a favourite quotation, too. Just you wait and see.

Veronika was standing at the kitchen window when I got there, waved hello and immediately disappeared, as if she had a surprise in store. My knees had stiffened up and my thighs were aching blocks of ice. My feet made a crunching noise as I walked up the path.

Indian mysticism, I thought. Ask him about that. How it comes over in the books.

It was Veronika who opened the door. She gave a shiver and hugged herself as she backed into the hall.

'You must have been freezing on your bike?' she said in a grown-up way.

I shook my head.

'As long as there's something to look forward to, you don't feel the cold.'

She gave a forced smile and made sure the door was properly closed behind me.

'Thank goodness you were home when I rang,' she said. 'I'm dying of boredom.'

'Home is basically the only place I ever am.'

'It may have been dull last summer, but it's nothing compared to this.'

'I know –'

I wiped my watery eyes. Everything was quiet out in the kitchen except for a transistor radio muttering something about

Adam and Eve. There were bowls of dates and walnuts, and a pile of books had cascaded across the table. The only Christmas decoration to be seen was a linked row of paper Father Christmases winding their way between the flowerpots on the windowsill, plus a couple of candles stuck in wine bottles.

Veronika started leafing vaguely through one of the books, poking at a join in the floorboards with her toe and saying nothing. She was wearing a striped jumper that stretched taut across her breasts.

She's still the same, I told myself. She hasn't changed in Stockholm, she'll come with me again to hear the night singers next summer. And she still talks the same, in that sort of natural, sing-song way, as if she never had to stop and think.

'Mum and Dad have gone for a long walk,' she said. 'So it's just us here.'

'U-huh,' I said, as noncommittally as I could.

'We can go up to my room if you like?'

I swallowed and felt myself go red. Up to her room straight away, as soon as I was through the door, before I'd even got my breath back. My face was starting to tingle. My cheeks were thawing and my earlobes felt as if someone was trying to set fire to them.

A mixture of wanting and not wanting.

'Why not,' I said, taking the plunge.

The room seemed bigger and more impersonal, the walls barer, but the advent star was shining in the window, as if time had stood still. A bit of make-up under the mirror, David Bowie in an apricot-coloured dress, reclining on a chaise longue on the LP sleeve. Veronika's bed was unmade. Her suitcase was open in the middle of the floor, the clothes thrown all over the place, knickers and tights strewn about as if she felt she could show me everything.

She curled up at the top corner of the bed with a pillow on her lap, like last time. Buttoned and unbuttoned the pillowcase, stroked the red embroidered flowers as if they meant something special to her. Flicked a look in my direction that I couldn't read. I sat down on the foot of the bed with my hands under my thighs. I couldn't think straight because it was just her and me and four walls. Everything I'd been thinking about all autumn, stuff I'd chewed on endlessly because she never got in touch, questions I'd turned over in my mind, again and again – now the whole lot was like a tangled ball of wool.

Had she in fact locked the door behind us?

'Quiet, isn't it?' I said.

'Do you think so?'

She put on the LP and tucked her feet up under her on the bed, humming the way she had in that checked chair at the library, fiddling with her bracelet. She hummed quietly, sort of to herself as if I didn't exist, picked at the pillow on her lap, whispered along to some of the lyrics, emphasised all the 'ee' sounds, followed the tune up and down. From the fretwork of holes in the advent star, little coins of light spread along the walls and up onto the ceiling in long rows. The further from the window they were, the larger, fuzzier and more extended they grew. On the wall opposite they disappeared completely, swallowed by the darkness.

I asked a bit about school and she answered yes and no and maybe, her mind clearly on something else.

Why wasn't she saying anything of her own? About that unforgettable night at Marsh Pool, the letters I'd sent and never received answers to, the months we'd been apart?

It was plainly something *else* bothering her. Something big that she couldn't come out with just like that, the thing she'd invited me over here to tell me.

'I'm getting some guinea pigs,' she said, looking down into her lap. 'The long-haired kind. Peruvian.'

She wasn't kidding.

'I'm going to feed them on carrots and hay. Have you ever seen a guinea pig eat carrots?'

I gave a desperate sort of smile. I picked up a belt from the floor and tested the pin in the various holes, tried to work out how much she'd grown since she bought it, experimented with rolling it up without leaving a hole in the middle.

'So you are coming to school here after all?' I asked in the end, unable to keep the question to myself any longer.

The blood pulsed at my temples.

My whole future.

'Since you'll have the guinea pigs, I mean,' I clarified. 'It's probably easier out here in the country?'

She just carried on sitting there, fiddling with the pillow, which she'd now taken halfway out of its case and found a loose end of thread to pull at. Presumably she felt a sudden urge to unpick seams.

Shouldn't think so, she said with a look, as if that was the stupidest thing I could have said at this point. With her mouth she said nothing, like she wanted to keep me on tenterhooks as long as possible, wind me slowly round her little finger.

The sense of bewilderment came over me again. Sitting here at either end of a bed with a wall of yes between us. As if all the longing served no purpose, just got in the way when you didn't need it any longer. I thought about Leo, thought about the tears that welled up when I handed him her flowers. I thought something must have broken inside him, something that might never be mended again.

Veronika was still playing with that bit of thread, pulling and tugging until the seam round the edge finally gave, then she worked open one corner of the pillow and plucked out a white feather, with which she gently stroked her cheek.

And that thing she still had pent up inside her? The whole reason why we'd had to come up to her room.

Out with it now! Just a little bit. Say I'm not like the others. Ask me to act as a brother or sister, anything you like. It doesn't matter if you stumble or have trouble getting to the point, if it doesn't come out quite as you'd planned.

'Do you believe in everlasting love?' she said.

I cleared my throat and tried to get her to look at me.

'I don't,' she answered for me. 'You can't help it if you fall in love with someone else. The ones who stay together all their lives are just frightened of change; you can't be in love with the same person for a hundred years. It's the ones who want to make something of their lives that get divorced.'

I nodded automatically and sat there with a sheeplike smile on my lips. I felt a hollow, rocking sensation as if I was on a raft. I stared at the frost patterns on the windows: billions of molecules petrified by the cold, ice crystals forming into stars, feathers, arrows and lines in all manner of symmetrical patterns, like secret messages from another time waiting to be decoded. Water molecules that have flowed in the rivers of the Amazon jungle, moistening the harpy eagle's palate as she stuck her claws into the black baby monkey, brought by the great current to Stoneacre and Veronika's window.

It's all been for nothing. She'll never come back here again.

What am I doing here? Shall I ask to lay my head in your lap for a while, ask if you can stroke my hair, wind a strand of it round your finger? Just for a minute?

'What did you get for Christmas?' she asked all of a sudden.

She looked alternately at me and at the pillow, from which she was now pulling more feathers.

Weird. From one instant to the next.

'We didn't really go in for it this year,' I answered honestly. 'There was nobody to dress up as Father Christmas. My father was ...'

'I got this jumper from Dad. Isn't it lovely!'

She came closer and held out her arm for me to feel the fabric. I had no sooner touched it than she shifted slightly, so my hand would make contact with her wrist.

A shiver ran through me.

And another –

There *was* something. That something that wasn't her.

She pulled her arm away and looked at me, a sharp, danger-ous look. Sat there for ages watching me through half-closed eyes, with something on the tip of her tongue. Then all at once she whacked the pillow, making the down fly. She kept on hitting it, ripped the seams open, emptied a great pile of feath-ers out between us, grabbed handfuls and tossed them up into the air as if she'd taken leave of her senses.

She was laughing excitedly. She threw more feathers, emptied out the pillow and tossed the last few up at the ceiling, letting them float down like snowflakes, to scatter their whiteness over the bed and us, and looked at me with those sharp eyes again.

A strange smile.

'Shall we take our clothes off?' she said.

Something leapt inside me.

She pushed a strand of hair back behind her ear. She looked ready to start any second. My throat constricted. I could feel the blush rising to my forehead.

There's the door.

Get out and be gone before her parents come back.

'How do you mean?' I stumbled.

'I don't know! Just take our clothes off. A sort of game.'

She pushed her hair back behind the other ear.

'Just something fun to do!'

Take our clothes off, here, her and me – as if nothing else mattered?

I could feel a tingling under my skin.

'You'll just make yourself unhappy if you take things so seriously all the time,' she said.

Her eyes on me all the time, like they were burning and dangerous.

From the corner: Why can't you ever simply join in, be spontaneous just for once? Are you going to hum and ha and hesitate all your life? What is there to lose, since she may not even be moving here? You'll never see her again.

'Do you want to see my new necklace, then?' she wheedled.

Before I had time to answer she'd pulled her jumper up to her neck to show me.

'Here. See?'

I couldn't believe my eyes.

That's what she's like – – –

And I'm allowed to see.

This is happening right now, it isn't a dream. We're sitting in her room with the door locked.

'Here!'

She held the jumper up with one hand and held the necklace out towards me with the other. Something silver on a long leather thong.

'Can you see what it is?'

I looked straight into her eyes and nodded, though I'd never seen anything like it before.

'A double-headed axe. From Greece. It was a present from Dad.'

I sat spellbound.

'It brings you good luck,' she said. 'Good luck in everything, including love.'

There was that smile again. Sharp and somehow poisonous, as if something uncontrollable was rushing through her. Or as if she was trying to trick me.

'Come on, look!'

She thrust the silver charm round to the back of her neck, pulled her jumper even higher and curved her chest out towards me. The thin, milky-white skin. The veins almost shining through, as if she was illuminated from inside. The hard, textured, flesh-coloured nipples.

Look at her.

She's ready for anything – – –

'Can you see?' she demanded. 'Come on, look! Daren't you look, is that it!'

I gave a laugh, an involuntary, idiotic laugh.

Here's your chance, the voice whispered in my ear. This is what you've been longing for all your life, fantasised about at night ever since the two of you parted at the sawmill. Ask if you can touch her, just once, find out how that softest of all soft places feels.

No.

She isn't herself any more, anyone can see that. Something's got into her, something's not as it should be.

What's that strange smile you've got, Veronika? Why are you doing this? Are you another person now?

Tell me you are.

Tell me you aren't!

'Forget it,' she said.

Gone.

I stared at the stripes on her jumper. Like a curtain that had fallen forever before the first performance had even started.

'Now it's your turn,' she said simply. 'You've got to show me, as well. Fair's fair.'

Light-headedly I pulled my thick sweater and vest up to my chin and looked down at my sunken stomach with ribs sticking out as if I was malnourished. Skinny, as pale as boiled ling, not a trace of hair or a hint of muscle. That stupid birthmark above my navel.

Veronika sat there calmly, looking, but she didn't laugh at me. She just looked, in an earnest, adult sort of way. As if she could take care of me.

'That's cheating,' she said after a bit. 'You've got to take your trousers off, too.'

'Take off my trousers?' came a voice like a parrot's.

'You're a boy.'

My thoughts were tumbling around my overheated brain. I undid my belt, didn't really know what I was doing any longer. Veronika was still calmly sitting there, her hands under her thighs as if to show me she wasn't going to do anything.

Go on, her nod told me, your flies as well, take it at your own pace. We're not in any hurry.

Some kind of barrier in me. Something intervening.

'I can't, not yet –,' I cheeped.

She pulled a weary face.

'Can't what? Why not yet?'

Somebody banging on the wall? Footsteps across a floor, hinges squeaking?

'Hello?'

It was Helena.

'We're here!' called Veronika, sounding normal again.

'We?'

'Klas is here. We're up in my room!'

I hastily buttoned up my trousers and refastened my belt.

Veronika moved back to her corner and tucked her jumper into her waistband, put a little cushion on her lap as if to cover herself. All around us there were drifts of feather and down, as soft and silky as angels' wings, as white as unfallen snow.

Don't ask me, she said with her eyes, I don't know what happened. Now everything's like it was before.

I was sweating under the arms, feeling relieved and swindled at the same time, pitched to and fro between the two. I could have got to see all of Veronika as she was. She would have stood there on the floor in front of me, naked and defenceless with her arms hanging at her sides. Her thick hair waving down her back.

Like a promise.

This is what I'm like, this is how I was made. You'll have to take me as I am.

Nothing – – –

'Are you really off home already?' said Helena. 'You're welcome to stay and eat with us if you want.'

There was no sign of Leo.

'I've got to get back, I'm afraid,' I said blindly.

Get anywhere. Out into the freezing cold where you belong. Back to the deep bog behind the sawmill to see if the Marsh Wife sticks her hand out this time.

'Well it's up to you, of course,' said Helena with a friendly shrug.

'I've promised to help out at home,' I lied. 'We've got live-stock to look after.'

Veronika said nothing. She'd poured a glass of carrot juice and was drinking it in a quiet, self-contained way as if it was nothing to her whether I stayed or not, or as if I'd had my chance but failed the test.

I closed the front door firmly behind me and hurried over to my bike beneath the solitary lamppost. Veronika was at the window looking out, just as she had been when I arrived, but she didn't wave goodbye. She stood there with the palm of her hand pressed against the pane and stared stiffly ahead of her, as if she was playing dead. Kept her hand in the same position, like a sign.

The frost flowers on the window, the white lace curtain, her smooth, pale face dimming a little more each time she breathed out.

Never being able to sleep. Going out to talk to the sleep-befuddled pigs in the middle of the night or lying alone, summoning up mental images of child psychiatric units.

I wound myself in the sweaty sheets and thought of boys with short-cropped hair and delayed puberty compulsively chanting nonsense or laughing to themselves in a clucking, hysterical way, twisting their hands spastically out of joint and smearing their faces with excrement, hurling themselves into walls and floors or tied down on narrow beds with green rubber mattress covers, naked so the attendants could come and masturbate them at nights in the hope that they'd reach sexual maturity one day.

Enuresis nocturna –

All the stars out there behind the blind, the silhouette of the bare, drooping birch branches against the window, the cold ticking in the walls.

Who would imagine it could be so quiet?

I changed the sheets and went down to make myself some hot milk with honey. Sat down on the fifth chair and drank it, nauseated by the rank pigsty smell that had impregnated the seat cushions and the whole kitchen. I was drumming Father's rhythm against my thigh without thinking about it, as if I had it in my blood.

Mum's lying in there asleep, all on her own in the double bed with the bedspread of crocheted squares still on Father's half, lying on her back with her palms turned upwards like when she was floating in the bathing lake that time. The alarm clock rings at five and the animals are waiting. Feeding, milking and mucking out for the ten thousandth time. Then see to the pigs and hens and empty the mouse traps for the cats.

I went and put my ear to the crack between the door and the frame. Heavy, relaxed, open-mouthed breathing, as if nothing could happen to her. I felt an urge to open the door and slip in, tiptoe over to the bed and stand there for a little while, see her chest rise and fall, accustom my eyes to the dark and see if she's wearing a nightdress, and if she's thrown off her covers in her sleep.

Your mum. The person who's done all she can, everything that's within her minimal power.

She's lying in there now, on the other side of the door. She isn't afraid; she can sleep without locking her door. She's breathing and dreaming we've sold Dower Farm and are going on holiday for the first time.

That time she put her hand on Father's arm and asked:

'Can't we take a few days off this summer? Go somewhere we can swim and have a bit of a break?'

'You know as well as I do that there's no such thing as time off in this place.'

'When the hay's in? Gotland maybe?'

'Pssh!'

I washed up my cup without a sound, put it away in the cupboard and went back upstairs. Lay down on my side and pulled my knees up to my chest, clasped them as hard as I could, feeling like an undeveloped foetus that should never have been born. I was longing for Mum to come and take my temperature like she did when I was little, lubricate the rounded end and push the mercury up as far in as she dared. The sweet smell of Nivea, her soothing hand on my hip, the feeling of having something dangerous inside you –

Who would have thought one could feel so alone?

Are the stars chiming like crystals tonight? Are the telephone wires singing now, is it cold enough out there? Singing for the spruces and the hares, and for the foxes who hear everything.

It was Veronika and her face.
I didn't know –

Like another person, she'd said. Different medication. That it would all be fine if they'd just let him home.

Like before. Start all over again.

I sat at my desk, biting my nails. Down by the pigsty the magpies were building this year's nest. Arranging the twigs they'd collected, continually bobbing their long tails, flapping about and making up to each other like a couple in love. For some reason they'd abandoned the house down by the road and started building afresh in the knotty Dung Birch. The male was forever flying off to the edge of the forest for building material, while the female perched in the nest to take delivery and tuck in place, inserting twigs at various angles or substituting new ones, taking charge of the construction project while he had to make do with the role of helper.

It was still January when I saw them flying in with the first sticks, as if to stake their claim to the best forked branch, but now they'd started in earnest, presumably knowing somehow that she would be sitting on eggs in two months' time.

Father got out of the car with a cigarette wobbling in his mouth and stood there surveying the weather. His moustache was gone and his face was as clean-shaven as in the wedding photograph on the bookcase. He looked up at the sky, into the forest, over to the fen, down to the Canal. It was neither overcast nor clear, everything was wrapped in a strange haze that almost swallowed up the tops of the spruces on the other side of the pasture. The sun spread an unreal, silvery-yellow light across the sky.

Father turned round and took a long, slow look down at the cowshed as if to retrieve something from his memory. He advanced a couple of steps towards the snow-covered scrap pile but then stopped, as if caught doing something foolish.

Mum turned the car and parked it the way it was always supposed to be when he was home, pointing in the right direction ready to drive off. Together they got out the cases and then they came this way, her first and Father a few metres behind, as if to be obstinate, or as if disowning himself.

'Anybody home?'

It was Mum calling, her voice happy and expectant, but I couldn't bring myself to answer. So Göran wasn't answering either? Locked in his room probably, laying out Idiot's Delight as usual. Father said nothing; he wheezed and coughed loudly, and seemed to think that was enough of a greeting. The cold air and cigarette smoke came streaming up the stairs.

I knelt down and smoothed out the edges of the rag rug, making sure the fringed ends were lying parallel and none of them had got tangled or were touching each other if they belonged to different knots.

It's going to be all right, the voice whispered reassuringly. You needn't be frightened any more, everything is as it should be.

When I came down to the kitchen he was sitting in his place with the newspaper open in front of his face like a detective, whistling tunelessly through his teeth to keep the silence at bay. Mum had her checked apron on like before and was frying ribs and cutting bread, steadying the loaf against her stomach.

Göran had found his dummy again and was sitting there kicking his feet in mid-air.

A string being pulled taut.

Sitting diagonally opposite each other at the same table. Not knowing what to do with my eyes or hands.

He rustled the newspaper and cleared his throat as if he was about to say something, tell us how he'd been, how it felt to be home again, maybe ask what *we'd* been doing.

'Now they're claiming there are more stars in space than grains of sand in the Sahara desert,' he said from behind the paper. 'That surely can't be possible?'

Was it the same voice as before? Wasn't there a touch of insecurity and entreaty in it, something conciliatory that said then was then and now is now? The very fact that he was asking rather than stating.

'It sounds well nigh incredible?' said Mum, over by the stove. 'What do you think, Klas? You're the one who knows everything.'

'Though where they found someone with time to count them all I can't imagine,' added Father, peering at me over the top of the paper.

'It'd certainly be tricky. I think they make mathematical calculations on the basis of the speed of light and its invisible radiation.'

He nodded.

'I think so too,' said Göran, still not tired of swinging his legs.

Father lowered the paper and regarded him with surprise, as if he wondered what on earth he had in front of him. A big boy with a dummy in his mouth. A boy who's going to have to retake his whole first year if he can't learn to sit still in class.

Mum was suddenly behind me, bending over my shoulder.

'Are you going to sit there chewing your fingers to shreds at your age?' she whispered. 'We might almost think you were nervous? See how you've made them bleed.'

'Don't worry about him,' came the comment from behind the newspaper. 'He'll cope, like I've always had to.'

I thrust my hands in under my thighs and looked at the snow dancing round outside, as if exempt from the force of gravity. Down in the cowshed, the light was already on. I caught glimpses of Alvar through the windows, a dark shadow moving about inside.

In the middle of the meal, Father put down his fork and tapped the underside of the table. He looked craftily at Göran and me as he chewed.

'I've got something here that might be of interest,' he said, nodding down at the fifth chair.

Mum's face brightened.

'Well that's not half bad?'

'They were meant as Christmas presents really, but things don't always turn out the way you want in this life. And better late than never; it wasn't much of a Christmas for me this year, as you may know.'

He brought out two parcels with bells and fir sprigs on the wrapping paper, and gold string round them.

'A little one for the big fellah and a big one for the little fellah,' he said, bowing as we took them.

Göran's was so big he had to lie down on the floor to open it. He ripped off the paper and stumbled over to Mum to show her an orange life jacket with a whistle on the chest. My parcel contained a pair of ice claws with turned wooden handles, and a leather cord linking them together.

'They're juniper,' Father nodded to me. 'They'll last you all your life.'

'Well that's not half bad,' Mum said again, switching on a smile.

'Let's hope you never need them,' said Father. 'But if you do get into trouble they could mean the difference between life and death, if anyone cares about that.'

'Shake hands and say a nice thank you, boys,' said Mum.

Father made a dismissive gesture; he wasn't finished yet. He reached for a bag and put a smoke detector in the middle of the table.

'That's for all of you,' he said.

'It's to wake you up if you're asleep when a fire starts,' Mum explained to Göran.

He nodded gravely.

'Had Klas better have it then?' he said. 'He sleeps with the ear protectors on.'

'Oh, we'll put it up in the hall where everybody can hear. Everybody needs to wake up if something's burning.'

There was feverish activity going on inside Göran's forehead.

'Why should something be burning?' he said, in a voice that didn't seem intended for anyone to hear.

'I thought I'd put it up straight away,' said Father. 'Trouble generally strikes when you're least expecting it. Sooner or later, everything burns.'

Who wants to lie awake under a wide-open eye? Have it trained on you whatever you do. A watchful, menacing eye that just gawps and glares, never blinks or looks away – like a hole into the void.

A black eye, boring blackly into blackness.

The very thought sent a shiver down my spine. It was as if it *wanted* something from me now, this very moment. As if my time had come.

You mustn't look at the eye tonight, the voice told me urgently. However tempting it seems. If you do, something will happen – and you won't be the only one to suffer.

Lying there waiting for what mustn't happen. Thinking about rope ladders and fire extinguishers, registering every movement and sound in the house.

Is there something brewing down there? Are things quietly building up to disaster? Is someone teetering on the brink? Wandering up and down, licking his mouth and biting his lips to shreds.

Time drags incomprehensibly slowly in the middle of the night. A snail in a kilometre-long pipe. Four sleepless people in the same house. The air hanging, quivering, behind locked doors. Clock hands that seem to have stopped.

Pretend nothing's happened.

The rats and mice are on their way now. That's the scuffling and scratching in the walls. The brown rats with their chisel teeth, eating their way through everything.

Come to me.

Crawl in under the covers and warm yourselves this cold night. After all I'm only lying here, waiting for time to pass. I can undress if you want to smell me or taste a bit, sniff at my orifices, lick my holes and creases clean, drink my body fluids, see what I really look like.

I'll lie here naked for you all tonight if you'll only come to me.

I've got it here. Xray 62 86 43, Yankee 14 42 61.

Dower Farm, Planet Earth.

This is my location: a minimal black square on the Swedish Grid. 6286.4 kilometres north of the equator, 1442.6 kilometres east of Greenwich, 148 metres above sea level. This is where my four walls, my floor and my ceiling are. I shall never live here.

If only I could lie among spruces and hares. Hold my breath for the tawny owl's mating call at night. Sleep with a soughing in my ears, sense the wind in the grass, never need to lock myself in.

The house smelt of butchering. That sweetish, ever so slightly putrid smell of raw pork that made you think of yellow pigskin with the bristles still on. Mum was standing there with her cardigan sleeves rolled up, mixing the filling for the smoked sausage in a big white enamel pail, thrusting her hands into the minced meat to work in the spices and barley grains with a squelching sound. The chunks of pig's head and liver were each boiling in their separate pans on the stove, and the intestines were all in a bright yellow washing-up bowl, waiting to be used as sausage skins. Piles of chops and ribs, pork pieces and knuckles, the hams ready for fine mincing and a big dish of blood for tonight's black porridge.

'There's enough to fill the freezer here,' said Mum. 'It should last us through the summer, just you see.'

She looked at me and at all the work she had done, probably wondered if I was going to help with anything, but as usual she couldn't quite bring herself to ask. It was as if she'd rather do it all herself than ask anyone for anything. As if she didn't want to be beholden.

'Almost all of it can be put to use if you've a mind to,' she said, frowning at the chopped offal she was going to make into lung hash, Grandma's recipe.

At that moment the door was wrenched open and Father came panting in, boots and all. He wiped the sweat from his brow and looked for something to fix his eyes on.

'It's no good,' he said. 'We'll have to pull the calf out.'

He looked at Mum with an expression on his face that said he had to have help but knew he had forfeited the right to ask for it. His hands were bloody and he had that black leather thumbstall on his ring finger.

'I'm a bit tied up, as you can see,' Mum said half-heartedly. 'Has it got to be this minute?'

He flapped his arms despondently.

'I can't sort this out. Everything's just piling up for me now.'

Mum said nothing. She just went over to the cleaning cupboard and took out his bottles of pills, then carried on with her sausage mixing.

'That's the last time I'm asking for anything in my own house,' he said. 'Just so you all know.'

His mouth puckered as if he had a nasty taste in it.

A sudden thrill, like a shooting pain, of wanting and not wanting.

'I'll come out with you,' I heard myself say. 'I can eat later.'

Father shot me an astonished look, and there was a sudden gleam of light about him.

'So you're ready right away?'

The distended heifer was lying in the stall nearest the door to the muck heap, groaning hard. She had a big white patch on her coat that looked like Gotland, but a bit rounder than the real thing. Maybe more like Lake Vänern in fact. The calf's front hooves were already sticking out of her, helpless and sort of pleading, like a pair of hands sticking out of a hole in the ice. Father had tied a rope round them and nodded down at the heifer as if to show who was to be the centre of attention.

'It's her first time. She's too narrow. That's why it's stuck. And she won't stand up, either.'

He went to get his pipe from the window recess, tapped it against the heel of his boot, then relit it and puffed. He scrutinised me a touch too long, as if to say that a down jacket and Lovikka mittens weren't suitable cowshed wear, but he didn't say anything. Presumably he was just grateful I'd come out with him. I could feel the steam rising from the heavy bodies. I liked the scent of the pipe smoke blending with the animal smells.

'She's called Beauty, too,' Father said. 'Like the one Our Lord did away with under the Spreading Oak last summer. We'll have to see what he wants this time round.'

I stood a bit behind him and to one side, to show I was ready but awaiting instructions. Waves were running through the heifer, invisible spasms clenching and relaxing, but they weren't the proper contractions, Father said. We'd have to wait a while and see.

Standing here, him and me, as we never have before. Listening to the drip of the water tap.

The cows were lying in their places along the shed, chewing the cud and waiting to be milked, indolent and bloated, in a kind of semi-slumber and apparently taking no interest in the outcome of the calving. Hanging above each stall was the cow's black chalkboard, recording its name and number, birth date and milk yield, and which bull had sired it.

A picture of Johnny came into my mind. What he'd been doing back in the spring. Why there are calves born with five legs or two heads. Whether it might be a monster whose life we were saving.

'It's high time we extended,' said Father, pointing with his pipe to show me what he was planning. 'Move the wall back eight or ten metres and the outer gable end the same. Five or six extra stalls we need, if this business is going to turn any kind of profit in the longer term.'

I looked for at least some hint of a smile on his face, but he was clearly serious.

'And a decent-sized new machinery shed next summer. And a combine harvester by the autumn. I'll help you out as much as I can. I've talked to the bank and sent for the forms from the County Agricultural Board.'

He sucked on his pipe, blew the smoke out of one side of his mouth in contented little puffs. A flourishing family firm seemed to have taken shape in his blind imagination. He saw us leasing extra land elsewhere, buying more livestock and bigger machinery, working together as father and son to make sure we would have a farm to hand down through the generations.

'You'll be well set up and in harness by the time I hand over for good, at any rate.'

He turned his head slowly and nailed me with his glassy stare. Perhaps he was demanding an answer? Perhaps he had caught himself out and could suddenly see the absurdity of what he'd just said? The next moment there was a muffled bellow from the heifer. It was as if the pains had taken her now, held her in their violent grip and would finally free her from the doubled-over calf. Her legs were twitching as she lay there, her womb and belly contracting in great convulsions. Her tail was erect, curving upward.

'Ready then?' cried Father and jumped up.

He passed me the end of the rope, braced his feet against the manure gutter and gave it all he'd got.

'Right, pull, this is it!'

And we pulled until our knuckles were white, wrapped the rope round our wrists and swung back and forth as if we were in a tug of war with death, Father in front and me a metre behind him.

'*And heave –*' he swung. '*And heave –*'

Half the front legs and the muzzle out, and Beauty bellowed and writhed, tossing her head and rattling her tether – but then everything stopped, the spasms settled, and the contractions ebbed away.

'It's no good,' said Father, throwing down the rope.

He wiped the sleeve of his boiler suit across his nose and shook his head dejectedly, as if there was no hope. An inarticulate cry of dissatisfaction rose from Beauty.

'You'll have to get the tractor,' he said.

I looked at him, bewildered.

'This calf's got to come out! Otherwise we'll have to get the vet over to saw it up *in situ*. If we don't want to lose them both.'

I unhitched the trailer and backed up between the muck heap and the cowshed wall, backing as close to the door as I dared. Father had extended the rope with a chain. He came out and fastened it straight to the tow bar.

'Now you go forward a bit so the chain's taut to start with,' he instructed. 'Take it nice and easy.'

I slowly raised the clutch and eased the tractor forward as gently as I could.

'Then you want bottom gear and just let it tick over. If your foot slips on the clutch you'll split her open and the whole thing will go to blazes. You're only going forward about twenty centimetres all told.'

He lit a cigarette and went back in. I slid even further down in the seat and pressed the clutch to the floor with all my weight, checked for the tenth time that it was first gear I'd engaged and thought about needing to take up the slack double quick. My left leg was shaking like an aspen leaf.

The calf and the rope and me, I thought. This is really it.

Father popped his head out and gave the signal: the contractions had started again. I was trembling as I raised the clutch, as cautiously as if there was a lighted fuse attached to it. I kept my eyes fixed on the front wheel, waiting for it to move.

'Steady! Steady!' I heard from the cowshed.

And the tractor wheels turned, millimetre by millimetre. The patch of snow on the tyres was just reaching the rounded crest and about to vanish down the other side. How far had I pulled the calf now? I crawled forward, feeling no resistance, thinking that the rope would be sure to stretch, crept infinitely gently.

'Woah, stop! For Christ's sake! It's coming!'

I turned off the engine and ran in with my heart in my mouth to see the calf lying there in the manure gutter, wet and shiny with its coat all matted.

Is it alive?

Father raised its head and put his fingers in its mouth, trying to keep the airways free. The heifer that was now a cow staggered to her feet and turned round with surprised and vacant eyes. She had a slimy string of yellowish membranes and blood dangling out of her.

'It's going to make it,' said Father.

And the calf began to show signs of life. It gave a little sneeze and started sucking on his fingers, thinking they were teats; tried to get to its feet but collapsed in a heap and lay there all long-haired and wet with big, sort of springy-looking ears. Father untied the rope round its front legs and carried it like a child in his arms over to the pen that he'd cleaned out and lined with a thick layer of straw. He knelt down and rubbed its coat dry, letting it suck his fingers as much as it wanted, one or two at a time, to encourage its sucking reflex even though it would never suckle.

'It's a heifer calf,' he said. 'She had a caul, just like you, Klas. You have to open it up pretty damn quick.'

'So it won't have to be slaughtered? If it's a her?'

He looked up.

'This one'll be a dairy cow. You could have it for fifteen years. Give her half an hour and she'll be able to stand up.'

Then he knocked three times on the hay trough on the wall, opened the calf's mouth again and blew long, deep breaths into it.

'That's what Father always did,' he said. 'It's meant to bring luck, so they say.'

I smiled at him and he nodded in return. He stood up and took off his cap, as if about to pray. He pushed his hair back off his forehead and looked meditatively out of the dirt-choked window, watching the snow that came drifting down in the reflection from the ceiling light.

'That means beestings pancake for pudding tomorrow,' he said. 'Like that, do you?'

A smile came over him. For a moment he looked as if he was trying to resist, but it came anyway, washing on of its own accord.

'Yes,' I said. 'It's not half bad.'

He lit his pipe and nodded in agreement. The calf tried to get up again, determined to stand on its own two feet as if it was born to run, only to crumple once more and lie there with an appealing look at Father.

Was that moisture in his eyes? Was he so pleased that the calving had gone well, the heifer was all right and the newborn calf was healthy?

'Beestings pancake with blackcurrant jam, that's the stuff, eh?' he said, nudging me in the arm.

I looked surreptitiously down at his red, swollen hand holding the gate and felt like touching it, gently stroking the knotted veins with my fingertips, feeling the leathery skin.

Soon I will, in just a little while. But you've got to promise not to be cross with me.

'So there we are,' he said. 'That's the fun over for this time.'

He climbed out of the pen and put his cap back on. From Beauty over on the far side came a desolate mooing in response, sort of broken and desperate, as if she wondered where her calf had got to.

You mustn't listen to the Salesman, promise me that.

He should be sent to Bog Island to count ravens, that's what. He'll stoop to anything if he has to.

Father gave a little cough and knocked on the door for the first time in what must have been several years. A thought rushed through my head: he wants to talk about my future. About Dower Farm and me and us.

I put my book face down and took a deep breath before I turned the key. He advanced into the middle of the room with a bag in his hand and scanned the walls as if to check something, or as if he'd forgotten what my room looked like.

'I'm reading about the lammergeier in the Himalayas,' I said accommodatingly. 'The most feared and admired bird that's ever existed. He drops bones onto mountain ledges so he can get the marrow out. A Swedish author's been there; he lived in the valley of the Buddha.'

Father nodded without interest. Extinguished his cigarette between finger and thumb and dropped the butt into his breast pocket. The radiator was bubbling and rattling away. His eyes were puffy and red-rimmed, the whites pink from sleepless nights or pills. A lump shifted in my stomach.

'I've got something here that you ought to be a bit interested in,' he said. 'If there's room for anything but birds in that head of yours?'

I forced out a smile and sat down again. In the bag he had a box of matches and a posh leather album with gold corners and his name printed on the front, sort of embossed into the actual cover like the lettering on the cover of a book.

'Most of them were taken here at Dower,' he said. 'You're in a few of them yourself, towards the end.'

He leant over my shoulder and opened the first page. Four black and white photos, each in their own frames, with something written under each one. Thin black ink, meticulously neat handwriting.

'That's my grandfather,' he said, pointing to a solemn-looking man with a middle parting and a Stalin moustache. 'He's the one I was named after. He died the same week I started school.'

I nodded dutifully, looked at the photograph and at Father's hand and wondered why he was keeping it on the picture for so long. I felt as if I'd never seen a bigger finger.

'You don't look all much like each other,' I said, meaning it as a compliment.

He didn't answer. Just breathed heavily by my ear, smelling of cowshed, hair tonic and cigarette ends.

'There were twelve children in that family,' he said. 'Their mother died when the youngest was born. Things weren't that easy back in those days, either. You're named after his father. He was called Klas.'

He lit another cigarette and carried on turning the pages, lingering over every picture as if he wanted me to read the captions and learn them all off by heart. Old gents and biddies with starched collars and permed hair, all very upright, their faces as scared as if it was the vicar behind the camera. A woman with her hands clasped in her lap and the kitchen table covered in flower arrangements; a man in a traditional Småland waistcoat and fur cap, out in the field with a horse-drawn seed drill. Then there were a couple of pictures of a young Father, slim and blond with a side parting and his hair combed flat, dressed for best in knee socks and a short-sleeved shirt buttoned right up at the neck. He was standing up straight with his fiddle in one hand

and bow in the other, laughing as if it was the most natural thing in the world.

'I'm about like you in that one,' he said, turning the page.

He stopped instead at a picture of some men in black hats and women in headscarves, lined up in front of a haystack holding scythes and rakes.

'That was how they did the haymaking back then,' he said. 'It's taken over at Calfpatch when they still cut the watermeadows. It was backbreaking, everything, in those days.'

'Yes, I can imagine.'

'There's the last picture of Father,' he said, putting his finger on a shrunken old fellow with a stick, under an apple tree. 'I'll never forget when they came to get him, he grabbed the top of the bed and they dragged the whole bedstead with him when they pulled him by the feet. He wanted to die at home.'

Father opened the window and knocked the ash off his cigarette, letting in cold air, and gestured to me with his other hand to carry on looking through the album myself. Pig killings and funerals; Grandfather's fiftieth birthday party at the Temperance Hall and Grandma's annual midsummer bath in the washtub behind the cowshed; sewing bees and parish catechetical meetings; a working party to raise the frame of the new pigsty, with the topping-out wreath up on the roof truss.

'There's a thing or two for you to look at in there,' he said, stepping to one side, as if presenting me with the album as a duty to be carried on. 'These are all your forefathers, think of that. If that's anything you might be interested in.'

I gave an involuntary smile. The next minute he was out of the room and on his way down the creaky stairs.

'Take lots of pictures!' he called back. 'Or one day you'll find it's too late.'

I went on leafing through the album, even though that must have been what he wanted. Stiff, yellowing sheets with grease-proof paper dividers, everything as neat and proper as in a book in a parish register, not a crossing out or an ink blot to be seen. I was there in some of the colour photos later on, sitting with Granny in the garden stripping currants off their stalks, helping Grandad earth up potatoes, or learning to swim with Father's hands at my waist. He had deathly pale legs and swimming trunks that were too small, bushy sideboards and hair that straggled way down the back of his neck. He was astride me, laughing into the camera, holding his hands at an angle so it looked as if he was about to press me down under the water as a joke. I didn't recognise myself in the picture; I must have repressed every second and felt it might just as well have been somebody else staring at me with petrified eyes.

Right at the back, a photograph of a football team was tucked in among postcards from the emigration museum in Växjö, and of the Treaty of Brömsebo. 'Series winners Div. VI Virdinge,' it said along the bottom. Twelve players and a bald coach, yellow jerseys, white shorts, black socks, old boots. The picture was square, the colours semi-bleached by time or the sun. The goal-keeper in the middle, his gloves on the ball. Out at the right-hand end stood Father, looking about twenty, thin faced and apparently as happy as the rest, but he was some way from the teammate next to him. They all seemed to have squeezed up as close as they could, squatting knee against knee or standing shoulder to shoulder to show they belonged together and had won the series as a team, but Father was standing on his own and didn't know what to do with his hands. Maybe he wasn't laughing either; maybe it was just a mask he'd put on, so the picture would get into the paper. Maybe he'd been the perpetual substitute, always waiting for someone to be sick or injured. The twelfth man, the bookish boy who wanted to be like all the rest. The boy who should have been a clergyman.

I shut the album firmly and sat there staring out of the window, as if struck by a vast emptiness. I stayed there, unmoving, for what must have been half an hour, looking at the tractor with the front loader that I'd had rides in when I was little, sitting there with my legs dangling over the edge, terrified that he'd release the bucket and not have time to brake; looking at the seed drill under the snowladen tarpaulin, the barbed wire fence that served no purpose as it rusted away there, the scrubby birches with the witches' brooms, the muck heap where the crows had gathered round a stillborn piglet.

Something had me in its grip. A pumping heat was gradually overpowering me from inside, as if someone had flicked a switch, brought a hidden fury back to life. I felt like wrecking something, punching my fist through the wall, breaking my foot with a kick to the chimney breast, throwing the window open so hard that it smashed into a thousand bits, tearing open the scab on my wrist and letting the blood spurt out.

I locked the door and walked round the room, circuit after circuit like a fired-up boxer on his way into the ring. I didn't know what to do. I picked up the coaching prize from boys' camp and hurled it as hard as I could into the mirror. The wall mirror that had been a christening present from Grandfather and Grandma and had hung on its hook all my life, remembering what it had seen.

Gone.

I lay down on the bed and let my gaze bore into the black eye on the ceiling. It just stared back, unremitting and ruthless, like a hole into evil and the void.

Like something pulling at you.

Forcing you to creep down to the cellar to check the shotgun and the elk rifle are in their places, that there are no marks in the dust round the lock of the gun rack.

To open the case of ammunition and count the cartridges in box after box but leave no sign of having been there.

'You don't seem to be eating much these days,' said Mum. 'You won't grow into a proper man if you don't eat?'

'I'll have to be something else then. Gynaecologists and astronomers don't have to be all that strong.'

She stuck out her bottom lip by way of answer, scrutinising me side-on with a mildly sorrowful look in her eyes.

'You're as thin as a rake,' she said. 'People might start thinking there's no food on the table here.'

Father looked up, as if roused from his reveries about wind and weather. He had been sitting there a long time, alternately tapping the barometer and looking up at the sky, tapping and looking up again to see if there'd been any change. Then he closed the oilcloth notebook and bored his eyes into me as if he was about to interrogate me. Something in the photo album, I immediately thought. The names of family members, what year this or that happened, who drowned themselves and who was appointed a lay assessor, who I think I am.

I picked up the paper to have something to fix my eyes on, ate my sticky porridge, adding the cold milk a few drops at a time so it wouldn't feel as if it was warm from the cow. My eye fell on an announcement about the inventory of songbirds at Marsh Pool that I was going to take part in over the summer. I'll finish the windbreak under the thickest spruce and go and take up residence there if Veronika doesn't come back, go out and count the songbirds, hoping for some Savi's warblers and river warblers, get to see the great reed warbler for the first time. Lie alone at nights waiting for the boom of the bittern, the African mimicry calls of the marsh warbler, the flitting shadows of the bats.

Father was staring at me intently, lips parted, as if ready to pounce any second, but nothing came. Just a slight twitching at the corner of his mouth.

'How about going out on our skis today, Klas, just you and me?' he said finally. 'The snow's just right, we may never get such a good chance again.'

Mum gave him a look of surprise. He seemed to me to be talking in an unnaturally slow, monotone voice, as you might to an ill person.

'Could you take both boys with you, in that case?' she said, putting her head on one side. 'Göran's big enough to go skiing now, isn't he?'

She reached over and stroked his arm as if to appeal to him, but he took no notice. He just stared straight ahead as if she didn't exist.

'Today it'll just be me and Klas,' he said to the wall.

It was completely still outside. The fine flakes of powdery snow lay like a mute covering over everything. Not even the plough ridges were visible, nor the road down to the Canal, nothing. Even the sky was as white as an eternity.

We made our way across the ditch and stopped side by side with the tips of our skis pointing out over the boundless fen. Our lungs were sending smoke out of our mouths. I was possessed by a strange sense that something was going to happen, though I couldn't explain why. In the mid-distance I could make out the clump of alders by the Canal as an ash-grey silhouette, but that was as far as you could see through the falling snow. The church spire that usually stuck up above the spruces to the north west was entirely hidden.

'We can go any way we want,' said Father and smiled a quivery smile. 'We've got several thousand acres in front of us.'

'As long as it's frozen solid enough to take our weight.'

And it had, for both of us. There was some occasional creaking under our skis, but the crust was so hard we could scarcely get the points of our ski poles through. Father took the lead and made tracks through the new snow, wielding his ski poles with his back straight, so strong that he hardly needed to bend his legs. He thrust in his poles and pushed like nobody's business. I had to resort to diagonal striding and double poling to keep up, but eventually I found a rhythm to stick to. I counted it silently to myself like a mantra, thinking about how it looked when they were skiing on TV.

'You won't get it better than this,' Father called over his shoulder.

'No –'

Across the potato field and over to the barley field where I had harrowed the stubble in the autumn, where the couch grass would carry on sending out its underground runners across the whole fen if I hadn't managed to destroy them once and for all. The couch grass that could take over every single field, branching like the nerves inside a human being, spread like the ground elder on an abandoned farm.

We were nearly at Fourways and he brought us to a halt, and had got out a handkerchief to blow his nose when a snow-white hare suddenly flew up out of the ditch and tore off towards the Canal like a shot out of a cannon. Father stiffened and watched the running hare, his handkerchief to his mouth and his eyes as wide as if he had just seen an apparition.

Then it was gone, swallowed up by the whiteness. Only the fresh prints stamped in the silence.

He stood there paralysed, biting his lips, and gave me a doubtful glance before he went forward to examine where it had been lying. He bent down and looked for a long time, put the back of his hand to the snow to feel if any of its body heat remained.

'It's like it's haunting me,' came the reaction. 'A Swedish hare, in the middle of the damned fen –'

He shook his head and peered in the direction the hare had taken. Licked his lips several times, as if they were itchy or dry.

'It's the one I shot last time, when you were with me,' he said. 'It was just here, on this very spot. I remember it as if it was yesterday. Something's not right.'

I didn't know what to answer. I put down my poles and retied my ski boots to have something to do, making sure the loops were exactly the same size and checking the bindings.

'I should never have fired that time,' he said in confusion. 'That was a big mistake. I think I shot him right through the brain. His head was just a pulp.'

He threw one hand wide, in a helpless gesture, still holding the pole, and turned to me with a tormented expression, licking his mouth. I could feel everything closing in on us.

The whole fen and nowhere to go.

'So it was h-here,' I stammered.

'Four years ago in March, wasn't it? If only it had died for good. Now it's off again!'

He turned his head once more and stared at the point where the hare had vanished. Lit a cigarette and took a few frantic drags.

'Four years, it's not that long when you think about it? Now it's here again.'

I was starting to get the creeps. We'd only been out for half an hour and I was already regretting I'd come.

'Perhaps we'd better go on?' I said.

'Go on? We should never have set out at all! That's the thing.'

I climbed across the ditch and out onto Nettlepatch, which sloped down towards the Canal. Turned back to show he was supposed to follow me.

'Let me go first,' I said. 'So you don't have to make the tracks.'

'Tracks?'

He leant on his poles and let his head fall forward, seeming suddenly to find it an enormous weight. He closed his eyes and grimaced, whimpered like a child and tossed his head from side to side as if trying to get rid of something.

Like out in the potato field that time, I thought.

'Listen now,' he hissed. 'Listen for Christ's sake, when the ravens are coming!'

I could hardly look at him. It was so utterly silent and still – like after a shot, when everything's holding its breath. As if the whole world was listening and the sky had ears. He rubbed his temples. Fished a few tablets out of his breast pocket and stuffed them into his mouth one after another, chewing and crunching.

'If only they'd leave me in peace,' he muttered. 'You've got to help me, Klas –'

The Canal was flowing serenely along its midstream channel, as black as tar against the snow and the fragile shelves of ice. We stopped in the middle of the bridge, took a few clumsy steps towards the edge and looked down to where the fish traps hung in summer. The wire cages we had come to empty so many times, cycling down after the cows had been milked and let out for the night, pedalling through the swarms of black flies at dusk and coming home to Mum with pike and bream on our bike carriers. The fish I could never bring myself to kill with a stamp of the foot or a twist to the neck.

I dared not get any closer but stayed at arm's length from him the whole time as I looked reluctantly down into the terrifying water and felt the goose pimples on my arms and back. Like on the edge of a sheer drop.

'If the ice hasn't closed over yet then it's not going to,' Father said after a while.

He shifted his poles a bit closer to the edge, leant over the makeshift wooden rail and extended his neck like a deckhand, as if he was looking for something under the bridge.

'What the hell must it feel like down there?' he said.

I shot him a surreptitious look.

'In the water?'

'In that infernal cold. And it never stops, just keeps on flowing, day and night.'

He shook his head, as if at something unendurable, and carried on looking down into the pitch-black water, his eyes screwed up as far as they would go, as if he was looking into a dazzling light. His jaws worked back and forth.

'The fish don't freeze,' I said. 'They never get a fever, either; their body temperature is always the same as the water. I read it in a book.'

He snorted and turned to me with a look that said he thought that was one of the stupidest things he'd heard in his whole life.

'The fish,' he said. 'Who the hell's worrying about the fish with all this going on?'

I took a step back, looked at the falling snow, the dry, powdery little flakes landing and melting instantaneously on the icy water. All around stood the silenced, wizened reeds, their feathery heads drooping. Here and there the bulrushes, with the previous season's cigars slit wide open: thousands of fluffy seeds waiting for the spring gales to spread them.

Father got out his handkerchief and blew his nose; he stepped away from the lethal rail and nodded that it was time to go on.

'Over to the other side?'

'That's right.'

At that moment we heard a dog barking in the alder clump. A Swedish foxhound that had got a scent, there was no mistaking it.

'Adder Hook Johnny,' I said. 'He'll be out with Punch on a day like this.'

Yeff! Yeff! Yeff! Louder this time, sounding more and more irascible.

Yeff! Yeff! Yeff!

Father and I stood stock still, our eyes wide. He was eying me nervously from the side, ears cocked for something he really wanted not to hear.

'It must be Johnny.' I whispered again, and that was as far as I got before a shot went off.

Then another, and an echo fading away.

The hare, I thought.

Father nodded grimly.

We came round the clump, Father first and then me, and found Johnny bending over something, hands on hips. He had stuck his rifle into the snow, its barrel pointing skywards.

'So you're up and about again?' he called. 'Not bad going.'

Father nodded and raised his pole in an awkward greeting.

'You've fucking well got to see this!'

The white hare was tossed down in the snow like a rag, head

first with splashes of blood behind it and a big red patch that had run out.

'So it was the same one,' Father said, partly to himself.

'I got him with the first shot,' said Johnny, prodding it with his foot. 'Didn't really need the second, so I didn't. He went straight down.'

Father stared at the hare with frightened eyes, as if it was a ghost lying there. He lit a cigarette and tried to smoke and bite his lip at the same time, rubbing both lips together and biting down on the lower one as if to numb something.

'It's hard going for me today,' he said, just like that.

Johnny gave a laugh.

'You should try it without skis then. Feels like I'm going through with every step. But then I must weigh as much as the two of you put together.'

Father's face remained impassive, and he looked down at the hare in front of him with distant eyes.

'It's more than that –'

'I'm not surprised,' said Johnny. 'But it's the hare we're talking about now, so it is. It's not every day you flush out a Swedish hare. Fine big lad he was, too. Tasty bit of meat.'

Just then Punch came running out of the clump of trees, went wild when he caught sight of the dead hare and dashed over to start tearing at it. He yelped and whimpered with excitement and his tail was going like a drumstick, but Johnny had his knife out and wanted the hare for himself. In a trice he'd cut open the belly and pulled out the intestines, stomach, liver and kidneys. Then he smashed the diaphragm and pulled out the heart and lungs, emptying out what blood was left.

Father pulled a face.

Now it was Punch's turn. He threw himself at the steaming

pile of innards, wolfed the heart down in one go and moved straight on to the rest. The blood ran juicily out of the corners of his mouth. Johnny was as thrilled as a child at the zoo and couldn't take his eyes off him.

'He's got the taste for it now!' he cried. 'He's got the taste good and proper!'

Punch licked his chops and soon there was nothing left but the rejected bits of gut and the stomach. Johnny patted him on the head and bent down for the hare, cut its ears off its head and its head off its body, wiped his knife on his trouser leg and brought out a pair of pliers, which he held out to me.

'You'll draw the teeth, then?' he said. 'So the dog won't do himself any damage.'

I recoiled as if a jolt had run through me. He gave a teasing grin, holding out the bloody head in one hand and the pliers in the other. Father looked at the hare's head and at me through eyes like narrow slits.

'Please yourself,' Johnny said dismissively. 'I'm not here to talk round a little swot.'

He opened the hare's mouth and tweaked out a tooth.

'*Aehh –*'

It was a whimper issuing from Father.

'You shouldn't have to see this kind of thing, Klas,' he hissed. 'You're too young for all this.'

Johnny gave him a quick look. Nipped off the last incisors and threw the head to Punch like a little ball to play with.

'Just you watch,' he said with satisfaction. 'That's the best thing they know.'

Punch sniffed at the head and carried it a little way off, like a treasure. Then he got his teeth into it and there was a loud crunch in his mouth as he bit. Bone and cartilage, eyes, the whole lot. Father put his face in his hands.

'You'll have to live with this for the rest of your life,' he said. 'We should never have come out today.'

Johnny raised one eyebrow with a knowing expression. He put Punch on the leash and patted him again.

'That just leaves us with some spruce twigs to find, to fill him out with,' he said, looking my way. 'You coming along, or plodding off home with the tenant?'

'We're going now,' said Father with a tormented look. 'We've seen all we had to, and more.'

Johnny gave an ironic salute, as if to one of his army superiors, picked up the rifle and hare and strode off towards the copse where the spruces grew. He left two black-tipped ears behind him in the snow, pointing in opposite directions.

'That's enough,' said Father. 'More than.'

We stopped at the Giant's Stone halfway home and stuck our poles into the snow. Father undid the rucksack and got out a bit of hessian sacking for us to sit on. There was a thermos flask for each of us, one of hot chocolate and one of coffee, and for Father she'd sent along a little bottle of cream wrapped in a knitted child's sock – as a memento or a hope, I supposed. Wrapped in newspaper there were two sturdy egg sandwiches and a big, rye-bread pretzel each, with cheese on. It was the first time Mum had made the same packed lunch for both of us.

'They're hickory, those skis,' said Father, nodding over at his. 'They'll last you all your life. They're tougher than juniper. They use it for sledgehammer handles. Sledgehammer handles and skis.'

I looked at him. He nodded again, as if to emphasise what he had said. It was only now I realised he had no gloves on, though it must have been ten below. His hands looked blue and frozen, but it didn't seem to bother him, or maybe he wouldn't be able to feel the difference anyway.

The fen was completely silent and deserted, a wilderness in shades of white. Not a snowflake in the air, not a spark of life anywhere. Over by the Canal road the Spreading Oak looked intimidatingly black with its bare winter branches, like a charred streak of lightning on its way up to the sky.

Sit here, him and me, on the same spot. Wonder to myself what he's not telling me. Take a bite and try to chew without a sound. See the steam issuing from our mouths and our cups, the separate clouds thinning and merging with each other before they become one with the air and are replaced by new ones.

'It was once the sea bed, where we're sitting now,' he said. 'Do you realise what that means?'

'That time passes and things change.'

He pretended not to hear.

'That people laboured away here digging out this Canal by hand to drain the water out so they could farm the land. How many cuts of the sod do you think it took? Given that it's ten kilometres long and seven metres wide? Klas was the one in charge of the whole thing, my great grandfather. If it weren't for him, we wouldn't have had much land to farm. The whole place is on drained land.'

'Yes, you've told us about it a few times,' I said, as kindly as I could.

'Well, it's time to say it again.'

He took a bite of his egg sandwich and pointed with his whole arm down to the Canal and over at the church and village to the north, as if to show how many fields all those shovel loads had amounted to.

'In the deepest parts they even had to build platforms and bring the mud up in stages, form a chain and pass it up to the top. And once the Canal was dug they had to reclaim the damn fen. Dig ditches all round and ditches down to the Canal to mark the boundary between wet and dry, and then ditches between the various fields – miles and miles of ditches before they could even start to think of sowing anything.'

He shook his head, the look in his eyes as bitter as if he had had to dig the whole lot himself in some earlier life.

'Backbreaking toil, for months and years. But it was either that or emigrate, if you didn't want to starve. Like choosing between dysentery and cholera. His brothers went to America and never came back. And now the land's sinking, year by year. One day, nature will reclaim the lot. Oxidation, they call it.'

I nodded down at the snow in front of me, drank my chocolate slowly and felt too jaded to dwell any further on the nineteenth-century's crop failures and famine.

'I've been slaving away here for forty years now,' muttered Father, summing up. 'And what do I get for it, d'you reckon? Soon it'll be your turn.'

I couldn't bring myself to contradict him; I could see it wouldn't make any difference anyway. He poured himself more coffee and slurped it noisily. He fed the rest of his sandwich into his mouth and looked at me reproachfully as he munched, as if he thought I should at least be showing a bit of gratitude that I had something to take over.

'Our teacher says agriculture could be the beginning of the end for mankind,' I said, trying to make it sound as if I was on Father's side. 'It would have been better if we'd carried on as hunters and gatherers instead of raising livestock for slaughter. And what's more, pesticides are killing the birds. The peregrine falcon and the sea eagle have been laying eggs with thin shells for twenty years. They crack when the parent tries to brood.'

He wasn't listening. He sat there with averted eyes, looking out at nothing, far away in his thoughts again. His jaws seemed to be chewing of their own accord, slowly and mechanically as if he was never actually going to swallow. Ice in his beard and empty, glazed eyes.

'Forty years –'

What are you thinking about Father, I wanted to ask. As you sit there? That it will all have been for nothing if I don't take over? That your whole life's been a waste? Could be something to do with the hare, maybe that's what he was turning over and over in his mind? But he'd come home with hares every winter and hung them up behind the brewhouse, gutted and headless just like Johnny's. With fragrant bits of their spruce-twig stuffing sticking out.

He extracted a lump of dough and egg from his mouth and fixed me with a look.

'I can't take much these days, Klas,' he said. 'You've got to help me.'

'Yes?'

'Have you ever seen a sow eat up her own new piglets?' he said, randomly changing subject. 'It's not funny, I can tell you.'

He ran his hands through his beard. His eyes misted, as if he was going to cry.

A perplexed and trembling smile.

Gone.

'It was as if the Devil had got into her. The blood was flowing and the cartilage was crunching in her jaws when I came in. It was a dreadful sight. And now this –'

I nodded automatically.

'She must have been sick?' he said. 'She was like a beast. It was the Devil's work. That was when he came.'

My face suddenly felt hot. I drew a five-pointed star in the snow with my finger while time stood still, taking care to make it symmetrical like it should be. As protection against all evil, it said in Veronika's book.

Father closed his eyes and pinched the top of his nose between two fingers.

'There are plenty of people who wouldn't have coped with what I've been through,' came the comment. 'Once I said I was as strong as a steer, but the steer's nearly done what he had to, now.'

He pressed his front teeth onto his scabbed lips and bit down until he made it bleed, and a bright little line trickled down into his beard. He shook his head, slowly, as if in the face of some nameless sorrow.

I picked the skin off my chocolate and drank it without a sound.

I mustn't turn into him, echoed the thought within me.

Anything but that –

A wind sprang up and bit at our cheeks, making our eyes water. The sun peeped out like a wintery full moon from behind thin veils of cloud.

How long had we been sitting there, not saying anything? Each absorbed in our own thoughts.

Father lit another cigarette and looked absently out over the fen. Down by the Canal, the embankments created by draining the lake in the eighteen-seventies could still be seen. I squinted into the sun and felt as if I could see the whole thing in front of me, through the flickering light of my eyelashes. Several hundred men in rough homespun trousers and slouch hats with shovels and spades out in the middle of the waterlogged mire, balancing on unsteady tussocks of grass, squelching through the mud with snowshoes on their feet and dripping turfs in their arms, plagued by horseflies and mosquitoes. Bark bread and rancid bacon for dinner, then evenings of coffee substitute and moonshine before they went to their rat-infested beds in the soiled hay.

Ssshh –

It was the telephone wires singing: a faint, wave-like song that came and went, rose and fell like something carried on the wind, faded away and then came back again, distant and close at the same time, rising higher and higher like a girls' choir humming in a church, in another age. Can you hear it Father? Hear that it's singing for us now, for the pigs and the hare and you and me. A girls' choir in a whitewashed church long before we came into the world, when the whole fen was under water and there were no fields. That's the song being borne in on the air now.

He sat there with glazed, empty eyes, quivering round the mouth. He poured out the last drop of coffee and pressed the stopper far too hard into the thermos. The bottle of cream in its child's sock lay untouched between us.

I awoke with a jolt. Switched on the bedside light and raised myself on one elbow, my eyes refusing to see clearly. I could hear one loud bash after another, echoing out and dying away.

Right, we're in for it again now. Someone's been lying awake in the boiler room for long enough.

I reluctantly pushed the blind aside and saw him furiously beating a threadbare old mattress, taking the beater right back after each stroke to get a good swing and smacking it down with as much force as if his life depended on it. He was in just his pyjamas and gumboots, with that awful headtorch on. The beam of light roved to and fro across the garden, like a restless spirit. His eyes were gleaming. The cigarette was bobbing at the corner of his mouth as if he was talking out loud to himself as he administered the blows.

The mattresses on the carpet-beating rack and a pile of rag rugs waiting their turn. There were sofa cushions and blankets tossed in a heap in the snow.

He stood there in a cloud of dust beating and beating, as if someone was forcing him. As if he had been lent powers or was at someone's mercy.

I'm not very keen on having a load of particles around me. It's time to get rid of those mites and fleas and lice, the whole lot. Beat and thrash until nothing's left. What does it matter if it's the middle of the night, if the house is full of vermin!

He threw a look at his watch as if to check he'd be finished before dawn. Then he gripped the beater firmly with both hands and resumed his beating. Every impact stung me inside, like little electric shocks of tears that couldn't get out.

So recently the frozen crust and the whiteness, and now they were gone. The ditches were sloshing and rushing, and out in the fields the plough-ridge stripes of bare earth grew broader by the day. The wind had turned, and there was a pale, silvery violet shimmer round the scattered clumps of birches that spoke of buds and sap. Mum had brought in twigs to decorate for Easter and put them on the table even though it was still a week to Ash Wednesday. The freezer was full and the Easter cards written and stamped, as if she was trying to anticipate something.

And the crows were on the wing. Tumbling about like mad among the tops of the spruces behind the cowshed, flapping to and fro with sudden changes of direction in mid-air, alternately corkscrewing their way up into the grey sky and plummeting down, excited by the thaw or uneasy about some impending disaster.

All at once, Mum was standing right behind me. She'd crept up without me noticing, like when you want to scare someone. She straightened out my shirt collar and put her arm round me. Stood so close I could feel her breast against my arm, smell the Helosan cream like when she used to bend over my bed to take my temperature.

'Bless me if I'm not going to take down the inside windows today,' she said. 'Shall we decide that, you and me, and let winter know we've had enough for this time?'

I nodded and felt all warm inside, as if my veins had dilated and the blood was surging round because she had come and was holding me. Without thinking, I rested my head on her shoulder.

Stand there for a while and watch the crows at play. Listen to the church service on the radio, hear her humming along beside my ear when the vicar started to sing. She gripped my shoulder and hugged me even harder, as if she wanted to comfort me or felt guilty about something.

Was she crying?

'I'm taking my kite out today,' I said, pulling away. 'Can't get much better flying weather than this.'

She put her head on one side and stroked my hair a few times, as softly and affectionately as if I was a little child.

'Yes, good idea,' she said. 'Just wrap up warm so you don't catch cold.'

I put an extra bit of fishing line in my binocular case, took the kite under my arm and was about to step into my boots when there were strange noises from the other end of the cellar. I crept very quietly along to the boiler room and put my ear to the crack: muffled groans and heavy thumps with little pauses in between – as if he was banging his head against the concrete wall. With every thump, the door vibrated.

'What have I done? Dear Lord ... tell me what I've done ... is it really ...'

Then the thuds stopped. What remained was a lamentation as keening and wretched as if he was almost at the end of his reserves of strength. Like a miner who has been trapped for days without food.

I felt a great lump in my throat.

He's lying in there now, on the other side of the door. Chewing his lip so the blood joins the flow of tears.

It was as if I could see him amongst all the clutter in the back corner, curled up and covered in sick, in his old cowshed gear. His emaciated face, his patched shirt stained with rust and blood, the clogged bits of sawdust in his hair. The handle was hanging loosely and the keyhole was empty: he had locked himself in but wanted someone to be able to open the door from outside.

'*What have I done? If You exist, help me now!*'

See what happens, said the voice. That's your father lying in there. The one you've tried to keep at a distance, told blatant lies to and made detours round, always been curt with and refused to humour. While you've locked yourself in your room with your books and sums to avoid seeing him and being held to account, crept down into the larder and pilfered like a rat as soon as he's closed the front door behind him. All this is your fault. If anything happens it'll be you that has to take over the whole lot, it's your punishment.

'*Dear Lord ... why are You doing this to me ... no end to it all ...*'

Then it all went quiet; the keening stopped.

Not the slightest sound.

The pounding in my ears.

I recoiled from the thought of looking in and finding him like that. Yet still I felt myself drawn to the keyhole, as if by some irresistible force.

No.

Just the empty kitchen settle with the ear protectors hooked over the back and the old Home Guard blanket kicked off in a pile at the foot end. The embroidery of the smallholder and his ox on its hook and the milking stool by the wall, some brown medicine bottles with their lids off. The pocket barometer he'd been given as a confirmation present.

There were no more thumps. Only whimpering, monotone crying from the corner, as if from a mistreated animal.

I walked along the Canal road with the binoculars round my neck and the kite over my shoulders, tracking the yellow-edged, mild-weather clouds with my eyes, feeling the warm wind come sweeping in over the Marsh Pool and inhaling them in long, deep breaths. I flared my nostrils and took in great lungfuls, as you do after a storm that has cleared the air.

Like a state of grace. To be able to breathe however you want. To be here. Walk, see, feel, listen.

Not go in there any more –

It had brightened up after the morning's rain. The sky arched over the fen like a sail. Dirty drifts of snow lingered along the stone wall, but down in the ditch, the coltsfoot was already in bud. The hazel catkins were out and the goat willows had developed their furry paws. There was a smell of frozen ground thawing and of manure: earth and ammonia. From over in the birch came the soft croak of the greenfinch and the untiringly boisterous spring jingle of the great tits: *do-di-do-di-do-di-do – do-di-do-di-do-di-do –*

The buzzards could come gliding over the edge of the forest any time now, as if they'd somehow known, down there on the Riviera, that vole numbers were on the rise round Raven Fen. In the aspen, the green woodpecker was yodelling at the top of his voice in the hope of finding a mate before he set about the task of hacking out this year's nest.

And the larks!

Fluttering like butterflies, wanting only to go up and up. It's all they know. Now there were three of them hanging over the fields, singing for their lives, rising with quivering wingbeats as if each was fastened on a piece of string that someone was reeling in, or as if their plan was to sing their way up through the sky. They rose and rose and warbled and sang, not even needing to pause for breath; it was as if they couldn't restrain themselves now the spring breezes would carry them, as they indiscriminately mimicked swallows, sparrows and curlews, incorporating it all into their endless lark's trill. Then they suddenly sank, gave in to their feather-light weight and descended in a series of jerks, one at a time, then spread their wings and floated to the ground like living parachutes to drop silently into their grassy grottoes – only to start all over again. Up, up on fluttering wings until they were hanging once more like three little crosses against the dazzling white sail of the sky, and their shower of warbling sound seemed to go on and on, merely rising and falling a little, in time with the wind.

I got the kite ready, checked the line and the wings and was about to hook the line to the bridle when a feeling came over me – as if I'd been caught red-handed. *As if somebody could see –*

I turned to look in all directions.

Are there eyes trained on me at this moment? Is someone watching everything I do? Eyes that make me feel weak at the knees?

What a load of rubbish! There's nowhere to hide out here, is there, in the middle of the fen with fields and grazing as far as the eye can see – just as long as there isn't anyone lurking in the ditch up ahead! Or sitting up in a tree in the spinney, just waiting for the right moment with telescopic sights, tracking me with the cross hair like a hunter and his prey, finger on the trigger, holding his breath.

Johnny, I thought.

He's the one spying on me, watching me. He's found out I saw him with the heifer.

Pff, it's just my imagination running away with me. Who'd have anything to gain by hurting me? Who could wish me harm? I haven't done anything, after all?

From an opening between the clouds: Shouldn't you stay at home while nobody knows how things are going to turn out? It might all depend on you this time – and it's a question of life and death.

I shivered, as if I'd seen a ghost.

You'll never escape me, the voice continued calmly. I am with you all the time, I am the eye that watches you everywhere, follows you wherever you go in life. I am the one who will make sure you can never be alone again.

I stumbled over to where a branch of stunted pine was draping the ground and sat down. Crouched among the stones on the slope into the ditch, and found a root end to fasten the kite to.

The eye fixed on me –

'I am me and the fen is the fen,' I said out loud to myself. 'The fen is the fen and the kite is the kite. Here am I and there is the eagle.'

I looked up over the edge of the ditch.

Nothing.

'Everything's as it should be,' I said into the wind. 'There's nothing to be scared of. It's only me here, not a living soul as far as the eye can see.'

Father – – –, came a rumble from the horrible opening in the clouds. He's the one who can see you, not Johnny or anybody else. He's the one following every step you take – because he can never be sure what you're going to do.

Father! Wasn't it him wailing in the boiler room just now?

Yes it was. Now is now and it's something else. Get out the binoculars to look, and you'll see. He's standing at the kitchen window back home. He'll never leave you. You'll never be rid of him whatever you do. He follows you wherever you go.

It made me jump to see his face through the binoculars; I thought for a second that I had got confused and was seeing things. That it surely couldn't be possible.

But it is. He's standing there now. Looking out over the fields and following the weather, like he used to, as if nothing had happened and all was as it should be.

I could only make him out vaguely; his face was blurred by the reflections of the trees and sky and distorted by the uneven glass. He didn't move a muscle but stood there as if turned to stone, looking down towards the Canal, framed in the white window, as indistinct as a photograph with greaseproof paper in front of it.

I turned my back on him and got to my feet, clambered out of the ditch and felt the wind tugging at the wings.

The kite and the wind and you, the voice flowed through me. The eagle and the line and me.

Now's the time. Hook on the line and get ready for the great voyage.

Come wind, spring up!

Come swirling force that nothing can resist! Come wind of winds and carry off everything, take me away from here, off and away to the thing no one knows anything about!

I want to be borne by the wind! I am the child with no backbone or teeth! I weigh nothing, I am as light as down and my lungs are pumping with hydrogen and helium! Nothing can hold me down, I am the skylark with a beak full of coltsfoot. I am the swift that never touches the ground!

Come angels and give me your hands, give me your smiles, see now who I am! Give me a sail, make the clouds my wings!

– – –

Can you see it all? You lot over there, on the other side of the fen? Can you see me flying? The slacker at Dower Farm who's never lifted a finger. It's my eagle, way up there, my wings, and he's going to take me along, too – like the harpy eagle in the Amazon jungle that carried off the newborn boy.

Took to the wing and disappeared –

Look now, Father! Get out the binoculars and you'll see me rise into the air! You've got to see me fly just this once! I'm taking off now, any moment, in a second I'll be on the wing – – –

Don't tell me you've already turned away, wandered off?

Don't tell me you've done that, Father!

There was a smell of hartshorn and cardamom right out into the hall, and of something slightly burnt. The heat came to meet me. The kitchen table was covered in bun loaves and biscuits, fresh from the oven and ready for freezing; on the worktop baking sheets of well-risen pretzel rings, waiting their turn.

The inside windows were still in place. On the radio cassette player Mia Marianne and Per Filip were singing that the pearly gates were open.

Important things, I thought feverishly. Something no one else is going to find out about. Something only I will know. The promise that came whistling with the wind.

Mum didn't say anything when she saw me, didn't turn down the music, ask me where I'd been all afternoon or whether I wanted to try the buns while they were still warm. She just went on rolling her dough, sticking her lower lip out and nodding in the direction of the front room, as if to say he was waiting for me, it was time now.

He was sitting smoking in the leather armchair with those awful dark glasses on. He had the old school atlas open on his knee like a departed dream. There was a smell of sweaty feet and urine. The chamber pot stood beside him on the floor.

'Is it you, Klas?' he said without turning his head.

'Yes, it's me.'

He nodded approvingly.

'You needn't be scared of me,' he said.

'No, of course not –'

'That's a fine kite you've got. I saw you from the window.'

On the table in front of him there were about fifty cigarette ends neatly arranged like the pieces in some game. The ashtray was more than full and the smoke was winding gently to the ceiling, all but unaffected by the shaking of his hands.

I cleared my throat.

'It's almost a year since I built it,' I answered obligingly. 'Sea eagle. The mightiest bird in all Sweden. He sees everything.'

Father nodded like before, slowly and absently as if in a kind of trance. He stared at the wallpaper in front of him and lit a new cigarette before he'd finished the last one. The sweat glistened on his forehead and his hair was plastered down across his skull.

'I had a kite when I was a lad, too,' he said in a slow drawl. 'Father must have burnt it. He wasn't much of a one for games.'

Then that strange smile of his was there again, empty and introspective, as if he was already in another world.

'I think he threw it on the Walpurgis Night bonfire,' he added. 'It was just as well. Sooner or later, everything burns.'

I didn't know what to say. His atlas was open at a map of Africa. His legs were shaking. I thought it looked like a horse's head, seen like this from the side, a dirty yellow horse's head with Lake Victoria as the eye. The Somali ear, the South African muzzle, the ocean all around it. Has that occurred to you, Father? The fact that it looks like this from way up in the heavens, when everything shrinks and resumes its proper proportions, and no work of the human hand can be detected? The sparkle in the sky-blue eye of the African horse.

'I thought the blackcoat was the one in charge,' he mumbled into the smoke. 'So it's the eagle, eh?'

A long column of ash fell from his cigarette onto the deep-pile rug. Outside the closed curtains, the branches of the weeping birch were flapping to and fro like a blurred shadow play, occasionally grazing the glass so you were aware how quiet it was inside. There wasn't even the ticking of the long-case clock; its weight was hanging as silent and still as a lump of lead.

'There's none as sharp as the eagle, none of the others can stare straight at the sun and not get blinded,' I said, raising my voice a little. 'Your eyes will get holes burned in them if you try. The sea eagle is the only bird that can't be killed by lightning. Fire has no effect on him. Thor can blaze away as much as he likes.'

Father didn't answer. He just sat still, tapping his clawlike nail on the glass of the pocket barometer.

I cleared my throat again.

'Don't you remember I told you about the kite, that time we were fishing for tench?' I said, unable to conceal my impatience. 'I said it was a sea eagle I was making. I told you! I said I'd got some chestnut sticks from up by the church to dry and use for the frame.'

He placed his smoking cigarette in the pile of ash, slowly took off his dark glasses and turned his head towards me, peering at me with glassy eyes – as if he had been looking into a fire.

'It's the spring equinox tomorrow,' he said, licking his cracked lips. 'So the light will be coming.'

I am as tough as juniper and as hard as stone.
You'll never be rid of me, if that was what you all thought.

The cowshed was ablaze. The flames were belching out of the windows and licking halfway up to the sky like enormous dragon's tongues. The flames fanned out across the fen, the roof trusses splintered like matches and the sheets of asbestos cement caved in and decapitated the cackling chickens. The cows pulled wildly at their red-hot chains, bellowed as if from the bottom of an abyss or a lake. Father was leaning over the well drinking scoop after scoop of water, as if he was the one on fire. Mum had turned her back and was breastfeeding Göran under the blossoming linden tree, as if trying to do everything she possibly could to protect him. Grandfather was chopping wood and didn't seem to have noticed the fire; he set chunk after chunk of it on the oak block and chopped away with his double-bladed axe.

Suddenly Veronika was standing on the other side of the barn, waving to me through the fire, shimmering like a mirage in the trembling heat and flames. She had her best dress on, and a bittern with outstretched wings in her hand. She held the bird aloft like a trophy and waved to me to come.

I reared up in the sweaty sheets. The phone rang again, more and more insistent with each successive ring. That means no one else can answer it.

'It's Alvar at The Point here – – –'

He sounded as if he'd run to the phone, or perhaps it was his heart, and that was why he was ringing. To ask for help.

'I wanted to speak to your mother really – – –'

He was breathing heavily and kept stumbling over what he had to say, obliged to start again several times before he could find the right words.

'The thing is, see – – – found a peaked cap down in the Canal – – – just a few minutes ago – – – was over at yours to see if the pike were anywhere near spawning – – – best if you folk drive down and check – – – out and get your mother – – –'

My stomach lurched.

'So you promise you'll run out to the cowshed and tell her right away? – – – – –'

I sat staring into the silent receiver.

Thinking that in there –

The little holes in their stupid circle, the rim of earwax and dust that had built up round the edge, the dirty fingermarks and smeared spots of grease, the scratches in the Bakelite that looked like a crooked A.

So it's happened now – – –

The thing that was never supposed to happen, was never to be mentioned; no one dared drop a hint or say a word.

Like a bare patch of white.

No it hasn't, not at all. Who knows what sort of cap it was? It could have been there under the snow in the reeds and has just emerged in the thaw. And the dowser isn't the sort of man to be relied on in matters like these. This is someone who eats dream porridge and sees visions when he's wide awake and divines the future with a sieve.

Father's out in the cowshed, helping Mum with the milking, anyone knows that! What would he be doing by the Canal this early?

I sat there feeling paralysed, staring at the aerial photo of the parish church with the chapel of rest beside it, at the scratch marks Göran had made in the wallpaper, the hole in the toilet door where Father had kicked it in; it was something he could never undo, it would always be there, like the carving in the rock, like an everlasting scar ...

I lifted the receiver again, but nobody was there to change their mind or take anything back, no misunderstanding was waiting to be sorted out. It just emitted its piercing, level tone, as if nothing had happened.

I got my trousers on and rushed out of the house, running in my socks along the edge of the field to the Canal, and suddenly there was a mob of lapwings around me. They whined and squawked, hurled themselves through the air and whipped the flats of their dark wings around my ears like warning messengers from death itself.

Naiiit, naiiit! Naiiit, naiiit, naiiit!

They dived frenziedly at me, swerving aside at the last moment, and tumbled in the air above my head scolding and shrieking as if they wanted to make me turn back home at any price.

Keep going! It could already be too late. It might all depend on you this time.

Naiiit – naiiit – naiiit – – –

My feet were aching with cold and the lactic acid was pumping in my thighs, but my legs just kept on running. As if they didn't know what else they could do.

A flickering flame inside me. Go on. Don't slow down or try to catch your breath, don't even think of stopping. Go on. Out into the furrows and straight across the field. Down to the black water that sucks and drags and never stops.

I staggered the last little bit in total exhaustion, crawled up the embankment and saw a pair of black boots down by the water. The Canal was flowing along nice and peacefully as if nothing had happened, carrying a few blobs of foam along with it and eddying round the boundary pole in mid-channel. The boots had been neatly placed on a rock, as if someone might come up out of the water any minute and step into them, or the way you might see a pair left by a ford in spring. His oilskin was folded up in the long, yellowed grass.

A bit further along, at the edge of the reeds, a Eurasian curlew stood stock still, pointing down into the Canal with its curved sabre of a beak as if it had news to break, having witnessed something unprecedented.

Not a sound.

I shuffled carefully down to the water and caught sight of the peaked cap, partly sunk in the mudbank. It felt like a punch in the stomach. Some splashes of blue or green and a few lighter, yellowish-white patches: his hands sticking out of his boiler suit. He was lying on his back a little way out in the marshy water, turned slightly away from me. His face glinted as the sun reached it with its longest rays. His eyes were wide open and had been able to see to the very last. His hair was swaying like sea-grass.

There were no bubbles rising, no steam or frosted breath. Just his body, winding without resistance in the flowing water.

A passing breeze ruffled the surface.

'Dad!' I shouted, not knowing what I was doing.

'Why don't you answer me? Answer me then!'

'D a d ! – – – – –'

I tried to reach down to the water, felt a compulsion to touch it, feel how deep it was where he was lying, whether I might be able to pull him up to the fresh air by myself, but I dared not get too close. I had nothing to hold on to and would be sure to slip down and get stuck in the mud, never be able to get myself out again. Have to stay there.

I found a stone and threw it in – as if to wake him. But the Canal merely swallowed it, letting it sink to the bottom like a bit of gravel in a water trough. The rings gently spread and faded, as if they'd never been.

My chest tightened.

I didn't want to be part of this.

From a reed beside my ear: It's over now. There's nothing you can change or undo, this is what had to happen.

It was as if something was pulsing through me, flowing hot and cold by turns. I was so cold I was shaking, yet was suffused with an inexplicable warmth. I couldn't think straight. I must have lost all sensation in my feet because I could feel nothing when I applied pressure to them, but I could see that my socks were soaked through, and stained in dark patches by soil and blood.

How can it be so utterly still? As if someone had put a bell jar over the fen, the sky and the fields, everything. There was only the Canal, whispering and running as it always had, the sliding black depths that would never stop, just keep running and running for an eternity of forevers, down to Marsh Pool, through the narrow channel in the reeds and across the long, thin bird lake, under the century-old echo of the humpbacked bridge and into the river on the other side, past the swidden land and the forest grazing, the water meadows and reclaimed farmland, through dark forest, outlying fields and boggy pools and all the way down to the coast, out into the mighty sea that one knew nothing about. Tens of miles over gliding black currents on the great waterway that never ends –

There's Father.

Lying in the numbing water, knowing nothing.

The spruce by the abandoned barn, I thought. Up there and hide, cross the Canal and stay on the other side.

I stepped into the boots, took the oilskin with me and ran to the bridge and into the clump of trees, crossed the wild animal tracks in the muddy soil and blundered about among the piles of stones and the thistles like a hunted fugitive before I finally saw the derelict barn on the crest of the slope ahead. I pulled off my socks, stuffed straw into the boots and quickly climbed up into the spruce standing alone among all the naked aspens, broke off some of the twigs thick with needles and arranged a bed so I could sit in the treetop. I wrapped myself in the oilskin and turned up the collar, and thought I could sense the smells from before – aftershave and pipe smoke – mixing with all the scents of the fen and the wind.

Why did you do it, Dad? Why didn't you say anything to us? *No goodbye no nothing –*

Didn't you want to know what I'm going to be when I grow up? Or give me your advice and feel proud one day? Do you remember when you showed me where the songthrush used to sing behind the cowshed when you were like me? When you pointed out the Plough and the Pole Star over the pigsty when we were clearing snow because the vet had to come in the middle of the night? Everything you wanted to show me and explain to me before I started school. When you taught me what icing and offside are. The difference between fractions and percentages. Between wheat and rye, sedge and timothy, acres and hectares.

The steps out into the icy black water, the stockinged feet sucked down into the mire, the decision not to fight it, just lie down and let it happen, feel the warmth come and your body go numb, make out the sky as a billowing light, far away. Then the bubbles rising from your mouth, that mouth which had decided to stay open and just keep swallowing.

Did you see your whole life in a second before everything went black? See when you were small and scared like me, see Mum and Göran and me among the flowers in the garden, all the animals we've ever had, see everything somehow from above before you were swept away? Did you think it was me who …

No.

I was going to cycle over to Hynne Ness for some eggs today. That was what I'd promised Mum before I went to sleep.

'Buy two dozen while you're there, or three if they'll let you. Then we'll have plenty to see us through Easter.'

The wicker basket she'd put out for me, with Grandma's linen teacloths for padding. The five kronor notes she'd folded and put in my trouser pocket.

There they are. I've got them, still folded in here just as they were. Fifteen kronor for eggs.

My cheeks and earlobes were glowing. My feet were starting to throb and prickle. Sensation was returning, my blood was racing – and the spruce murmured as I put my ear to it, whispering and purling as if from some underground waterfall. I thought it must be the sap rising, the meltwater defying the earth's pull to make the branches send out shoots, the buds burst and the spruce trees flower, like in Paradise.

I leant against the rough trunk and looked out over the fields, following the black watercut of the Canal as far as I could. Away to the north, the church spire stuck up like a chalk-white arrow above the endless dragon's back of the spruce forest. In the south, there was a glimpse of the Marsh Pool between the trees, perhaps still iced over, but ready any moment now to swallow the last layers of ice and give the birds back their water.

Out in the fields, hundreds of gulls and lapwings were hunting for worms where there had once been a lake: bright white dots against the cold soil, like the stars in the sky when the bittern boomed and you told me about the boy who disappeared.

As long as they don't turn up with their blue lights flashing, I thought. As long as they never come here.

FREEDOM
TO **WRITE**
FREEDOM
TO **READ**

This book has been selected to receive financial assistance from English PEN's Writers in Translation programme supported by Bloomberg and Arts Council England. English PEN exists to promote literature and its understanding, uphold writers' freedoms around the world, campaign against the persecution and imprisonment of writers for stating their views, and promote the friendly co-operation of writers and free exchange of ideas.

Each year, a dedicated committee of professionals selects books that are translated into English from a wide variety of foreign languages. We award grants to UK publishers to help translate, promote, market and champion these titles. Our aim is to celebrate books of outstanding literary quality, which have a clear link to the PEN charter and promote free speech and intercultural understanding.

In 2011, Writers in Translation's outstanding work and contribution to diversity in the UK literary scene was recognised by Arts Council England. English PEN was awarded a threefold increase in funding to develop its support for world writing in translation.

www.englishpen.org